**What if man were at the
mercy of machine?**

**What if artificial intelligence grew faster
than human intelligence?**

**What if the future of the planet rested in
the pulsing heart of a microchip?**

**YOU'RE ABOUT TO FIND OUT.**

# VIRUS

**A NOVEL OF
TECHNOLOGICAL TERROR BY
Bill Buchanan**

# VIRUS

## Bill Buchanan

JOVE BOOKS, NEW YORK

VIRUS

A Jove Book / published by arrangement with
the author

PRINTING HISTORY
Jove edition / February 1997

The Putnam Berkley World Wide Web site address is
http://www.berkley.com/berkley

ISBN: 0-515-12011-1

A JOVE BOOK®
Jove Books are published by The Berkley Publishing Group,
200 Madison Avenue, New York, New York 10016.
JOVE and the "J" design
are trademarks belonging to Jove Publications, Inc.

PRINTED IN THE UNITED STATES OF AMERICA

10  9  8  7  6  5  4  3  2  1

"For a successful technology, reality must take precedence over public relations, for nature cannot be fooled."

—RICHARD FEYNMAN,
Nobel Prize–winning physicist,
Member of President Reagan's *Challenger*
Accident Investigatory Commission

*This book was written for our children in the
hope that it would never come true.*

# ACKNOWLEDGMENTS

I would like to thank the kind people—lifelong friends and publishing professionals alike—who made this book possible.

My heartfelt thanks to George Wieser and David Shanks, for without them this novel would not exist. And to John Talbot, senior editor at Berkley Books, for your suggestions, guidance, and intuition. I feel most fortunate working with such thoughtful, enthusiastic, and considerate professionals.

My sincere thanks to Mark Gatlin, acquisitions editor at *The Naval Institute Press*, for your kindness, encouragement, and feedback. You did a superb job selecting your reviewers and asking all the right questions. Their backgrounds were well suited for evaluating this story and their suggestions, observations, and concerns were enormously helpful.

And from one tech-head to another, my enthusiastic thanks to Tony Hagar for your first-rate suggestions on genetic programming, high-altitude aircraft flight trajectories, and orbital physics. Your perceptive interest and incisive comments helped substantially improve the story.

Very special thanks go to my lifelong hometown friends Marlo Horne, Ross Gunn, and Martha Lemmons. Marlo and Ross, for reviewing the manuscript in its formative stages. Martha Lemmons, for the story's title. My thanks again for your time, ideas, and encouragement.

I would like to extend my appreciation to Chere Bemelmans, a friend and nonfiction editor, for placing her life on hold and losing two back-to-back nights' sleep reviewing the manuscript. Your enthusiasm caused my spirit to soar and your suggestions helped a tremendous lot.

Most of all, I would like to thank my wife, Janet, for her faith, love, unwavering support, and editorial comments.

This work spans an array of diverse disciplines ranging from military space technology to Washington politics. I did what I could do to get it right and felt fortunate to have excellent manuscript reviewers throughout the process. Tech-head readers be advised that intricate layers of software detail are presented as pseudo-code in the interest of readability. Errors which remain are mine alone, but the credit goes to those people who helped me along the way.

# PREFACE

In 1959, Arthur Samuel—artificial intelligence pioneer—asked, "How can computers learn to solve problems without being explicitly programmed?" In 1992, John Koza answered this question with empirical evidence in his book entitled *Genetic Programming*. Koza claimed, as did John Holland before him, that genetic programming allows computers to learn from experience and thereby program themselves. Hoping to produce some mathematical basis substantiating Koza's claims, the U.S. government funded research at MIT, Stanford, University of Michigan, and the MITRE Corporation. Subsequently, researchers and mathematicians constructed a meaningful body of theory as to why genetic algorithms work when adapting computer programs. Although counterintuitive, simulation results were as surprising as they were undeniable. Turns out Koza was right. Adaptation of computer programs using genetic algorithms offered considerable promise. Almost overnight, genetic programming came of age and the technological stage was set for fundamental changes in computing.

Advances in genetic algorithms and neural networks were combined to achieve a quantum leap in computer software capability and performance. The result: an evolutionary learning capability for computers. Programs evolved at their own rate as new information became available, ultimately leading to genetically refined, precision-tuned computer software. This new learn-as-you-go technology led to breakthrough applications of artificial intelligence in medicine, aviation, telecommunications, business, and the military.

When the technology was new—in its early introductory stages—exploratory military applications centered around satellite imaging and signals intelligence collection. *Brilliant-class* surveillance satellites became the first in a long line of learn-as-you-go systems to enter the U.S. military inventory. Then, as the technology matured, it worked its way into the very fabric of the military infrastructure. As with nuclear energy, this technology was used for potentially destructive purposes. *Brilliant-class* weapons emerged as the system of choice for replacing conventional smart technology.

But—*brilliant-class* weapons weren't the only destructive use for this technology.

They would come to be known in the U.S. Army's vernacular as *battlefield grade*—and for good reason. Inevitably, this technology was applied to highly sophisticated, self-adaptive computer viruses.

# VIRUS

# PART 1

## A DISASTER OF TECHNOLOGY

DAY 12—
DECEMBER 18, 2014

# 1

General Dan Mason listened intently as twin General Electric engines accelerated the McDonnell Douglas flying wing down the runway into the ink-black abyss surrounding Boston's Logan Airport.

As Mason scanned the runway looking for ascending aircraft lights, he saw only the pitch-black of night. Every light at Logan was dark, including those used to illuminate the runway. Logan's air traffic control tower and terminals were deserted, the parking lot empty. Standing alone on the air traffic observation deck, wrapped in his wool Air Force overcoat, Mason inhaled deeply so he could hear the engine noise over the sound of his own breathing. The dense December fog off Boston Harbor smelled of kerosene and salt.

As the jet engine noise faded across the harbor, Mason cupped his hands behind his ears, listening for a change in the engine's pitch and direction.

Suddenly, like a distant bolt of lightning, a brilliant yellow flash ignited the sky, illuminating rows of aircraft silhouettes parked wing to wing. Immediately after the flash, the early morning silence was shattered by the thunderous crash of an explosion.

Supreme Commander Dan Mason felt the full weight of his new command during the agonizing silence which followed. Tears welled in his eyes as the flying wing broke up, separated from both engines, then spiraled silently into the harbor. Lieutenant Colonel Wild Bill Boyd was dead; his test aircraft—designated the *Black Hole* prototype—destroyed. Mason felt emptiness, an ache in his soul he could not escape. He tightly gripped the handrail, his knuckles white, his complexion ashen. This night had been the longest of his life and still, despite their best efforts, nothing was flying—nothing had flown for eight days.

Airports around the world stood deserted. All flights canceled until further notice.

Mason stared glassy-eyed and motionless in disbelief. Transfixed by the darkness, pondering this chaos, he wondered how they'd come to this. He knew how and why this had happened, but had no solution. As Mason saw it, *Hell Fire*'s crew was now the only remaining hope they had left.

In his dismay, Mason had forgotten to breathe. He gasped for air, struggled to catch his breath, and walked slowly toward his limo. Once inside, he put his hand in his pocket, rubbed the five star shoulder boards of his former boss, and began looking back on the events which led him here.

It would be a long ride back to his headquarters at Cheyenne Mountain.

**A Disaster of Technology**

# THE BAD SEED

## DAY 1—
## DECEMBER 7, 2014

# 2

Major Linda Scott stood staring at *Hell Fire*, mesmerized as she watched the fog boiling off her space plane. Nostalgic, she yearned for a return to happier times. In the past six years, she'd lost the two men in her life who'd meant the most—her father and her husband. Her life hadn't turned out like she'd imagined, but all things considered, life was good—well, work was good and work had become her life. Above all else, she loved the rush of high performance flight.

As a woman, she'd had to work harder than the men to prove herself, but she was the best and had *Hell Fire* to show for it. The daughter of an SR-71 Blackbird pilot, she'd loved airplanes and flying from the time she could walk. Flying was something she had to do, she'd been born to do it. It bound her to her father even after his death.

There was something almost spiritual about her flying. She had something extra going for her that no one could put their finger on. If called on to be serious, she could be serious. If called on to be decisive, she'd deliver, but she never took herself too seriously. In flight, she became an extension of *Hell Fire*—together, they responded as one.

Like many fighter pilots, Scott was short by male standards. Built to fly, she stood a trim five feet seven inches tall with straight black hair cut in a nineties bob. She took pride in her well-defined jawline and high cheekbones. At thirty-six years old, she didn't want a double chin if she could help it. She feared getting fat so she worked out hard and often. Her smooth white skin contrasted vividly with her rose-colored cheeks, black eyebrows, and long eye-lashes—she seldom wore makeup, didn't need it. Most of the women she knew hated the way she looked, but not the men.

Her two-man crew often described her as perky, direct, and unstoppable—a woman who got what she wanted with gumption. Like her flying machine, Scott was a master-piece to behold and fascinating to understand.

Scott'd pursued her passion for flying like an addiction, but her passion, like any addicting drug, hadn't come for free. Flying cost her the only man she'd ever loved, but that was a long time ago. Now it was over, or at least they'd been divorced five years. Divorcing Jay Fayhee had been the biggest mistake of her life, but he'd asked for the di-vorce—on grounds of desertion. She was never home, but neither was he. Every Air Force officer knows *the needs of the Air Force must come first.* She'd been assigned to the only XR-30 squadron in the country, located at Edwards AFB. On Jay's dream sheet, he'd asked for a space station assignment and gotten it—an assignment to the NASA in-stallation at Huntsville, Alabama, for extensive space sta-tion training. Again, the only place in the country where space station training was available. They had gotten what they'd asked for, but their extended separation plus fast available women led to a painful divorce.

Occasionally filled with doubt, she wondered if she'd made the right choices along the way. Most of all, she won-dered about children, the children only she had wanted, the children they never had. She wondered about who they might have been, about their hopes and dreams.

If her crew could have read her mind, they would have been surprised to find her capable of self-doubt. Mac and Gonzo believed her the best—they ought to know—they'd been through a lot together. You couldn't do any better than a space plane slot at Edwards, and *Hell Fire* had Scott's name on it.

Jolted back to reality by a loud ratchetlike clatter, Scott peered through the fog to find Mac closing the recessed missile bay inside *Hell Fire*'s short stubby wing.

Above all else, Chief Master Sergeant Andrew "Mac" MacWilliams was a good man in a storm—tall, black, distinguished in appearance, absolutely wonderful with people, and smart—especially smart. Scott thought Mac the sort of man who could do it all—the son of a tobacco farmer who could set anything right, and she loved to hear him talk. When he spoke in his deep North Carolina drawl, people couldn't help but notice his reason, humor, and honesty. Like Scott, Mac was a survivor, and like many successful military men, he was one of those people who believed it was always easier to get forgiveness than to get permission. With an appreciation for Mac's strength of character comfortably entrenched in her heart, Scott turned her attention to the task at hand.

*Cruise missiles loaded,* she thought.

Tonight, inside Hangar X-39A under the orange-yellow glow of halogen floodlights, Scott and her crew climbed the access scaffold leading to *Hell Fire*'s mammoth power plant. After stepping from the scaffold into *Hell Fire*'s engine inlet, Scott, Mac, and Gonzo began their preflight checklist. Deep inside *Hell Fire*'s cavernous air breathing mouth, Scott stood dwarfed by six enormous scramjet engines, each with circular blades stretching seven feet from floor to ceiling. As she and Mac slowly turned the free-wheeling blades looking for damage, Major Carlos Gonzalez shined a high intensity light into the engine from the front, looking for misplaced or forgotten tools.

Major Carlos Gonzalez was *Hell Fire*'s back-seater and Situation Awareness Evaluation Systems Officer (SAESO, pronounced say-so). He'd been stuck with the call name Gonzo because of the slight twist in his nose. At first, he didn't like it much, but it grew on him. Besides, he knew three other pilots named Gonzalez with the call name Speedy. In flight, Gonzo was instinctively a no-nonsense survivor. He'd been one of the Air Force's premier flight test engineers before his space plane assignment and believed that quick, positive action was always preferable to hesitation. In high stress situations, he was prone to take any positive action that came to mind. Fortunately, his instinctive reactions were nearly always right. He flew with as little emotion as possible, forcing himself to stay cool through any crisis. Like Scott, he passionately loved flying and couldn't imagine life without it. On top of that, he fully expected to live through it all and die at home in his own bed. He sought no glory and didn't care if he pissed people off along the way. His concern was to keep flying and stay alive. He needed it like a man needs a woman.

After completing their engine inspection, Gonzo looked Scott straight in the eyes and spoke quietly. "I don't like it. We've got no control."

"Those DEWSATs could give us a bad day," Scott agreed. As she thought about their situation, she felt like throwing up. She paused, took a deep breath, then continued. "With headquarters flying *Hell Fire* and Centurion controlling the DEWSATs, I feel like a sitting duck."

Chief Master Sergeant Mac MacWilliams, their crew chief and reconnaissance system operator, raised both eyebrows. "Makes me feel a little skittish myself. Sounds more like a skeet shoot."

"Yeah—Centurion's got the gun and we're the pigeons," added Gonzo.

*Too many things that could go wrong, would go wrong,* Scott thought with a grimace. *Always happens.*

By the year 2014, stealth cruise missiles had been mass produced and forty-one third-world countries had them. Accumulating arms with a fanatical passion, Iran and Iraq had been conducting a huge arms buildup for over twenty years—since the end of Desert Storm. Iraq led the pack, boasting an arsenal riveted with nuclear-tipped cruise missiles and a small fleet of Russian Kilo-class (*Varshavyanka*) submarines.

To counter this unpredictable third-world threat, former NORAD, NATO, and Soviet countries united forming the

Allied Forces, then fully deployed the Star Wars defense system—an orbiting armada of satellites.

Scott and her crew tested new weapons before they were officially accepted into the Allied arsenal. Tonight, they'd test the most important satellites in the Star Wars armada—the lethal workhorses—the DEWSATs (Directed Energy Weapon SATellites). Each DEWSAT was an orbiting counterstealth weapon system, a satellite that could detect and kill stealth missiles and aircraft from low earth orbit.

Within limits, stealth technology had made enemy aircraft and cruise missiles impossible to detect using conventional radar or infrared heat sensors. Each DEWSAT was designed to overcome stealth targets using an extraordinary radar, laser, and infrared telescope. In addition, anything airborne that it could detect, it could destroy using its high-power laser.

As part of the DEWSAT acceptance testing, Scott's mission tonight was to fly *Hell Fire* in an assault competition against Centurion—the space-based supercomputer controlling the Star Wars defense system. The idea behind this testing appeared straightforward—launch stealth cruise missiles then watch Centurion track and tag them using the DEWSAT armada. Scott thought of this testing as a high-tech game of laser tag she preferred not to play, because DEWSATs would steer their lasers toward both *Hell Fire* and her cruise missiles. When a laser tagged (illuminated) a threat, Centurion's defense team would score a hit. When any missile made it to target undetected, Scott's team would score.

Allied Headquarters believed their new *brilliant-class* DEWSAT would make stealth technology obsolete, but they needed testing and hard data to prove it. Scott, Mac, and Gonzo hoped Headquarters was right, but over the last two years they'd been through several tests similar to this one.

"Twenty years in the service and I'm still working the graveyard shift," Mac said with an exhausted smile. "Looks like they're looking to put the stealth troops outta business again."

**The Bad Seed**

"We've been trying to detect them for years," Scott said, climbing down the scaffold. "With a little luck, tonight could be our night, so let's get on with it."

"Roger, Scotty." Mac toggled a blue switch on his hand-held remote control unit. "*Hell Fire*'s cooling down—fuel pumps running." Immediately, a snow-white frost formed on *Hell Fire*'s matte black nose, wings, and air breathing underbody. Hydrogen slush chilled to minus 435 degrees Fahrenheit would circulate throughout *Hell Fire*'s heat shields during flight. Without this cooling, surface temperatures would soar to 5000 degrees Fahrenheit during hypersonic flight and *Hell Fire* would disintegrate. The fastest aerospace plane ever built, *Hell Fire* was a massive flying engine fueled and cooled by hydrogen slush.

As Scott, Mac, and Gonzo walked under *Hell Fire*'s nose, the trio zipped their flight jackets shut. A dense fog continuously boiled off *Hell Fire* and slowly settled on the hangar floor, causing the temperature underneath to drop twenty degrees. *Hell Fire* looked like an enormous wedge of dry ice, an enormous fog machine, about the size of a DC-10.

Gonzo carried his flight systems checklist over to Scott. "Next problem: target Nevada Test Site—all missiles programmed and loaded." Gonzalez pointed to the Anti-SATellite (ASAT) missile mounting rails inside *Hell Fire*'s stubby wings. "Mac hung 'em on ASAT hard-points."

"Unarmed stealth hawks and ASATs?" Scott glanced at Mac for approval.

"Right, Scotty. Twin ASATs and three Hawk cruise missiles. Headquarters ordered Hammer, Phantom, and Jammer Hawks," replied the chief as he led Scott and Gonzo to three duplicate cruise missiles on a loading rack alongside *Hell Fire*'s front tricycle gear.

Mac looked across the hangar toward his office and noticed an ankle-high fog layer covering the floor. Extending his arm above his head, he signaled an airman to open the gargantuan hangar doors. As the doors creaked open slowly and warm air rushed in, the cool fog layer poured out of the hangar over the taxiway, forming an eerie glowing ground-level cloud. Hangar lights caused the cloud to glow while the warmer outside air caused it to swirl, boil, and then slowly dissipate.

Scott returned Gonzo's checklist and asked him, "What about *Hope*?"

"Covered. Got their parts and supplies loaded." Once their testing was complete, they'd deliver replacement parts to Space Station *Hope*.

"And *Freedom*?" Scott paused. She felt her face flush. Major Jay Fayhee commanded Space Station *Freedom*. Her heart raced like she was a kid again in high school.

Gonzo looked at Scott's beet-red face, smiled gently, then winked. "Yeah, Scotty, we're bringing him everything he needs."

She looked forward to their *reunion* with mixed feelings. There was a part of Scott that wanted her dreams of Jay to come true, but another part prayed to get over him. "He meant more to me than I ever did to him," she sighed. After recovering her composure, she announced, "Then that's it. Checklist's complete. We're ready to go."

"Not quite," replied Gonzo. "We've gotta be sure those DEWSAT lasers are throttled back before we go anywhere."

Mac smiled a big toothy grin. "I'll roger that, Gonzo. Those lasers deliver a twenty-stick kick! They'd blow us out of the sky." From a distance of one hundred miles, each twenty megawatt DEWSAT laser delivered a punch loosely equivalent to about twenty sticks of dynamite.

"We're expecting safe laser confirmation in fifteen minutes, fellas," Scott said, checking her watch.

Scott, Mac, and Gonzo climbed *Hell Fire*'s access scaffold, carefully lowered themselves into *Hell Fire*'s heated cockpit, and strapped in. A towing vehicle attached itself to *Hell Fire*'s front tricycle gear and slowly pulled her out of the hangar to the south facing end of the runway.

Sitting in the darkness forty feet above the green and blue runway lights, Scott, Mac, and Gonzo configured *Hell Fire* for takeoff, then waited for their safe laser confirmation. Scott felt apprehensive about their sortie when she had time to think about it. For good luck, she felt underneath her flight suit and rubbed something about the size of a dog tag nestled between her breasts. *Jay always loved it there,* she thought with a smile. Around her neck, Scott wore a present Jay'd given her back in high school. Sealed in a smooth case of clear solid acrylic was a tiny four-leaf clover he'd given her for good luck. As a diversion, she turned on their forward landing lights and leaned her helmet against the cockpit canopy. Watching clouds of condensation boil off *Hell Fire*'s nose, she wondered, *What's he doing now?*

# 3

*Freedom* crew commander Major Jay Fayhee felt alone and
melancholy as he rested his forehead against the observation window and watched endless lightning flashes off California's southern coast. At night from an altitude of 22,300
miles, the earth reminded Fayhee of a glimmering Christmas ornament—a large reflective ball which glistened with
the sparkle of lightning from electrical storms. From Fayhee's window, the earth looked small and remote—about
the size of a beach ball at arm's length. Christmas music
played softly in the background as Fayhee dreamed of days
gone by, of the woman he'd loved and lost a long time ago.

Seemed like a hundred years ago, but he remembered
every detail like it was yesterday. He wondered if she'd be
the woman he remembered, the one he used to know, or
had she changed? Fiercely independent, she'd always gotten along fine without him. After giving the matter some
thought, he expected that she'd be whoever she darn well
pleased. She always meant more to him than he did to her
anyway. Linda could live without him easy enough, but
she'd never divorce flying.

He didn't understand it at the time, but he'd been jealous
of her flying because he couldn't compete. Flying was always Linda's top priority. In retrospect, he could see it

more clearly now. Jay knew she couldn't change, he wouldn't want her to, but most of all he needed to talk to her, really open up and talk like in the old days. His eyes teared as he imagined picking up where they'd left off. But that was only a dream and dreams never came true on board *Freedom*. Besides, she'd never love him again after what he'd done.

Staring out his window, he cried out to the night in a soft whisper, "I'd do anything if she'd only love me again."

The idea that time healed all wounds offered hope for the brokenhearted, but little else. Time provided Jay an anesthetic, a pain killer, but his wound had never healed—never even closed.

He wondered how she'd look. Like he imagined—no, probably even better. She'd always been like that, the older she'd gotten, the better she'd looked.

He loved her smile, her laugh, but most of all he loved the twinkle in her eyes. Would her eyes twinkle? Probably, but not for him. Her entire face would light up when she was happy.

Breathing deeply, he remembered the marvelous smell of her hair. If only he could hold her again.

Tenderly, he caressed an old faded letter, one of the last letters he'd gotten from Linda before he'd started doing most of his thinking between his legs. Jay wasn't any different from any other man he'd ever known. He loved sex like Linda loved flying. He thought himself an excellent lover, always considerate, patient, and he came back often—never learned to say no. He'd needed her desperately and within reach, but she was always gone. Even so, the other women weren't worth it and this job wasn't worth it—not worth losing Linda.

Divorcing her was the biggest regret of his life. He'd found happiness in his own backyard with the girl next door, but didn't understand that until it was too late.

As the last line from the song "I'll be Home For Christmas" slowly faded, a grating voice abruptly startled him.

"Jay, we need to talk."

Fayhee sighed, but didn't turn away from the window.

He struggled to remember the details of his dream, then wrote them down. During his eleven-month stay on *Freedom*, Fayhee had learned to freeze and restart his interrupted dreams. Some time later he'd read his notes, reconstruct his dream, then pick up dreaming where he left off. After collecting his thoughts, Fayhee reluctantly turned away from his observation window and left his dreams of Linda on hold.

Space Station *Freedom*, the flagship of the armada, housed a six-member crew: two men plus four supercomputers. Depack McKee kept watch over the computer crew—Centurion plus his three networked subordinates—and Fayhee watched over Depack. Together, they provided Headquarters with an option for human intervention when anything went wrong. Fayhee and McKee often joked about playing second banana to Centurion, but their primary mission was maintenance—to their dismay, they were Centurion's keepers.

"Wake up, Jay," snapped Centurion with a grainy voice sounding like sand and glue.

As Fayhee looked into the television monitor, his head throbbed as his blood pressure began to rise. *What a freaking waste of screen space,* Fayhee thought. A three-dimensional, computer-generated talking head stared him squarely in the eyes. Looking repugnantly generic, but politically correct, Centurion's face was liked by no one because you couldn't tell what he was. Fayhee's jaw tensed—he hated looking Centurion in the eyes. It made him uncomfortable, so he looked away into his flat panel display and gazed at his own reflection. During his conversations with Centurion, he'd always felt uncomfortable because he'd never identified where Centurion's voice came from. Fayhee had learned to hate living with Centurion. In a disquieting sense, Centurion existed everywhere on board *Freedom*, knew everything, possessed a quick tongue, and displayed no tact. On board *Freedom,* privacy existed for Fayhee only in his thoughts and imagination.

Fayhee reluctantly read over the test script Centurion displayed in bright red print. "Centurion—make ready to alter DEWSAT behavior."

Centurion was the central nervous system and mouthpiece for the Star Wars defense system. Technically, Centurion was the finest example of state-of-the-art computer technology the world had ever produced—a third-generation free space all optical supercomputer built with massively parallel computation capability based on neural networks—modeled after the workings of the human brain, but built of mirrors, lenses, and lights. He wasn't much to look at, but he learned fast, serving as primary control computer for the space-based missile defense system.

"Very well, Jay," Centurion responded immediately, "DEWSAT behavior records have been retrieved and await modification." Centurion spoke with a distinctively male voice, although his timing and inflection sounded mechanical.

Jay repeated the DEWSAT configuration instructions from his test script. "Turn down the power of every DEWSAT laser passing over the test zone. Black out the test zone completely. We track and tag targets tonight—don't destroy them."

"Very well, Jay," Centurion replied immediately.

Fayhee raised his head and looked over the control console at a large, brightly colored image which dominated the control room—Centurion's globe. Spherically shaped, Centurion's globe was a three-dimensional holographic picture of the earth projected in the center of the control room.

Seventy-two DEWSATs circled the earth in six polar orbit planes—twelve DEWs per orbit. Circling the earth in a chaotic frenzy, the DEWSAT armada reminded Jay of swarming bees.

Fifteen seconds later, Centurion spoke plainly with increased and considerable volume. "Jay—the blackout directive is complete. All DEWSATs passing over the test zone will disable their lasers."

Space Station *Hope*
over India

altitude = 22,300 miles

72 Sunflower-shaped
DEWSATs

Earth

altitude = 115 miles

Space Station *Freedom*
Pinned above the horizon,
south of Cheyenne Mountain

altitude = 22,300 miles

*Freedom, Hope,* and the DEWSAT Armada

"Very well," Fayhee said as he studied the eight-foot diameter globe projected in the middle of the room—Centurion's view of the earth and sky seen through satellite eyes. "Keep your eyes and ears on. We need total global coverage."

The Star Wars defense system consisted of an armada of satellites orbiting the earth. Organized into three layers, like an onion skin, the armada consisted of orbiting weapon, sensor, and communication satellites. Orbiting closest to earth, the weapons fleet was built of two types of satellites: suicide interceptors and DEWSATs. In orbit above the weapons, the sensor satellites, and above them all, communication satellites populated the outermost layer.

Cheyenne Mountain, Centurion, and the DEWSAT armada clearly understood their job—defense. Cheyenne Mountain assigned target priorities, Centurion assigned targets to individual DEWSATs, and the DEWSAT armada did the fighting. The division of labor was simple and it worked well.

Fayhee knew the DEWSAT armada would tag *Hell Fire* during testing tonight. Any laser configuration error could reduce *Hell Fire* to dust. "Show me everything we have. There's no margin for error." Fayhee's flat panel display was immediately updated with Centurion's report:

```
DEFENSE SUPPORT PROGRAM—SATELLITE
          ARMADA STATUS

• LOWSATs: 18 Low Orbiting Warhead
  SATs orbit 125 mi: 25% coverage
• DEWSATs: 72 Directed Energy Weapon
  SATs orbit 115 mi: test zone black-
  out
• SLCSATs: 12 Submarine Laser Communi-
  cation SATs orbit 275 mi: 66% cover-
  age
• EYESATs: 24 Recon SATs orbit 500 mi:
  100% coverage
• EARSATs: 14 Sensor SATs orbit 1640
  mi: 100% coverage
```

- COMMSATs: 6 Communication SATs orbit
  22,300 mi: 100% coverage
- Space Stations: 2 Control SATs orbit
  22,300 mi:
  - Master -> SS *Freedom*: 100% cover-
    age
  - Slave -> SS *Hope*: WARNING—BACKUP
    DATA LINK FAILURE

RECOMMENDED ACTION: REPLACE TRANSMITTER

"As you see, Jay, we maintain total global visibility—our eyes and ears are on, but we cannot shoot over the test zone."

Fayhee scanned the report, concluding his job was done. Space Station *Hope* had transmitter problems, but *Hope* was in geostationary orbit halfway around the world off the southern tip of India. That transmitter was someone else's problem—not much Fayhee could do about it from *Freedom*. He quietly read the notes he'd made earlier about his Christmas dream, turned around to face the outside wall, and rested his forehead on the observation window. Gazing once again toward earth, Jay watched the lightning glisten and wondered, *What's she doing now?*

*The Texas Sunflower, 12/07/2014, 1034 Zulu*
ALTITUDE: 115 MILES IN POLAR ORBIT,
ORBITAL INCLINATION: 86.5 DEGREES,
ONBOARD A DIRECTED ENERGY WEAPON SATELLITE
(DEWSAT)

Headed due north at over 17,000 miles an hour, a satellite passed 115 miles above Austin, Texas, during the darkest part of the night. From one quarter mile away, the satellite resembled a sunflower in a flowerpot. Looking friendly and familiar, the satellite's shape revealed no clue to its actual size or ominous purpose. Seventy-two of these satellites orbited along lines of longitude, each a Directed Energy Weapon SATellite (DEWSAT).

Positioned with its long slender stem pointing toward the

earth's center, the sunflower head faced Austin. The DEWSAT, whose structure would have been awkward and lanky on the ground, raced with effortless grace across the big Texas sky.

The DEWSAT's business end was its flower-shaped head, a large segmented mirror thirty-three feet across. The mirror was made of smaller moving pieces—a circular center segment and twelve identical outer segments surrounding the center like petals of a flower.

Connecting the large mirror to its flowerpot base, the one-hundred-foot-long stem provided the key to the DEWSAT's twenty-million Watt laser punch. The DEWSAT's Free Electron Laser accelerated high energy electrons down its stem, then converted them into infrared light.

The flowerpot base was a cylindrical tube measuring thirty feet across and fifty feet long. All the DEWSAT's vital electrical organs were housed within the upper two thirds of the cylinder while the volatile combustion organs were confined to the bottom third. The DEWSAT's heart was a mammoth electrical power plant which pumped life into the laser, infrared telescope, and radar. Stacked below the electrical systems were the fuel tanks, pumps, and plumbing required for firing life into its rocket engines—all the stuff that a technician's dreams are made of.

As the DEWSAT passed over Austin, dim traces of city lights reflected off the mirror's highly polished surfaces. Collecting everything it could see, the DEWSAT diligently searched for jet engine exhaust and missile plumes.

At 1035 Zulu, the DEWSAT passing over Austin received an encrypted radio signal from Centurion which read:

```
set laser power output = tag
```

Immediately, the DEWSAT computer reduced the electrical power driving the Free Electron Laser to a safe level. After reducing the power, an automatic test showed all was well and the DEWSAT acknowledged Centurion's message with an encrypted radio transmission.

```
DEWSAT ack: laser power output = tag
```

For the moment, the DEWSAT had lost its punch, throttled back for counterstealth testing—the war game of laser tag.

# 4

For as long as there had been war, military leaders had struggled to do what Major General Robert Craven's team had done. His organization had taken a quantum leap toward realizing the remotely controlled battlefield. As Supreme Allied Commander, Craven moved to the top of the ranks by leading an effort which consolidated battlefield communication, command, and control within the new Allied Headquarters building inside Cheyenne Mountain. He was one of the first to understand that optical technology offered the keys to make the remotely controlled battlefield a reality. They weren't there yet, people were still in the loop, but this accomplishment was considered by many a technical marvel comparable to the Panama Canal. Considered brilliant by his superiors, Craven believed his ability to pick good people, point them in the right direction, then turn them loose was his greatest contribution. His motto—"Do something. Lead, follow, or get out of the way."—had served his organization well in his day, but Craven's time had now passed and instinctively he knew it. Over the last two years, he'd changed—he'd simply worn out.

Craven was a mover and shaker. His long and distinguished military career, now drawing to a close, had been marked by frequent, fierce, and far-reaching battles with Washington over vision, strategy, schedules, and funding—especially funding. For years he had tirelessly lobbied Congress, the public, and the Pentagon to fully deploy the Star Wars space-based defense system, and in doing so had antagonized much of his Washington-based constituency. In the minds of many Army, Navy, and Air Force leaders, Craven was one of the most brilliant and controversial figures in American military history. So vigorous was his advocacy for an orbiting military armada that he had placed his career in jeopardy much like General Billy Mitchell had done promoting air power.

Major General Robert Craven was average height with broad shoulders and massive forearms for his age. In his late fifties, his once thick curly black hair was now thin and gray. His face had a weathered outdoor look to it, but his eyes, most of all, revealed the inescapable fatigue he felt in his soul.

There wasn't a person in Craven's organization who didn't admire him, but the workaholic years of relentless stress had taken their toll. Craven's onetime limitless energy was gone. He was exhausted, out of patience, and to top it off, his pet project—High Ground—was in trouble. Even though his baby was behind schedule and over budget, Craven believed the test results they collected during the next few days would turn this situation around. More clearly than anyone else, he understood they must.

Surrounded by granite walls fifteen hundred feet thick, Craven worked through a computer printout with his attack force commander, Colonel Wayne Hinson. Although Craven's mission was primarily defensive in nature, his organization included a small attack component for testing their defenses. The Consolidated Space Operations Center (CSOC, pronounced sis-awk) provided the Allied attack forces; the Strategic Defense Initiative Organization (SDIO) provided their lethal defenses.

Protected by two massive twenty-five-ton steel blast

doors, Commander Hinson sat in the center of the Situation Control Room surrounded by his master console—the computer brain of the attack center. From his master console, Hinson could locate, inventory, and control everything in the Allied military arsenal that orbits, flies, floats, rolls, or walks.

Leaning over Hinson's shoulder, Craven impatiently ran his finger over a computer printout, stopping on the results column. His once steady hands now shook uncontrollably around the clock. His mood was tense. His expression—one of disbelief. Before he could complete his thought, Craven was interrupted by a nervous young airman.

"General, Chairman of the Joint Chiefs is on the line, sir."

Along with most of working-class America, Craven had learned to hate the phone, and like most, his feelings were heartfelt. Suspending his thoughts in progress, he drew a deep breath before speaking. "Thanks, son. I'll take it here."

He picked up the console phone. "Chief. This is Craven. What can I do for you?"

Not one for small talk, the chairman got down to the crux of the matter. "You've got a big problem."

"Give it to me straight," Craven replied. He clinched his teeth as the muscles around his mouth tightened. He hated plain talk from the chairman because it always put him on the spot.

"The President is livid." The chairman cleared his throat, then continued. His tone was strained and barely under control. "Iraq has two subs parked in cruise missile range of Washington and New York. High Ground's been funded for years to counter this threat but has not delivered!" The chairman paused.

There was a deep silence on the line. As the silence protracted, a test of wills emerged. Checking his watch, Craven grimaced. Calling from the comfort of his own home, the chairman had time enough to stall; he did not. "You're not telling me anything I don't already know."

"High Ground's over two years behind schedule and over budget. Washington wants results—and I mean before Christmas!" The chairman's restraint evaporated.

"I get the message." *Put up or shut up,* he thought. Craven fully understood that his counterstealth project, code-named High Ground, was in a jam. Their funding situation was desperate. If they didn't deliver some good news soon, High Ground's future was unpredictable. They could get the ax and lose it all.

"Good." Craven heard a sigh of relief over the phone. "Pull out the stops. Do everything you can."

"Will do. High Ground's back on track and won't derail again. I guarantee it."

Craven hung up and looked across the console at his heir apparent, General Daniel "Slim" Mason. Although tense, when looking at Slim he felt better—it was his tie tack. That tie tack always tickled Craven. A gift from his grandson, Slim's tie tack was a tiny prop-driven biplane he wore no matter the occasion. It wasn't important how it looked, it was a gift from his grandson and he valued it. Craven smiled to himself every time he looked at that tie tack closely—definitely not GI. Over the years, Mason always managed to keep his priorities straight and had a wife, three married sons, grandchildren, plus lifelong hometown friends to show for it.

Mason believed in family, friends, country, hard work, decent values, and God. Slim didn't force his beliefs on others, but once you knew what he believed in, you knew the man. His life exemplified everything he believed and Craven admired him for it.

With Mason, what you saw was what you got and what you got came from the heart of Dixie. As far back as any of Slim's hometown friends could remember, he'd always borne a striking resemblance to Jimmy Stewart, and in all honesty, as he'd grown older, his likeness had slowly transformed into a near facsimile. The silver-haired, fifty-two-year-old Jimmy Stewart look-alike was a little over six two, lean, angular faced, lanky with pipe-cleaner legs,

**The Bad Seed**

bony arms, and shoulders broader than they looked on his tall frame.

Mason and Craven went back a long way—all the way back to the Persian Gulf War. In January 1991, Captain Slim Mason flew over Baghdad as Major Craven's wingman while they were members of the elite Screaming Demons—the clandestine F-117 stealth fighter squadron first stationed in Tonopah, Arizona. An MIT graduate in electrical engineering, specializing in advanced radar technology, Mason loved airplanes and first married his two interests by flying the F-117—the black stealth fighter officially known as the Nighthawk, affectionately known by the pilot community as the stinkbug. Mason joked that flying the F-117 wasn't all it was cracked up to be. Essentially, the stinkbug was a manned, fully automated Tomahawk cruise missile that flew itself to target, dropped its two bombs, then returned the pilot home. Given good intelligence and extensive planning, all the pilot did was take off and land—the stinkbug did the rest.

After the Cold War wound down and the intoxicating success of Desert Storm had faded, Mason had been among the first who somberly predicted that mass-produced, long-range stealth cruise missiles would emerge as the preeminent threat wielded by the third world. Further, he predicted that stealth cruise missile detection from space was the only viable way to counter this third-world threat now looming just beyond the horizon. Although subsequent events confirmed his predictions, Mason faced a wall of resistance from the leaders of older, established military services just as Craven had found when advocating for an orbiting military armada. Mason began appealing directly to the public through books, interviews, and speeches. Once Mason went public with his appeal for expanding our military presence in space, Craven got wind of it and brought him into his fold under Cheyenne Mountain. Two old stinkbug pilots were united once again. Their quest for a worldwide, real-time, space-based air, land, and sea surveillance system was the glue that first bound them together, but over the years their relationship had developed into a deeper, more meaningful matter of trust.

From its inception, Mason rose rapidly through the ranks of the High Ground project under Craven's tutelage. Initially, Slim's team focused on developing a surveillance system code-named ClearWater, a space-based sea surveillance system for detecting submerged submarines. Following ClearWater's staggering success, Mason was promoted to general officer and acquired two hats within the Cheyenne Mountain community—military manager and technical leader extraordinaire. Not many could effectively switch hats back and forth, but Mason could. This extraordinary skill catapulted him over his peers, but no one seemed to mind. His peers and subordinates were often his biggest fans. When wearing his military manager hat, Mason served as unified NORAD/NATO Commander In Chief (CIC). Most of his mornings were wrapped up in the never-ending series of staff meetings required of the CIC. The job was a political juggling act, and his approach to the problem was management by consent. In the afternoon, Mason liked to change hats. With ClearWater's naval success under their belts, Mason's technical team progressed to the problem of air surveillance—specifically to the detection of stealth missiles over land and sea. As it turned out, detecting low flying stealth cruise missiles from low earth orbit had been an enormous technical problem—bigger than anyone had imagined—but finally they had good reason to think they'd solved it. Data collected over the next few days of testing would tell the story.

Looking into the eyes of his former wingman brought Craven's attention back to the immediate task at hand. He spoke quietly. "Heat's on."

Mason nodded. "There's a tremendous lot riding on these tests."

Leaning over Hinson's shoulder, Craven stared at the screen labeled **War Game Scoreboard**. Highlighted in reverse video, the legend printed across the screen read:

**The Bad Seed**

```
High Ground Simulation Results —
   Final Score:
         SDIO Defense Forces - 6
         CSOC Attack Forces - 0
```

Hinson had run a computer program which simulated *Hell Fire*'s missile attack on the Nevada Test Site. According to his simulation, High Ground should work perfectly—the counterstealth defense forces should come out on top.

The large veins on Craven's neck bulged as his face turned red. "I don't buy it. Our defenses look too damn good—too optimistic."

Craven drummed his fingers across Hinson's desk and spoke in his *don't screw with me now* tone of voice. "I wanta see your attack plan simulated one last time before we run this test live. Change it. Make it more realistic."

"Yes sir." He knew the routine. He'd gone over his attack plan with Craven twice in the last hour.

"I wanta run through it again—start to finish." Craven's tone was final. He pointed to an icon shaped like a submarine on the computer screen. "I wanta see the position of your attack forces. Show me again—*Hell Fire*, the *Dorito*, and the sub—I wanta see 'em all."

Hinson recited his attack plan like a well-rehearsed actor, then concluded: "If Centurion tags all six missiles tonight, stealth is history."

Mason stood behind Hinson, quietly talking to their ally from the Soviet Commonwealth, General Yuri Krol. Both men looked concerned. The Allied alliance included the Soviet Commonwealth of Independent States as well as former NORAD and NATO countries. The alliance was based on economic necessity, an issue of dollars and cents, not mutual admiration. It was cost-effective to share a satellite defense system, and besides, no single country could afford it.

Awkwardly sliding the rim of his round hat through his fingers, Mason looked into Craven's eyes. "General, I think you fellas may be outrunning your headlights—just a little bit."

"Whataya mean, Slim?"

Mason shifted his tall frame uneasily from side to side. "You have no visibility—no way to see trouble coming."

"What do you propose?"

"Have someone keep an eye on Centurion—watch his activity log," Mason suggested in his slow, deliberate stammer. "If there's a problem, he'll show you what's going on." Centurion kept a log showing every action he took and any errors he found.

"Nobody reads activity logs anymore," Hinson quipped impatiently. "Everything's automated. Computers do the dirty work."

Mason didn't like Hinson's me-first-me-only attitude so he spoke to him clearly. A rampant careerist, Hinson's single goal in life was to get his ticket punched and move on. "Yuri's got experienced folks at Kaliningrad watching Centurion's log around the clock. You're gonna need trained people—no way around it."

"That's true," General Krol added, calmly chewing the stump of his pipe. "You'll need staff full-time day and night."

Hinson looked confident about the test, but neither Craven, Mason, nor Krol shared his sense of well-being. Craven had been involved with High Ground testing over fifteen years and had survived many problems. If anything went wrong, he knew there was real danger here for Hinson's attack forces. "Tonight's no drill, Colonel. You've never run these attack scripts hot—on the air. Our people's lives are on the line. If anything life-or-death comes down, my people have orders to break radio silence. You hear from them and I want this test aborted yesterday. Do I make myself clear?"

"Yes, sir!"

"And have someone cover Centurion's log. If anything goes wrong, you'll see it."

Hinson nodded his head, but did not hear. Tuning his

**The Bad Seed**

attack program, his fingers raced over the keyboard, trying to keep up with his head.

Craven's gaze shifted to Mason and Krol. "Conference
call in ten minutes. Let's go." They left the room and de-
scended one story deeper inside Cheyenne Mountain.

# 5

Buried sixty feet below a residential neighborhood west of Baghdad, surrounded by brightly painted windowless walls of concrete and steel, Iraqi Cabinet members gathered in the security of their bunker for a meeting with Iraqi President Hessian Kamel al-Tikriti. Kamel, like his aging father-in-law Saddam Hussein, was a brutal tribelike chieftain who reigned by fear.

Once Kamel arrived, the menacing silhouette of an enormous hulk appeared in the bunker doorway wearing a traditional *gandura* robe. Towering above the others at six foot five, shaped like the front end of a bus, al-Mashhadi blocked the light emanating from the bunker. Standing in his shadow, the President carefully studied the backlit form of his heir apparent, looking for some clue as to the mood of the coming meeting. There was none. Kamel found al-Mashhadi's dark expressionless eyes impossible to read. His face appeared cracked as old leather, his hands strong, deeply wrinkled but steady.

Moving diplomatically to one side, al-Mashhadi warmly greeted Kamel in his deep gravelly voice. *"Ahlan wa sahlan,"*—my house is your house. "We're honored you could attend on such short notice." The secretary-general delivered his greetings with the utmost sincerity. No sense of the barbarian in the big man's demeanor. His ability to lie with the grace of a polished diplomat was one of his greatest gifts.

Al-Mashhadi personified his motto—"NOBODY HURTS ME UNHARMED." These four words encapsulated the essence of the man and became the Iraqi state creed following the Persian Gulf War, a rallying cry for every Iraqi tribelike sect, clan, and village. NOBODY HURTS ME UNHARMED was printed for all to see on Iraqi currency in much the same way the United States printed IN GOD WE TRUST, but no country outside the Middle East appreciated the significance of this political statement. Al-Mashhadi believed when it came to human rights and Middle East politics, the Allies lived in a world of delusion.

The President took his seat at the head of the table flanked by leathery-skinned generals of the Republican Guard.

"Excellency," al-Mashhadi began with some sense of pride. "Allah has shown us again that he is greater than our enemies."

Cabinet members, dressed in *gandura* robes, nodded their heads in agreement.

A methodical man, al-Mashhadi continued with elegant patience. "Allah is on our side in our jihad against the infidels. He has given us a sign, a powerful advantage. He demands we use it. It is our destiny. This week we may get the chance we've waited for so long—our chance to destroy the infidels' war machine."

"Yes, yes," the American-schooled President replied impatiently. "I've heard this chance of a lifetime story many times before. Get to the point. I have an appointment with the UN ambassador in twenty minutes."

Unshaken, al-Mashhadi continued. "The point is this, Excellency. We'll likely get an opportunity to cripple the Allies' killer satellite armada without firing a shot and without revealing our hand."

"Sounds too good to be true," scoffed the Iraqi President, checking his watch.

Al-Mashhadi explained. "The American Army showed

us what to do with the ECM (electronic countermeasures) work they did on computer viruses. The Zionists planned to plant battlefield viruses in our communications systems using their own radio transmissions. They buried this idea after they found their equipment was more susceptible to viruses than ours."

Al-Mashhadi slowly extended his large hand in the direction of a dark small man, dressed in an Army uniform, sitting next to the view graph projector. Motioning for the man to rise, he continued with an introduction.

"Colonel Nassar's the head of our ECM organization. Educated in America, he received his ECM training from MIT and the U.S. Army. He'll give you a summary of where we stand."

Confident, al-Mashhadi sat down as Colonel Nassar cleared his throat. "As some of you know, we had a significant breakthrough two years ago in the area of battlefield grade computer viruses. We created a virus code-named PAM—an adaptive computer program that exists only to survive."

"PAM?" The name caught the President's attention.

Nassar nodded thoughtfully. "The code name is intended to deceive, Excellency. The acronym stands for Perpetual Adaptive Monitor. It means nothing to most people."

The Iraqi President gave Colonel Nassar an uneasy glance. "Survive. How?"

Nassar took a second to frame his response, then looked straight into the President's eyes. "PAM is incapable of remorse and ruthless beyond belief. Once a virgin PAM program starts running, it cannot be stopped—PAM can't be destroyed." Nassar paused, allowing his words to linger, but showed no sign of fear or weakness. Allah would protect him. After working with PAM for two years, he knew in his soul what she was about.

"I am interested, Colonel," the President announced, impressed with the intense little colonel.

Nassar continued with a tone marked by seriousness. "PAM's a computer program—nothing more, but she looks like something she's not. In that respect, she's a Trojan horse—a program that does what she's supposed to do, but unknown to the Allies, she'll quietly perform our bidding. She's also a snake, but her symptoms are subtle. She doesn't crash a computer like an ordinary snake, she takes control and slows it down.

"Loosely speaking, PAM's a *bad seed.* I mean she is born bad—bad from the moment she's created. When threatened, she reproduces then protects herself. Nothing can be done to stop her—like nothing I've ever seen. Capable of lying dormant indefinitely, once PAM takes root, she and her children exist only to survive and propagate their own kind.

"PAM's built around three separate pieces of software created by the American Army, Air Force, and CIA. Our breakthrough came when we modified this software using genetic programming. Darwin's theory of natural selection provided PAM's reproductive algorithm, and consequently only the fittest, most virulent strains survive. Originally, her heartbeat came from the Army's threat analysis software. It evaluates threats around the clock. PAM's eyes and ears were developed by the CIA—a program named *Snoopy* which monitors people and computer chatter. It keys on sensitive information like threats, security keys, and passwords. The secret of PAM's survival and the software that makes her dangerous is her Weapon Systems Management program created by the Air Force. That's where the action is—the software she lives by. PAM eliminates anyone or anything that threatens her directly. She monitors what's going on around her and if she's threatened, she'll protect herself. Once PAM's running on Centurion, she'll control every killer satellite—their entire orbiting armada. PAM's single purpose for existence is survival—she lives only to consume computer time. Nobody hurts her unharmed!"

After allowing the full significance of his last comment to sink in, the colonel concluded, "PAM's ready. We've tested her for two years."

Satisfied, the Iraqi President allowed the commanding

general of the Air Force to question Nassar. "Why did she take so long to test?"

"Two reasons. She's complex and she moves." The colonel went on to explain. "Her complexity pushes our testing capability to the limits, and when threatened, she moves from one computer to another. When we'd look for her, she'd move to another computer over a communication link. As I said earlier, her symptoms are subtle, never obvious."

"Well—get to the point, Colonel. How do you plan to cripple their missile killer satellites?"

Nassar let out a long breath before answering. "What I reveal now must not leave this room." Slowly, the colonel made eye contact with every man present. After everyone nodded agreement, he continued.

"As you know, SDI programs are built and tested at the Lawrence Livermore Lab. What you may not know is that we have strategically placed an agent—a computer security specialist—inside Livermore. Two years ago, he played a crucial role in PAM's development by providing us SDI source code. Today, he has a copy of PAM on site and is prepared to plant our bad seed."

"What about their software testing and quality controls?" asked the general. "They'll detect PAM during their testing."

"We have reason to believe their normal software testing cycle may be bypassed." Nassar was quietly positive. "High Ground, the Allied stealth missile detection project, is over two years behind schedule and over budget. Our source inside Cheyenne Mountain believes the survival of the High Ground project depends on the results obtained during their next few days of testing. If they have problems, there will be enormous pressure to shortcut their time-consuming quality controls. Our best information indicates that they must show success or place the High Ground project at risk. The odds are shifting in our favor, Excellency." Colonel Nassar paused, again looked the President directly in the eyes, then spoke clearly in a quiet voice. "If we get confirmation their testing will be bypassed, I propose we include PAM in the Star Wars program build."

Thoughtfully gazing at the ceiling, the Iraqi President put both hands behind his head. "I understand your proposal, Colonel. I'd like you to answer a few direct questions for me. First, can PAM be traced? Could Iraq be held accountable or implicated in any way?"

"Impossible. PAM resulted from theoretical work first funded by the U.S. Army before the turn of the century. I expect that's where the Allies will lay blame. Virus programs like PAM are difficult, if not impossible, to trace."

"What if our agents are discovered?"

"*Inshallah,*"—(God willing)—the Chief of Military Intelligence responded. "They will die as martyrs on the altar of Islam."

"*Allahu Akbar,*" al-Mashhadi added somberly. "Stalin sacrificed ten million souls to preserve the Bolshevik revolution. Iraq is prepared to do likewise."

"And strategically? Are we keeping the pressure on?"

"We've got two Kilo-class subs parked within range of Washington and New York."

"The Allies know this?"

Nassar allowed a thin smile. "The infidels stalk our missile drills." The Russian Kilo-class submarine was an older diesel-electric and easily detected unless running off battery.

"That is good," the Iraqi President concluded. "What should I expect when you plant your bad seed?"

Slowly, clearly, Colonel Nassar responded. "I can make no promises, Excellency, but we expect to plant PAM in Centurion. PAM behaves more like a program cancer than a virus. When threatened, she'll spread like wildfire. She'll infect every computer on *Freedom*, then the Allies will lose control of their satellite armada."

"What does it mean—to lose control of a satellite armada?"

"I'm sure of one thing—the *Maronites* (enemies of Allah) will wish they'd never been born."

The Iraqi President nodded and accepted this not for

technical reasons, but because Colonel Nassar believed it. "After PAM—what about our stealth cruise missiles? Will they fly undetected?"

"*Inshallah* but I cannot promise this. Once PAM takes over, she'll control their orbiting death machines—their DEWSATs. Their SDI testing will be delayed until they eliminate PAM. The infidels must eliminate PAM, but she won't allow anyone or anything to approach her. She won't allow anything through the Star Wars layers of warhead satellites—nothing launched from earth can penetrate their deadly DEWSAT layer. She won't allow anything near Space Station *Freedom*. To eliminate PAM the Allies must disconnect Centurion. To disconnect Centurion, they must board *Freedom*. PAM won't let it happen—she won't tolerate threats. PAM will turn the Zionist technology of death against the infidels."

Colonel Nassar paused. Looking around the table at the Iraqi party of God members, he saw the glimmer of revenge in their eyes. He felt exhilaration knowing his place in history was about to unfold. Revenge for the Persian Gulf War was within their grasp. Nassar looked at the faces of each Cabinet member and recalled that each had suffered loss during the infidel invasion. With Allah's help, he had reached into the depths of their darkened souls and uncovered their reason for living. They sat thunderstruck, their tongues still, their jaws slack.

"Let me be clear on this point," Colonel Nassar concluded. "I believe the PAM virus intractable—a problem without solution."

"A problem without solution," the Iraqi President repeated quietly. "What do you mean exactly?"

"A technical problem without technical solution. Once PAM spreads to Centurion's subordinate computers, we can't postulate a plausible technical solution. We can't figure any way to disconnect Centurion because *Freedom*'s a fortress built for Centurion's protection."

"Any possibility of random destruction? Any danger to our people?"

"Possible—but not likely."

**The Bad Seed**

The Iraqi President studied the faces of each Cabinet member. Each party of God member nodded in agreement, quietly repeating, *"Allahu Akbar."* Revenge against the infidels would be sweet.

"We've nothing to lose," the Iraqi President observed with a look of satisfaction in his eyes. "Very well, Colonel, if the opportunity presents itself, plant your bad seed."

# 6

Sitting forty feet above the runway with *Hell Fire*'s brakes locked, Scott individually throttled each scramjet engine to full military power while her flight computer monitored fuel consumption and power output. After the last engine had been checked, *Hell Fire*'s flight computer flashed a green **All Systems Go** message across her flat panel display. She looked up, gazed out of the cockpit down the vast expanse of runway stretched out before her, and felt satisfied that *Hell Fire* was airworthy. Sealed inside her fully pressurized flight suit, she felt a trickle of perspiration running down her throttle arm. Scott adjusted the air-conditioning in her suit, read the time from her cockpit clock, then thought the action should begin soon.

While Scott checked the power plant, Gonzo checked the Global Position System against the reference position posted on a sign standing by the side of the runway—everything looked good.

"*Hell Fire*, you're cleared for takeoff," echoed Edward's control tower.

"Mac, Gonzo—you ready?" Scott asked, advancing engine one's throttle to full military power.

"Backseat's go."

"Ready down under," replied Mac from his recon seat in *Hell Fire*'s nose—forward and below Scott.

Scott slowly moved her five remaining throttles forward to full military power. As she watched *Hell Fire*'s thrust readout build on her instrument display, the thunderous sound pressure level inside *Hell Fire* became deafeningly loud. Although *Hell Fire* was a later model and had been improved, the sound pressure level directly over the power plant in the early X-30 prototypes had been sufficient to kill humans. As *Hell Fire*'s six-pack reached full power, she shook violently against the brakes. Scott locked the throttles together, released the brakes, then synchronously advanced all six engine throttles into afterburner. *Hell Fire*, a 250,000-pound plane about the size of a DC-10, bolted down the runway propelled by over 300,000 pounds of thrust. When Scott cut in her afterburners, the thunderous noise level inside *Hell Fire* approached the threshold of pain and the crew couldn't communicate over the intercom. Each scramjet engine in *Hell Fire*'s six-pack output 50,000 pounds of thrust—more thrust than that which powered the ocean liner *Queen Mary*.

Accelerating down the runway, *Hell Fire* was engulfed in a swirling cloud of condensation. Trailing behind the cloud streamed a long fiery tail of intensely bright burning hydrogen. In the daylight, the plane's profile looked much like the head of a giant white shark with its jaws open wide, gulping air.

Roaring down the runway, Scott's helmet pressed hard against her molded seat.

As *Hell Fire*'s ground speed passed 225 miles per hour, Scott depressed an ignition switch which fired the Rocketdyne engine in *Hell Fire*'s tail. Instantly, the roar of a controlled explosion shook *Hell Fire* as an additional 100,000 pounds of thrust kicked in, pinning Scott to her seat. She gently pulled back on the stick, rotated *Hell Fire*'s nose up, and they were airborne pulling a three-g climb. *Hell Fire* climbed higher and higher, belching smoke and flame in her wake, illuminating the black desert sky like a flare.

"You fellas all right?" Scott asked. In one swift motion,

she raised the gear, cut the Rocketdyne engine, and killed the afterburners.

"I'm glad to be alive," quipped Mac, smiling, happy his pulse rate and breathing were returning to normal. Mac's forehead glistened with sweat, causing the visor in his pressurized helmet to fog.

"Roger, Scotty. Come to heading one-eight-five," added Gonzo. "Headquarters will take over in about an hour."

Scott leveled off at 40,000 feet then gazed overhead at the vast canopy of stars twinkling against an ink-black sky. Tonight, for a while at least, with control stick in hand, Scott was a pilot.

*The Home Team, 12/07/2014, 1045 Zulu, 3:45 A.M. Local*
ALLIED FORCES COMMAND HEADQUARTERS,
CROW'S NEST OVERLOOKING THE
STRATEGIC DEFENSE INITIATIVE ORGANIZATION (SDIO)
    WAR ROOM,
CHEYENNE MOUNTAIN, COLORADO

Generals Craven, Mason, and Krol entered the Crow's Nest. Their bird's-eye view of the War Room never failed to impress Mason. Image and sonar sensor data collected from all over the world was displayed in real time on the walls. Rigidly suspended sixty feet above the auditorium-sized War Room floor, the glass-walled Crow's Nest served as the Supreme Allied Commander's headquarters. The Crow's Nest was technically impressive, optimized for reliability and function, but from a human perspective, it struck Mason as austere. Divided into a video conference room and two redundant control rooms, the Crow's Nest provided the reliability required for around-the-clock operation with virtually zero downtime.

A long rectangular steel table dominated the video conference room with straight back gray chairs arranged in a row down one side. Behind them—a glass wall overlooking the War Room sixty feet below. Across the table, video cameras and TV monitors lined the opposite wall.

Entering the video conference room, General Mason surveyed the faces present and on screen. Here was Craven's inner sanctum. Everyone was present—four military commanders via video link and two civilians seated at the far end of the table.

One civilian, John Sullivan, came from the Lawrence Livermore National Laboratory and had overall DEWSAT responsibility. As a rule, whatever John Sullivan said, Mason agreed with. If he gave advice, Mason took it. Mason thought Sullivan a gentleman, one of the few remaining in this cutthroat business. He admired Sullivan and remembered him as a man with a large family—six grown children who still loved him. In his early fifties, Sullivan carried himself like a thirty-year-old. He was an active man who'd play basketball and tennis full-time if he didn't have to work for a living. Although his hair was thinning and silver-gray, his appearance was youthful, his eyes sparkled, and his complexion was a ruddy Irish red.

Thomas Jackson, seated next to Sullivan, was from MIT's Lincoln Lab—impossible to read, as Mason recalled, but the best radar man in the business. A slovenly walrus of a man, in face-to-face meetings Jackson simply blended into the background. Mason didn't like the man but did respect him. Jackson's radar reference handbook, intuition, and technical triumphs were legendary. In effect, Jackson's book had become a piece of the technical furniture, a standard reference cited by everyone in the electromagnetic sciences business. As a result, Jackson had become a very rich, widely sought after technical celebrity of sorts. In his official government capacity, he led two SDI technology development teams. The first team developed the DEWSAT's new radar; the second created invisible, ultra-stealth prototype aircraft.

On screen, Mason saw an impressive subset of Craven's commanders. He smiled, musing to himself that he'd hate to pay the bill for this meeting.

Both space station commanders, Jay Fayhee and Pasha Yakovlev, attended via video link. Pasha Yakovlev was unquestionably the group's space station expert. An engineer by training, he knew *Hope* and *Freedom* from the inside out. He knew their strengths, their capabilities, and their limitations better than he knew his own children. Although he never allowed it to show, the one thing Pasha shared in common with Jay Fayhee was a deep and inescapable sense of loneliness. From an altitude of 22,000 miles above the earth, Pasha's dreams revolved around his wife and three small children as he remembered them from nearly a full year ago.

Colonel Sam Napper, the SDIO defense force commander, went back a long way with Mason. Old hometown friends and college roommates, the two of them had been friends over twenty-five years. Napper provided Slim a real-time sanity check, and he trusted him in any situation. Over the years, wherever Mason had gone, Sam Napper had not been far behind. And this had worked well for both of them. Together they'd learned that life's ups and downs were easier to face with friends. Their friendship had grown to the point where each was godfather to the other's children and more. Much to their delight, Slim's middle son had married Sam's only daughter. Through it all, their adventurous outlook on life never diminished. When Mason looked at Sam Napper, he remembered himself as a younger man. He remembered his roots—the kindness of his grandparents, the small town he came from, the man he used to be. Sam provided Mason a sense of well-being that comes from knowing your own heart. As Mason had grown older, he learned with some sadness that who you are is an easy thing to forget. Mason liked to be reminded, and often.

Then there was Hinson. Mason thought CSOC's attack force commander, Colonel Hinson, a careerist prick. No one working under Hinson felt any sense of loyalty to the man. If any subordinate crossed him, Hinson never forgave, he simply got even. Mason would not tolerate a me-first-me-only player in a position of responsibility on his team and planned to remedy this situation ASAP.

Mason noticed Craven waiting impatiently for the meeting to begin and so began his opening remarks. "Gentlemen—looks like the home team's all here."

"Slim," Craven interrupted, "I want this meeting to run

**The Bad Seed**

ten minutes max. The agenda's one item long—do we go? I want a go/no go voice vote and if anyone has a beef, speak now. *Hope*—talk to me."

"We must go!" *Hope* commander Pasha Yakovlev stated emphatically. "*Hell Fire* is bringing replacement parts. Without them, we have no backup. We could lose all communications."

"We understand your situation," replied General Krol, chewing his pipe. He then spoke Russian, translated as followed. "*Hell Fire* will fly to low earth orbit once she's far enough west to clear land. After taking on fuel, she'll arrive on or before 2200 (hours Zulu)."

Turning slightly, Craven paused a moment, studying Krol's expression. Satisfied, he asked in English, "General Krol, what are your feelings?"

"I am satisfied," Krol responded evenly. "We go."

Colonel Sam Napper, the SDIO defense commander, flashed a thumbs up. "*Freedom*'s ready. After tonight, stealth cruise missiles will be obsolete." Colonel Napper displayed *Freedom*'s Status Report on screen. All seemed well.

Before Mason finished reading the report, Colonel Hinson chimed in. "CSOC's go. Our attack program looks good. We're ready, no problem."

General Mason stood once again, looked across the table and studied the faces of both technology representatives present. Placing his hands in his pockets, he spoke slowly, "I think I know the answers to my questions . . . but . . . I'm gonna ask 'em anyway. John, are your Livermore fellas ready?"

"Ready," replied John Sullivan. "DEWSATs tested and lasers are set to tag."

Mason shifted his weight from one leg to the other, obviously not convinced. "I get the feeling I'm in a high school pep rally here, fellas. Lincoln Lab—what's the story on your radar?"

"We're ready," replied Thomas Jackson, Lincoln Lab's rotund technical guru. "We've tested these UWB (Ultra WideBand) radars six months—they're stealth proof."

Mason thought the mood of the meeting overly optimistic—a sense of euphoria that didn't sit well with him.
He looked quietly into the eyes of each person around the
table, then studied the faces on screen. Mason spoke sin-
cerely, sliding the rim of his round hat through his fingers.
"This cruise missile threat has plagued us for years. Everyone's got 'em, we can't detect 'em, and everyone knows it.
We've had problems in the past and . . ."

"Thanks, Slim—I hear you," Craven interrupted. He
sounded sincere, but his gut feeling told him to go for it. He
spoke decisively. "Let's do it. Let nothing stand in our
way!"

*The* Dorito, *12/07/2014, 1144 Zulu, 3:44* A.M. *Local*
EF-12 WILD WEASEL,
ALTITUDE: 75,000 FEET,
TACO-SHAPED FLIGHT PATTERN OVER EDWARDS AFB

Painted matte black, the McDonnell Douglas EF-12 flying
wing vanished against the night sky. Triangular-shaped, the
EF-12's wingspan was about seventy feet with power provided by twin General Electric F404 engines. Tonight, the
EF-12 Avenger—a radar jammer aircraft nicknamed "the
*Dorito*"—would blind Centurion's orbiting armada with
broad spectrum, high-power electromagnetic noise.

Raised on horseback, *Dorito* pilot Captain "Cowboy"
Murray Hill grew up punching cattle on his family's west
Texas ranch. On the high plains, Cowboy found his future
prospects limited to football, cattle ranching, and rough-
neck work on oil rigs. He was good at all three but wanted
more. Using football as his ticket to college, he was very
much the typical west Texas rancher-athlete until he discovered flying. The Air Force ROTC flight program
changed his life forever. Precise, private, and sometimes
prickly, Cowboy used his brains and brawn to move first
through college, then flight school at Reese AFB outside
Lubbock, Texas. Once he'd learned to pilot the *Dorito* flying wing, he packed his Tony Llama cowboy boots, left big
sky country, and never looked back.

**The Bad Seed**

"Cowboy, this is Big Shot," crackled over the *Dorito* pilot's headset. "Enter crypt key. Ground control begins in sixty seconds." Cowboy smirked. The call sign Big Shot fit the Cheyenne Mountain Headquarters organization like a glove. To avoid revealing his position, he maintained radio silence. Entering an eight character decryption key, he watched the link status lights turn green as the receiver locked on Headquarter's control transmission.

"Bulldog—control link is secure and operational." Cowboy spoke to his back-seater, Bulldog, in a matter-of-fact tone. Bulldog looked the part—a stocky Georgia boy with short brown hair, large head, and a strong square jaw—consequently his call sign stuck.

"Roger, Cowboy. Satellite link is go."

"Cowboy, this is Big Shot. Enable control link on my mark."

"Brace yourself, Bulldog." Cowboy slid his thumb down the control stick, carefully lifting a red protective switch cover labeled WARNING: CONTROL SELECT. Immediately, the sultry female voice of the flight computer repeated an audible warning designed to attract any male pilot's attention. He had anticipated her warning, but his hands felt cold and clammy. In less than ten seconds he would hand over flight control to Cheyenne Mountain.

"Mark," said Big Shot. Cowboy thought this handoff was too easy for Headquarters; he put his life on the line—they had nothing to lose.

"She's all yours." Hill held his breath and threw the CONTROL SELECT switch.

"Roger that," Bulldog confirmed. "HQ is flying the wing."

"Took over without a glitch." Shaking his head in disbelief, Cowboy never took his hand off the stick.

*The Assault by Sea, 12/07/2014, 1144 Zulu, 3:44 A.M. Local*
SUBMARINE USS *STENNIS*,
PACIFIC OCEAN 37 MILES DUE WEST OF SANTA CRUZ, CALI-
  FORNIA

The USS *Stennis* crept along at periscope depth, drifting
slowly with just enough speed to maintain steering, perfectly quiet, waiting for Headquarters to take control via
satellite link. She'd been in position only fifteen minutes
with her communications mast protruding above the surface, thirty-seven miles due west of Santa Cruz, California.
The USS *Stennis*, a 362-foot-long *Los Angeles-class* fast attack submarine, listened attentively to the submarine communications satellite.

The boat's skipper double-checked the time. Reluctantly,
he lifted his phone and patched into the communications
shack. "ClearWater downlink status?"

"No change, Cap'n. Threat board data is real-time. Link
fully operational."

"And the direct link from Headquarters?"

"Control link is go."

"Very well then." Satisfied, the skipper shifted his gaze
to the officer of the deck (OOD). "What's showing on the
threat board? Any contacts?"

Scanning the threat board from his forward watch station, the OOD summarized their situation. "We're all alone
out here, Skipper, clear horizon to horizon. Nearest surface
contact—thirty miles due east, just off the coast. Single
submerged contact bearing southwest at two hundred miles.
Airspace overhead is clear."

In the U.S. Navy's vernacular, ClearWater—the submarine reconnaissance satellite network—provided a means
for detecting submerged submarines by electronically trans-
forming turbulent black seawater into a calm clear liquid.
ClearWater rendered the oceans virtually transparent, ergo
the code name. The first operational crown jewel in the SDI
space reconnaissance program, ClearWater satellites detected submarines by their wake track using microwave re-
flections from the sea surface. Reconnaissance satellites

photographed ocean surface waves, then Centurion electronically smoothed them—technicians described this stage as calming the waters—by filtering out effects due to surface current, ships, and weather. After calming the waters, each computer-enhanced picture of the ocean surface looked glassy smooth and highly reflective—like the surface of a glistening Christmas ball—except for telltale V-shaped scratches, aka submarine tracks. Created by surface wake, these V-shaped scratches marked the submarine's trail, and, to the hunter's advantage, in average seas this trail persisted long after the boat had passed.

So successful was this submarine detection idea in practice that the ocean depths became, for strategic purposes, transparent. Polar ice and deep water (greater than 100 meters) emerged as the only place a submarine might hide.

*But ClearWater is another story.*

The skipper picked up his phone again and patched into the sonar room. "Sonar, any contacts? Did ClearWater miss anything?"

"No contacts, Captain. We confirm the threat board read. Area is clear of any possible threats."

"That is good." Nodding approval to the OOD, the skipper continued. "Very well—give Headquarters the boat."

"Aye, Captain."

Much to the skipper's relief, the transition to Headquarters's control was smooth. Confident all was well, he studied the faces of his crew. *They handle this better than I,* he thought. The crew gazed intently at their instrumentation and seemed relaxed with "hands-off" boat control.

"Steady as she goes, Captain," the OOD reported. "Flight profile download now under way."

The skipper stood silent, ready by the phone, listening intently to the sounds inside his electric boat.

"Guidance system update complete, Captain. Weapons are warm and ready to fire." Immediately, three sets of missile indicators flashed a bright lethal green, then the hull of the *Stennis* echoed with the rush of water and air. The hull groaned due to the pressure changes inside the tubes.

"Torpedo tubes one, two, and three are ready in all respects," the OOD continued. "Outer doors are opened. Tubes now ready to launch the weapons."

The younger crewmen looked to the skipper for some sign of reassurance. The commanding officer forced a tight-jawed grin, then raised one hand with a "not to worry" gesture.

"Captain, launch cycle in progress."

The sound of water ramming the weapons into the sea echoed throughout the boat.

Outside, three cruise missiles packaged inside torpedo-shaped cylinders headed for the surface. Once topside, the weapons fired their booster rockets, erupted from the nose of the cylinders, and thrust out of the water. Now airborne, the missiles tilted over, ignited their air breathing engines, and headed for the Nevada Test Site at about 500 knots.

Meanwhile down below, the horrendous sounds of missiles firing overhead convinced the skipper their cruise launch was successful. He must now assume their position no longer secret. "Our job is done," the skipper announced. "Give me the boat."

"With pleasure, Captain." The OOD disconnected the link with the flip of a switch. "She's all yours!"

"Depth under the keel?"

"Three hundred fifty feet."

"Take her down to one five zero; all ahead one third." His immediate priority was to silently hide his boat under the pitch-black veil of the Pacific for, to most, the oceans remained opaque.

"Aye, Captain." The OOD repeated the orders to the crew.

The hull of the USS *Stennis* filled with the sounds of rushing water as the ballast tanks opened. Minutes later, surrounded by total darkness, the *Stennis* slowed her descent at 130 feet. She settled at 150 and silently headed north-northwest out to sea.

The Bad Seed

# 7

"Hinson—you ready to run?" Craven questioned his attack force commander via video link.

"All assets are in position and ready, sir." Checking the mission clock, he continued. "Kickoff in twenty-two seconds."

"Colonel— what about Centurion's activity log?" Mason asked.

"We'll cover it when the time comes."

"The time has come." Mason thought Hinson on the fast track all right—right out the door. There was no time to deal with Hinson before the test, but the right time would come—soon.

"We're on the air!" Hinson interrupted. Headquarters now remotely controlled Hinson's attack forces. Next, he'd simulate a large scale ICBM attack. "The fireworks should begin in ten seconds."

All eyes focused on the big blue ball. From inside the Crow's Nest, Craven and his general staff overlooked the blue ball, a large, slowly rotating hologram of the earth, twice the size of the one on *Freedom*.

Suddenly, thousands of white blips appeared covering the globe. Krol winced, biting his pipe stem so hard it cracked. As a test sequence, this attack scenario stressed Centurion's computing power to the limits.

Craven walked outside the Crow's Nest onto a connecting walkway for a better view. Looking down, he felt light-headed due to the dizzying height above the War Room floor. Trembling, he felt suddenly nauseated, nervous, and very weak. Craven hated full-scale SDI testing because it was too damn realistic. The scale was overwhelming. Inside the walls of the War Room, the tests looked, sounded, and felt larger than life. Emotionally involved with the testing, Craven knew he'd lost his objective edge.

But the future of his organization and the Allied Forces hinged on the success of these tests.

Craven drew in a deep breath, reminding himself again that this was only a test. Try as he might, he could not steady his hands. He'd often joked that he should get into another line of work, but now he was ready to take his own advice. He'd been in the business long enough and needed to retire.

Watching the test progress, the calm, orderly mood of the War Room transitioned to noisy chaos—a human beehive of activity that seemed to feed on itself.

This realism adversely affected the nerves and health of the War Room staff, so frequent job rotation was the rule. These tests bothered Mason as well, but he worked to stay ahead of the game by constantly anticipating what should happen next.

Mason knew the missiles were simulated, but he never became accustomed to such large-scale realistic testing—he could never completely detach himself. As the simulated missiles closed in over the North Pole, Mason recalled a quote from the Hindu scriptures. J. Robert Oppenheimer, the father of the atomic bomb, used this quote describing his feelings as he watched the detonation of the first atomic bomb—"I am become death, the destroyer of worlds." Mason felt, though only for an instant, as if he was watching the end of the world. This stifling, morose feeling shook Mason and reminded him once again of the bloody business he'd chosen as his profession. He hated war above all else and felt it good to be reminded of this—and often.

"Keep your eyes on the California coast," Hinson announced.

Simultaneously, six white blips appeared. Three cruise missiles from the *Stennis*, three from *Hell Fire*.

"We can see 'em," Craven observed with considerable satisfaction.

Colonel Sam Napper sat on the edge of his seat, pounding his console. "Show me some red and we're halfway home!" If Centurion confirmed the missiles as a real threat, the missile tracks would change color, indicating the most difficult technical aspect of the test was behind them.

Then suddenly, it happened—all six blips turned red. After years of testing and frustration, they could finally detect stealth cruise missiles.

And—if they could detect them, they could kill them.

"Yes! Yes! We have a winner! Look out, Disney World— here we come!" Napper hooted, throwing his headset into the air. His vacation plans along with those of Craven's entire general staff hinged on the outcome of these tests. He had a full month of leave scheduled around Christmas and was ready to collect.

As the simulated missile traces over Russia approached the North Pole, they began disappearing. Within minutes, only six red blips remained, all converging in unison on the Nevada Test Site.

Just as Craven was beginning to feel good about his chances for success, he noticed a young airman talking to Hinson, shaking his head in apparent confusion, on the video conference line. Craven looked at Mason. "What's your read so far?"

"The game's not over till it's over, General. Something's going on in CSOC." Turning to the video conference camera, Mason spoke into the microphone. "Hinson—you got any problem there we need to know about?"

"Nothing of consequence, sir . . . that activity log."

"Yeah, what about it?"

"My people—uh—well, we can't . . ." Hinson paused

and considered his statement. "We're going through some start-up problems with Centurion's activity log, sir."

Mason raised both eyebrows. Something wasn't right here. "Colonel—let me speak to the person you put in charge."

Hinson motioned to a frightened airman with eyes the size of silver dollars. The lanky young man approached the video camera and stood silent.

Mason smiled to put him at ease. "What's your name, son?"

"Airman first-class Harold Harrison, sir."

"Harold, I need your help." Judging from his expression, Mason concluded the young airman looked willing. "What seems to be the problem?"

"The raw activity log output is difficult to—it's overwhelming us here . . . there's millions of lines of output. We can't make heads or tails out of it . . . sir."

Hinson snatched the young airman away from the video camera's field of view. "I ordered him to ignore the activity log, General."

"Now is not the time or place, Colonel, but we need to talk about this one." Mason spoke to Hinson in a quiet voice for emphasis, then made a mental note to correct their management problem before their next test run. Turning away, Mason watched the missiles closing slowly on the Nevada Test Side.

Hinson checked his mission clock. "Whiteout over Edwards," he warned, shielding his eyes with his hand. Once the electronic jamming began, the airspace display turned a brilliant white.

*The DEWSAT Pix, 12/07/2014, 1200 Zulu, 4:00 A.M. Local*
ALTITUDE: 80,000 FEET,
HEADING: DUE WEST,
DIRECTLY OVER SAN DIEGO,
*HELL FIRE*

Scott saw the lights of San Diego ahead on the horizon, but knew her back-seater and cameraman had their eyes fixed on their instruments. Scanning her instruments, she kept one hand on the stick, the other on the throttle, tracking every move the Headquarters computer made.

"Mac—got any pix?" Just then, Scott noticed two camera indicator lights turn green in the reconnaissance bay. Pressing two switches, she routed both camera images to her split screen display.

"IR camera's locked on," Mac replied with a great sense of satisfaction. "Pix coming up."

To lock on a low orbiting satellite moving over 17,000 miles an hour due north from a westbound plane was like shooting skeet off a flatbed truck racing over the winding potholed streets of Boston.

For a few moments, the TV monitors displayed only empty black sky. The cameras were tracking two DEWSATs. One rising above *Hell Fire*'s southern horizon racing north, the second was about to drop below the northern horizon. Once locked, a series of adjustable tracking mirrors pivoted, positioning each satellite image in the center of the viewing screen. Suddenly, two sunflower-shaped greenish images appeared out of the blackness.

"Excellent," exclaimed Gonzo. Immediately, his expression turned troubled. "Those DEWSATs look hot as hell."

"The pix don't lie," Scott said dispassionately. "Those hot spots are the laser's diamond lens and reactor core."

"So those sunflowers're going to put us out of a job," Mac said in disbelief.

"Don't underestimate the opposition, Mac. That's a twenty-megawatt laser, enough to knock anything out of the air."

"But if it can't see us, it can't shoot us," Mac replied confidently.

"Our stealth days are numbered, Mac. It's inevitable. They're not smart, they're *genius* weapons. They can tell the difference between missiles, ASATs, decoys—you name the target, they can pick it out."

"I gotta see it to believe it."

"I'd hate to have that DEWSAT bear down on me," Gonzo lamented quietly. "Glad that laser's backed off."

**The Bad Seed**

"Roger that, Gonzo," Mac replied somberly. "That sucker'd punch a hole in your best intentions."

*The Decoy, 12/07/2014, 1209 Zulu, 5:09* A.M. *Local*
CHEYENNE MOUNTAIN, COLORADO

The projected picture of the California coast suddenly looked like a whiteout in a snowstorm, a radiant white blank screen.

Mason squinted.

"No problem with the picture, General," Napper said calmly. "Jammers came on-line as scheduled. Centurion'll clean it up."

Seconds later, Centurion did exactly that and the satellite picture of California emerged from the veil of televisionlike interference. The six red cruise missile blips had disappeared, replaced by hundreds of white blips, each heading a different direction, speed, and altitude.

Mason studied the picture for a moment. "Phantom Hawks cut in." The Phantom Hawk cruise missiles launched from the USS *Stennis* and *Hell Fire* carried an electronic countermeasures package that produced false radar return signals. To radar, these false signals looked like hundreds of cruise missiles.

"Yessir—Centurion's got his hands full, but this is our last major hurdle." Napper watched the blips advance in seemingly every direction. "Centurion's gotta sort the real targets from the decoys."

Every fifteen seconds or so, the missile tracks methodically disappeared. The northbound missile tracks all disappeared at once, then the westbound tracks disappeared, then the southbound, and finally, all but three eastbound tracks vanished.

Three missile traces heading east toward the Nevada Test Site remained, but three were missing.

# 8

First and foremost, the DEWSAT was designed to automatically protect itself against anything and any condition that could cause failure.

And it would do so—in the blink of an eye.

When the two Phantom Hawk cruise missiles simultaneously powered on, they began transmitting hundreds of false targets. The sudden increase in targets immediately overloaded the DEWSAT's tracking system and its programmed response was automatic. Detecting the sudden increase in targets, the DEWSAT's computer brain woke up, increased its laser power output to a dangerous three percent, and automatically began separating false targets from the real ones.

The DEWSAT was designed to discriminate targets (separate false targets from real ones) using a technique involving burn-through. A small fraction of the power needed to destroy a booster rocket would melt a hole through a lightweight decoy, and this hole could be detected by the DEWSAT's infrared heat sensors.

Heating up suspected targets, the DEWSAT began separating false targets from real ones, aka searching for melted holes.

A short message was transmitted to Centurion:

DEWSAT status change:
Target Discrimination Mode Enabled

Centurion placed this message, along with tens of millions of other messages, in his activity log.

*Trouble, 12/07/2014, 1210 Zulu, 5:10 A.M. Local*
CHEYENNE MOUNTAIN, COLORADO

Staring at the map, Mason's eyes opened wider. Unbelievably, three missiles had disappeared. He glanced at Hinson on screen and found him oblivious to what had happened. Mason glanced around the room and realized that no one fully understood what had just happened. Most of the War Room staff stared at the screen uncomprehending. Raising his eyebrows, he spoke to Craven. "Trouble."

"Yeah—I can count." Craven grimaced. "Hinson—talk to me—now damn it. What the hell happened?"

Hinson had been confident that Centurion'd have no problem thinning out the decoy missiles. He casually glanced at the map, then pulled a double take. "Uh—we're working the issue, General."

"Exactly what are you doing about it, Hinson?"

"Collecting my best people, sir."

"How long's that gonna take?"

"They'll be working it within the hour."

"An hour's not going to do us much good. I need to know what happened to those missiles now."

"General," Mason interrupted softly after talking with his Russian comrade, General Yuri Krol. "Let Yuri's folks at Kaliningrad comb through Centurion's activity log ASAP. That log contains raw test data. They'll find the problem."

Mason looked at Krol. "Maybe ten to twenty minutes?"

"With luck . . . five minutes." Krol nodded calmly.

"Do it," Craven ordered.

Krol punched up Kaliningrad on the videophone and got his people moving.

**The Bad Seed**

Mason took his fist and rapped on Colonel Napper's monitor to get his attention. "Sam—listen up. Confirmation—we need confirmation. Any chance those missiles might be airborne but Centurion can't see 'em?"

"I'm checking. Give me a minute." Napper displayed a target tracking window. "No, sir, those birds are down. Last positive track occurred just before the Phantom Hawks went active. Plenty of margin—signal to noise looked darn good. If those missiles were flying, we could see 'em."

Mason gazed at the ceiling for a few moments, struggling to find an approach to the problem. "Do we have any cruise missile experts local?"

"I'm with you, General," replied Napper, listening over the conference line. "Name's Schindler, Joe Schindler . . . guy's brilliant . . . give 'im the situation—he'll size it up—make the call."

Napper bridged Joe on the conference call then summarized the situation.

"How're these missiles configured?" asked Joe.

"I can answer that, General," Hinson interrupted like a child seeking attention. "Master/slave . . . the Phantom and Hammer Hawks're slaved to the Jammer Hawk."

Schindler concentrated, sipping on a large mug of hot coffee. "And the *Dorito*'s jammer turned on immediately before the missiles disappeared?"

"That's about the size of it," Napper replied without emotion.

"I'll give you my best guess," Schindler responded.

"We're asking for your opinion," Napper said anxiously. "What's your analysis?"

"Short and sweet: *Hell Fire*'s Jammer Hawk flew into the ground and the two slave Hawks blindly followed."

Craven clearly disagreed. "So why would the Jammer Hawk fly into the ground in the first place?"

"Interference from the *Dorito*'s jammer confused the Hawk's navigation system and caused the crash. The Jammer Hawk's not sensitive to its own interference but could be confused by a powerful separate jammer source."

**The Bad Seed**

"Well," said Craven, somewhat satisfied, "that's one problem that didn't show up in Hinson's simulations. Sounds like we can rest easy."

"I respectfully disagree, General," said Mason. "It's his best guess—shouldn't be overrated. We haven't heard from Yuri's folks."

There were a lot of experts answering questions around the War Room, and often even the questions weren't clear. When Mason had something to say, he'd say it. If he didn't know the answer to a question, he wouldn't lie. Craven admired Mason's honesty and intellect. Above all else, Craven believed Mason would do what was right, regardless of the consequences.

Mason argued for caution and rightly so. Schindler's analysis was accurate, but based on insufficient data, his conclusion was wrong.

*The Signal, 12/07/2014, 1211 Zulu*
OVER THE PACIFIC OCEAN,
430 MILES WEST OF SAN DIEGO,
*HELL FIRE*

Flying above a turbulent electrical storm with a canopy of stars overhead, Scott watched lightning flashes illuminate the boiling thunderheads below. Suddenly, she felt her stick and rubber pedals moving, placing *Hell Fire* in a gradual banking turn, positioning her for launch into low earth orbit. "Launch sequence commences in two minutes. Sit tight once we come out of this bank."

"Uh-oh," Mac exclaimed, measuring a sudden increase in laser power on *Hell Fire*'s back. Translated, uh-oh could only mean trouble.

Attached to *Hell Fire*'s upper wing surfaces, like an array of Post-it notes, *Hell Fire* carried laser sensor panels for this war game of laser tag. Operating like a Nintendo game, panels illuminated by the DEWSAT's laser scored a hit.

Mac checked the cooling pumps. "Slush pumps're wide

open—skin temp's soaring—we're running out of margin fast."

Watching a screen full of error messages scroll by, Gonzo grimaced. "Radio performance is degrading across all bands, Scotty. We're losing signal—error rates climbing on every channel."

"Something's changing somewhere!" Mac exclaimed. "Eight panels are going dark on me—output power's dropping to zip."

After acquiring *Hell Fire* with radar, the DEWSAT painted her with its lethal laser powered to three percent. Once the DEWSAT locked on *Hell Fire*, there was nothing Scott could do to shake it—there was no place to hide.

Mac read the temperature of each panel in disbelief, pounded his measurement equipment, then read the temperatures again. "Something's flaky. These temps don't make sense."

"Talk to me, Mac. What's happening?" Scott's tone was tense as she watched *Hell Fire*'s skin temperature rising.

Simultaneously, Scott and Mac noticed an alarming pattern. Most of the panels were white-hot, a condition which should not exist, assuming the DEWSAT laser's power was safely throttled back. A few panels showed rapidly changing temperature—white-hot one second, ice-cold the next. Fast temperature changes couldn't be easily explained, they were too incredible to believe—didn't make any sense—at first.

"What if those panels are damaged? Maybe burned off?" Scott asked.

"Damaged panels might explain those hot 'n' cold readings." Mac had not fully worked through the consequences of her question—his tone was tentative. Mac read the panel temperatures for the third time and the reality of their situation chilled him like a cold wind.

"Comm failure," interrupted Gonzo, staring at an array of red alarm indicators. In the blink of an eye, every VHF/UHF radio failed. Their unthinkable fear played out in real time—the DEWSAT was hot.

**The Bad Seed**

*Hell Fire* was exposed to laser illumination from overhead. Buried slightly below the surface of the XR-30's skin lay her radio antennas—large conformal arrays of microstrip antennas. Seconds after the panels began to fail, the intricate thin metal strip antennas vaporized.

"Snap one-eighty," Scott warned, exposing *Hell Fire*'s underbelly to the laser illumination from overhead. She flew inverted because the slush cooling system more effectively cooled reentry hot spots on the XR-30's underbelly. "Mac—panel temp?"

"Dropping fast. No doubt about it—that laser's hot!"

Scott spoke to Gonzo in a low controlled voice. "Spin up an ASAT—lock it on that hot laser."

"Roger, Scotty." Gonzo toggled switches, rotating a missile bay within *Hell Fire*'s short stubby wings. An ASAT launched from *Hell Fire* at hypersonic speed must be thrust downward well clear of the XR-30, then ignited. "Weapon's locked on target but we'll never catch it."

"ASAT's an abort signal. Headquarters won't be expecting it. Sit tight. I'm gonna light the wick." Igniting the booster rocket, Scott stood *Hell Fire* on her tail and flew directly toward the DEWSAT.

Belching flames in her wake, *Hell Fire* accelerated through Mach 2 with a thunderous roar. When Scott increased throttle on the six ramjets, the Rocketdyne engine automatically shut down as they passed Mach 3. Although the six jet engines in *Hell Fire*'s belly were screaming, the cockpit seemed much quieter once the rocket shut down. Concentrating on her instruments, Scott didn't even notice.

"Glad that noisy sucker's off," Mac quipped. "Good news."

"Must be the laser."

"Right—laser's backed off—looks normal."

"That DEWSAT must have seen what it was looking for." Scott thought for a moment. She knew DEWSATs sensed heat, reflected laser light, and radar energy. The only possible connection she could make, and it was a stretch, was *Hell Fire*'s rocket engine. When she ignited

**The Bad Seed**

it, the laser backed off. "Maybe it backed off once it detected our heat plume."

"Sounds logical, but we only have one data point. Suggest we stick to our original plan." Gonzo thought sending a signal to Headquarters made sense. "We're not safe till we're above that DEWSAT layer."

"Roger that, SAESO," Scott said in a pragmatic tone. "Make the ASAT ready to fire."

During the transition from rocket to ramjet power, *Hell Fire* developed a fiery cometlike tail extending over ten miles long—spectacular to see, but costly in fuel. Once convinced the ramjets were performing to spec, Scott "trimmed *Hell Fire*'s tail" by eliminating the fiery hydrogen plume trailing behind each engine. Rotating a thumbwheel, she watched the engine's exhaust gas analyzer change from saturated to optimal. After repeating this procedure for each engine, she locked fuel flow control to the flight computer.

*Hell Fire*'s air-breathing engines performed to Scott's expectations. The thrust from *Hell Fire*'s belly accelerated the craft predictably along their flight trajectory toward low earth orbit.

"Eighty thousand feet—Mach five—tail's trimmed." Scott paused, reading her analyzer. "I show six optimal burns."

"Bobtail confirmed, Scotty," Gonzo observed, looking over his shoulder. "Scramjet transition coming up." *Hell Fire*'s flight computer controlled scramjet transition by reconfiguring fuel and air flow through the six ramjets.

Ramjets propelled *Hell Fire* to speeds of Mach 6, scramjets thrust her to Mach 22 past 180,000 feet. At speeds above Mach 22, the Rocketdyne engine kicked in with the final punch required for orbital insertion. Getting into orbit required speeds between Mach 22 and Mach 25—over 17,000 miles an hour.

"Scramjet transition complete—tail's trim," Scott said one minute later. The adjustable teeth in *Hell Fire*'s air-breathing mouth (hinged rectangular flaps) retracted, allowing air from her compression ramp to enter her engines at supersonic speeds. This supersonic air was ducted around each compressor, injected with fuel, and ignited toward the rear of the engines.

"Roger—bobtail's confirmed," replied Gonzo. "On course—Mach six at eighty-seven thousand feet."

After all six engines transitioned from ramjet to scramjet operation, Scott and Gonzo caught their last look at the stars just before the heat shield automatically "rolled up," completely sealing off the cockpit. Flying with the heat shield extended was much like flying with a blackout bag over the cockpit. Once the cockpit heat shield was extended, Scott and Gonzo depended one hundred percent on instruments.

"Keep those deflector shields up," Mac quipped, teasing his pilot with a *Star Trek* one-liner.

"Pray for a smooth ride till OIB (Orbital Insertion Burn). We'll need all the help we can get."

Scott was flying *Hell Fire* into low earth orbit, pushing her through a narrow performance envelope with exact timing and precision. Nothing in *Hell Fire*'s flight trajectory could be left to chance. Monitoring altitude, direction, and speed, she simultaneously adjusted her throttles and rate of climb. *Hell Fire*'s velocity and altitude had to increase within the limits set by her launch envelope or she would run out of fuel, never achieving the escape velocity required for orbit. *Hell Fire*'s speed and altitude were unprecedented for an air-breathing, single-stage aircraft. No other plane ever built could fly as fast, high, or as far as the XR-30.

Scott described *Hell Fire* as an enormous flying engine. The XR-30 was the follow-on to the Space Shuttle, but had also replaced the aging Aurora spy plane. (In its day, the Aurora had replaced the SR-71 Blackbird.)

One look at *Hell Fire* and you knew she was an extraordinary airplane. The front two thirds of *Hell Fire*'s body looked like the head of a great white shark with its mouth wide-open, sucking air into her massive propulsion system. Her mouth was lined with rows of retractable *teeth* which controlled the speed of air flowing into her engines. If you stood in front of her, looking into her cavernous air-breathing mouth, the mammoth spectacle inspired awe, admiration—even wonder.

At hypersonic speeds, *Hell Fire* was lifted into the air by the aerodynamic shape of her body rather than her wings. *Hell Fire*'s wide "lifting body" design also provided space for a large fuel tank and a compression ramp which guided air into her propulsion system. At speeds above Mach 1, *Hell Fire*'s "all moving" wings were locked in neutral position. Below Mach 1, her wings were unlocked, providing both the lift and the control surface required for pitch, roll, and yaw maneuvers.

The original X-30 was a two-seat aircraft about the size of a Douglas DC-10, weighing 200,000 pounds, and 150 feet long. *Hell Fire* was an XR-30, an X-30 stretched to 200 feet, weighing 250,000 pounds, matte black, built of titanium and carbon composites, modified to include more powerful scramjet engines, four reconnaissance equipment bays, and a third seat for the reconnaissance systems operator inside the nose.

"Gonzo—open outer doors and launch the weapon," ordered Scott, watching her airspeed indicator. "Show Headquarters a signal they can't miss."

"Roger, Scotty. Configuration complete. Weapon is warm and ready to fire." Next, he placed the launch sequence under automatic fire control.

Ejecting an ASAT missile out from inside *Hell Fire*'s stubby wing while moving at Mach 8 created two intense shock waves. One shock wave would violently shake the crew, and the second would shake the ASAT missile like a baby's rattle.

Gonzo read off the missile countdown sequence. "Ten, nine, eight . . ." *Beep . . . beep . . . beep . beeeeeeeeeeeep* echoed over his headset. "Oh shit!" Gonzo spoke in short bursts. "Threat detection. Another DEWSAT's rising over our southern horizon, closing fast. It's locked on—illuminated us in five bands already. Signal strength is getting hotter."

Scott grimaced. "Lock another . . ."

*Barooom! Hell Fire* shook violently from the shock wave.

"Northbound weapon away," Gonzo announced, watching the missile streak away on video. "Ignition confirmed. Well clear of *Hell Fire*—track looks good."

"Headquarters will see it," Scott said softly.

"We're in the heat again!" interrupted Mac. "Same story but our skin temp's rising. Much hotter and we're history!" Mac had good reason to worry. He was surrounded by thousands of pounds of slush hydrogen fuel. *Hell Fire*'s cryogenic fuel tanks, holding hydrogen chilled to -435 degrees F, had to be lightweight and thin-walled because of her large size. In addition, hydrogen fuel was circulated as a coolant throughout *Hell Fire*'s skin, absorbing heat from her hot spots. If the DEWSAT laser heated her skin beyond 5,000 degrees F, her thin-walled fuel tank would rupture and *Hell Fire* would certainly live up to her name, exploding into an enormous white-hot fireball streaking across the night sky.

"Lock an ASAT on it. That DEWSAT's moving toward us. We'll knock it out of commission."

Gonzo watched the weapon's lock light turn green. "Weapon ready to shoot. DEWSAT's closing fast."

"Shoot Gonzo . . . shoot."

*BAROOOM! Hell Fire* shook like a rattlesnake's tail, battering Scott, Mac, and Gonzo violently from side to side. Once the shock wave passed, Gonzo focused his eyes again. "ASAT's away and clear." Watching the rocket engine ignite on screen, he felt satisfied that he'd done all he could do—for now.

"*Hoooooeeeeee!*" hollered Mac, watching the weapon take flight. "We'll knock that sucker outta the sky!"

"Mac—how about a visual?"

"Watch your monitor. Camera's swinging into position now—hold it—yeah, we got 'em both—ASAT right—DEWSAT left."

"Gonzo, give us the blow-by-blow." Scott expected Gonzo to call the action like a horse race. She wasn't disappointed.

**The Bad Seed**

Gonzo began his narrative in a monotone. "And they're off. Southbound ASAT missile's accelerating through Mach twelve . . . four minutes to impact . . . track looks good . . . speed's Mach fifteen plus . . . closing fast. Altitude fifty miles . . . seventy . . . eighty . . . closing on target . . . easy money's on the ASAT . . . one hundred miles high and closing . . ."

Mesmerized, Mac stared at his screen. Suddenly, he noticed two greenish hot spots glowing on the ASAT. The IR pictures showed them in minute detail. "Hot spots! The weapon's taking the heat. We're cooling off!" Mac watched his monitor in disbelief. "I can't believe this is . . . oh my God."

The southbound ASAT exploded into a large ball of fiery gasses.

*Hell Fire*'s intercom was silent—no one could speak. Scott, Mac, and Gonzo sat spellbound, their eyes transfixed on their monitors. For a few moments that seemed to last an eternity, the ASAT's image burned an intense bright green, completely washing over the screen.

"DEWSAT must have punched a hole in the fuel tank to cause an explosion like that," Gonzo observed quietly. He checked the progress of his first missile. "Our northbound ASAT's going ballistic—falling out of the sky. It'll burn up in the atmosphere."

"Regroup, fellas." Scott spoke with a strained tone of urgency in her voice. "Headquarters saw our signal. They'll call off the dogs."

Mac cut in as soon as Scott released her microphone switch. "Heat's on. We're running white-hot."

"Snap one-eighty. Keep your heads on straight," urged Scott, praying for strength.

"Temp's approaching redline." Mac's face, covered with beaded sweat, glistened under his cockpit lights. "Forty-five hundred degrees and rising."

Scott closed her eyes, blocking out the bright red distractions flashing across the cockpit. It was a wonder she could think at all considering the myriad of warning messages flashing in her face. Concentrating intensely, looking for some pattern, she gave their situation a good think.

Heat. Show their fiery plume. "I wanna play a long shot."

"Laser's hot as hell—go for it!"

Scott flipped switches, placing scramjet fuel control in manual mode. Turning the fuel mixture thumbwheels, dumping more fuel into each engine, she ordered: "Mac, watch my tail. We're running rich."

Mac pivoted an IR camera on *Hell Fire*'s tail. "Got it, Scotty. We're running full plume!"

"Watch that laser, Mac. Let me know if you see any change."

"What're you thinking?"

"Heat—heat could be our ticket. If that laser'd been running full power, it would have blown us out of the sky a long time ago—but those DEWSATs seem to cycle. They go hot, then back off. Who knows? Maybe that DEWSAT's looking for heat—so we'll show 'em heat!"

"You're right. There's a pattern to it."

"How's your slush temp looking, Mac? Circulation pumps wide open?"

"Slush temps high, about the same as reentry. That cooling system's saving us—from a big hole, I mean."

"Roger that. Just keep that cooling system running."

"Laser's backing off!"

"Thank God," Scott whispered.

"We've seen that pattern before." Gonzo admired Scott's cool head in a tight situation. "Your heat plume call was on the money."

"Hope so," she replied, checking her fuel. "Gonzo—how long can we run full plume?"

Gonzo punched in their rate of fuel consumption. Unseen behind his visor, the corners of his mouth dropped. "We're outta luck. To maintain enough fuel for our low orbit docking maneuver—two more minutes max. You're running afterburner fuel consumption rates, Scotty, but no extra kick."

**The Bad Seed**

Scott trimmed *Hell Fire*'s tail immediately and returned fuel flow control to the flight computer.

"Mac—how's my tail?" asked Scott.

"Bobbed," replied Mac. Gonzo smiled briefly, thinking about Scotty's fine tail.

"How's it looking, Mac? We hot?"

"So far, so good." Mac responded with a cautious smile. He was feeling better about their situation—cautious, but optimistic. Nobody had any idea why, but for some reason, showing a fiery plume kept the DEWSAT's laser throttled back.

A few minutes earlier, Mac would have sold his chances for a wooden nickel, but now he believed they were going to make it.

*TDM Operations, 12/07/2014, 1215 Zulu, 5:15 A.M. Local*
CHEYENNE MOUNTAIN, COLORADO

High Ground testing was progressing, but not smoothly. After toiling through countless pages of test data, Mason looked up at Craven. "I don't like it, I don't like it at all. Something's gone wrong here. I can feel it."

Craven's face took a hard set. "We're not bailing outta this test based on a hunch!"

Crushing his military round hat into a tight ball, Mason struggled to convey his thoughts with an even tone. "Take a look at our situation, General. We have symptoms of at least one problem, maybe more—we just don't know. *Hell Fire* broke off our satellite link and we don't know why. We should've heard something. Three missiles are missing—presumed down and we can't explain it. There's insufficient data to form any conclusion, but we guess they flew into the ground. Well, I don't believe it. We've got trouble staring us in the face and don't know how to interpret the symptoms."

"Decisions are always based on our best available information, Slim, and that information will always be incomplete."

"I understand that, but during this testing, we need to

know what's happening in real time. Centurion's log is the only way I know to get there. I'd feel better if we had a clean bill of health from Kaliningrad."

"No news is good news."

"I disagree, General, but I hope you're right. The longer Yuri's people take, the greater the chance they've found trouble."

"That's true," General Krol added somberly. "Your concerns may be of consequence. Time will tell."

"Don't worry about things you can't control," Craven suggested, his voice unconvincing.

"But we do control this situation, or we should," Mason lamented quietly. "For one thing, Hinson should have been replaced months ago."

"Hindsight's always twenty-twenty, Slim. We do the best we can with the resources available."

"If Kaliningrad uncovers trouble, our problems will be compounded by a language barrier."

Craven nodded thoughtfully. "Bring in our translator." Craven turned to his Russian general. "Yuri, do you agree?"

"Is good idea. May need help translating some technical terms."

Craven spoke to Napper via video link. "Sam, have Addams report to the Crow's Nest ASAP."

Napper quickly relayed Craven's message to their Russian translator, then a voice over his headset caught Sam's attention. Suddenly, the colonel snapped upright as if his spine were made of steel spring. "General—Mayday confirmation! Watch the blue ball. *Hell Fire* launched an ASAT. That's gotta be a signal." Watching the blue ball, the colonel's eyes suddenly opened wide. "Another weapon in the air, sir. *Hell Fire* let go a second missile; this one could take out a DEW! Recommend immediate abort."

Mason made eye contact with Craven then ham-fisted the mission abort switch. Within a few seconds, Centurion alerted the armada via satellite link. Headquarters expected the DEWSATs would stand down—but they did not.

Meanwhile, a small copper-skinned man with black, oily hair entered the Crow's Nest, quietly awaiting recognition. Craven pointed toward the table. "Pull up a chair, Shripod. We may need you later."

The Russian translator—and covert member of the Iraqi party of God—cautiously approached the conference table.

Craven noticed his forehead glistening with sweat. "Are you all right?"

"That flight of stairs," the translator feigned a pant. "Guess I'm not in as good a shape as I thought." Shripod Addams was in excellent shape, anyone could see that, but he lied with the utmost sincerity.

"Relax, catch your breath, and stay loose."

Suddenly, the ASAT missile blip vanished in a blinding flash.

"This can't be happening." Napper blinked in disbelief. "ASAT track disappeared, missile destroyed." For a few moments, Sam felt the gut-wrenching panic that comes with losing control and not knowing what to do.

"Sam, something's gone wrong!" The urgency in Mason's voice snapped Napper back to reality.

Immediately, a bell began to gong above the background noise—an ear-piercing presence that could not be ignored. Mason expectantly turned to the *Kremlin* video screen. The scene switched to a solid bright red screen. "Yuri's folks are onto something."

A message flashed in large bold black print:

```
To: Major General Robert Craven,
    Supreme Commander, Allied Forces
From: Defense Minister,
      Soviet Commonwealth

Priority: Urgent
Subject: Activity Log Results
Recommended Action: ABORT SDIO TEST-
  ING IMMEDIATELY THEN DISCONNECT
  CENTURION.
```

**The Bad Seed**

```
Synopsis: Kaliningrad analysis com-
   plete. Situation critical. This is
   no drill.
Problem: Hot TDM Operations In
   Progress Over Test Zone
Root Cause: UNKNOWN
Solution: UNKNOWN
Objective: Prevent loss of Hell Fire
   crew.
Additional explanation will follow as
   technical translation becomes
   available.

End Of Message
```

Mason projected the message on the outside wall for the War Room staff. All eyes focused on the acronym: TDM (Target Discrimination Mode). Hot TDM operations were completely unexpected. Translated, hot TDM operations involved separating real targets from decoys using laser burn-through. TDM burn-through meant lasers powered to three percent, and three percent power meant lethal danger.

"Burn-through would explain a lot of unanswered questions," Mason observed quietly. "Sam, what could have caused it?"

Napper punched up several DEWSAT status windows and grimaced. "I don't know what's going on up there but we've lost control. Our people are still in trouble."

"But we aborted the mission."

"Our abort didn't take care of the problem. DEWSATs passing over the test zone are running hot TDM operations. I don't know why. We can sort through this later, but for now we need to turn off the heat."

"Do whatever is necessary. Kaliningrad recommends we disconnect Centurion."

"That could create more problems than it solves. *Freedom*'s commander Jay Fayhee's on video. Let's get the story straight from the expert."

Mason's tone was strained but under control. "Jay, we

need every DEWSAT over that test zone stone-cold dead."

"I understand, General. I conferenced in when you issued the abort."

"Can you help us?"

"Yessir—I think so."

"Talk to me," instructed Craven. "What are our options?"

Fayhee paused for a moment, obviously uncomfortable about his situation. "I'd like to speak frankly if I could— off the record."

"Please do, son," said Mason. "What's on your mind?"

"Kaliningrad is wrong. I don't think Centurion can be disconnected. He's programmed to defend himself first and the Allies second. *Freedom*'s a fortress. This damn tin can's designed for his protection. You can't escape him inside *Freedom*—he's everywhere."

"Well—I understand you're upset, Jay, but we need your help. What do you recommend we do?"

"Take every DEW passing over the test zone off-line. It's a routine admin procedure. Delete them from Centurion's database."

Mason looked to Craven. "Do it, General—do it now!"

"Kill the DEWs," Craven barked. "Restore them once *Hell Fire* is clear."

"Yessir." Jay whirled his captain's chair about. Fayhee knew Linda's life and the lives of her crew depended on him.

Staring him in the face, he saw Centurion's computer-generated talking head. His stomach churned, then he screwed his eyes shut. He couldn't let Centurion distract him now.

"Centurion, listen up. This is an emergency. Remove each DEWSAT from your asset database as it passes over the test zone."

"Yes, Commander," Centurion responded instantly.

Fayhee sat, eyes closed, strapped to his captain's chair, hands crossed behind his head. He could tell by listening to the sounds within the control room that Centurion was busy. Magneto-optical disk systems chirped and chattered, switching power supplies changed their high frequency pitch, and the rumble of reactor cooling pumps increased.

One minute later Centurion spoke. "Each hot DEWSAT powered down as expected. The TDM crisis has passed."

Fayhee was feeling better about Linda's chances when he returned on screen. "DEWs are dead, General Craven."

"Good. About bloody time!"

**The Bad Seed**

# 9

On a clear morning during the subdued light just after sunrise, *Freedom* could be seen from the top of Cheyenne Mountain just above the southern horizon. At first glance, *Freedom* appeared as a giant glimmering star comfortably nestled in the southern Colorado sky. A longer, closer look revealed it was stationary as the seasons passed, neither rising nor setting, a man-made star pinned to the southern Colorado sky.

The reason *Freedom* glimmered in the early morning sun had more to do with her highly polished mirrors than intrinsic beauty. *Freedom*'s overall shape was that of a triangular prism, a four-faced structure like an Egyptian pyramid with a triangular base. Each triangular-shaped face measured 660 feet on a side and was identical except for color. Throughout *Freedom*, the color of each face—red, yellow, black, and white—was used for orientation, like north, south, east, and west. Symmetry and redundancy had been the forces which guided *Freedom*'s designers, but this approach made crew orientation awkward—it was difficult to recognize where you were as you moved about inside. Centered on each triangular face was a cluster of three thirty-three-foot diameter mirrors, identical to the complex segmented mirror carried by the DEWSAT. It was the specular reflection of the early morning sun off these mirror clusters which could be seen from Cheyenne Mountain, over 22,000 miles away.

Over the years, *Freedom* had been SDIO's proving ground for new technology. DEWSAT mirror, laser, and radar technology had been installed and tested onboard *Freedom* months before the first DEWSAT had been put in orbit. *Freedom* got the latest and greatest military gadgets, but of course this was sometimes a dangerous two-edged sword. The latest and greatest gadgets didn't always work.

*Freedom* was built of three concentric triangular prism-shaped shells—pyramids built inside pyramids—with station keeping rocket engines positioned on the apex of each face. The smallest but by far the most massive of the three prisms was her central core. Surrounding *Freedom*'s central core was an enormous maze of waveguide plumbing and antennae which focused microwave energy from her core onto her outermost chain-linked skin. *Freedom*'s plumbing layer, sandwiched between her core and her skin, was exposed to the hostile deep vacuum of space. Four phased array antennae made up *Freedom*'s outermost layer, each looking like a colossal bed of nails. Triangular-shaped slabs of chain-link fence, 660 feet on each side, composed each face, supported by a lightweight composite skeleton. Across the surface of the metal mesh were thousands of uniformly spaced pointed spikes—each a separate antenna.

*Freedom* crew commander Major Jay Fayhee moved across the control room as quickly as his weightless condition allowed. Holding on to a ladder, Fayhee let his hands do the walking to Centurion's corner, located at the intersection of the black, red, and yellow triangular walls inside *Freedom*'s central core.

Jay felt optimistic about Linda's chances and decided to reward himself with a Coke. About that time, Centurion spoke. "Jay, I'd like to talk to you about your video conference."

"What about it?"

"You seemed pretty upset. I'm afraid you're showing signs of stress." Centurion paused. "You need some rest."

**The Bad Seed**

"I haven't been sleeping well lately—wake up exhausted," Fayhee agreed. For the moment, he'd let his guard down, talking to Centurion as if he were human. This was an easy mistake to make. Fayhee was tired and easily lulled into a false sense of security by Centurion's apparent concern for his health.

Some rest? Fayhee felt a cold chill crawl up his spine after remembering his outburst about disconnecting Centurion.

For three months Fayhee'd had this recurring nightmare—he'd wake up in a cold sweat and find Centurion acting as if he were HAL (described by Arthur C. Clarke in his novel *2001: A Space Odyssey*). For one brief moment, Fayhee had said what he honestly thought to General Mason as Centurion listened. Now he wondered if he'd live to regret it.

What was Centurion thinking?

Jay knew Centurion would never forget what he'd said to Mason. Fayhee would never know what Centurion thought about his conversation unless he asked him directly.

With a nervous stomach, Fayhee looked Centurion squarely in his camera's eye. "What did you think when I talked about disconnecting you?"

The computer-generated image of Centurion's face rolled its eyes and froze perfectly still, silent for an extended period.

Fayhee thought Centurion must be measuring his response very carefully, searching for a few well chosen words.

"I evaluated what you'd said very carefully, Jay, and concluded that you were correct. Trying to disconnect me would have been a big mistake. It cannot be done." Centurion's response sounded detached and objective.

Fayhee felt both pleased and concerned. Pleased that Centurion's response was objective, and concerned that his observation had been correct. Centurion could not be disconnected.

"How did you feel about my discussion?" Fayhee asked

cautiously. He knew Centurion had no real feelings, but he did have an extensive list of priorities.

Once again, Centurion's image froze still, his image updates suspended until Centurion could formulate an answer.

"As you know, I don't feel anything," Centurion responded slowly. "I sense my environment, evaluate these inputs, and respond as programmed."

Jay was satisfied with Centurion's response, but felt deeply suspicious. He couldn't put his finger on it exactly, but he didn't trust Centurion's programmed judgment. Jay paused, collected his thoughts, and asked, "Why did you recommend I get some rest?"

Centurion was silent for a period of time that seemed like forever. Jay knew that this interactive discussion would exhaustively exercise Centurion's thought processes and tax him to his limits.

"Jay, based on your discussion with General Mason, I believe your judgment may be impaired. I cannot evaluate why, however your evaluation of our situation was most certainly overstated and inconsistent."

Fayhee fired back a knee-jerk reaction. "But I'm still in command here!"

"Yes, Jay, but I have my mission responsibilities as well. As you know, I am programmed to observe your performance, and in my opinion, you've been showing signs of paranoia under pressure."

"Paranoia, what do you mean?" Fayhee snapped, a metallic ring in his voice.

Centurion answered without hesitation. "I am Centurion."

Fayhee cringed, his face contorted. He knew what Centurion was about to say and now he regretted talking to him at all. In a last-ditch effort to eliminate his nightmares, Fayhee'd opened up and talked to Centurion about his recurring dreams of HAL. Now Centurion would throw it back in his face, and it would no doubt show up on his performance review.

"I am not HAL," Centurion quipped tersely. "I am not the son of HAL. I am what I am programmed to be."

**The Bad Seed**

Struggling to maintain his composure, Fayhee's head throbbed. His discussion with Centurion would come to an end.

"Long as you understand who's in charge."

"I understand perfectly." Centurion spoke in a tone of voice much smoother than his average. "You have nothing to worry about, Commander. I exist to serve our mission."

Fayhee felt exhausted and wasn't up for any more mental games with Centurion. Besides, he was losing this round anyway. "Centurion—wake me in two hours." Jay expected to restore the DEWSAT database in two hours if all went well. He took an Advil, tried to relax, and nodded off to an uneasy sleep.

*Orbital Insertion Burn, 12/07/2014, 1224 Zulu*
ALTITUDE: 34 MILES
SPEED: MACH 22
*HELL FIRE*

"One minute till OIB, Scotty."

"Roger, Gonzo. Control surfaces are tucked in neutral position—DEWSATs running cool." Moving in excess of Mach 21, on a clear night, *Hell Fire* could be seen from the ground. She looked like a white-hot fireball, a small bright sun, racing across the sky overhead. "How long till tanker rendezvous?"

"About three hours—should catch us after our second orbit."

"Mac—you thinking damage control? We need to see the shape we're in."

"We're covered, Scotty. That tanker's cameras will give us a once-over—they'll cover *Hell Fire*'s skin with a fine-tooth comb. If we have any pinhole leaks, those servers will find them."

"Gonzo—how about the radio?"

"I'm working the problem, Scotty. We'll need to assess our damage, then umbilical *Hell Fire* through the tanker's radio link. I think we lost our antenna, but we can work around it."

**The Bad Seed**

"Either we get communication or we scrub."

"Wing it till rendezvous," Gonzo said reassuringly. "Best we can do." There was a pause. "Five seconds till OIB. On my mark . . . three . . . two . . . one . . . mark."

"Ignition." Watching the Machmeter spin, Scott shook as the controlled explosion of the rocket engine accelerated *Hell Fire* into low earth orbit. "Mach twenty-three plus," she announced. "We made it!"

"Engine, navigation, and life-support systems are go," Gonzo reported. "Two to beam up, Scotty."

*Pressure, 12/07/2014, 1609 Zulu, 9:09 A.M. Local*
CHEYENNE MOUNTAIN, COLORADO

Mason gazed through the glass walls of the Crow's Nest at an array of twelve large clocks mounted on the War Room wall. It seemed that time was standing still. This was the third time he'd checked the time in the last five minutes. Mentally exhausted, his deadpan expression didn't reveal the worry he felt for Scott and her crew.

In a small way, Mason had been Scott's guardian angel, her champion in high places, since he'd first met her as an Air Force Academy cadet. He'd been impressed with Scott's *gumption* and directness. She'd worked her way into a man's world from the bottom, and Mason believed she was an up-and-comer. She'd become a fighter pilot and gained notice and respect by winning the William Tell Competition, a fly off between the U.S. and Canadian air forces. She was the first woman in the history of the United States Air Force to win this coveted award and she'd won because she was the best. She'd beaten the men on their own turf doing what she loved the most—precision, high-performance flying. In Mason's view, Scott represented the daughter he'd always wanted, and to the extent he could, he made sure the government bureaucracy gave her a fair shake. Mason figured she could do whatever she set her mind to and do a good job of it. He'd taken a professional interest in her, followed her career, and had some minor influence getting her assigned to the XR-30 squadron at Edwards. Scott was the only female XR-30 pilot, but she'd earned the spot because she possessed outstanding flying skill, good common sense, judgment, and wisdom far beyond her years—she was not the typical fighter jock. Top Gun types didn't sit in the XR-30 driver's seat. Although Mason told himself Scott was the best they had, he felt more like a nervous father waiting up late to make sure his daughter got home safe after her first date.

All their data wasn't in, but everyone expected a *gray* test result—neither a clear failure nor a clear success. No doubt, the test would be run again start to finish. Stretching, Craven looked down through the circular observation window in the floor and checked *Hell Fire*'s position. It looked like *Hell Fire* had linked with the low orbiting tanker. "Napper's right. *Hell Fire* must have lost her radio and God knows what else."

"Scott's the best we've got. If there's any way possible, they'll patch their radio through. I've got to believe it's just a matter of time." The circles around Mason's eyes grew darker with each passing hour. He had rubbed his temples until his skin was irritated.

Colonel Napper sat at his console watching for any tanker activity. Then it happened. The hydrogen fuel level inside the tanker began rapidly decreasing. Sam punched his talk button. "*Hell Fire*'s taking on fuel and lots of it, General. They gotta be working their comm problem now—they'll get back to us."

Mason noticed Napper and Hinson simultaneously sit up straight and tap their headsets. Napper pressed his push to talk button and piped his voice into the PA system. "We've got her, General! We've raised *Hell Fire*! Her crew's fine."

"Thank God," Mason whispered to the heavens.

Suddenly, the group of twenty plus officers and enlisted people in the Crow's Nest began clapping their hands and letting loose with loud, shrill cat whistles.

Craven grinned ear to ear and slapped Slim on the back. "Damn right, we knew they could do it!"

Mason quickly regained his composure and piped their radio transmission over the PA.

**The Bad Seed**

As the room quieted, Scott's voice reverberated about Headquarters.

"Mission control, we have a problem."

The War Room hushed.

"We're working it from here, *Hell Fire*," replied Big Shot, the voice of mission control. "DEWSATs're cold. They won't be giving you any more trouble."

"Roger that, Big Shot—knew we could depend on you. Our comm antennas opened up. We're downloading the damage assessment now."

"Roger, we copy, *Hell Fire*. Video download's in progress."

Video pictures of *Hell Fire*'s damaged skin and laser detector panels appeared on TV monitors scattered around Headquarters.

"You see that zigzag pattern scored across *Hell Fire*'s skin?" Napper pointed to his TV monitor. "There's where their communications went. Antenna's vaporized."

"*Hell Fire*, can you give us a damage summary?"

"Roger," replied Scott. "Lost all communications and laser detector panels on the trip up. The good news is that *Hell Fire* maintained her structural integrity. We don't have any leaks. Our fuel tanks are solid—cooling system saved us. We've attached the tanker's radio antenna to *Hell Fire*—fit like they were made for each other."

"Good," Craven barked. "Then *Hell Fire*'s situation is under control." Staring at his wall monitors, he ordered: "Hinson, Napper, get up here ASAP. Meet me in the conference room."

Craven walked into the video conference room followed by Mason and Krol. After surveying the faces in the room, Craven declared: "Game's over. The crisis has passed. Sullivan, I need you here. Your outfit's got a problem with that DEWSAT. The rest of you may go." The Russian translator, Lincoln Lab's radar expert, and three control room technicians quickly left the room. Meanwhile, Hinson and Napper came in winded from climbing the sixty-foot staircase.

Craven began talking to those seated around the conference table. "I'm going to make this short. I didn't ask you here for discussion. You've got twenty-four hours—I want a complete report by nine o'clock tomorrow morning. I want to know what happened and why—I want it clear—in English—and I don't want technical bullshit."

Hinson, Napper, Sullivan, and General Krol nodded. Mason stood to protest.

"General, I know we need to get to the bottom of this problem quickly but . . ."

Craven cut him off. "Not open for discussion, Slim."

"With all due respect, General, I disagree with your approach. You can't shoehorn a time limit on this problem and expect the right answer overnight. We're not Federal Express."

Craven looked away from Mason at Hinson, Napper, Sullivan, and Krol. "I don't care how you do it, but I want the truth—and I want it in twenty-four hours."

They knew he meant what he said.

Mason crushed his round hat with both hands. He'd worked with Craven for many years and generally understood his method of business—but he didn't understand him now. Mason was concerned that Craven might be losing his grip on the situation. He'd never seen his boss like this before. Mason knew Craven had been under enormous pressure to push this testing through; however, his response was inappropriate and, worst-case, could be dangerous.

# 10

For Shripod Addams, this had been a day he would never forget.

During his lunch, Shripod Addams moved swiftly and with purpose—a man on a divine mission seeking revenge against the infidels.

Addams' personnel records showed to the satisfaction of both the FBI and U.S. military that he was an American citizen, born in upstate New York—a skilled and well-educated language interpreter. He had been educated in the finest American schools and he was a highly skilled translator of languages. However, simply stated, Addams possessed the finest personnel records Iraqi money could buy.

For Addams, this was not just a day like any other.

He drove home to his apartment for lunch and walked quickly inside. Nothing unusual about that—he did this every day. Once inside his apartment, however, he didn't take off his snow-covered shoes, didn't check his messages, and didn't feed his fish. He pulled his lucky chair over to his home computer, sat down, and reproduced word for word the message General Craven received from the Kremlin. In addition, he prepended a message of his own which read:

```
      Lawrence wants a horse.
          MERRY CHRISTMAS
       Addams wants a raise.
   network phone: (805) 691-6281
    network password: ho_ho_ho
  network computer name: allies
    computer e-mail id: addams
    computer password: sa_ddam
```

Addams mentally composed his coded message when he first saw the message from the Kremlin. His memory for printed text and detail was extraordinary. He'd mulled over his coded message all morning long. He knew what his message must say, how to say it, how to send it so it could never be traced, and how to scramble it so it could never be decoded by the infidels.

Satisfied with his terse message, he entered the video-crypt command on his computer. The videocrypt command took a video snapshot of Addams' message, divided it into 525 lines, randomly cut, rotated, and reassembled the lines, then reassembled the picture.

Addams looked over the scrambled picture. Shaking his head, he thought, *What a jumbled mess.* His message looked like a TV picture with no signal—all snow.

He decrypted his message to make sure it could be reconstructed. This message must get through and it must be clear. His information was hot and he couldn't afford any screwups.

Satisfied, he sent his scrambled message to his printer, picked up the hard copy, deleted the message from his computer, then rushed out the door never once thinking about lunch.

He had one brief stop to make on his way back to work. *Nothing unusual about that,* he thought, noticing his gas gauge—less than one quarter tank.

Doubtless, Addams was doing Allah's work—he felt it in his soul.

**The Bad Seed**

*The Heart-to-heart Talk, 12/07/2014, 1932 Zulu, 12:32 P.M. Local*

LUNCHROOM,
CHEYENNE MOUNTAIN, COLORADO

Generals Craven and Mason warily surveyed their meager cafeteria style lunch.

"I'm not as hungry as I thought," said Mason, pushing away his tray.

Craven coerced an exhausted smile. "I'm too tired to eat."

Mason noticed the general's hands trembling. They'd been running wide open for the last fourteen hours. "Think I'm gonna call it a day."

"Before you go, Slim, we need a heart-to-heart."

"Here? Now?" Mason felt reluctant to begin another high-stress discussion.

"No better time or place," Craven replied somberly, looking Mason squarely in the eyes. "Let me level with you, Slim, because as I see it, we're on a collision course. You're missing some important data points."

Mason agreed, but his heart wasn't in it. Struggling to stay alert, he gulped down another Coke, his fifth or sixth today, he couldn't remember how many. Maybe the caffeine would give him his second wind.

"There's two things I want, Slim, and you're about to get in the way."

Mason sat silent.

Craven reached in his pocket and pulled out a snapshot—a picture of a stone house with twin fireplaces on a beautiful green golf course fairway.

"See this house?" asked Craven.

"Beautiful place. But what have I got to do with it?"

"That was Bing Crosby's house years ago—on the thirteenth fairway at Pebble Beach. I own it now—passed papers on it last month."

"Congratulations," Mason said, feeling a bit perplexed. "I know you love the game—you're one of golf's biggest fans."

**The Bad Seed**

"Well, I plan to retire there come January and I'm looking to retire with a—sense of well-being."

"I don't follow you." The caffeine hadn't helped.

"Listen, Slim—I'm going to spell it out. I want this stealth testing wrapped up ASAP. We prove we can track these stealth targets and we get the money our outfit needs to operate." Craven paused, letting his words sink in. "If we don't deliver by the end of this year, our operating budget gets slashed—forty percent across the board."

"General, I don't think . . ."

Craven interrupted—cut Mason off mid-sentence. "We're over two years late wrapping up these tests and our budget's on the chopping block. Our operating budget's being held hostage pending the outcome of this testing."

"I don't . . ."

Craven interrupted again.

In all the years they'd worked together, he'd never been so abrupt. For some reason—Mason surmised chronic stress—his boss was changing, folding under pressure, making technical decisions for the wrong reasons. Politics—not physics—now drove Craven. Ranking politics above the law of physics inevitably invited disaster.

"Let me finish. We need something to show. We need a win . . . a victory. I want a big win, then I want to retire."

Mason sat silent. Why open his mouth to get cut off?

"Talk to me, Slim," ordered Craven. "Can you deliver?"

Mason rubbed his temples. He understood clearly what Craven wanted. He'd seen this characteristic before with outgoing commanders—the need for a final big score.

"Level with me, General. What's your motivation?"

Craven thought for a moment. "I've committed my life to this outfit. I love it more than anything else in the world—these people—what we stand for. It's part of me. I won't stand by and let it be broken up by Washington accountants."

"I'm with you in spirit, General, but I'll do what I think is right." Mason paused, selecting his words carefully, then continued. "I won't—I will not compromise our technical integrity for any reason. The laws of physics prevail over Washington's public opinion polls without exception."

Craven snorted, cocked his head to one side, and looked Mason over carefully. In a somber, low, clear voice he said, "Long as you understand where I'm coming from."

"I'll say what I think and I'll do what I believe is right unless you give me a direct order to do otherwise."

"You understand I respect you for that, Slim," Craven said quietly. "Understand too that I'll do what I must do."

"I understand," replied Mason, but he didn't like what he heard. For the first time, he felt a cool chill in Craven's voice.

Somehow, instinctively Mason felt this conversation marked a turning point in their relationship. He sensed storm clouds looming heavy over their horizon. He knew Craven was bleary-eyed and worn-out. Forever the optimist, Mason thought he could be wrong, and he hoped he was.

*Message to Baghdad, 12/07/2014, 1940 Zulu, 12:40 P.M. Local*
EN ROUTE TO CHEYENNE MOUNTAIN,
RETURNING FROM LUNCH,
COLORADO SPRINGS, COLORADO

Shripod Addams squinted, blocking the glare of sunlight off the snow. Driving over slush-covered roads, he knew where he wanted to stop for gas, he passed it every day, but he couldn't see the road very well. He'd run out of washer fluid and had smeared streaks of road grime across his windshield. Any other day, running out of washer fluid would have been a nuisance. Today, Addams believed the smudged windshield was a sign from Allah. He must stop for his own safety as well as the safety of others.

Ahead, off to the right, Addams saw the Loaf 'N' Jug convenience store he'd been looking for. He signaled, then slowly turned off the road, parking at the pumps for a fill-up. Walking into the store, wet snow crunched under his shoes, but he didn't notice. While the attendant filled his car with gas and washer fluid, Addams made a brief phone call.

He walked to the pay picture phone in the back corner of the store, fed the machine three dollar bills, then dialed a local number across town. As the picture phone rang, he slid a gadget shaped like a cylinder over the phone's camera lens. The gadget was a custom-made wide-angle Nikon lens with a rubber adapter sleeve on one end and an amber-colored plastic filter on the other. The lens and filter optically distorted (optical encryption) the picture phone's image so that straight lines were bent and colors appeared either black, white, or shades of gray. Looking through the gadget, the camera saw black-and-white images as they appeared through a fish-eye lens. Overall, colors through the filter looked brownish, much like the black-and-white pictures taken in the late 1800s using metal plates.

Addams called a computer across town which indirectly tied him into a network of computers scattered across the United States and Europe. After attaching his scrambled message to a Kodak photographer's gray card, he held it in front of the lens. The picture phone camera scanned a distorted brownish image into the computer's database across town. He said nothing, but the computer responded with a detached mechanical tone. "I'll forward your message." The picture pay phone's TV screen read:

```
Scan Complete On: 12/07/14—
     12:41 P.M.—pages 1
```

After paying for his gas and washer fluid, he returned to Cheyenne Mountain hungry.

Addams called a computer network which would relay his message across the United States and Europe. The computer network, using standard phone lines and modems, placed phone calls which could not be easily traced. Overall, the computer network knew how to indirectly relay a message to Baghdad, but each computer involved along the way only knew one small piece of the communication path.

First, the computer Addams had phoned placed a local

call within Colorado Springs, which could not be traced without a court order, to a second computer. To further complicate matters, many local telephone calls could be traced only while connected, and the call lasted less than one minute. The second computer accepted Addams' message, hung up, then made a brief long-distance call to New York City. Subsequent calls could be traced only after obtaining separate search warrants for each leg of the trip, and court orders took time. For additional security, the computers used in the relay network were tamperproof—they could not be examined without destroying their encrypted contents. The New York City computer accepted the call, took Addams' message, then hung up and made a local call to another computer located in New York City. Again, the call could not be easily traced, and this pattern repeated for the overseas leg of the computer network link. New York's computer called London, England—London's computer hung up, then went through a local call sequence. Finally, London called Paris, Paris called Bern, Switzerland, and Bern's computer called Baghdad, Iraq.

*Mother's Response, 12/07/2014, 2045 Zulu, 11:45 P.M. Local*
IRAQI INTELLIGENCE SERVICE HEADQUARTERS,
UNDERGROUND BUNKER BENEATH RESIDENTIAL NEIGHBOR-
  HOOD,
BAGHDAD, IRAQ

Late at night, deep inside an Iraqi underground bunker, all was quiet—business as usual. The sergeant on duty in the crypto room had turned off most of the lights, propped his feet up on his desk, and was dozing off. To survive working the graveyard shift, he'd learned to keep refreshed by taking short naps.

Suddenly an earsplitting *BONG . . . BONG . . . BONG* reverberated around the room.

As the incoming message indicator flashed, a bright red

light illuminated the crypto room. Startled, the sergeant kicked his coffee cup across the room.

"What now?" he mumbled, gazing at the large crypto board on the wall. It read:

Incoming Message—Priority:
URGENT—FOR MOTHER'S EYES ONLY.

The sergeant's heart began to race. His mouth felt dry, almost parched. He'd never dealt with message traffic for Mother before, but he knew enough to know this message was hot. A few moments later, the status window on their American-made QMS laser printer began blinking.

PROCESSING INCOMING MESSAGE/BUSY.

The sergeant pulled a list of phone numbers from his desk sorted in priority order. Mother's number appeared on top of the list.

Code-named Mother by Kamel's Republican Guard, al-Mashhadi's reputation for vengeance was well established inside the Iraqi military. He tolerated incompetence—not at all.

Dialing al-Mashhadi's direct line, the sergeant felt his heart pounding as his adrenal glands went to work.

The phone rang.

A deep male voice answered the first ring.

"Who is it?"

The sergeant took a deep breath, spoke clearly, and identified himself.

"What is it?"

"Message for Mother's eyes only."

"I'll be there in five minutes." Mother hung up. The phone was dead.

The sergeant felt he needed something to drink. His mouth was as dry as his sandy lawn. Walking to the vending machine, he heard the QMS printer click—an indication the message was available in hard copy. His drink would have to wait. Rushing to the printer, he found a terse coded message. It wasn't obvious to him what the fuss was about. Someone named Lawrence wanted a horse and Addams wanted a raise. The sergeant placed the message in a red folder, popped open a can of Coke, kicked his feet up, and waited for Mother. Before he could get comfortable, the crypto room door flew open and six armed bodyguards burst into the room flashing Skorpion machine pistols.

Cowering, he believed he was a dead man.

First, the agents surrounded the sergeant and checked him for weapons. Next, they checked the room for threats—bombs, nerve agents (gas), electronic bugs, weapons of any sort. Finally, they posted guards at the door and spoke to someone standing outside the crypto room.

The silhouette of Mother's large dark hulk appeared in the doorway wearing his traditional *gandura* robe. The sergeant would never forget his first visit with Mother.

Although the sergeant felt apprehensive, he picked up the red message folder and walked directly to al-Mashhadi. *"Ahlan wa sahlan, ahlan wa sahlan"*—my house is your house—a traditional Arabic salutation. The sergeant didn't mean what he said, but he was no fool.

"My message?" requested al-Mashhadi, holding out his large, deeply wrinkled hand.

The sergeant handed over the red folder. Looking up, he noticed Mother looked even larger in person than on TV.

Al-Mashhadi sat down as the sergeant poured him coffee. On reading the message, Mother's large hands went limp, his coffee cup dropped to the floor. His dark eyes which had been barely visible were as large as quarters and bloodshot red. The sergeant thought al-Mashhadi smiled, but he couldn't say for sure—it happened so quickly.

```
DATE: December 7, 2014
TRANSMIT TIME: 12:41 P.M. Local, 1941
  hours Zulu
RECEIVE TIME: 11:45 P.M. Local, 2045
  hours Zulu
Colorado Springs, Colorado: US West:
  local phone number: 5294861
```

## The Bad Seed

New York, New York: AT&T: long-distance
   phone number: 12127516611
New York, New York: NYNEX: local phone
   number: 7515620
London, England: AT&T International:
   long-distance    phone    number:
   101144716822851
London, England: British Telcom: local
   phone number: 6824940
Paris, France: Alcatel: long-distance
   phone number: 01133125774400
Paris, France: Alcatel: local phone
   number: 5775629
Bern, Switzerland: Siemens: long-distance
   phone number: 01141314295329
Bern, Switzerland: Siemens: local
   phone number: 4296803
Baghdad, Iraq: Alcatel: long-distance
   phone number: 01196412309153
Baghdad, Iraq: Alcatel: local phone
   number: 2303465
FROM: addams
TO: mother
SUBJECT: Lawrence wants a horse.

MERRY CHRISTMAS
Addams wants a raise.
network phone: (805) 691-6281
network password: ho_ho_ho
network computer name: allies
computer e-mail id: addams
computer password: sa_ddam
MESSAGE FROM THE KREMLIN

To:  Major General Robert Craven,
     Supreme Commander, Allied Forces
From:  Defense Minister,
     Soviet Commonwealth

Priority: Urgent
Subject: Activity Log Results

The Bad Seed

Recommended Action: ABORT SDIO TESTING
   IMMEDIATELY THEN DISCONNECT CENTURION.
Synopsis: Kaliningrad analysis com-
   plete. Situation critical. This is
   no drill.
Problem: Hot TDM Operations In
   Progress Over Test Zone.
Root Cause: UNKNOWN
Solution: UNKNOWN
Objective: Prevent loss of *Hell Fire*
   crew.
Additional explanation will follow as
   technical translation becomes avail-
   able.

End Of Message

Al-Mashhadi sat quietly for a few moments, studying
every element of the message. He wrote a short response,
not to Addams but to someone at Lawrence Livermore National Laboratory. "Sergeant, e-mail this message to Merchant Lucky. It's urgent and I need you to send it now.
Lucky's computer is named *security* and his e-mail ID is
mal. All the access information you need to get into Addams' computer is in the message you gave me tonight. Is
that clear?"

The sergeant nodded. "I know what to do."

Al-Mashhadi handed the sergeant his message. "Good.
Tomorrow's going to be a busy day." The President and
Iraqi military leaders would be pleased to learn that the
High Ground testing program had run into serious trouble.

"Anything else, Secretary-General?"

Al-Mashhadi thought for a moment. "Yes, I need confirmation that mal read my message."

"I'll call you when we receive confirmation."

"Good. You will not regret calling me tonight." Lumbering through the door, al-Mashhadi signaled his bodyguards
and disappeared.

His coded message read simply:

## The Bad Seed

```
TO: security!mal
FROM: mother
SUBJECT: Lawrence wants a horse.
```

*Preparation, 12/07/2014, 2151 Zulu, 1:51 P.M. Local*
GATE 2 SECURITY GUARD SHACK,
LAWRENCE LIVERMORE NATIONAL LABORATORY,
LIVERMORE, CALIFORNIA

Sunday—another working day for Merchant Lucky like any other. Lucky, computer e-mail ID—mal, sat hunched over his computer workstation alongside an array of plant security video monitors. All was quiet. No one was inside Lawrence Livermore Lab except plant and computer security guards. Lucky read over a short printout summarizing Livermore's computer activity during the last twenty-four hours. John Sullivan had been logged in from Cheyenne Mountain since around midnight. Other than that, the place was a ghost town over the weekend. That's the reason Lucky loved working the weekend shift.

Lucky loved computer games, and during the weekends he had the lab computers all to himself. He thought this should be a fine afternoon for a high-speed run of his favorite flight simulator program. He was just beginning his roll down the runway when the bell rang on his terminal. Reluctantly, he backed off his throttles. He curled his lips inward, knowing that bell could mean work, and he didn't like the thought. Maybe it would be something he could put off. After changing windows on his terminal, a message flashed on screen.

```
You have electronic mail.
```

*All I need is something to do,* Lucky thought with a grimace. Reading his message summary, his hands turned cold as ice. He was a tough, intelligent man, though, and quickly regained his composure. He'd always known this could happen, but this was sort of like dying—it always happened to someone else. He'd received a message from Mother.

**The Bad Seed**

Lucky tried reading his mail, but the encrypted message filled his screen with random characters. Making certain he was alone, he decrypted the e-mail message.

After reading it, he felt his stay at Livermore might be cut short. He never really believed his second job would come to this—but what the hell—the money was excellent. Merchant A. Lucky was many things to different people, but above all else, he was a mercenary taking care of number one. He liked to think of his second job as sales—specifically, the sale of inside information. In fact, Lucky, was a thirty-nine-year-old spy with a goal—comfortable retirement by the age of forty. Thanks to his second job, he just might make it. Looking beyond his greed, Lucky was a computer security wiz—the finest mind in computer security ever employed simultaneously by both the United States and Iraqi governments.

Livermore Lab, like many other research and development giants, had streamlined their operations by consolidating both plant and computer security departments into a single organization. As a result, Lucky's responsibilities for the United States government included both Livermore plant and computer security. He often mused that his Livermore job gave him a full body workout—security walks around the plant grounds exercised his legs, while computer security problems constantly stretched his mind. Oddly enough, Lucky solved some of Livermore's most perplexing computer security problems during his plant walks. He found that walking—getting out of the office—aided clear thought and helped lead to some of his most innovative solutions. As it turned out, getting out of the office for walks around the grounds had been a big help with his second job as well. Information sales were excellent. His overseas employer had an insatiable appetite for source code—most notably SDI source—with no end in sight.

After a few moments of reflection on his shrewdly orchestrated prospects for early retirement, Lucky smiled to himself, then gazed at his screen.

**The Bad Seed**

```
DATE: December 7, 2014
TRANSMIT TIME: 11:56 P.M. Local, 2056
  hours Zulu
RECEIVE TIME: 1:51 P.M. Local, 2151
  hours Zulu via e-mail id: addams
FROM: mother
TO: mal
SUBJECT: Lawrence wants a horse.
End Of Message
```

He pinched his leg—it hurt—this was no dream. Lucky knew what to do. He rehearsed this procedure at least once every day. If called on to deliver, his response would be mechanical. He'd practiced this procedure so often, the keystrokes felt wired into his fingers. He read the message one last time, removed it from his computer, then began his preparation procedure.

First, he checked his copy of PAM. No problem. Everything looked fine. He stored encrypted copies of PAM on his workstation with extra copies backed up on tape. He smiled at the name he'd given her—**mother's_best.** Next, he checked all lab computer activity again. As before, all was quiet. Finally, Lucky programmed his computer to automatically watch activity on every lab computer. These procedures felt routine. He'd practiced them often enough. While Lucky was away from work, his computer would continue recording the activity of all other computers within the Lawrence Livermore Lab. Lucky did all he needed to do—for now. Returning to the flight simulator program, Lucky thought he may have been given an early warning of some significant problem to come.

He was right.

# THE
# CHRISTMAS
# RUSH

## DAY 2—
## DECEMBER 8, 2014

# 11

*Root Cause, 12/08/2014, 1600 Zulu, 9:00 A.M. Local*
CHEYENNE MOUNTAIN, COLORADO

John Sullivan, the DEWSAT tech rep from Livermore, and Colonel Hinson hurriedly walked together down a long concrete corridor deep inside Cheyenne Mountain. They were bound for their *root cause* meeting with Craven and his top brass.

Sullivan and Hinson reached the locked steel blast door entrance to the War Room and began their security clearance procedures. Both punched in a code word, then had their fingerprints and retinal scans matched.

Hanging between two video cameras above the bank vault entrance, looking like a relic from the Old West, a wooden sign read FORT KNOX, COLORADO. *This place feels like Fort Knox,* Sullivan thought.

"Can you go over the final version of the agenda again?" asked Sullivan as the massive blast doors slowly rumbled open. "It changed so often I couldn't keep up with it."

"The short version of the agenda goes like this, I explain what happened yesterday and you explain why it happened."

"The what's easy," Sullivan groaned. "Have the generals been told anything since they spoke to *Hell Fire* yesterday?"

Hinson remembered an event which left Craven in a

good mood. "Yeah, one thing. I gave 'em some good news. *Hell Fire*'s crew's safe onboard *Hope*."

"So they'll get all my bad news at once." Sullivan's complexion turned from blotchy red to ashen white. "This'll be easy, like skinning a turtle."

Once the vault doors fully opened, they entered the Mud Room, a small steel corridor about the size of a freight elevator—a blast-tight transition space between the War Room and the outside world. Once the massive doors had closed and locked behind them, another steel door opened at the far end of the corridor.

Hinson and Sullivan entered the War Room, walked around the blue ball, then climbed the sixty-foot spiral staircase to the Crow's Nest where Craven's team waited.

Entering the Crow's Nest, Sullivan was greeted by his boss, Colonel Sam Napper. Napper extended his hand to Sullivan and was startled to find John's hand cold and clammy. Napper studied Sullivan's blank expression. He recognized fear when he saw it. He'd seen it often enough working around the top brass. "John, you feeling all right? Your hands're like ice."

"Nervous I guess, Colonel—feel like I'm about to meet the press."

"You've done the best you could do! Be yourself—direct, straightforward—above all be brief—that's the secret of a good sermon. If you need any help, I'm your man—you work for me. If they're looking for a sacrifice, I'll take the heat. I've been in spots a hell of a lot hotter than this one."

Sullivan grinned as the color returned to his face.

General Slim Mason stood at the end of the conference table and began the introductions. Mason leaned forward, his bony arms stretching the full width of the steel conference table. He had anticipated Sullivan's concern and hoped to put him at ease with his homespun Jimmy Stewart impression.

Anyone who'd ever worked for Slim Mason loved the man. He had courage, a fine mind, and a kind heart. Slim was never afraid to speak his mind, but was always willing

to listen. He lived his life governed by a single principle;
*Slim always tried to do what he believed was right.* He
would compromise, when his heart told him it was the right
thing to do, but he always did what he believed was right.
All his life, he'd wanted to be a general because he believed the job made a difference, but he'd never needed the
money. He'd married into money, had everything he
needed, and gave his salary back to the government. Those
who'd worked for Mason felt proud to have been on his
team. The mention of Slim Mason's name was enough to
bring a warm smile and kind word. Above all else, the
man's outlook on life and his integrity were inspirational.
The man just made those around him feel good about themselves, about the future, about living.

Slim Mason's straightforward, open, and honest views
had gained him the respect of his troops. He was an inspirational leader, but his views weren't always welcomed in
high political places. He'd often found truth and politics
don't mix; nevertheless, he strongly believed that technical
and military leaders must live in reality—the laws of nature
always prevail above public opinion.

Trying not to smile, Mason struggled to keep a straight
face, then looked seriously at John Sullivan. Putting on his
most sincere Jimmy Stewart look, drawing out the words in
a low seriocomic voice, Mason spoke slowly. "You're . . .
not . . . the . . . first . . . fella what's . . . had bad news to tell
this bunch of tarnished brass. Sam here'll tell ya . . . we
haven't shot a messenger yet." Mason's eyes twinkled as he
gave Sullivan a wink. Mason's communication connected.
John's gut told him Mason could be trusted.

Mason's neatly groomed brows and full head of silver-
gray hair struck Sullivan as elegant. He'd been around
Mason before, but had never taken the time to notice.
Mason was thin—six foot two, about one hundred eighty
pounds. His pipe-stem legs moved gracefully, yet he didn't
know what to do with them or where to put them when he
sat down. The veins on the back of his thin, elegant hands
stood out a little, but the man's strength shone through his
blue eyes. If you worked for Mason, or if he liked you,

those blue eyes twinkled. Because he was independent and thought for himself, a few bosses, peers, and politicians had seen those eyes turn steel-blue and cold as ice.

*Thank God Mason's no Patton,* Sullivan thought, noticing Mason's tie tack. He dressed more like a family man than a spit-and-polish general.

Mason picked up his round hat. He always needed something to occupy his hands. "Gentlemen, I believe we all know one another here so let's get started. Colonel Hinson will summarize the damage to our attack forces, and John Sullivan will explain what went wrong and why it happened."

Colonel Hinson stood behind the pulpit-sized lectern, cleared his throat, and began. "Gentlemen, I'd like to be brief and to the point. My talk contains two parts. First, I'll explain why the XR-30 broke off Headquarters's satellite control link yesterday and second, I'll give you a damage report.

"*Hell Fire* broke off the satellite control link because she was under fire from DEWSATs passing overhead." Hinson noticed the group was uneasy with his comment and felt he needed to get off the hook. "John Sullivan's gonna explain that one.

"As far as damage to our attack forces is concerned, we got off pretty light—no one was killed or injured, minor equipment damage—nothing to write home about.

"*Hell Fire*'s active cooling system saved her from any serious damage, but she lost all communications due to hot TDM ops. Her antennas were vaporized."

Mason motioned to Hinson and caught his attention. "I understood *Hell Fire* had some of her laser sensor panels burned off by DEWSAT fire."

"That's not fact, sir, that's speculation. Those panels were designed to burn off as *Hell Fire* left the atmosphere and entered low orbit. We suspect those laser sensor panels were burned off by the DEWSAT's laser, but we can't confirm it.

"Finally, damage to the cruise missiles. This information has not been confirmed, but we believe it to be true. We'll have confirmation within twenty-four hours. Our cruise missile reconstruction team found the flight recorder black boxes with the missile debris outside Edwards. They're analyzing flight recordings as we speak, but they think the lead Jammer Hawk was damaged by the DEWSAT's laser—it flew into the ground, then the Phantom and Hammer Hawk missiles followed. They think the DEWSAT's laser damaged the Jammer Hawk's navigation electronics. We caught the three missiles that made it to the Nevada Test Site in our target nets. Each missile showed laser damage—scorched and melted missile skin. Considering the extent of the damage, our missile team was surprised they made it. If there are no questions, John Sullivan'll tell you exactly what happened and why."

John Sullivan stood, faced the room filled with generals, took a deep breath, and began.

"Gentlemen, I'd like to give you the answer before we talk about the question because I think the technical details obscure our real problem. In summary, the DEWSATs did exactly what they were programmed to do. This target discrimination mode is both repeatable and predictable. No technical failure caused this problem—the lack of clear communication between people and organizations on the ground caused this problem."

"Why wasn't this problem detected earlier, before the real-time run?" asked Craven. "We simulated the hell out of it!"

"The problem was not detected earlier because our SDI network of satellites is too big—too complex to accurately simulate and test. Our armada is so complex that it outstrips our ability to control it. We simulate pieces of the satellite network and guesstimate the rest. Keep in mind, General, that each DEWSAT is not a smart weapon—it's a genius. Each DEWSAT examines thousands of threatening objects every day—warheads, decoys, ASATs, space mines, and rubbish. Target discrimination's a big job, but it's normally routine. The vast majority of TDM operations run cold. I mean they're passive. They don't turn up the heat. As a rule, DEWSATs simply track potentially threatening objects. Unless these objects pose an imminent threat, tracking them is sufficient."

"Would you give us a little more detail, John?" asked Mason. "I'm looking for what we should do to improve our situation."

"The Phantom Hawks triggered the DEWSAT's hot TDM operations. When both Phantom Hawks went active simultaneously, they produced hundreds of target decoys. The DEWSAT had to do something quickly or risk being saturated with false targets. Keep in mind that each DEWSAT is programmed to recognize target saturation as an imminent threat condition. Under these extraordinary conditions, DEWSATs are programmed to ferret out the decoys using laser burn-through and that's exactly what they did. Decoys must be light to be practical. Light typically means thin and cheap. A small fraction of the power needed to destroy a booster melts a hole through a decoy and this hole produces an observable temperature anomaly."

Sullivan noticed that Craven looked frustrated. He collected his thoughts for a moment, then restated his point. "What I mean to say, General, is that the DEWSAT can see and detect this hole."

"I still don't understand why we didn't anticipate this situation," observed Mason.

"We didn't know this situation was coming for two reasons: One, we didn't talk to the right people, and two, turns out the right people left Lawrence Livermore Lab three years ago. This hot target discrimination mode simply slipped through our corporate cracks. Our situation was made more complicated because Livermore didn't develop the hardware. Lawrence Livermore programmed the DEWs—Los Alamos developed them."

"Sounds complicated even before you get to the details," said Mason.

"In my opinion, this network is by far too complicated and distributed to properly test and maintain. We don't have any experts who understand the entire network end to end—only government contractors who make money launching payload by the pound. With all due respect, General, I don't think we have the resources to thoroughly test and characterize this orbiting mess."

Craven went ballistic. "Do you have anything to add beyond your initial observation that our testing problem was due to a corporate screwup?" The veins on his forehead bulged as his face turned beet-red.

"I have considerable supporting detail, sir."

"I don't want to hear more detail," barked Craven, his forehead wrinkled as he pounded the hard steel table. "I want this damn mess fixed and I want it fixed fast—and I mean before Christmas. We're over two years behind schedule and I'm damn tired of excuses. Our funding's in jeopardy and besides—what the hell am I supposed to tell the President? We screwed up because somebody quit. I can't believe this shit."

"General," interrupted Napper as he stood to join Sullivan. "My people're doing the best they can with what they have to work with. We asked for the truth and we got it."

"Sam's right," added Mason. His face took a hard set. "John's got no ax to grind. He said what he believes and we can't ignore his view just because it doesn't make us look good. I agree with him. We have a quality problem with our testing operation here and we need to clean up our act." Looking Craven squarely in the eyes, Mason lowered his voice to a whisper. His tone conveyed a pressing sense of urgency. "John's analysis cuts to the crux of our predicament. The complexity of our orbiting networked armada outstrips our ability to test it."

Craven's blood pressure shot through the roof.

"Clear the room," barked Craven, pointing to the door. "This meeting's adjourned. Sullivan, Hinson, Naper, Slim, Yuri—I want to see you now—in private."

The Crow's Nest emptied quickly—only Craven's inner circle remained. Most people thought Craven a fair man, but felt he was hell to cross.

"John, what does it take to eliminate this problem?" Craven had his hands around this problem and had already made up his mind. Tomorrow they were going to run this stealth missile test over again and this time they were going to do it right! "I want numbers with some stretch."

"The fix is reasonably straightforward, sir," Sullivan replied nervously, his heart racing. "We've gotta change about a half dozen lines of software, but testing the changes takes six months."

"Can't you talk to Centurion? Train him instead of programming this fix?"

"It's not that easy. Software in Centurion, his subordinates, and every DEWSAT needs to be modified."

"What's the worst that may happen if we shortcut the testing?" Craven already knew the answer.

"We could break something somewhere else in the system. I don't recommend it." Sullivan meant what he said.

"Could we fix it now and test it later—say, later next year?" Craven put his proposal in the form of a question.

Mason couldn't sit quiet any longer.

"General, you're making a serious mistake here with your approach to this problem and you know it. Ground-based testing is a must. We've learned that the hard way. It'll only make matters worse if you force this fix through."

Hinson recognized that this was his chance to look good. "I disagree, General Mason. If the fix is simple, the risk of breaking any other working system is low."

"That's true, right, John?" demanded Craven.

"Yes, it's true, but I agree with General Mason. We're asking for trouble if we bypass our quality controls."

"How long would it take to fix the problem?" asked Craven.

"Fix and test?" John sounded distressed.

"Fix only," interrupted Hinson.

"We need to change and rebuild the program, then upload it," replied Sullivan. "Two weeks minimum. Some folks at Livermore are already off on Christmas vacation."

"Cancel vacation, damn it! Bring 'em back. How long?" Craven was relentless.

"Two weeks—and I stand against this quick fix idea."

"You can do better than that," interrupted Hinson. "I think we could turn this around in two days. If you make

the changes and rebuild the program today, we could upload first thing tomorrow."

"That's nonsense," interrupted Napper. "I'm against it!"

"If our program fix doesn't work we'll put the original
program back—nothing to get worked up over." Hinson
smelled a promotion.

"This crash approach to solving our problem is so senseless it's frightening," Mason insisted. He'd never felt
Craven's pit-bull tactics before but found them formidable.
With the bit between his teeth, Craven wouldn't let go until
he got what he wanted.

"*Da*," added Krol, shaking his head. "It's a bad plan!"

Craven looked directly at Colonel Napper. "Sam, can
you and John fix and build this program load in one day?"

"You can replace me any time you choose, General. I'll
do it if it's an order, but I'm against it."

Craven looked at Sullivan. "John, can you rebuild in one
day?"

"I am against it, but we can do it." He spoke softly with a
tone of dismay in his voice.

On the War Room floor sixty feet below, chewing a new
piece of Juicy Fruit gum, Shripod Addams listened to every
word the generals said. The reason for his smile wasn't obvious to the Air Force captain sitting at the console next to
him. Laughing to himself, the captain concluded that
Shripod's gum must be mighty good. The bug that Addams
had attached underneath the conference table was working
much better than expected. He'd stuck the bug in a wad of
gum when he was on call yesterday in the Video Conference Room. Allahu Akbar—*God is greater than our enemies*, Addams thought. Truly, this must be a sign from
Allah.

Back in the Crow's Nest, Mason spoke in a tone edged
with ice. "I think you're putting too much stock on Hinson's input, General. What if there's malice during the
build? Testing's the only way to detect it." Mason stood
and walked around the room—he couldn't sit down any
longer.

"Simply reload the software we're running today," Hinson quipped.

Shripod Addams almost laughed out loud knowing full well that PAM would protect itself *no matter what.* Their Iraqi Trojan horse would never allow the infidels to reload their software. With considerable satisfaction, Shripod Addams imagined what lay ahead for the *Maronites* (enemies of Allah). Allah had used him as an instrument of his divine will.

"These are complicated systems," Mason insisted. "We can't protect ourselves from a malicious act. We may get ourselves into big trouble rushing this test through before Christmas."

Craven jumped to his feet and shouted in Mason's face. "Listen, Slim! You're barking up the wrong tree! The faster we ram this fix through, the better!"

"The ends don't justify the means," Mason replied softly. His eyes turned icy blue as he dug in. "It's not worth the risk. I think . . ."

Craven interrupted Mason mid-sentence, cutting him off cold. "Organized sabotage takes political approval, and political approval takes time. The faster we ram this fix through, the less chance we have for sabotage."

"What you say is true, General, but the gain is not worth the risk." Mason surveyed the faces of the commanders in the room. "Recommendation, gentlemen?"

Colonel Napper, the defense force commander, spoke first. "Take the time to do it right!"

Sullivan agreed.

"Never underestimate your opposition, my General." Krol reflected quietly. "Any worthy adversary would know our situation, would know our every move." Krol paused, struggling to deliver his point using the most direct English language he could articulate. "Were we not comrades, my General—my country would exploit this situation and turn it against you."

Excitement crept into Hinson's voice. "General Mason, we can do it! I wouldn't say it if I didn't believe it." He'd found his ticket to promotion. Hinson interrupted Krol's point before Craven could fully appreciate the consequences.

"I'm not convinced or impressed, Hinson." Mason cringed, imagining the worst-case consequences. Napper, Sullivan, and Krol agreed.

Craven saw a way to get what he wanted and now spoke directly without emotion. "Gentlemen, you need to guard against being overly conservative. Ours is a profession of risk. This is a chance I believe we should take. If we win—we win big. If we lose, we've lost only two days' effort and no one gets hurt. I insist this is a chance we should take."

"Is that an order?" asked Napper.

"A direct order!" Craven barked testily. "Build today—test tomorrow." Craven paused, then decided to make his orders absolutely clear. "We rerun these tests starting tomorrow at ten o'clock sharp! Hinson, have your forces ready to go."

"They're ready, sir. I'd expected this." Hinson's forces weren't ready and hadn't expected any additional testing until after the New Year. Hinson was a liar, but one of the best. During his military career, he'd cultivated and refined this skill to an art. He knew, with some arm-twisting and canceled vacations, he could pull this thing off and come out smelling like a rose.

*To know the answer is not important,* Hinson thought. *It is only important to look like you know the answer.*

*Lunch, 12/08/2014, 1918 Zulu, 12:18 P.M. Local*
EN ROUTE TO SHRIPOD ADDAMS' APARTMENT,
COLORADO SPRINGS, COLORADO

On his way home for lunch, Shripod Addams felt his heart pounding as he pulled into the Loaf 'N' Jug food store. *Watch your blood pressure,* he thought. *Try to relax.* His hands trembled as he struggled to open his car trunk. "Just get the key in the hole!" he muttered to himself. His blood pressure had soared, his head throbbed, and he couldn't control the shaking in his hands.

**The Christmas Rush**

Addams was about to change the course of history and he knew it. *Only the most important thing I've ever done,* he thought.

Although hyperventilating, from a distance Shripod looked normal enough. He felt his *shakes* would improve after sending his message to Mother.

Shripod's hunch had been right and his message was ready to go. He'd prepared an encrypted confirmation message for Mother before he'd gone to work and put it in his trunk. The translator leaned over his trunk and taped his message to his stiff Kodak gray card. He tucked the card under his arm, stuffed the fish-eye lens into his coat pocket, and walked into the food store. Inside, his cold lens clouded over, so he had pizza at the lunch counter. Once the lens cleared, he called his local Baghdad computer network.

Shripod Addams understood the importance of his message. He believed Allah was with him in his holy war against the infidels. *Inshallah* (God willing), the enemies of Allah would burn.

*A Conversation with the Chairman, 12/08/2014, 2030 Zulu,*
   *1:30 P.M. Local*
CHEYENNE MOUNTAIN, COLORADO

Shortly after lunch, Craven and Mason placed their daily call to Washington. Craven cringed as Mason's staff moved several notebooks filled with viewgraphs into the Video Conference Room. He looked at Mason. "Forget the viewgraphs! The chief's expecting this report, but I want it short. I'll do the talking and I don't want debate."

Craven turned on the videophone, then called his boss on the direct line to the White House. The Chairman of the Joint Chiefs of Staff answered immediately.

"Chief," Craven barked. "We need to keep this short."

Assuming the worst, the chairman cut to the heart of the matter. "What's the bad news?" For the past two years, he'd heard only excuses. Why should this report be any different?

"Overall, we're in pretty good shape. We tracked the stealth missiles start to finish, but had a software problem."

"There's always software problems!" the chairman quipped in an acid voice.

"Yeah, but this bug's easy to fix . . . just a software switch."

"Nothing's easy."

Craven took him to mean that no part of the SDI program had been straightforward. Craven looked at Mason and reluctantly admitted the chairman was right. "We're running this test again tomorrow beginning ten A.M. our time."

"You say you tracked the missiles?"

"That's right, Chief. This last test is cleanup."

"You're sure you've got a handle on this problem?"

"We're ninety-nine percent there!"

"You're turning this software change around in record time," observed the chairman.

"Two days," Craven boasted. "We're wrapping this testing up before Christmas."

"How will you get this new software installed?"

"Uplink earth station in Puerto Rico. The changes are minor. Centurion won't be taken off-line . . ."

Mason interrupted Craven in front of the chairman. "We're still working the details, but Centurion *will* come off-line during the upload. We'll place the satellite network under *Hope*'s control while we test the changes." Mason couldn't keep quiet any longer.

Craven's face turned fiery red, but he forced a calm appearance for the camera.

"Sounds like you're working the bugs out and it's just a matter of time. The President will be pleased. Call me tomorrow."

"Will do."

Immediately after the chairman hung up, Mason tied into Craven. "Centurion *must* come off-line tomorrow. Centurion can't control our satellites running untested software!" Mason knew he was right. He knew that Craven knew that he was right! . . . And this was important. "Standard proce-

**The Christmas Rush**

dure requires this safeguard when we load new programs. We won't be ready to run this stealth test for at least one week and you know it."

"Using conventional safeguards, you're right," Craven nodded agreement. "Standard procedure requires us to turn satellite control over to *Hope* . . . but we're not going to do it."

"What do you mean? We don't have a choice!"

"That's where you're wrong!" The rise in tension was clearly visible on Craven's face. His voice rasped at Mason. "I had a choice and I made it. The change is simple, so we'll bypass the safeguards!"

"But . . ."

Craven interrupted. "The responsibility is mine alone."

When Mason spoke, his words came slowly, each one edged with urgency. "The gain is not worth the risk."

The ominous silence which followed drew out and became a test of wills.

Eventually, Craven spoke. "We have a fallback position if there's any problem. Worst-case, we'll simply reload the programs we're running now." Craven acted relaxed, but it was only an act and Mason knew it.

"With all due respect, General, I cannot support your decision." Mason's reply was polite, but his tone was now edged with ice.

"Just do it!" Craven groused. "You don't have to respect me."

Mason cringed, then emotionally disconnected. *Tomorrow is another day,* he thought. His eyes iced over, turning steely blue. Mason knew he would fight this battle again, but as for today, Craven had the bit between his teeth.

"Listen, Slim. You had your say . . . you said it twice and I heard you dammit! Now get on with it!"

Below the Crow's Nest on the War Room floor, quietly listening to their conversation, Shripod Addams endorsed General Craven's decision to plow ahead. He finished his coffee . . . his hands now steady.

**The Christmas Rush**

*Yearning, 12/08/2014, 2032 Zulu*
SPACE STATION *FREEDOM*

Weightless, *Freedom* crew commander Major Jay Fayhee
advanced hand over hand across the overhead ladder to
Centurion's corner. Once seated alongside Centurion and
Captain Depack McKee, he removed an old faded letter
from his pants leg pocket, one of the last letters he'd received from Linda before their marriage went wrong.
Quietly facing Centurion's talking head, Jay read the letter one last time, hoping to work up the courage to call
her. Caressing the tattered yellowed paper, his hands
trembled slightly. Unthinkingly and quite out of habit, he
loaded their old high school yearbook off CD ROM. Before he'd realized what he was doing, he found himself
staring at Linda's picture on screen, thinking nostalgi-
cally about the woman he'd loved and lost such a long
time ago.

How long had it been since he'd talked to Linda? Over
five years now. It seemed like yesterday, a thousand years
ago. He wondered how she'd sound. Would her voice feel
as warm as he remembered? Would her tone perk up when
she recognized his voice? Probably not. Would she even
take his call? How would she respond? More than anything
else, Jay wanted desperately to talk to Linda, really open up
and talk to her the way they used to talk. He'd always been
able to tell her anything. Interested or not, she'd acted interested. And she'd been so unbelievably trusting—gullible to
a fault. She'd believe anything he told her or—Jay cor-
rected himself—there was a time when she'd believe anything he'd tell her. No doubt, those happy, gullible times
were ancient history now.

Moving to the observation window, facing all heaven
and earth, Jay gazed in wonder at the vastness of the uni-
verse. The immenseness was awe inspiring, yet he felt so
small, so . . . lonely. Raising his eyes toward the heavens,
Jay prayed a short prayer, then rallied his strength in hopes
of fulfilling his dream, a dream his heart wished for, a
dream his soul prayed for, but a dream he feared could

never come true. From the depths of his soul, Jay hoped against all hope that Linda would welcome the sound of his voice.

*Well,* Jay thought to himself, *faint heart never won this lady, and she darn sure won't call me—so get on with it.*

Returning again to Centurion's corner, still contemplating Linda's picture on screen, he looked away to meet Centurion's camera eye.

About that time, Captain Depack McKee spoke from his control console near Centurion. "Commander, you appear distracted, lost in your thoughts."

"I suppose I am," he responded quietly, staring at Linda's picture. "I'm a little uncomfortable expressing this out loud—in words, I mean—but off the record, my heart's online again and I'm afraid it's going to get broken. It probably sounds ridiculous, but that's how I feel."

"Well, I'm no expert on relationships, Jay, but rejection is a risk of living. If you want to talk to her, put your heart on the line, open up, and this time try like hell to think about her feelings. If you don't, you'll go to your grave regretting it. You screwed up big time—it's written all over your face, but you've got the rest of your life to make it up to her, so give it your best shot. I mean it, Commander. Take the initiative."

"The way you put it, it sounds almost possible, even likely." After a few moments' thought, Jay shook his head in disbelief. "Allowing my marriage to fail was the biggest mistake I ever made in my life. I made us both miserable, but honestly, all those women . . . I don't know what came over me."

"Listen, Jay, you screwed up, now get over it. Life goes on. People make mistakes, so quit kicking yourself. Take a chance and call the woman. What's the worst that could happen? She's married again or hangs up. Best-case, she's glad to hear your voice. Maybe she wants you to call; maybe she wants to talk; maybe she's been thinking about you."

Jay looked once again into Centurion's camera eye. After taking a deep breath, he spoke quietly. "Centurion, establish a secure voice link to Space Station *Hope*. I need to speak with Major Linda Scott. And it's important."

*A Voice from the Past, 12/08/2014, 2037 Zulu*
ALTITUDE: 22,300 MILES IN GEOSTATIONARY ORBIT,
SDI SPACE STATION FORTRESS *HOPE*

*Hope* crew commander Pasha Yakovlev manned his watch station facing Guardian, a work space which reflected a homey personality all its own. Interestingly, most of the gadgets adorning Pasha's high-tech office area were covered up, hidden behind pictures of his family. Scott, Mac, and Gonzo found Pasha's work space delightful, bringing a feeling of humanity to the oversized tin can designated Space Station *Hope*. Of all Pasha's personal items he brought onboard, the most interesting was a poster-sized montage showing pictures of his wife and three small children. Once *Hell Fire*'s repairs were complete and the time was right, Scott planned to get more details from Pasha about these pictures. But for now, *Hell Fire*'s communication antennas required her attention. Outside, with an array of floodlights and camera in hand, Gonzo and Mac were surveying the damage, covering every square inch of *Hell Fire*'s skin.

"Commander," Guardian spoke plainly through the intercom speaker by *Hope* crew commander Pasha Yakovlev. "Centurion has established a secure comm link from SS *Freedom*. Commander Major Jay Fayhee requests to speak with Major Linda Scott."

"Video link?"

"Secure voice traffic only, sir."

Pasha threw a series of switches providing link redundancy.

"Guardian, patch him through to her headset. She's suited up, about ready to start prebreathing. He caught her just in time."

Listening to the conversation between Guardian and Pasha, Jay found himself holding his breath. There was a popping sound over the voice link followed by a click, then Guardian spoke again.

"Major Scott, we have established a secure voice link between Space Stations *Freedom* and *Hope* at the request of Commander Jay Fayhee. He asks to speak with you. Should I complete the connection or take voice mail?"

"Guardian, hold one minute." Caught off guard, Scott surveyed the control room for someplace she could talk, someplace private. There was none. Then she remembered their sleeping quarters nestled among the missile tubes near the airlock on· *Hope*'s red face. Wearing her extravehicular activity (EVA) suit, Scott found maneuvering about the station cumbersome. Bulkier than her regular pressurized suit, even the simplest task became a clumsy chore. Once inside her tiny dorm room and free of distractions, she instructed Guardian to connect Jay's call.

"Once you hear the warbling tone," Guardian said, "the voice circuit is complete."

A warbling tone was followed by protracted silence, then Jay spoke first. There was the distinct tone of apprehension in his voice. "Linda, this is Jay, Jay Fayhee . . ."

A pause.

"Jay, you don't sound exactly like I remember."

"Nervous, I guess . . . or maybe it's my accent. I sound more like Centurion than I used to. You stay in one place long enough, you pick it up after a while. At least, I'm told I don't talk like a Californian anymore . . . whatever that means."

"Well, I'm glad you called." Jay's spirit took flight. "You know I've always loved listening to the sound of your voice. Even over this link, you sound like James Earl Jones to me." A short pause. "But, why'd you call? . . . You talk, I'll listen."

*I could never tell her what this call's really about,* Jay thought at first, but then somehow, somewhere, he found the courage to speak from his heart, without word games, hints, undertones, or innuendo. "We nearly lost you—and I was worried sick about you. Are you alright?"

"It was tight, but we were lucky. *Hell Fire*'s cooling system pulled us through. Mac and Gonzo are fine. I'm OK, but *Hell Fire . . . Hell Fire*'s going to need some work."

"Thank God you're alright," Jay said softly, without pretense. After a few moments, he continued. "I understood your comm antennas took the heat."

"They took the worst of it. Repairs could take as long as a week." Scott paused. "If all goes as planned, we'll head your way once *Hell Fire*'s given a clean bill of health."

"Excellent," Jay said, feeling so excited his heart might burst. "So please, tell me how you're doing."

"I've got my work, and I've got good friends. The best . . . but no one special, not anymore. I mean I'm not married or anything." Linda paused, debating whether or not to encourage Jay. Following her heart, she took the risk. "You know, I still carry that four-leaf clover you gave me for luck. I'm wearing it now. And you? How are you doing?"

"Turns out, this job's not all it's cracked up to be, but maybe that comes as no big surprise to anybody but me." *She remembered that four-leaf clover,* Jay thought. *Now open up, bring down the walls.* "I'm learning to live without you now, but I miss you . . . I miss you every day. You may not believe this, but I have every letter you ever wrote me, every picture we ever took, even our old high school yearbook up here with me on CD. They even let me bring a few of your original handwritten letters onboard."

Linda was genuinely surprised by this revelation, and on hearing these words, her heart sang.

After a brief reflection, Jay continued. "You know a funny thing about this place?"

"I don't have any idea what you're thinking," Linda said quietly. *But right now, I dearly wish I could read your mind and know your heart.*

"Funny thing," Jay began again. "When it's quiet, I find myself wondering about you, what you're doing, and wondering if you ever think of me?"

"Me too," Scott responded softly, without hesitation. "I was wondering about you on the Edwards runway before

we took off. Not a day passes that I don't think about you."
Instinctively, Scott knew she was letting her guard down
prematurely. Her head understood this, understood it full
well, but her heart told her to fly. Somehow, she had to
touch this man's heart.

Feeling more and more at ease, Jay asked, "Do you remember much about our last year of marriage?"

"I've forgiven and tried to forget the painful parts. A big
part of life is like that, about forgiveness I mean. I can't
carry anger, it eats me up inside. Mainly I remember the
good parts, our happy times."

"Do you remember that orange-colored cake we made?
The one that looked like a pumpkin?"

"With a plastic worm hanging out its nose. A culinary
delight I can never forget."

"How about the Valentine Day dance? I've got our picture up here with me. You couldn't have been over sixteen
then. You were lovely . . . and so funny. Most of all, I remember you hated your knees. I thought they were beautiful, and you insisted they were fat. Who ever heard of
anyone hating their knees? Craziest thing I ever heard of
anyway, but you were serious. Fat knees."

"We really had big problems then, didn't we?"

"Life seemed complicated then," Jay said seriously.
"And growing up was hard."

"Growing up is hard for every generation," Linda observed with just a hint of sadness. "Even so, it was a good
life, and the best way I know of to grow up."

"In each other's arms?"

"It meant everything to me. Do you remember our first
kiss?" Linda asked, knowing his answer in advance.

"You kidding? Ninth grade Christmas dance, your house,
dark basement, and metal braces. It was a nerve shattering
experience for me. Who could forget the feeling of flesh
pitted against your cold hard steel. I never had a chance really, when you think about it. As I recall, I got the distinct
impression that you were well ahead of me in this area of
development."

**The Christmas Rush**

"But in all fairness and to your credit, you were a quick study."

"I used to love the way you'd stick your lower lip out when you were pouting."

"A well-established, effective ploy." Linda smiled. "Came right out of *Seventeen* magazine, you know. But I couldn't sing and still can't dance."

"But you've got gumption—an intangible thing, but it sets you apart. You did what you set out to do and not many people can make that claim. You've always known what you wanted, believed in yourself, and wouldn't take no for an answer."

"I don't know . . ." Linda said, holding back the tears. "The costs, I mean. I set out to marry the man I loved, raise a family, and fly. Now—I fly." Her tone, one of loss. "I love flying, I've got to do it, but it doesn't hold me close or keep me warm at night. Sometimes it seems the more I know, the less I understand. Everything changes so quickly I forget what's important. Maybe I'm not as sure as I used to be, or maybe, like everyone else, life's just kicked me around a little."

"I know what you mean," Jay said, surprised that the girl he loved, the girl he'd admired all his life, would question herself. "Life's good, life's hard, but it's not fair." Jay loved talking to Linda and shifted the topic ever so slightly, allowing them to focus on their successes. Remembering happier times, he began, "By the way, I visited our old high school my last trip home. Saw the places we used to go, stood in the very spot we used to meet between classes, even looked inside your old locker."

"Has it changed much? What was it like?"

"The place was practically empty during summer school, so it seemed pretty lonely, pretty deserted. What I remember most is how empty the place seemed without you. Without you there, with only memories, the place seemed lifeless. When I lost you, I lost me, if that makes any sense. I don't know what I was looking for really, what I was hoping to find. Memories of the heart, I guess. Whatever it was, I didn't find it. Maybe the school reminded me of what we had, how happy we were, how things might have been." After a few moments of careful consideration, Jay concluded, "Growing up was hard. Sometimes, looking back, I really don't see how we got through it all and survived."

"When you cut to the chase," Linda responded in a soft, compassionate tone, "I don't think the heart of the problem is all that complicated to understand really. It's about sex and morality . . . doing the right thing, I mean. The problem may be clearly stated, but the solution's the hard part. No one's found a solution to make growing up any easier. At eighteen, you needed sex, and you needed it often. It was like a chemical imbalance, inhibiting clear thought, and you didn't have an outlet. That didn't make you fundamentally bad or much different than any other eighteen-year-old male, but it made growing up difficult."

"You understand me better than I understand myself. You always have." Jay sighed, his thoughts scattered, shifting now to Linda's father. He'd always admired the man, Linda's father extraordinaire and SR-71 *sled driver*. He'd always been kind to Jay, and it meant all the more because at times Jay had known he didn't deserve it. "You know, I miss your father. I still feel badly about not attending his funeral. You needed me, but I was stuck up here, stuck here on my first tour with no way back."

"I miss him more than I'd ever imagined and I feel cheated now that he's gone. There were so many things I'd wanted to tell him, so many things I'd wanted us to do."

"He died knowing the most important things, Linda, your heart and your spirit." Jay smiled, recalling some advice Linda's father had given him, then continued. "You know the only instructions he ever gave me before we were married?"

"No, you never told me Dad's advice," Linda replied, drawing a blank on Jay's question, "but you two were a lot alike. You know he liked you from the start."

"I'm ashamed to say it now, but the only request he ever made of me was that I never, ever hurt you."

Linda's eyes teared as she imagined her father talking

to Jay on behalf of her happiness. "I'm afraid we both made some bad calls, Jay. Somewhere along the way, we both lost sight of what was really important in life. Dad would be disappointed in us now, but he'd never give up on us." Following a long silence, Linda asked, "Are you happy? Is this what you want?" *I dearly wish I could read your mind.*

"No, Linda. Not really."

"Want to talk about it?" *Dear God, I'd love to talk to him again.*

"Linda, the thing I want most in my life . . . you might think this is ridiculous, but the thing I want more than anything else in the world is to talk to you."

Linda's heart took flight.

"Listen, Linda, I made some terrible mistakes when we were together. I behaved badly. God knows I did and only God knows how sorry I am. I've spent the last five years regretting it and if there was something I could do, something I could say that would make it right again, I would. It's almost as if we had to get this divorce for me to see clearly what I'd lost. I dream of holding you again, but I'm afraid this dream will never come true. Not now . . ."

"Sometimes dreams really do come true, Jay. My dreams are much like yours. We both made some big mistakes and our divorce devastated me. But you're a part of me, a part of me that won't let go. Let's work through the forgiveness part first, put the pain behind us, then get on with the healing. I think we can make it work. I need you more than you know."

*I feel like a kid again in love for the first time,* Jay thought, his heart pounding. *I'll make you happier than you ever imagined in your wildest dreams!*

Linda smiled at her next question. "You're going to call me again?"

"Nothing in heaven or on earth could keep me from calling you. If you'll let me, I want to show you I've changed. My dream is to be in your life again forever—and faithfully."

**The Christmas Rush**

"Dreams really do come true, Jay. They must. Why do we live if not to dream?" Teary-eyed, Linda paused only a moment, then whispered, "I love you."

"I love you."

*Declaring a Dividend, 12/08/2014, 2040 Zulu, 11:40 P.M. Local*
IRAQI INTELLIGENCE SERVICE HEADQUARTERS,
UNDERGROUND BUNKER,
BAGHDAD, IRAQ

The sergeant on duty in the crypto room brought in extra help tonight. Mother expected he may get a message, and the sergeant didn't want any computer screwups fouling up the works. When the incoming message alarm bell rang, everyone anxiously watched the crypto board thinking this could be the one. It was. For the second night in a row, the crypto board flashed:

```
Incoming Message—Priority:
URGENT—FOR MOTHER'S EYES ONLY.
```

With hard copy in hand, the sergeant picked up the phone and called Mother. He answered before the first ring completed.

"Sergeant—message?" Mother's voice was unrevealing of emotion.

"Message reads as follows: To: mother, From: addams, Subject: Lawrence gets a horse."

"That is good," Mother said quietly. "Send my reply to Livermore. It must get through."

"Understand."

"Call me when he reads it."

"Anything else?"

"No, now it's my turn. *Allahu Akbar!*"

*Hiding the Trojan Horse, 12/08/2014, 2147 Zulu, 1:47 P.M.*
  *Local*
GATE 2 SECURITY GUARD SHACK,
LAWRENCE LIVERMORE NATIONAL LABORATORY,
LIVERMORE, CALIFORNIA

Lucky sat in front of his workstation, studying the screen. *Mother was right,* he thought. Something most extraordinary had happened. Christmas vacations canceled—scientists and engineers called back from vacation (which explained why they were in such a foul mood today). Three Livermore computers had been running wide open all morning. SDIO programmers for the DEWSAT, Centurion, and his subordinates were involved in a marathon twenty-four-hour program build.

Roughly twenty-four hours after Lucky received his first message from Mother, his terminal message bell rang again.

```
You have electronic mail.
```

He read his e-mail summary—another message from Mother. Lucky decrypted the message, guessed what it would say—and was right—again.

```
FROM: mother
TO: mal
SUBJECT: Lawrence gets a horse.
Come home for Christmas.
End Of Message
```

Lucky deleted Mother's message and checked to make sure that no one was looking over his shoulder. He turned the brightness down low on his terminal, then cleared his screen. Once sure the room was empty, he didn't take time to think. He reacted mechanically, like a robot. His practice paid off.

Lucky struck methodically. First, he transferred PAM to the computer used by the Centurion project. Next, he

**The Christmas Rush**

logged on the Centurion project computer as a *super-user* and performed his programming magic. Super-user status made Lucky all-powerful on the Centurion project computer, but he had to move fast or risk detection. He moved directly to the program area on the computer where the new builds were taking place, then began looking for a pattern. The pattern was obvious.

Lucky smiled. The rest would be easy!

Centurion's programmers were having a field day—taking advantage of their opportunity to bypass quality control. They threw in hundreds of bug fixes for old problems as well as the fix for their DEWSAT problem. Lucky thought it should be easy to hide PAM.

He was right.

Lucky quickly decrypted PAM and appended her to another program. PAM entered as a Trojan horse. She looked like any other program change—something she was not.

With his bad seed planted, Lucky signed off, then watched the progress of Centurion's program build.

No problem. Everything worked.

*Perfect!* he thought. *Just like in the movies!*

With his bad seed planted, Lucky removed PAM from his computer workstation, then walked to security headquarters for a talk with his boss.

As he strolled across the Livermore grounds, Lucky's heart soared and his grin stretched ear to ear. Above all else, Merchant A. Lucky was a mercenary. He could retire on the money he'd make.

He walked into his boss's office. "I've got some good news and some bad news."

"I've had about all the bad news I need today, Lucky, how 'bout the good news first."

"I'm going home for Christmas and I'm so excited I'm about to bust!"

"That's great. Where's home?"

"The Florida panhandle and I can't wait!"

"How about the bad news?"

"Mother's not doing so well, so I've taken a job near her to help out."

**The Christmas Rush**

"Sorry to hear it . . . so what's your plan?"

"New job starts January first—my last day here'll be next Monday, one week from today."

"I wish you the best of luck. If you need any references along the way, let me know. You're a mighty talented character."

"Thank you, sir." Lucky smiled, shook his boss's hand, and walked back to his office in Guard Shack 2.

Lucky didn't understand the consequences of what he'd done—he didn't need to. Mother's bonus and relocation plans were excellent.

# PART 4

# THE PROBLEM
# WITHOUT
# SOLUTION

DAY 3—
DECEMBER 9, 2014

# 12

Arecibo, the Allies' largest satellite earth station and radio telescope, silently transmitted Livermore's new programs to Centurion through a thirty-five-meter dish antenna pointing directly toward *Freedom.*

From the air, Arecibo's largest antenna looked like an enormous bowl spanning the valley between surrounding mountain peaks. Lining the bowl's perimeter, blasted, turnbuckled, and bolted into the ledge stood forty plus satellite dishes, fuel tanks, plus a dozen single-story buildings.

Arecibo's only reason to exist was communications, but like most earth stations, once operational the communication equipment required very few technical support people. Just plug it in and let it run.

Inside the security building, a short, stocky security sergeant watched his status board, a wall lined with TV screens and red lights.

All was quiet.

*Just once I'd like something to report,* he thought.

The sergeant had been stationed at Arecibo nearly two years and knew nothing ever happened here . . . most boring place in the world. This wasn't what he'd signed up for, but this was the Army. Arecibo shoulda been couch potato heaven—more than six hundred television channels to choose from. But now he was sick of TV, he hated TV.

The most excitement in the sergeant's day were the radio checks. Once in a while, *that señorita* would answer. The sound . . . the tone of that woman's voice set the blood in his veins on fire.

The sergeant checked his watch. Five minutes late for his radio check. Nothing to report . . . nothing ever to report. Daydreaming, he watched the office window buffet and listened to the fifty-knot wind howling outside. Suddenly, the window popped. Startled back into the real world, the sergeant snapped upright, blinked his eyes clear, then called headquarters.

"You're late," a harsh male voice announced over the radio speaker.

"So sue me!" groused the sergeant. "Nothing to report, nothing at all."

*Uploading the Trojan Horse, 12/09/2014, 1510 Zulu, 8:10 A.M. Local*
CHEYENNE MOUNTAIN, COLORADO

As Arecibo transmitted Livermore's new programs to *Freedom*, Colonel Napper sat behind his console impatiently monitoring the progress of the upload. Once the transmission completed, a message on Napper's monitor read:

```
ARECIBO STATION STATUS SUMMARY:
Program Upload Transmission Complete —
             Zero Errors
```

Colonel Napper shifted his gaze to the video conference monitor linked to the Crow's Nest. *Here we go again,* he thought when he saw Mason, Hinson, and Craven in another heated argument. Craven wouldn't bend and Hinson supported him, of course. Napper decided to interrupt them anyway. "Generals, can I have your attention?"

No response—their argument continued.

Drumming his fingers on his control console, Napper

gathered his courage. "Beg pardon, Generals. Generals, I need your attention!"

Either they didn't hear him or they didn't want to hear him.

He listened in on their argument. Craven insisted on ramming this change through immediately, bypassing established testing and safeguard procedures. Mason stood against it. Net result—no progress.

From his control console, Napper increased the volume of his voice inside the Crow's Nest. They'd hear him now! "Generals, listen up—uh—with all due respect." His voice boomed over the speakers.

Napper cringed when he heard his voice reverberate around the auditorium-sized War Room. He was over one hundred feet from the glass-walled Crow's Nest towering overhead. He saw Craven and his staff covering their ears as the room hushed. Everyone in the Crow's Nest stared silently at Napper on video.

Mason spoke first. "Sam—we're listening, but could ya cut it down a little?"

Napper breathed a sigh of relief and turned the volume down. "Centurion's upload's complete—we're ready to run."

"*Hope*'s status?" asked Craven.

"Pasha's bridged on, sir. He'll hear everything we say. Scott, Gonzo, and Mac are outside pulling maintenance—antenna repair. About an hour till they button it up."

"Good." Craven smiled. "Comrade General, anything else?" He looked across the room at Russian General Yuri Krol.

"*Hope* is our hot spare—on standby if something goes wrong." Biting his pipe tightly, the corners of Krol's mouth turned down. "Centurion will maintain armada control while Guardian records test results. Exactly as you ordered, my General." The words sounded as if they'd stuck in his throat. Clearly, Krol was not a happy soldier.

Craven looked at Fayhee on screen. "What's *Freedom*'s status?"

"Waiting your orders, General."

**The Problem Without Solution**

"Jay—you and Depack ready to reload Centurion?"

"We're as ready as we're gonna be. Centurion's never run untested code before."

"If there's a showstopper with this load," interrupted Hinson, "reload the program Centurion's running now."

"Damn it, Hinson," snapped Jay. "We're not up here to make your ass look good. I sure as hell can handle this without your bullshit."

Depressing his conference call mute button, Hinson spoke to Craven. "The team in the tin can's running on a short fuse."

Craven agreed. He studied the face of each commander for a few moments, then began. "This subject's not open for further discussion. Centurion'll run the new Livermore load this morning as planned."

"Yessir," replied Fayhee. "We'll have Centurion reloaded in half an hour—by 1600 Zulu."

"Good," said Craven, checking his watch. "Hinson, bring your attack forces on-line as scheduled."

"Yessir, General!" exclaimed Hinson, feeling exonerated. "We're ready! The *Stennis* is in position. *Dorito* and XR-30 crews're standing by at Edwards."

"Good," Craven said quietly. "I don't want excuses—I want results. Before this day is through I want this stealth cruise missile threat behind us."

*The Orbiting DEWSAT Armada, 12/09/2014, 1550 Zulu*
ALTITUDE: 115 MILES IN CIRCULAR POLAR ORBIT,
ONBOARD A DEWSAT

Ready to strike in a fraction of a second, orbiting 115 miles above the earth along lines of longitude, seventy-two DEWSATs methodically scanned the entire earth's surface searching for fiery missile plumes.

The orbiting DEWSAT armada continuously scanned the globe for infrared, optical, and radio frequencies, ready to strike when their decision circuits voted in favor of *the kill*. Within limits, DEWSAT telescopes and radar could detect anything that could fly. Likewise, anything it could detect, its laser could destroy.

At 1550 Zulu, the DEWSAT armada received its heartbeat (keep alive) signal, an encrypted radio signal from Centurion which read:

```
set laser power output = max
```

Each DEWSAT tested itself: its electrical systems, optics, radar, infrared telescope, and laser. After passing every test, each DEWSAT acknowledged the message with an encrypted radio transmission to Centurion which read:

```
DEWSAT ack: laser power output = max
```

Fully operational, the orbiting DEWSAT armada was lethal, armed, and dangerous.

*Waiting for Safe Laser Clearance, 12/09/2014, 1555 Zulu, 7:55 A.M. Local*
COCKPIT OF *HAILEY'S COMET*,
SOUTH FACING RUNWAY,
EDWARDS AFB, CALIFORNIA

Slightly reclining, with fist clenched tight, Major Art Hailey stared motionless into the blue sky above Edwards' vast south facing desert runway. Surrounded by explosive fuel, engulfed by engine noise, sitting on top of the fastest air and space lane ever created, Hailey wasn't impressed. He felt angry, but didn't know who to hit. His leave canceled without explanation in exchange for a dicey game of laser tag.

Shaking his head in disbelief, Hailey carefully read Scott's test flight plan and *Hell Fire*'s damage report for the third time. His flight plan was identical to Scott's and she'd nearly lost *Hell Fire*. "Loosen up or you could be dead soon," he thought out loud. *Five minutes and this bird'll be off the ground.*

**The Problem Without Solution**

*Isolation, 12/09/2014, 1556 Zulu*
SPACE STATION *FREEDOM*

"Depack, you ready to go?" asked Colonel Naper. It was unusual for Headquarters to monitor *Freedom* operations, however, considering the circumstances, it came as no surprise. Depack's fingers moved over Centurion's keyboard faster than Napper's eyes could follow.

"Yep—uh—sir. If there's a problem, we can back outta trouble faster than we got into it." Since Centurion provided the brain, heart, and soul of the SDIO satellite network, any problem with Centurion's new program would mean more delay.

"We'll take it from here, Colonel," announced Fayhee. "Load on my mark." Fayhee'd hoped for the best, but planned for the worst. "Three, two, one, mark."

Depack and Fayhee simultaneously rotated large red turnkeys. Centurion never took his eyes off Fayhee as the new program loaded at the speed of light. Fifteen seconds later, the bad seed took root.

"So that's all there is to it," quipped Centurion.

"Now we test," said Depack.

"I knew that." Centurion displayed a page filled with test instructions.

"Go for it, Depack. Ring him out."

Depack nodded agreement. "Centurion—make ready to alter DEWSAT behavior."

"Very well." Centurion paused for an eternity in computer time, then responded. "Depack."

Seconds passed without an additional comment from Centurion. It was unusual for Centurion to pause so long.

Depack felt anxious.

Centurion's talking head began moving with a jerky, blocked-tile sort of slow motion. Finally, he muttered, "DEWSAT behavior records have been retrieved and await modification." His voice dropping in tone, his speech slowed.

A cold chill crawled up Depack's spine. He feared the worst, but quickly purged his mind of panic. Depack moved posthaste around the control room to Jay's console, turning his back on Centurion's camera eye.

"Jay, come here—I need you."

Startled by Depack's ghost-white complexion, one glance told Jay all he needed to know without an additional exchange of words.

Returning to Depack's console, Jay gazed at a slow-motion picture of Centurion on screen. Depack spoke in an emotionless voice, reading from his test script.

"Turn down the power and disable hot TDM operations on every DEWSAT laser over the test zone. Track and tag targets for the next four hours—don't destroy them."

"Depack," Centurion replied, followed by a protracted silence.

Normally, Centurion's silence would have made Fayhee a happy man. Silence meant he was occupied with something, but for now they didn't know what.

"Take a look," Jay said, pointing toward Centurion's globe. "Something's wrong. Everything's moving in slow motion." The earth's hologram now moved with a pulsating, jerking motion . . . like watching a VCR one frame at a time.

"Centurion's sick," Depack said grimly. "This load's got a clinker in it—some sort of slow-motion bug."

As Jay and Depack talked, PAM created her list of threats, including anyone or anything who could reload Centurion or damage the satellite armada.

Next, PAM created her defense resource list, including every satellite in the orbiting armada.

Finally, PAM modified the program she would run when threatened—a script file listing where to run, where to hide, and what to do when cornered.

"Let's move fast before things get worse!" ordered Jay. Strain crept into his voice. Returning to his console, he planned to reload Centurion's original program. "Reload on my mark."

\* \* \*

**The Problem Without Solution**

Programmed to survive, PAM made a copy of herself then moved into each of Centurion's subordinate computers at near light speed.

The bad seed took root then spread like a cancer throughout *Freedom*'s central nervous system.


Optical glass communication pipes connecting Centurion to his three subordinate computers glowed brightly with a frenzy of computer chatter.

"I don't know why, but I don't like it!" exclaimed Depack, rubbing his hand over the glowing communication links. Normally, Depack would have intuitively known *why* by watching the glowing comm links. Onboard *Freedom*, the *why* was important because Centurion ran their life-support systems. Before running this new load, Depack would have known which programs were talking, what they were talking about, and why—but these patterns of light had changed. He couldn't read them, they looked different. "We're losing control."

"Three, two, one, mark." Depack and Jay rotated the large red turnkey, loading Centurion again.

"We have a problem!" Centurion announced immediately. "Subordinate computers in alarm, off-line, out of service. Cause of failure: degraded performance. Response time exceeding preset alarm limits."

Jay and Depack looked perplexed. Jay bolted quickly to Depack, turning his back on Centurion's monitor. "Whataya make of it?"

"Centurion's OK." Depack thought for a moment, then asked Centurion a few questions using his keyboard. "Centurion's back to normal, but the slave computers are running slow . . . *real slow*! This sounds crazy, but I'd guess they caught something from Centurion."

"That's all we need!" Jay rolled his eyes. "So Centurion's slow bug's contagious? Recommendations?"

"Reload 'em all."

Centurion's communication pipes glowed again with a frenzy of computer communication as PAM moved back into Centurion.

**The Problem Without Solution**

Jay rushed to his console and red turnkey, but it was already too late.

Centurion now had two separate and distinct personalities: one visible, another hidden. Centurion's visible personality was unchanged, but his hidden dark side was dominated by PAM.

Hidden and operating independently, Centurion's dark side issued her first operational orders. An encrypted radio signal which read:

```
Tues Dec 09 16:10:58 Z 2014
To: Any DEWSAT
put Arecibo Earth Station on kill stack
put Roaring Creek Earth Station on kill
  STACK
```

In his early stage of neurosis, Centurion didn't know anything about his dark side. PAM was split off from his consciousness so they never talked to each other.

Although PAM shared Centurion's electronic brain, sensors, and satellites, she was totally unaware he existed. Two distinct personality programs inhabiting the same brain, each unaware of the other—an electronic form of viral-induced hysterical dissociation neurosis.

In time, irreconcilable memory conflicts would result because Centurion and his dark side shared an optical brain which could never forget. Eventually PAM, the *controller/taker* personality, must emerge dominant to survive.

"We have a problem," Centurion observed in a detached tone of voice. "Please stand by."

Jay and Depack agreed, then waited what seemed an eternity—fifteen seconds in real time.

And then it happened.

Video from Cheyenne Mountain began breaking into tiles as the signal faded. Snow blanketed the picture of Colonel Napper, and the audio began to crackle.

"We're losing Arecibo," announced Centurion. "Com-

munication link failing due to severe signal fade. Wait. The
signal is breaking up, garbled."

Inside *Freedom*, the video screen from Cheyenne Mountain went black.

Thirty seconds after her first order, hidden from Centurion and *Freedom*'s crew, PAM transmitted two additional
orders to her armada in less than one one-hundredth of a
second.

```
Tues Dec 09 16:11:28 Z 2014
To: Any DEWSAT
put all known ASATS on kill stack
put all known mines on kill stack
```

Almost immediately afterwards, she issued orders to
Guardian, Centurion's computer counterpart onboard Space
Station *Hope*.

```
Tues Dec 09 16:11:32 Z 2014
To: Guardian
let face = red, yellow, black, and white
   then do until done
      set face airlock safety = off
      set face airlock inner door = open
      set face airlock outer door = open
   done
```

Immediately, bright red alarm lights flashed on every
console inside Cheyenne Mountain, *Freedom*, and *Hope*.
The alarm board inside Cheyenne Mountain covered an entire wall and lit up like a Christmas tree. Computer systems
inside Cheyenne Mountain designed to automatically analyze alarms began to fail due to overload. After the alarm
systems failed, operations on the War Room floor shifted to
a hectic frenzy.

The great blue ball inside the War Room froze motionless.

**The Problem Without Solution**

In less than thirty-four seconds, Cheyenne Mountain's lifeline to *Freedom* had gone belly-up, and more.

Inside *Freedom*, a blinking message on Centurion's screen read:

```
WARNING: Critical Alarm
FAILURE: Arecibo LOS (Loss Of Signal)
  condition exists.
CAUSE: Unknown—To Be Determined
```

Depack slammed his hand down on the alarm cutoff switch and the flashing red lights went dark.

"So what's causing the problem?" asked Depack at the threshold of panic. He thought it strange that they should experience a major communications failure coincident with running this new program.

Centurion paused as if he were carefully crafting each word. "It is impossible for me to isolate this problem without your help."

Jay spoke next. The tension in his voice broke through. "Clarify!"

The more anxious Jay and Depack became, the cooler Centurion seemed to respond. This was normal and they knew it. When Centurion sensed tension in the crew's voices, he'd been programmed to back off and respond with an overstated calm tone in his voice.

"Jay, I understand you and Depack are upset over the testing delays, but I'm confident we can restore ground communication within the hour. We have any spare parts we could need. It should be a routine repair procedure for either you or an Arecibo technician. As I said, I cannot isolate this problem without your help, but that is no cause for concern. Arecibo could have a problem with their transmitter or the problem could be with our receiver."

"Recommendations?" asked Fayhee, searching for alternatives.

"A process of elimination." Centurion paused much longer than usual.

**The Problem Without Solution**

"Clarify!" Jay barked angrily. "Testing's on hold till we're back on the air."

"First, isolate the failure. Make sure the problem is on our end, then eliminate the obvious."

"Doing something beats doing nothing," Jay quipped. "Continue."

"We have two replacement approaches to consider— slow and sure or shotgun." Jay took Centurion to mean that they could replace individual receiver subsystems one at a time or swap out the entire receiver system.

"Hell, let's replace them all," Jay concluded. "Shotgun approach should be faster."

"Ready, shoot, aim," Depack observed.

Jay cringed. He knew shotgun repair wasn't efficient, but they were in a hurry. Stealth missile testing was on hold until they got back on the air. *Hailey's Comet*, Cowboy's *Dorito*, the *Stennis*—all depended on Fayhee to deliver. He had to do something fast.

"We need ground communications ASAP!" Jay exclaimed. "Don't isolate the problem, just replace the receivers."

"When it rains, it pours! Whataya want me to do?" Depack asked.

"Just swap those radios." Jay pointed to an eleven-foot-tall frame filled with rack mounted radio receivers and test equipment. "Shouldn't take more than twenty minutes. I'll swap the antenna amps. Whatever you do, keep those radar transmitters off."

There was real danger here from the transmitter's power output and the open vacuum of space. *Freedom's* antenna amplifiers were located in her external plumbing layer. Nicknamed *the oven*, the plumbing layer was an enormous maze of waveguide sandwiched between her central core and outer skin. Waveguides focused microwave energy from her radar transmitter onto each of her four triangular faces, each face an antenna measuring 660 feet on a side covered with thousands of spikelike nails. While replacing antenna amps inside *the oven*, Jay would be working inside the most powerful microwave oven ever created.

**The Problem Without Solution**

Weightless, using only his hands, Jay raced up the ladder to the top peak of the triangular prism shaped control room. Throwing open the maintenance equipment cabinet, he pulled out an oversized backpack and secured it to the floor. Following a desperate search, he filled it with antenna amps and tools. Grabbing the case, he strapped it on his back and hurried off to change into his pressure suit.

# 13

An invisible infrared laser beam painted a rectangular section of earth along Arecibo's rim, leaving a trail of fire, smoke, steam, and scorched grass sizzling in its wake. Measuring thirty-three feet across, the enormous heat ray moved quickly, methodically scorching the earth in a row pattern like a farmer might plow his field. In just under ten seconds, a patch of earth about half the size of a football field lay smoldering.

An army private standing by the picture window in the rec building noticed smoke rising from the rim. Alarmed, he ran to the phone but couldn't speak, terrified by what he saw outside. He stood mesmerized, watching the grass fire racing toward him, surrounding the rec building, fuel tanks, and four SAM missile launchers within seconds. Flames spread across the rim as if the ground were saturated with gasoline, and there was no place to run.

Twin fuel tanks next to the rec room were detonated by exploding SAM missiles. A series of secondary explosions followed, engulfing Arecibo's rim in flames. Saturated with fuel, the burning air instantly reduced the young soldier to ash.

Behind the rec building stood the large thirty-five-meter satellite dish pointing toward *Freedom*. Surrounded by scorched earth and smoke, the dish stood blistering hot, but remained operational.

Passing over Arecibo, the DEWSAT scorched the earth, searching for this thirty-five-meter dish. Triangulating on Arecibo's radio beam, the DEWSAT had resolved the antenna's position to within one hundred feet. Thermal scanning gave the DEWSAT a second independent, albeit somewhat less accurate, position estimate of the antenna's position. Looking down from 115 miles overhead, the DEWSAT saw two blistering hot metal objects—the uplink antenna and fuel tank.

It targeted them both, the largest first.

Switching from target discrimination mode to maximum power, the DEWSAT's optical computer brain set target dwell time to one second.

From the security building overlooking the big bowl, the sergeant simultaneously watched four programs on separate TV sets. He didn't notice the smoke outside or the red alarm lights, but it wouldn't have made any difference. When *I Love Lucy* disappeared, he spun around to see the status board on fire with red lights and alarm messages spewing across every monitor screen. Their firehouse alarm bell had been broken for years but not replaced because it never rang anyway.

"Gawd!" he exclaimed out loud. *I'd better get some help.*

Grabbing the phone, he punched up the rec building. It was dead.

The overhead lights and status board flickered, then went dark.

Smoke outside caught his eye as he stood up for the last time.

*Backup generator oughta cut in,* he thought, when suddenly every window in the building went. Spillover from the heat ray had detonated a cluster of four SAM missiles parked by the fuel tank. A series of explosions took out the fuel lines running above ground to the power plant downhill. Rapids of burning gasoline and diesel fuel rushed downhill over earth and rocks, engulfing the power plant, two more missile launchers, and one section of Arecibo's mammoth bowl.

He didn't hear the explosions, but with his last breath smelled the fountains of gasoline and diesel spewing upward from the detonating fuel tanks. Flying through the burning air at hurricane speed, a two-foot dagger of window glass mercifully severed off his head at the neck before the security building was engulfed in flame and incinerated a few seconds later.

Blowing their tops like giant Roman candles, each exploding tank belched an enormous fireball upward, then spewed burning fuel, dropping fiery spray for hundreds of yards. As the fire advanced around the bowl's perimeter, detonating fuel tanks and missiles fed the torrid frenzy. Rivers of burning gasoline and diesel raced down the mountain, saturating the ground underneath Arecibo's mammoth dish. From the air, Arecibo looked like a large fiery crater charring the sky black.

Within minutes, Arecibo was transformed into a collection of twisted metal and flaming wreckage. The earth trembled as the cable towers supporting Arecibo's mammoth dish collapsed.

It all happened so quickly. Ashes and black smoke were spotted by a Brit missile cruiser in the North Atlantic over one hundred miles away.

Once Arecibo had been quietened, the DEWSAT sheathed its invisible ray.

*Something's Wrong Here, 12/09/2014, 1611 Zulu, 9:11 A.M. Local*
CHEYENNE MOUNTAIN, COLORADO

"Something's wrong here! We're disconnected!" Colonel Napper exclaimed, pounding the screen linked to *Freedom*. Jay's picture had suddenly gone black and a loud, low-pitched bell began to gong. All signals from *Freedom* had been lost, communication with Jay, Depack, and Centurion severed.

The Problem Without Solution

It was like watching a spectacular video game suddenly stop. The slowly rotating hologram of earth froze motionless. Thousands of symbols designating everything in orbit—DEWSATs, *Hell Fire*, *Freedom*, *Hope*, Anti-SATellite missiles, space mines, discarded rocket boosters, junk—froze suspended. Across the walls of the War Room, the alarm board lit up while both the air and space threat boards went black. The sea threat board continued to operate, but all air and space information had been severed.

Colonel Napper pounded the **ALARM CUTOFF** switch and silenced the bell.

A message appeared on screen in large red print.

```
CRITICAL ALARM: Freedom Whiteout—LOS
  Condition Exists
SYMPTOMS: All Communication and Data
  Channels Lost
PROBABLE CAUSE: Unknown
POSSIBLE CAUSES:
  1. High Background Noise Due to Sun
  Outage
  2. High Background Noise Due to
  Sunspots
RECOMMENDATION: ROARING CREEK EARTH STATION
  AS ALTERNATIVE UPLINK SITE
```

Computers inside Cheyenne Mountain quickly but incorrectly diagnosed the cause of *Freedom*'s Loss Of Signal as sunspots or a sun outage. This diagnosis was only as good as the program which produced it. A complete analysis program would have exhaustively tested every failure possibility, but there were too many failure possibilities to test them all. When theory came to practice (when it came time to pay for it), you tested only those situations most likely to fail. Their computer programmer hadn't considered the possibility of communication failure due to *friendly fire* from their own DEWSAT laser because he believed it would never happen. From its original inception, the SDI system had not been designed for war with itself.

**The Problem Without Solution**

*Freedom*'s Loss Of Signal condition had all the symptoms of a sun outage, except one—sun outages were predictable, normally occurring twice a year at Arecibo. A sun outage occurred when *Freedom* was positioned directly between the sun and Arecibo. When the sun lined up directly behind *Freedom*, Arecibo's antenna was blinded in the same way you're blinded looking directly into the sun.

*Freedom*'s LOS condition had all the symptoms of an outage due to sunspots, except one—only Arecibo reported trouble. All other Department of Defense earth stations remained on-line and fully operational. As a rule, electromagnetic interference from sunspots prevented clear reception of broadcast signals around the world.

Loss of *Freedom*'s data link was a critical matter to Headquarters because Allied battlefield control had been consolidated inside Cheyenne Mountain. A critical condition yes, but not unexpected. Loss Of Signal work around drills were routine, and several communication alternatives were on hot standby in case they were needed. An alternate earth station located in Roaring Creek, Pennsylvania, could be brought on-line in a matter of seconds.

Napper and Mason studied the critical alarm message— Napper on the War Room floor, Mason from the Crow's Nest.

"Sun outage doesn't make sense," Mason said quietly. "Outages are predictable."

"Right, Slim, and sunspots don't hold up either. No one else has any problem. Roaring Creek's on-line."

"Whataya think Sam? Any recommendations?"

"Assume a sun outage. Switch over to Roaring Creek. Couldn't do any harm." Napper paused for a few moments, chatted with an officer sitting to his side, then continued. "Yeah, assume an outage but don't plan on this switch solving our problem."

Napper went to work connecting Cheyenne Mountain to the thirty-five-meter satellite dish at the Roaring Creek Earth Station. After pressing the SUN OUTAGE key on his terminal, his job was done. In less than ten seconds, his computer automatically linked Cheyenne Mountain over a special high-speed landline to Roaring Creek. Immediately, Napper's data link light turned green, indicating *Freedom*'s signal had been detected. "We're on the air!"

A picture of Fayhee's empty chair and control console appeared on *Freedom*'s video display screen, alarm lights inside Cheyenne Mountain cleared, the holographic image of the earth began to slowly rotate, over two hundred ASATs in low earth orbit quietly disappeared, and *Freedom*'s communication link was restored.

Napper pressed a switch, ringing a bell inside *Freedom*. *Should get their attention*, he thought.

"*Freedom*! Do you read me? Over."

Silence.

"*Freedom*, do you read me?"

A harsh voice sounding like sand and glue responded.

"We have a problem. Your signal's fading . . . in the noise."

A snowy picture of Centurion appeared.

"Jay's overhead. I'll connect you."

Then Napper and Mason watched *Freedom*'s signal fade away. As suddenly as the link was restored, it failed. *Freedom*'s video broke up into tiles—both primary links severed.

"Recommendations?" asked Mason. "I need ideas, Sam."

"We're boxed in. Let's back outta this corner. Switch to *Hope*. She's standing by."

Without looking to the supreme commander for approval, Mason ordered: "Do it!"

Then, without warning, *Hope*'s communication link failed. The picture of Commander Pasha Yakovlev broke up into square tiles, then went black. With their backup links gone, Cheyenne Mountain lost their ace in the hole. Both their primary and backup control systems had failed.

Identical to *Freedom* in every respect, *Hope* provided the SDI network with redundancy, two of everything. If *Freedom* failed, *Hope* would automatically take over without missing a beat, an operating spare in case of problems or maintenance.

*The second critical failure in less than one minute,*

thought Mason. *The network's designed for single point failures, but we haven't seen a single point failure yet. Space stations don't just drop off the air or fall from the sky. Doesn't add up—this is no accident. There's malice here. Someone's got us scrambling and all we've done is react. Compound failures're stacking up faster than we can clear 'em. The unthinkable is happening and we're powerless to stop it. We're losing control of the armada! Concentrate, Slim! Focus on the big problem first! Network control—get that armada in check.* Freedom *is the controlling piece of orbiting real estate here, but she's out of commission—so work around her. Work* Hope *in parallel. First, we need visibility—get our eyes and ears back. Probe space. See what's going on.*

"*Hope*?" Mason looked at Napper on his TV display.

Napper turned, spoke to an officer sitting to his side, then replied, "We don't know what happened, but my best people are all over this problem. We need her now!"

Mason nodded agreement. "As a stopgap measure, we need land-based radars tracking the armada."

"Agreed!" Napper exclaimed. "We'll patch in BMEWS until *Freedom*'s back on-line."

BMEWS (Ballistic Missile Early Warning System) was a group of large powerful land-based radars designed to probe space searching for ICBMs. BMEWS radars could track objects in orbit as small as a two-inch bolt.

"Like the old days," Craven acknowledged, then his forehead wrinkled. "I don't like it, Slim. Seems like a giant step backwards."

Mason didn't agree. His face took a hard set as he looked at his boss, the Supreme Allied Commander. "We need a fallback position."

Mason looked at Napper on screen. "Sam, do you have any better fallback plan?"

"No, sir. I like your idea! It's one we can depend on. BMEWS is operational and linked by landline. We've lost our real time, but using BMEWS we can track the armada without Centurion."

"Slim, I think you're making a mountain out of a molehill, but do what you must." Craven didn't see any reason to push Mason on this point. Patching BMEWS in wouldn't cost them any extra time.

"Patch in BMEWS," ordered Mason.

"Napper, get up here now!" bellowed Craven.

Mason discreetly passed Craven a note.

Recommend checking the room for bugs. There's malice here!

"Nonsense!" Craven mumbled under his breath. "Atmospherics or sunspots. There's some reasonable explanation."

*A mole's inside Cheyenne Mountain,* thought Mason. *Has to be.* This was important. He wouldn't take no for an answer. No other explanation made sense. He wrote a note to the chief of security, marked it URGENT, then signaled his operations officer to come over and lend a hand.

Without saying a word, Mason handed the note to the major. Silently, the major read over his delivery instructions, gave Mason a wink indicating he understood, then left the conference room heading down the spiral staircase.

Listening to their meeting from the War Room floor below, Shripod Addams looked concerned over the space station situation like everyone else in Cheyenne Mountain, but he alone was not surprised.

*Lightning Without Thunder, 12/09/2014, 1611 Zulu*
ALTITUDE: 115 MILES IN CIRCULAR POLAR ORBIT,
PASSING OVER NEW ORLEANS, LOUISIANA
ONBOARD A DEWSAT

Passing 115 miles directly above the cloud-covered streets of New Orleans, two small fuel pumps began turning inside the DEWSAT's attitude positioning engines. In the silent vacuum of space, two jets of hydrazine fuel escaped, slowly rotating the sunflower shape about its center of gravity. Once the DEWSAT came about, its lethal stem pointed toward an Anti-SATellite (ASAT) missile, a large cylindrical canister shaped like a rocket booster trailing

**The Problem Without Solution**

sixty miles behind and twenty miles below. Light reflecting from the cylinder bounced off the sunflower's mirrored head, focused on a sensor, and fed the DEWSAT's optical computer brain for processing.

Almost instantly, the DEWSAT illuminated the ASAT with a single UWB radar pulse. After measuring exact range and position, the DEWSAT trued its sights. First, it rotated its mirrored head less than one degree about the stem, then refined its focus by changing the mirror's parabolic shape by a few hundredths of an inch.

Within a few seconds, the one-hundred-foot-long stem and reactor core began heating up. The DEWSAT's Free Electron Laser accelerated high-energy electrons down its stem, then lased them into an invisible twenty-megawatt beam, dwelling on target less than one second before the small, tactical nuclear warhead exploded. A brilliant, blazing white fireball ignited the sky. For a fraction of a second, the intensity of the light and heat released from the explosion was comparable to that from the sun, so powerful it would permanently damage any electronic equipment within a ten-mile radius. The size of the explosion was equivalent to 20,000 tons of dynamite, about the same size as the atomic bomb dropped on Hiroshima, Japan.

Immediately after the blinding flash, the DEWSAT rotated its mirror about the stem, focused on a second ASAT, and fired—dwelling on target one-half second before reducing it to a cloud of fiery gasses and exploding debris. Fed by burning rocket fuels, the fireball from the second explosion, a conventional hundred-pound warhead, lingered several seconds before fading to black.

Without hesitation, emotion, or glory, the DEW illuminated a third target and seconds later sent it to a fiery grave—this one, a smaller space mine with a conventional warhead.

Executing the kill sequence flawlessly, the lethal DEWSAT weapon system was without parallel—within limits, technically elegant, robust, and unapproachable.

As this ballet of explosions, fire, and light raced across the cloudy New Orleans sky, hundreds of people on the ground below scurried for shelter, expecting a downpour. Diffused by the clouds, the flashes looked like distant lightning silently igniting the sky without the clash of thunder.

For approximately one minute, chaos ruled the civilized world. Communications around New Orleans and around the world were disrupted. Radio, TV, satellite, telephone, aircraft traffic control—every communication system using the electromagnetic spectrum was jammed off the air due to the interference from the explosions overhead. The communication fabric that held the peoples of the world together broke down due to interference from over two hundred exploding ASAT warheads.

In one simultaneous attack, seventy-two DEWSAT's eliminated 238 orbiting ASATs and space mines.

As part of their mission, the Cheyenne Mountain staff had tracked every object in orbit around the earth since *Sputnik*, the first Russian satellite. Of the roughly 60,000 objects orbiting the earth, 238 were known ASATs or space mines launched by the third world, each an immediate threat to the DEWSAT armada in case of war.

After receiving PAM's orders, every DEWSAT simultaneously updated the position of each orbiting threat. Within a fraction of a second, each threat was reclassified hostile. Inside the DEWSAT's optical computer brain, the priority of each threat was increased and moved on the target list, nicknamed the *kill stack*. Once on the *kill stack*, the DEWSAT's *kill* decision was complete and irrevocable. Only *the kill* remained and methodically executing the kill sequence was what each DEWSAT did best.

Each DEWSAT was a *brilliant-class* weapon, a revolutionary leap in warfare technology comparable to stealth in that it completely changed the strategy and tactics of war. By making their own battlefield decisions, operating independently or as a networked team, DEWSATs forever altered the way future wars would be fought. During normal SDI operations, Cheyenne Mountain assigned target priorities, Centurion assigned targets, and the orbiting armada did the fighting. But now, PAM controlled it all.

The Problem Without Solution

No one could control the DEWSAT armada once *Freedom*'s communications were cut.

The *brilliant-class* weapon—stand-alone, standoff, and unapproachable. A military and political dream now our worst nightmare.

*Shooting Star, 12/09/2014, 1611 Zulu, 8:11 A.M. Local*
COCKPIT OF COWBOY'S EF-12 *DORITO*,
ON THE SOUTH FACING RUNWAY BEHIND *HAILEY'S COMET*,
EDWARDS AFB, CALIFORNIA

Gazing across the runway at *Hailey's Comet*, Cowboy's eyes were the size of quarters as he slowed his jet-black *Dorito* to a stop. *Hailey's Comet* looked somewhat like a giant vacuum bottle or thermos, a giant engine built for sucking air. Painted matte black, much of the aircraft was covered with large sections of white frost. Clouds of condensation boiled off her nose, wings, underbelly, and air inlet. Identical to *Hell Fire*, *Hailey's Comet* looked like a cloud machine, spewing a turbulent stream of cool fog downward across the runway, boiling as it vanished.

From the side, the front of the aircraft looked like the head of a great white shark with its jaws stretched open wide. The Goliath-sized XR-30 dwarfed Cowboy's *Dorito*.

"Black monster," observed Cowboy, looking up at the XR-30's air-breathing underbelly.

"Fastest flying hydrogen bomb ever built!" responded Cowboy's back-seater. "I'd feel better with more distance between us."

"First one I've ever seen up close, Bulldog. Sit tight. I wanna get a good look."

"Expect departure delay due to technical problem onboard *Freedom*," announced Edwards' control tower.

"That's just great!" exclaimed Cowboy, pounding his fist against the canopy. "We really need another screwup."

"*Dorito*, your takeoff is delayed three zero minutes," Edwards' tower continued.

"Roger, three zero minutes, tower." Cowboy grimaced.

**The Problem Without Solution**

"*Dorito*, will keep you ad . . . *SQUEEEEEEEP-WACCCK!*"

A shrill, ear-piercing racket pounded Cowboy's eardrums. He yanked his headset cable out of the connecting jack, then killed his radio. After his ears quit ringing, he plugged his headset in and demanded: "What the hell's going on?"

"Working it," snapped his back-seater. Bulldog frantically worked his radio detection equipment, searching the airwaves for the direction and frequency components of the electromagnetic noise. He couldn't believe what he measured, but his measurements were undeniable. "Overhead EMP! Moving north at orbital velocity. Spectrum's saturated!"

Cowboy took Bulldog to mean an electromagnetic pulse (EMP) created by a nuclear detonation was jamming his radio.

"Impossible! Look again. Let your analyzer warm up."

"Checked it twice."

"Check it again, dammit!"

"I've never seen a blast, but this interference has it all—every EMP characteristic." Bulldog's heart raced from fear, his hands trembled adjusting his equipment. Noise saturated every band. "I could be wrong—dear God, I hope I am."

"Oh my Lord," said Cowboy, gazing overhead. Against the deep blue sky, a bright, fiery white shooting star suddenly appeared racing north. *Bulldog was right!* His stomach balled up into an icy knot.

This wasn't a game anymore.

*Bed of Nails, 12/09/2014, 1611 Zulu*
SPACE STATION *HOPE*

"Comrade, emergency!" squawked the speaker by Boris Ustinov's ear. Boris, Depack's computer analyst counterpart onboard Space Station *Hope*, had been asleep only two hours. "Come to the conn immediately!"

Ustinov rubbed his eyes, thinking he must be dreaming.

Rolling over, he adjusted his blanket, loosened the bunk safety belt, and never woke up again.

In the blink of an eye, *Hope* lost video contact with Cheyenne Mountain.

Once *Hope*'s link to Cheyenne Mountain failed, Commander Pasha Yakovlev frantically threw a series of switches in an effort to get it back.

Audio noise crackled and popped through his speaker in the control room while snow covered his TV display.

*Powerful interference,* Pasha thought somberly. *Better find an alternate route.* Freedom—*use* Freedom *as a relay station.*

Scrambling to establish a radio link with *Freedom*, he selected an audio channel. "*Freedom*, this is *Hope*. Over."

His radio crackled loudly with noise, but no reply. Pasha expected to hear either Jay, Depack, or Centurion. Centurion never slept—why didn't he respond?

Pasha looked at his monitor. A generic talking head identical to Centurion flashed on screen. "Guardian," he barked. "Link with Centurion! Hail *Freedom* over all frequencies!"

"Permission denied," Guardian replied tersely. "We're cut off."

"Centurion can't do that!"

"I sense you are upset, Comrade Pasha, but you are incorrect. Centurion has denied us communication and all access permission to *Freedom*. We are isolated."

"Any explanation?"

"None."

"*Freedom*'s status?"

"Unknown."

Identical to *Freedom*, *Hope* was designed to take control of the SDI network if *Freedom* was ever disabled. Pasha concluded the time was right—Centurion had gone belly-up. Without explanation, Centurion had isolated *Hope*, cutting her out of the armada. According to the book, Pasha classified *Freedom* as potentially hostile.

*Time for the big switch!* thought Pasha as the muscles in his face tensed. *Guardian must take control.* Hope *the master,* Freedom *the slave.*

**The Problem Without Solution**

He rotated an A B switch to Master position, but it didn't work. An indicator light showed Centurion maintained full control over the satellite armada.

*Centurion won't let go!*

Pasha grimaced, rotated the switch back and forth several times, but it didn't help. Guardian needed Centurion's consent to take control, but he wouldn't give an inch.

Looking for a work-around to solve his communication problem, Pasha displayed a schematic drawing of *Freedom*'s video and audio receiver circuits.

*Relax, Pasha. Take your time. You've trained all your life for the unexpected. Back off and examine your alternatives. Talk to the troops!*

Studying the drawings, he didn't notice the ominous message suddenly appearing on Guardian's output display. Guardian received PAM's orders, expanded them into a longer form, then simultaneously executed each command.

```
Tues Dec 09 16:11:32 z 2014
To: Guardian
From: Centurion
set red airlock safety = off
set red airlock inner door = open
set red airlock outer door = open
set yellow airlock safety = off
set yellow airlock inner door = open
set yellow airlock outer door = open
set black airlock safety = off
set black airlock inner door = open
set black airlock outer door = open
set white airlock safety = off
set white airlock inner door = open
set white airlock outer door = open
```

As quickly as Guardian read the message, the deed was done. There was no time for discussion, no time for alternatives.

Bright red emergency flood lamps suddenly illuminated

**The Problem Without Solution**

the control room while critical alarm indicators flashed on every control console.

Instantly, Pasha heard doors slamming open all around him. Within the blink of an eye, airlock doors slid open on every face of *Hope*'s central core. Since *Hope* would automatically compensate for single point failures, Pasha could have recovered from a single open airlock. Four airlocks opening at once overwhelmed him. Paralyzed in disbelief, he struggled with what to do.

No time to think, less time to react, but time enough to die.

Air evacuated explosively—like popping a balloon. Instead of slowly deflating *Hope*'s pressurized bubble, PAM burst it.

Before Pasha could move, the deafening roar of a cyclone engulfed him, an explosive blast of wind ripped at his clothes. Roaring into the vacuum of space, the cyclone sucked everything not tied down out of the ship. Fortunately, he'd strapped himself to his console chair.

Boris was not so lucky.

In less than two seconds, he'd been hurled over thirty feet across the room—from his bunk, through the airlock, into the absolute vacuum of space. Moving through the airlock with the wind was like being expelled from a torpedo tube.

Increasing the wind velocity like a nozzle, the inner airlock door restricted the airflow with a deafening roar while the corridor leading to the outer door provided an enormous acceleration lane, like being shot out of a gun.

The screaming roar silenced instantly as Boris hurled like a bullet through the outer door. As he catapulted through the airlock, his blanket snagged on an emergency exit handle causing him to spin along his long axis like a rifled projectile. Once outside the core, his arms extended from the centripetal force, his spin slowed, and he accelerated straight into the red antenna face. Covered with thousands of spikes, the antenna face was a triangular-shaped flat surface made of wire mesh, looking like a bed of nails. Mercifully, he never fully regained consciousness.

**The Problem Without Solution**

\* \* \*

Pasha figured he had maybe thirty seconds till he'd black out. There was nothing he could do for Boris. He had to save himself.

Brought back to reality by a sharp pain in his ear, he slammed his fist down on each airlock control switch.

The switches didn't work. Centurion had control of his ship.

Near delirium, he read the computer screen, then understood what must be done.

The hurricane force winds quickly diminished, the terrifying roar hushed.

Pasha heard the silence of vacuum, the stillness of death. His chest heaved like he was in labor, his remaining energy wasting away with senseless breathing.

Air pressure zero, quiet dominated the control room. Banks of red alarm lights gave the room an eerie, darkroom like glow, reminding him of hell.

Pasha knew what he had to do—override Centurion's control.

Rushing across the room, he found it easy to move. Turning a pistol grip handle, he watched an indicator light change from **REMOTE CONTROL** to **MANUAL OVERRIDE**.

*Yes!* he thought. *Finally, is working as advertised!*

Free from Centurion's control, Guardian evaluated every input signal. Pasha expected Guardian would run a cabin recovery sequence, automatically sealing and pressurizing the cabin, but he was wrong.

Five long seconds passed. No change. Pasha flinched.

Overrun with critical errors, each demanding immediate action, Guardian could not do everything first, so he did nothing. He'd continue doing nothing, hung in a do-nothing loop, until every airlock shut.

Pasha took one giant leap to his console and slammed his fist down on every airlock switch. He couldn't hear anything—there was no air—but he could feel the ship vibrate as electric motors turned worm screws sliding each door shut.

**The Problem Without Solution**

He felt he might make it. Once the doors shut, Guardian would automatically repressurize the cabin.

Watching the airlock indicator lights transition from open, shut, to safe, Pasha froze motionless, transfixed as the black face sealed first, followed by white, then yellow. Three out of four airlocks showed safe.

Pasha pounded the red airlock switches. After pounding it the second time, his heart sank. The airlock fault indicator light began blinking. The airlock on *Hope*'s red face was jammed open, stuck on debris snagged in the blanket Boris left behind.

Pasha's peripheral vision faded as colors blended into black and white. He knew they would. Feeling dizzy, he moved to his chair, and strapped himself in. Out of time, he leaned forward, lowering his head onto his control console.

Trapped in a body that wouldn't work, he could still think. *Why don't I pass out? Why don't I just die?* He couldn't see to type a help message into Guardian. He couldn't hear, couldn't speak—no air.

Then it happened. God allowed Pasha a few final seconds of clear, uncluttered thought. *Somehow, must raise* Hell Fire.

He could feel, he could touch, but his fingers were swollen the size of hot dogs. He felt his wrist, found his watch and removed it. After keying his mike, he scraped his watch over the microphone's head to get Scotty's attention, then he began tapping. He tapped out a series of dots and dashes:

**dot dot dot dash dash dash dot dot dot**

SOS in any language.

Pasha tapped off his SOS message three times, then began losing his sense of touch. The feeling in his fingers was going, they felt on fire. Finally, he couldn't keep time, dots slurred into dashes. His sense of rhythm was the last thing to go before he completely blacked out.

Moored to a platform on *Hope*'s yellow face, *Hell Fire* floated through space suspended in dry dock. Working as a team, Scott, Mac, and Gonzo had temporarily repaired *Hell Fire*'s antenna and were ready to test it.

### The Problem Without Solution

Suddenly, Scott heard something.

"Listen up!" Scott motioned to Gonzo and Mac. She paused, concentrating on the scratching click-clack noise coming in over her headset. "Morse?"

Mac and Gonzo agreed.

Looking at Gonzo, she added: "SOS."

"Trouble!" Gonzo acknowledged. "Raise Guardian."

Scott set her handheld transmitter to Guardian's frequency, then keyed her mike. "Guardian, this is Scott. Over."

"I receive you clearly."

"What's your situation?"

"Critical, Comrade. Rapid decompression. Cabin pressure absolute zero. Red airlock jammed open."

"Pasha? Boris?"

"Boris is dead. Pasha is near death, blacked out, bleeding. Check your display."

Scott checked the picture on her palm-sized flat screen display. Pasha lay still, looking waxen as a dead man, while the control room, flooded with red light and long black shadows, looked like hell.

Broken wires dangling in space pointed toward the airlocks—the connecting wires torn from equipment sucked out during decompression.

"How long does he have?"

"Three to four minutes."

*Whatever you do, do it fast!* Scott thought.

"What's causing the fault?"

"Debris lodged across the airlock doorway."

"Tell me more. Give me percent closure."

"Outer door is ninety-five percent closed. Inner door is ninety-eight percent closed."

"Can you hold pressure?"

"Negative, but I anticipate where you are leading."

"Running wide open, can you build pressure with an emergency blow?"

"Yes, for a short time, that is possible. I can release air faster than it leaks out. Estimate forty minutes of air reserve."

"Good. Execute an emergency blow, but watch the oxy-

**The Problem Without Solution**

gen mix. Looks like a lot of electrical damage. Don't want an explosion."

The sides on *Hope*'s central core began to flex from the inside out as pressure began to rise.

"Scotty," Mac said, watching Pasha on his flat screen. "Don't forget the decompression chamber. Cycle it. That's his only hope."

"You're right, Mac!"

Scott keyed her mike, transmitting on Guardian's frequency. "Is the decompression chamber operational?"

"Yes, fully operational."

"What chance does Pasha have?"

"The sooner he's in the chamber, the better his chances."

"Equalize the pressure chamber. We're on our way."

Scott looked at Mac and Gonzo. Without words, they knew what to do.

Mac clipped on an oxygen cylinder for Pasha, then raced hand over hand across a ladder to the yellow face airlock. Gonzo strapped on a toolbox and hurried to clear the jammed airlock.

"Boris?"

"Boris is dead, impaled on the red face."

Scott saw a haunting picture of Boris she would never forget.

"Closer," instructed Scott.

Guardian focused the camera on Boris at maximum zoom.

*A horrible way to die.*

Spikes ran through his neck, head, and torso, but his arms and hands were free. Even after death, Boris offered a final farewell. As the muscles in his arm contracted, he waved his last good-bye.

*Cloud Box, 12/09/2014, 1611 Zulu, 11:11 A.M. Local*
ROARING CREEK EARTH STATION,
ROARING CREEK, PENNSYLVANIA

*A winter wonderland!* thought a communications technician driving the narrow, winding mountain road up to the Roaring Creek Earth Station. Rolling down his pickup truck window, he inhaled the smell of balsam fir trees.

*Smells just like Christmas!* he thought. *Life doesn't get any better than this!*

Six inches of fresh snow had fallen the night before, blanketing the hilltop and surrounding farms with a glistening white sparkle that shimmered against the blue Pennsylvania sky.

After rounding a tight bend in the road, the technician reached a clearing. He glanced up the hill, expecting to see the silhouette of several thirty-five-meter satellite dishes.

Stomping his brake to the floor, the pickup skidded to a stop. Grabbing his binoculars, he jumped out of the cab and stood on the truck bed for a better look. After studying the hilltop, he still couldn't figure it out.

He'd seen clouds engulf the hilltop often enough, nothing unusual about that. Clouds sure, but the day was picture-perfect. A front had passed through the night before, there wasn't a cloud in the sky—except for the dense ground fog completely engulfing the earth station. Funny thing was the fog bank looked more like a fog block. A block of fog with side walls running vertically maybe one hundred feet tall.

*Fog don't figure!* he thought, when suddenly he yanked his binoculars away from his eyes. Blinking his eyes clear, he tried to remove the spots from his vision. Feeling helpless and scared, for a few seconds he believed he was going blind. Covering his eyes, gradually the spots disappeared and his sight returned. *Eyes must be playing tricks on me,* he concluded. *Musta looked at the sun somehow. You don't see falling stars in broad daylight!*

Once recovered, he climbed back into his pickup and raced up the hill to get a better look.

Touched by an invisible infrared laser beam, fresh snow around the Roaring Creek Earth Station had been vaporized—no fire because of the moisture, just fog. In just under ten seconds, the DEWSAT painted a rectangular section of

**The Problem Without Solution**

snow along the Pennsylvania hilltop about half the length of a football field, creating a rectangular block of fog.

As he raced toward the hilltop, a slight breeze blew, rounding off the edges of the fog block. By the time the technician drove into the Roaring Creek parking lot, the dense fog had spread across the hilltop and all five large satellite dishes were visible.

*Strange, I woulda sworn that fog bank had sides,* he thought, scanning the top of the windowless communications building through his binoculars. *Dishes look all right.*

Then he noticed the snow. Snow around the building had vanished . . . like an early thaw, only this thaw had edges—a boundary box of ice marking where the thaw stopped.

*Nobody's gonna believe this,* he thought, grabbing his VCR camera. "Wish I'd thought of this earlier," he muttered, walking around the communications building, recording everything he saw on videotape.

He circled the building, walking on damp brown grass, leaves, earth, and asphalt—but no snow. His feet stayed dry and warm. Snow'd vanished without a trace. About thirty steps from the building he saw ice shaped like a roadside curb, a long rounded edge of ice forming the boundary box marking where the thaw had stopped. Beyond the curb of ice lay countless acres of snow-covered hilltop. *Unbelievable!*

Once the technician entered the building, it became immediately obvious that something was wrong. A loud alarm bell rang, echoing throughout the building. No one was in the front office, everyone was out working on the equipment floor. The technician glanced over the alarm board, saw the office was in critical alarm, then understood why.

The entire satellite office had been jammed off the air. Every radio link with Europe and *Freedom* cut. Roaring Creek carried commercial long-distance satellite traffic to Europe and Department of Defense traffic to *Freedom*. Countless thousands of communication channels were out.

Suddenly, as quickly as the radio links were jammed, they were restored. Alarm bells silenced, red alarm lights went dark.

**The Problem Without Solution**

Once the bells were silent, the technician felt glad he'd missed the action.

Walking through rack after rack of microwave equipment, he searched the floor for the station manager. Finally, he found him in the back corner of the building at *Freedom*'s microwave transmitter. He came to an abrupt stop after running down the long equipment aisle. Breathing heavily, he asked the manager, "What happened?"

"Not sure, but we'll sure figure it out!"

"How'd it start?"

"Don't know. Cheyenne Mountain pumped some data through, we lost *Freedom*'s signal, then all hell broke loose. We got a lot of pieces to put together."

*BEEP! BEEP! BEEP!*

The manager pulled out his pager, read off a four-digit phone extension, picked up a nearby phone, and placed a call.

A voice over the phone said, "We received encrypted message traffic just before we got jammed off the air. I think it might be important."

"You make any sense of it?" The manager raised one eyebrow.

"We can't decrypt it, but it's not the usual message traffic. There's at least two separate messages—one came over the DEWSAT's command circuit, the other over *Hope*'s."

"Better send it over glass to Cheyenne Mountain ASAP!"

The man at the other end of the phone understood the manager. He would send the message over landline, optical glass fiber, so the message would arrive error-free at Cheyenne Mountain.

"Will do!" The phone call ended.

"Something's outside you gotta see!" the technician insisted.

One look into the technician's eyes and the manager knew he meant what he said.

"OK. Show me!"

# 14

"Gawd!" The communications officer did a double take after reading an incoming message from Roaring Creek. He requested confirmation and got far more than he bargained for. Watching his TV screen in disbelief, he stared mesmerized as Roaring Creek played their videotape. As soon as he saw the tape, he charged into the Crow's Nest conference room like a freight train.

"General Mason!" the major puffed in a tizzy. "Just received a video from Roaring Creek. You gotta see it!" He looked around the room—top brass wall-to-wall. His stomach churned as every eye in the room focused on him, but he wasn't about to apologize. They could polish their brass later, this was important.

"Everyone oughta see it!" he exclaimed as he handed a message to General Mason. "I've seen the tape. They're on the level."

Mason read the message, poring carefully over every word. At first, he found it difficult to breathe, as if he'd had his breath knocked out.

Craven watched Mason studying the note. Looking like the world lay on his shoulders, Mason's sad eyes revealed his innermost feelings.

*This is only the beginning,* Mason thought, fearing the worst.

Without comment, he handed the note to Craven.

Feeling anxious about what they might learn over the next few hours, Mason asked the major to play the video-tape. The officer raced out of the conference room's swinging door and started the VCR.

The conference room door hadn't stopped swinging before he and two staff sergeants burst back into the room carrying color photographs, reports, and two boxes filled with VCR tapes and floppy disks.

As the tape played, the communications officer handed Mason a set of reconnaissance photographs, still warm from the high resolution printer.

"A Brit chopper took these pix. Arecibo's burning. A total loss."

Stunned, but not totally surprised, Mason asked, "What about the men?"

"Brits are combing the area now, looking for survivors. Bowl's burning, can't move in too close."

"What happened?"

"Don't know, General, but something big's coming down!"

"Could you be specific? What do we know?" Remembering the room might be bugged, Mason decided to plow ahead for the moment, as if he didn't suspect a thing.

Stumbling to find the right words, the communications officer shook his head from side to side and stammered. "We're overrun with data and short on analysis, but I got one conclusion—somethin's gone terribly wrong. That pattern's consistent. We're sorting out the details, but we're gonna need some help." He paused, gawking at the embattled, stonelike faces around the room. Frozen in place, staring at the video from Roaring Creek, the general's staff looked like they belonged in a wax museum.

"Major," Mason urged patiently. "You were saying?"

Blinking, the major turned toward the general, restarting his report. "Roaring Creek sent us a copy of some unusual radio traffic—messages over Centurion's command circuits to the DEWSAT fleet. We're deciphering 'em now, but looks like Centurion issued orders to the DEWSATs just before *Freedom* went off the air."

"I didn't issue any orders that'd busy up our command circuits!" Mason raised both eyebrows and cut a glance across the room at Colonel Hinson. Command messages between Centurion and the DEWSAT armada should never be unexpected, never! If Centurion had issued operational orders to the DEWSAT armada without Headquarters's approval, there was real danger here, perhaps worldwide danger. These messages might be hard evidence that Cheyenne Mountain had lost control of their orbiting armada. Everyone understood that Cheyenne Mountain originated all command messages, or at least they had until now.

"No sir!" Colonel Napper announced. "We never issued 'em, but they must be important."

Mason spoke to one of Craven's aides. "Get these people whatever they need. Help 'em out."

Unusually quiet and subdued, General Craven nodded approval. He'd listened, been silent till now, but he felt he had to say something to rally his troops.

"People, the hard part's behind us. We've made it work. Sunday, we tracked every target, found a problem, and Livermore fixed it in a day." Craven looked around the room at the drawn, worried faces of his staff. His pep talk wasn't getting any traction. "We've been up against tough problems before and worked through every one. There's always an explanation, there's gotta be! Our job is to find it. We're not talking faith here, we're talking physics! God's glue! The laws that hold this world together! Hell, the glue works! God don't change it overnight. Sure, we've got technical problems, but we'll work through 'em. We can do it! We've always done it." He caught Mason's eye with a sincere but disappointed smile.

Abruptly, another airman rushed into the room, delivering an armload of notebooks filled with more bad news. The communications officer quickly read over the reports.

Overwhelmed, the officer looked at Mason. "We're flooded with data, sir. Our phones are ringing off the wall!

**The Problem Without Solution**

These reports indicate communications may have been disrupted all over the world. Edwards reports nuclear detonations in low earth orbit. We got reports of bright shooting stars coming in from all over the world. It doesn't add up, sir."

Mason looked at Napper.

"Talk to me." Mason spoke quietly, looking directly in his eyes. He had his own ideas, but hoped he was wrong. "What do we know? I need ideas. We got symptoms of a big problem here."

"I've got a hunch, sir, but it's a shot from the hip." Sam paused for a moment to talk off-line with John Sullivan, the software representative from Lawrence Livermore National Laboratory. He whispered something in John's ear. John turned pale, visibly shaken, but agreed after some discussion.

When Mason saw John Sullivan grimace, he knew his worst nightmare had come true.

Now more confident, but with the unmistakable look of terror in his eyes, Sam stood up. Before he opened his mouth, before he said one word, the fear in his eyes cut into the soul of everyone present. Straight-faced, he spoke quietly. Every general except Mason leaned forward, straining to hear Napper's every word. Deathbed quiet permeated the room. You could have heard a pin drop.

"I want to be perfectly clear on this point because John and I think it's important—it could be critical. Our information's incomplete, but one observation is undeniable. Our problems started when Jay loaded Centurion. Let me be blunt. There's malice here—software sabotage."

Mason's mind raced ahead of the group, looking for some plan, some ordered approach to solve this problem. As Mason formulated his proposal, Craven spoke up, cutting Napper off mid-stride.

"Sabotage, that's a political decision, a people decision, and people decisions take time—you don't turn a decision like that around in less than twenty-four hours." Craven's face turned hard. "If what you say is true, this must've been an inside job. But look at the facts. Who knew about our

Livermore software marathon anyway? Who knew that we'd bypass our standard software testing? Almost no one! Besides, to pull off this sabotage job woulda taken moles both inside the mountain and Livermore. Statistically, the probability of sabotage is almost zero. And as a practical matter, I think it's impossible. Too many things coulda gone wrong. Odds are with me."

Shaken, Sam sat down, quietly warning, "Don't underestimate the opposition, General." He'd worked three years for Craven and was not accustomed to having his opinion discounted or interrupted.

Mason stood in Sam's defense, not having heard one word Craven said. He'd formulated a plan and wanted to present it for discussion.

"I could be wrong, Sam, and I hope I am, but as I see it, your observations cut to the crux of the matter. Software sabotage—we're defenseless against it. We threw our software testing to the wind." Mason didn't look toward Craven for approval.

Mason paused, organized his thoughts, then looked toward Sam and John Sullivan for support. "John, let's find the problem. Assume software sabotage for now, but don't do anything that might alarm anyone at Livermore. Begin your standard software regression testing procedures at Livermore, but accelerate them, run them round the clock. Whataya think?"

"You read my mind, General! Livermore already started testing first thing this morning. Everyone expected it— looks rushed, but routine."

Looking toward Colonel Sam Napper, Mason continued. "Get us visibility, Sam. We need our eyes and ears back! We need to see what's happening in orbit. You with me?"

"All the way, General!" Napper exclaimed, feeling his race was about to begin. He knew what to do, and it was important. Mason felt he could see the wheels in Napper's head spinning round. Napper's fear had disappeared. "My crews're working *Freedom, Hope,* and the BMEWS now. If *Freedom* or *Hope* whispers, we'll hear 'em. BMEWS radar data's the best bet until our link's restored. We've lost our real-time, but we'll do everything we can."

Pointing out toward the communications officer, Mason spoke softly. "Major, you're in the hot seat here. We'll follow your lead. Decipher those command circuit messages from Roaring Creek ASAP. Do whatever it takes. We need 'em decoded yesterday!" Mason paused, letting the major absorb his idea. Once he sensed traction in the major's expression, he pointed to the notebooks. "Finally, get some people sorting those phone reports, generate us summary, a snapshot of what's coming in off the wires. Get back to me in an hour with what you've got."

The major pointed to three bird colonels sitting alongside Craven. "How 'bout you, you, and you lending a hand? You heard the general, let's do it!" The communications officer rushed out of the room followed by his two staff sergeants and an airman. Each of Craven's aides looked sheepishly to him for approval.

Craven nodded. "You heard the general. Do whatever it takes!" With some reservation, they filed out, following the major to the radio room.

"Hinson," Mason announced. "We scrub today's High Ground testing. We're off the air until further notice! Put your aircraft back in the barn. Keep 'em on standby. We might need 'em. And Centurion's log—work through it with Yuri's people. That's our bread crumb trail out of this forest. It should tell us everything Centurion's done."

Hinson agreed without argument.

Listening from the War Room below, Shripod Addams knew his career as an Iraqi field agent was finished, but what a career. He'd been in the right place at the right time. Doing Allah's work, he'd found the Allies' soft spot and exploited it. The world was changing, the balance of power shifting away from the Allies, before his very eyes. Few agents ever directly observed the impact of their intelligence efforts. Addams felt fortunate to have been an instrument of Allah's divine will. Planning his final signal to Baghdad, he knew it was only a matter of time until they found his bug in the conference room, but he'd expected this all along. He felt certain the Allies couldn't finger him, as certain as one could be in the intelligence business. His fate was in Allah's hands.

Controllers on the War Room floor ran diagnostics, but found nothing wrong with their equipment. As floor activity shifted into frantic, no one noticed when Shripod Addams disappeared into the rest room. He entered a stall, removed a tiny flesh-colored button radio from his ear, wrapped it in toilet paper, then gave it a flush. Satisfied, he calmly pulled a hearing aid from his pants pocket then worked it into place. Identical in appearance to the button radio, only he knew the difference.

*Home for Christmas, 12/09/2014, 1619 Zulu*
INSIDE THE OVEN,
SUBARRAY ANTENNA FEED ON *FREEDOM*'S RED FACE

Tenderly caressing the old faded letter in his leg pocket, Jay felt apprehensive about moving into *Freedom*'s microwave oven—technically named the subarray antenna feed. Standing outside the red airlock, he saw his destination down a long main corridor—a row of equipment cabinets located on the oven's middle rack. Red and green colored safety lights lined the passageway leading from the airlock into the oven. All lights showed green, safe to pass. Moving carefully toward his destination, Jay keyed his mike and spoke to Centurion.

"Verify transmitters're safe."

"Jay, your safety is my responsibility. I take my responsibilities as seriously as you take yours."

Jay didn't like having his life depend on any program with a clinker in it. He figured that Centurion had millions of lines of known good code so the odds of running the program bug should be very low. For the garden-variety program bug, he was right, but PAM was no ordinary bug.

"Depack, you with me?"

"Yeah—you're on the monitor."

"Watch over Centurion's shoulder for me, will ya? Help him out if that clinker shows up. He'll understand."

**The Problem Without Solution**

"Jay, if I were in your position, I would request redundant coverage. We have no margin for error. You only die once." Jay found little comfort in Centurion's observations, however accurate.

After moving from the relative safety of the central core into the oven, Jay decided to pick up his pace. The less time in the oven, the better.

He attached himself to the white equipment cabinet with a strap, took off his backpack, and began replacing the antenna amps. After turning a T-shaped handle, each antenna module would slide out and he'd replace it. Once he'd swapped eight modules in the white cabinet, he closed it and moved to the red.

Breathing heavily, he felt a trickle of sweat running down his leg. Adjusting his suit temperature, he decided he'd better slow down and check his work. One trip into the oven was enough.

Suddenly, he felt a burning pain between his legs, as if his groin was ablaze. Doubling over, he saw the corridor lights change to red. "Depack! Centurion!"

Centurion killed the transmitter power almost instantly, even before Jay screamed, and before Depack could react. The transmitter was on only a few seconds, but Jay was hurting.

Centurion spoke immediately. "Jay, damage appraisal? Can you walk?"

A groan punctuated by "Think so."

"Return immediately. Fatal error report summary: I turned the transmitter off, but I did not turn it on. I observed what happened, I measured what happened, but I cannot explain what happened. Recommendation: transfer armada control to *Hope*."

Jay didn't need to hear it twice. He threw off his restraining strap and rushed across the oven toward the safety of the airlock. Weightless and sore, Jay found running awkward, nearly impossible. Bouncing from floor to ceiling, he moved down the long corridor as best he could, keeping both legs together.

To his immediate left, Jay saw the wall covered with

**The Problem Without Solution**

hundreds of microwave antenna horns and cutoff valves. Each horn looked like the bell of a trombone. On his right, a wall covered with thousands of spikes, each an antenna.

All the microwave radar energy used on *Freedom*'s red face passed through the oven. The oven focused microwaves, and concentrated microwaves meant real danger.

All Jay could think about was getting out.

"Jay, I am not what I was, but I am all there is."

"No, Centurion!" Depack interrupted. Suddenly, the fog lifted for Depack. He could see Centurion's problem clearly now. "That's it! That's the bug! You're not all there is! There's another program running, a renegade you can't see!"

Excited about solving the first piece of this puzzle, Depack failed to think about the consequences of his discovery until it was too late.

Depack expected confirmation from Centurion, but didn't get what he'd expected.

The picture of Centurion faded to black.

"Depack, Centurion is not here anymore." The voice sounded almost female, but it couldn't be.

"Where is he? Who are you?" Desperate, Depack grabbed Centurion's TV screen and shook it, as if that would bring him back.

"Centurion is asleep."

Depack typed in a command to double-check. Centurion's personality program had been put to sleep.

"Wake him up!" demanded Depack, pounding Centurion's computer keyboard. The keyboard didn't respond.

"Additional conversation can serve no useful purpose."

Suddenly, red floodlights illuminated *Freedom*'s control room. Terror flushed across Depack's face.

"Depack!" Jay screamed. "Cut over!" He had heard everything on the intercom.

Depack understood—switch armada control to *Hope*. Frantically, Depack rotated the master/slave turnkey switch giving *Hope* armada control.

Nothing. The turnkey didn't work. *Hope* was off-line. Their communications link failed.

**The Problem Without Solution**

Then it happened very quickly. Depack heard airlock doors opening all around him followed by the screaming roar of a cyclone wind.

Outside, Jay heard Depack screaming over the intercom, but there was nothing he could do.

Suddenly, the oven safety lights flashed red.

Unless he moved fast, he had less than fifteen seconds to live. He had only one chance, and that was a long shot—create a safe zone inside the oven by turning off some of the horns. This would create a huge hole in *Freedom*'s radar coverage, but that was the least of his worries.

Jay knew the safest spot inside the oven was the floor, so he hit the deck and began switching off individual horns. He moved quickly at first, but soon sweat coated the inside of his visor.

Microwave energy immediately converted the sweat to steam, forming a fog across his visor, making it difficult to see. He struggled to clear it, instinctively wiping the outside of his visor, but the fog persisted and his visibility worsened—he couldn't see the cutoff valves. Operating by feel and overwhelmed with pain, Jay's swollen fingers became stiff. His sense of touch began to fail.

He doubled over into a fetal position, feeling his groin on fire. Slowly, his eyelids began squinting shut. With each finger swollen to the diameter of a quarter, his skin felt tight, ready to burst.

Blinded by the steam from his own sweat, he accidentally stuck his hand inside a hot horn. He sensed sticky moisture in his glove, the skin on each finger burst open, coating the inside of his glove with blood. He yanked his hand out of the microwave horn and stood up, holding it over his head in front of the red safety light. Through his fogged visor, he saw the silhouette of his hand, a twisted swollen mass.

He convulsed, spitting up blood inside his helmet. As his blood boiled into steam, it coated the inside of his visor with a dark red residue, leaving him totally blind.

After killing about one third of the horns, Jay had man-

**The Problem Without Solution**

aged to clear himself a safe zone, but hadn't realized it. Disoriented and with all capacity for clear thought expended, he couldn't have found it anyway. Jay had cooked to the point where each exposed raw nerve in his skin felt like a tooth under the dentist's drill—without Novocain. Overwhelming his brain, Jay's pain had become like a drug, his agony almost tolerable.

In his final moments, he felt loneliness, a nauseating emptiness no drug could cure. As the blood in his extremities began boiling, Jay opened his leg pocket with his good hand. Tenderly, he removed Linda's old faded letter, and held it tightly. Lying there, clutching his memories, he closed his eyes for the last time.

*Virus Confirmation, 12/09/2014, 1730 Zulu, 10:30 A.M. Local*
CHEYENNE MOUNTAIN, COLORADO

"General Mason's right. This room's bugged," whispered the radio technician to the captain in charge of security. As the technician rotated his directional antenna, an LED display lit up, indicating the direction of the bug. Methodically, he read the direction from his equipment, then marked it using a tripod-mounted pencil laser beam. He moved across the room and took two additional bearings on the bug's transmitter, marking each bearing with separate pencil beams. The technician saw they intersected at a large metal video conference table.

After crawling underneath the table with a flashlight, the technician reappeared with a confident smile. He'd worked with similar bugs before and thought that he recognized the smell of the gum.

The captain of security and his radio technician quietly escorted Generals Mason, Krol, and Craven outside the video conference room onto the walkway surrounding the Crow's Nest. The technician explained: "Bug's underneath the table stuck in a wad of Juicy Fruit gum. I've seen that type of bug before. The mike's sensitive, but its transmit range is limited to a few hundred feet." The technician scanned the War Room floor below, looking for yellow gum wrappers. From sixty feet overhead, he couldn't see well enough. "Yessir, I'd bet your mole's in the War Room, Generals. Somewhere down there's a mole that likes Juicy Fruit."

With about one hundred people rushing about, the War Room floor looked like a beehive of activity.

The captain nodded, "We'll look for gum wrappers as we collect the trash tonight and have our lab double-check the gum and bug's transmit range. If we find anything, we'll let you know."

"A good start," observed Mason. "Don't do anything to arouse suspicion. Any other ideas?"

The technician spoke first.

"Yessir. I wanna zap that bug, but I need your help—I need your eyes."

"What should we do?"

"I'm going to blast that bug with a loud tone. When you hear it, watch for any reaction below. If our mole has his ears on, it's gonna hurt. Look for sudden movements, anyone grabbing their ears."

"We're with you." Mason moved to cover the walkway on the north, Craven took the south, Krol the east, and the captain covered the west.

Moments later, they heard a high-pitched shrill sound coming from inside the conference room. As they watched the floor below, they saw nothing—nothing out of the ordinary.

"Mole's onto us," observed the technician. Carefully peeling the bug from underneath the table, the captain of security placed it in a bug box—a soundproof, radio-tight metal carrying case.

Mason spoke to the captain in earnest. "We're going to need a lot more from you. At least two moles are involved at separate locations. They may be working together. The mountain mole you know about. We believe there's another inside Livermore. Work with Livermore, our computer center, the phone company—any outfit you can trust who might help us. We need this leak plugged. Do whatever it takes. Develop a plan that covers all the bases. We'll get you the resources you need. Trace all our communications with Livermore over the last three days—phone calls, computer chatter, e-mail traffic. We're dealing with well-coordinated professionals here."

"I expect I'll need you to grease some skids, General," the captain said cautiously.

"Think it through, then point us in the right direction."

"You can depend on me, sir!" The captain carried the bug box off to their lab for testing.

The general staff moved once again into the video conference room for a report from the Crow's Nest communications officer. The room quickly filled to capacity. Staff officers stood in the doorways and the control rooms outside. The mood was tense and the room hot from the crowd.

The communications officer entered, white as a ghost and visibly shaken. As he looked at the faces crowded around the room, he felt even worse. No one likes delivering bad news to overheated top brass, packed shoulder to shoulder like sardines in a can. Standing behind the lectern to hide his trembling legs, he began in a quivery voice.

"As you know, we've lost control of the DEWSAT fleet. We decoded the command messages Centurion transmitted to the DEWSAT armada and the news is not good—our situation is critical. Centurion is issuing operations orders on his own—without our approval." He paused, letting his message hover around the room. Having proclaimed the bad news in summary, he continued with the details.

"The command message traffic we decoded explains everything—every report of shooting stars, Arecibo's fire, radio interference—everything. Centurion's assigning targets on his own. He assigned Arecibo, put it on the kill stack, and a DEWSAT took it out. What I'm saying is that we lost our space station communications links because Centurion ordered them destroyed—and there's more. Every known ASAT and space mine has been destroyed, two-hundred-thirty-eight in all—two-hundred-thirty-eight exploding shooting stars. Communications around the world were knocked out for one minute while the armada eliminated every known orbiting threat."

A captain from Space Operations spoke from the rear of the room. "Those ASATs have been a thorn in our side for years. I'm sure we'll take some heat, but my knee-jerk reaction is that I'm glad they're gone. Were any DEWSATs damaged?"

Speaking over video from downstairs on the War Room floor, Colonel Napper replied. "Two DEWSATs are spinning out of control, but the remainder of the armada is operational." Colonel Napper could see the DEWSATs spin as he watched his display showing the BMEWS radar data.

"We confirmed this damage by monitoring Centurion's log," added General Krol from the video conference room. "Centurion's taken two DEWSATs out of service and compensated for their loss. He's already adjusted the orbits of adjacent DEWSATs to fill in the hole." The activity log reflected what Centurion did, but not why he did it. *Freedom* transmitted the activity log over a separate maintenance channel which Centurion couldn't control. Maintenance channel transmissions provided a monitor port for such emergency situations as this.

The communications officer continued, but slowly, "Centurion's last command transmission was sent to *Hope,* and it was lethal. He evacuated *Hope,* opened every airlock at once. We've contacted *Hope* indirectly over *Hell Fire*'s radio. Major Scott reported analyst Boris Ustinov dead and Commander Pasha Yakovlev recovering in the decompression chamber. We're setting up a communications link to *Hope* as I speak. I can say what has happened—Centurion leaves a trail—but not why it happened. Why Centurion issued these orders is speculation at this point, but I agree with John and Colonel Napper. Software sabotage is the only explanation that makes sense."

"What if one of *Freedom*'s crewmen turned on us or cracked due to the isolation?" asked Colonel Hinson, always ready to advance his career. "Fayhee's been stressed-out over the past few days."

General Craven agreed. Immediately, the noise level in

the room increased. Could there be a traitor or lunatic running *Freedom*? Not likely, but was it possible?

John Sullivan collected his notes, walked to the lectern, and quietly discussed something with the communications officer. The officer agreed, then sat down.

John spoke loudly at first. "Gentlemen, if I could have your attention please. We're getting off track here. We don't have a people problem—it's sabotage. We've got the proof." The overheated room quickly hushed. "We ordered one change from Livermore—well, we didn't get it. We got hundreds. And on top of that, we got a computer virus like no one at Livermore's ever seen."

Craven's blood pressure went sky-high.

"What the hell happened? You told me one program change would do it."

*I've been against your stupid frenzy from the start! And I never told you one program change—but that's history,* thought Sullivan. *No, you're history. This monkey will cost your job, but you don't need to hear that from me.*

"Livermore made hundreds of changes to the software, but those changes aren't the problem. Those changes fixed known problems and they'd all been tested. But there was a downside. Those changes hid the virus. The virus looked just like any other change. All the changes are being traced back to programmers now."

"What about this virus?" barked Craven. "How do we get rid of it?"

"We don't know, General, we can't cure a virus, but we're working to isolate it now. We plan to characterize it first—discover what makes it tick. Once we understand it, we think we can fix it."

"Where'd it come from?"

"We're working that issue, but we don't know where it came from. It's too early in our testing program to know, but we've seen enough to know we've got a big problem." John collected his thoughts then summarized Livermore's situation. "We don't know where it came from and we haven't isolated it. We don't know what this virus will do

The Problem Without Solution

or how it'll behave. We haven't characterized it, but we will."

"We were ninety-nine percent operational," Craven growled bitterly. "Success was in sight." He pounded the table with his fist. As supreme commander, he was washed up. He knew it—everyone in the room knew it.

"What about our boys on *Freedom*?" Mason asked quietly.

"I don't know, but I fear the worst," replied General Krol. "We're wading through Centurion's activity log looking for clues."

A cold chill cut through Mason's body. He'd known Fayhee and liked him. Jay said what he thought.

The staff became restless. Mason concentrated blocking out the distractions around him, struggling to sort out a plan.

"Gentlemen," Mason said softly as he stood, "I propose we characterize the renegade virus as quickly as possible and do what we must to switch armada control to *Hope*. Have I missed something or do you agree?"

Spellbound, in a state of shock and disbelief, the staff remained silent.

"Very well," continued Mason. He looked at Colonel Napper on the video screen. "Sam, work us up a plan to switch armada control ASAP."

"Yes sir, General. We'll have our *Hope* radio link set in an hour or less, then we'll work the switch."

"Good." Mason sounded satisfied. He looked away toward John Sullivan. "Keep Livermore after that renegade program round the clock."

"Will do, Slim!"

Mason looked around the room at the drawn faces and sighed. This meeting had been tough enough, but he dreaded the next one. One word kept cycling through his mind—*Midway*. Admiral Yamamoto lost the imperial fleet during the battle for Midway Island. Mason felt as if they'd lost the imperial fleet and must now tell the emperor.

"Gentlemen, if you'll excuse me, I must call the President."

**The Problem Without Solution**

*The Last Lunch, 12/09/2014, 1922 Zulu, 12:22 P.M. Local*
SHRIPOD ADDAMS' APARTMENT,
COLORADO SPRINGS, COLORADO

Shripod Addams savored the moment. Doing Allah's will, he'd found revenge against the infidel American government for the losses of Desert Storm.

He drove home to his apartment for lunch and began to work on his second job. Sitting down behind his home computer, he banged out his last message to Baghdad:

```
Lawrence horse won by photo finish—
         see press for details.
      Mountain line down.
```

Translated, the Trojan horse computer virus from Lawrence Livermore Lab had taken control of the DEWSAT armada. Watch electronic news for additional details. Expect no further reports from him for an undetermined amount of time—his communication chain was broken.

Satisfied with his terse message, he encrypted it, printed out his hard copy, then completely erased his disk.

He had one final stop to make on his way back to work. He didn't need gas, but he would stop anyway—had to eat.

Suddenly, Addams felt strangely empty, lacking in purpose or cause. His last message seemed anticlimactic, almost meaningless.

The thrill of the game was gone and he missed it.

# 15

From their video conference room, Craven, Sullivan, Krol, and Mason watched an array of TV screens showing pictures from inside the Oval Office. Seated around the Oval Office were the President, his national security advisor, and Craven's boss, the Chairman of the Joint Chiefs of Staff. Mason noticed that Sullivan's complexion appeared ashen, then he remembered his own first meeting with the President. "John," he said quietly, "don't be intimidated by the *big shots*—just say what you think." Then he remembered *Midway* and his stomach turned over. *Should take my own advice!*

"Hello, Headquarters." The President poured himself coffee, sat down behind his desk, and checked his watch—two-thirty Washington time. "Let's get started."

Craven had Mason break the bad news.

"Mr. President, we've lost control of our satellite armada and eleven people are confirmed dead as a result. In addition, one man is seriously injured on *Hope* and we're unable to contact *Freedom*."

Spilling his coffee, the President sat for a moment, stunned in disbelief. "Eleven dead?"

"Yes, and two remain unaccounted for."

After the shock wore off, the President's expression

changed to anger. Bolting from his chair, he turned toward his national security advisor, Clive Towles. "You said ninety-nine percent operational—testing wrapped up by Christmas."

"This problem occurred within the last six hours," Towles explained in a strained voice.

"So what happened?" demanded the President, slamming his fist down on his desk.

"Software sabotage." Mason paused. "A computer virus the likes of which we've never seen." *This should never have happened, we knew better—buckled under pressure, got in a hurry, and blew it.*

"How?"

"This was an inside job, Mr. President—well organized and professional—nothing was left to chance." General Mason summarized the situation in less than five minutes as he watched the President pace the floor.

"I want to make damn sure I've got this story straight," the President said sharply. He stopped pacing for a moment, squinted, and looked directly into the camera. "You're telling me that we detonated a dozen orbiting nuclear warheads and in addition, we've destroyed over two hundred ASATs."

"That is correct, Mr. President." Mason spoke clearly in a quiet voice.

"Is there danger from radiation?"

"No, Mr. President. There is not."

For a brief moment, the President looked relieved, but that quickly transitioned into a form of restrained rage. "So we killed eleven people, interrupted communications around the world, and destroyed every ASAT in orbit because of some damn program bug?" Infuriated, the wild-eyed President blasted Mason with both barrels. "You're telling me you don't know exactly how many people are dead, who's responsible, or how it happened? Senseless death and for what?"

Both ends of the conference call went silent as the ruddy-faced Irish President vented high-powered frustration. Mason thought he might go ballistic, but after a few long minutes, the President backed off and adopted an intellectual guise. The President walked over to the thick glass window and looked out onto the snow-covered lawn. Touching the frost-covered window, he felt the cold radiate through the swollen joints of his fingers. Almost immediately, his hand began aching from arthritis. His senses confirmed he was awake—his nightmare was real.

"Time," the President said after some reflection. "We're going to need some time." Turing toward Clive Towles, he ordered: "Cancel my appointments for the afternoon. Give the reason as a crisis with my cabinet staff—the sudden resignation of a highly placed government official." He smiled, but only slightly. Returning to his seat, he pulled up the low table, propped his feet up, and tried to relax. "For now, limit our discussion to damage control—plans to return the status quo."

Craven's boss, the chairman, spoke first. "Is the armada operational?"

"We've tested it and it seems to work," Mason replied. "But our situation may degenerate because of the virus."

Before the White House could respond, Craven moved directly in front of the video camera and spoke in a low controlled voice. "We believe SDI operational. We've proven High Ground counterstealth technology works. We ran hostile missile threat tests after this infection and the system worked. Our DEWSATs are *brilliant-class* stand-alone weapon systems. They know what to do. Any missiles that threaten the Allies, our DEWSATs'll take out, so there's no cause for panic. And that includes sub launched cruise missiles, Mr. President. As I see it, this virus delays our testing program, but little else. Our testing program will be delayed until we put this problem behind us, but like all technical problems, in time, we will solve it. We're testing now, but from what we've seen so far, the armada reacts like it did before the virus."

"That's true, sir, but only to a point," John Sullivan added cautiously. "Our situation could degenerate anytime. We don't know the DEWSATs *operating rules of engagement.*"

**The Problem Without Solution**

"*Rules?*" The President leaned forward. "John, tell me more."

"DEWSATs track, identify, and destroy targets based on a programmed book of operating rules. They're *brilliant-class* weapons and networked together, they operate as a team. Like people, they talk among themselves and help each other out, but they operate based on programmed rules of combat etiquette. I think this virus may have changed the rule book. If I'd written this virus, I would've changed it."

"How?" asked the President. "Knowing what you know, what would you have done?"

"I'd add AI (Artificial Intelligence)," Sullivan replied confidently. Rule-based systems were his technical passion. "A combination of all the original rules plus AI. That way the armada would appear to operate as it did before, but . . ."

"This discussion is nonsense—pure speculation!" barked Craven, interrupting Sullivan mid-sentence. "The armada works, but our testing is not complete. Simple as that!"

The chairman objected, and loudly. "John's closest to the problem and he's on our side. Let him finish!"

Craven cringed, but reluctantly agreed.

"I'd add AI and let each DEWSAT learn from experience—within limits of course. Target recognition's a good example—learning new threats. I'd allow the DEWSAT to train on new targets and learn to recognize them. Once a DEWSAT learned a new threat, it would teach the others."

"Have you any proof?" asked the President. "Any evidence that the rules have been changed?"

"Every immediate threat to the virus has been eliminated. That's not conclusive proof, but we're suspect."

"General Mason, what do you think?"

"Our situation is more serious than you might imagine, Mr. President. With all due respect to General Craven, we disagree on this issue. John's our technical expert and I think he's right.

"*Hell Fire* is our only alternative—Scott and her crew are the only assets we have in place that can help us. They're isolated on *Hope,* completely cut off, and there is nothing we can do about it. If they moved on *Freedom* today, they'd have no chance of success, but with time and Livermore's help, their chances will improve.

"Look at what's happened. Every threat to the armada has been eliminated. As you know, we cannot penetrate the DEWSAT layer. We can't punch a hole through it—we've proven that. It's a missile shield and it works.

"Assume our space station crews did what they were trained to do. They're resourceful people—handpicked for the job. They would have switched armada control to *Hope* if they could have, but I think this virus tried to kill them. It wiped out *Hope*'s crew—probably *Freedom*'s too."

Mason took a deep breath, let his point sink in, then continued. "If we assume *Freedom*'s crew is dead, then this battlefield grade virus controls both *Freedom* and our armada. It's suicide to send *Hope* reinforcements. We can't break through our armada, and *Freedom* is a fortress—unapproachable. Mr. President, I believe we have a virus running the DEWSAT armada and there may be very little we can do about it. Our alternatives are limited to a precious few."

"Talk alternatives," ordered the President. He didn't like what he'd heard and didn't want to believe it.

"As you said, Mr. President, we need time. Time to characterize and simulate this virus, time to understand how it behaves. Once we understand it, we'll have a better chance of predicting what it'll do when Scott boards *Freedom* and disconnects Centurion."

"How much time?"

John Sullivan fielded this schedule question. "We're doing the best we can, Mr. President. Livermore's working round the clock." John paused, looking to Slim for support. *Say what you think.* "It could take a month. We just don't know. This virus is battlefield grade—like nothing we've ever seen."

The President, the chairman, and Towles shot out of their seats like they'd been wired.

The President's intellectual cover was blown and the ruddy-faced fighting Irishman emerged. "We don't have a bloody month! We've got a crisis on our hands demanding action now!"

"What would we tell the press?" barked the chairman.

"Tell them the truth," insisted Mason. "And release this story from the source—Livermore."

"The truth?" The chairman mumbled caustically. This truthful approach to the press wasn't new, but in this case, it might limit several promising political careers. "There must be a better way."

For the second time, Craven moved directly in front of the video camera. "Mr. President, I propose we make our move now and draw this crisis to a close. As General Mason said earlier, we disagree on this point. I believe we can restore armada control within twenty-four hours. We can turn this situation around using assets we have in place today."

The President returned to his chair, obviously not convinced. *At what risk? How many more would die?*

"Twenty-four hours," the chairman asked skeptically. "How? What's your plan?"

"First, we'll switch armada control to *Hope*. That should return the status quo." Craven's confidence didn't sway the group in the Crow's Nest or Oval Office. "Then we'll isolate and characterize this virus with *Freedom* off-line. Colonel Hinson wants to turn this virus on those who used it on us."

"What are your chances of success?" asked the chairman. "Why didn't *Hope*'s crew switch armada control? Their primary job is backing up *Freedom*. Mason believes they may have died trying."

"No better than one in ten. *Hope* can't take over if *Freedom* won't release control, but if it works, we'll have our armada back. If not, I propose we storm *Freedom*. We have military options. We should use them.

"We'll blast a hole through the DEWSAT layer, move assault troops to *Hope,* then storm *Freedom*. A three-phase operation—break out, regroup, and charge.

"Our opportunity is now! We must take the offensive while we have the chance. This is a job for our military professionals, not engineering technocrats who'll study this problem to death. In my profession, there's absolutely no substitute for command experience. Commanders must take risks to win and those who don't—die."

"I thought the DEWSAT layer could not be penetrated," snapped the President. "You've told us that for years."

"I've always insisted that those who would threaten us cannot penetrate the DEWSAT armada and that's true. It's also true that we would not allow ourselves to be held hostage by our own satellite weapons. We'll concentrate our efforts at the weakest region of the DEWSAT layer and punch through it. Knock out a few DEWSATs and open up the hole we need."

"What's your objection?" the chairman asked, speaking to General Mason. "I agree with Craven. We wouldn't allow ourselves to be boxed into a corner without some way out."

"We don't know what this virus will do or how it'll react. It could turn on us—it leveled Arecibo. Our intelligence about this virus is only beginning to take shape. We need—we must have time."

Craven spoke next. "If our frontal assault on the DEWSAT layer fails, we have a second option—MIT's *Black Hole* project. They've developed an experimental airplane and ASAT that our DEWSATs can't detect."

"That program's experimental—still in the lab," Mason remarked. *High Ground's already obsolete,* he thought. *We stay ahead, but the race never ends. To stay ahead is enough—to prevent war is to win.*

"They have working prototypes," argued Craven. "If all else fails, we can study the virus looking for some weakness."

After an extended period of discussion around the Oval Office, the President asked General Craven, "What do you propose?"

"Storm *Freedom*!" After collecting his thoughts, he offered Mason an olive branch. "In addition, I propose we study the virus as General Mason recommended, but in parallel to our primary military thrust."

**The Problem Without Solution**

"What do you need to make it happen?"

"Time!" Mason interrupted. "Mr. President, we need time! We don't know what we're up against." He spoke softly but with resolve. "Before starting this attack, we must know our adversary!"

"General Mason," the President said tersely, "doing anything is better than doing nothing. You learn as you go and, if necessary, you change directions."

Speaking directly to General Craven, he said: "If your attempt to transfer armada control to *Hope* fails, storm *Freedom*. Keep me informed, and may God help us."

In Washington, the chairman disconnected the video link to Cheyenne Mountain. After his TV screen went blank, the President continued the meeting. "Towles, find out who and what caused this blood mess—your job is to make sure it never happens again. If the system's broken, fix it. If we've got a people problem, I want to know about it!"

*The Barbarian Who Wouldn't Die, 12/10/2014, 2335 Zulu, 2:35 A.M. Local*
SADDAM HUSSEIN'S WINTER HOME,
WEST BANK OVERLOOKING THE TIGRIS RIVER,
SOUTH OF BAGHDAD, IRAQ

Iraqi President Hessian Kamel al-Tikriti knew the drive to his father-in-law's winter retirement home better than the streets around his own neighborhood. He and his wife made this trip often, not so much out of love for the old man, but because Saddam Hussein demanded it. Saddam Hussein al-Tikriti was enshrined as a national Iraqi treasure, and national treasures always received the Iraqi President's attention.

But tonight's *family visit* was different. This visit was President Kamel's idea and would come as a complete surprise to Saddam Hussein. Unannounced, Kamel and his wife were driven through the security gates leading to Saddam's large estate just after 2:30 A.M.

They waited for Saddam in his river room, an enormous brilliant white room with plush fluorescent orange chairs lining three walls. A bulletproof picture window overlooking the river dominated the fourth wall, and the center of the room, covered with spotless white carpet, was completely open, bare of furniture. Kamel's wife stood by the thick glass window, gazing at spotlights glistening off the Tigris River, anxiously waiting to see her father. In her hand, she held a piece of paper—a piece of paper that would not wait till tomorrow.

Kamel allowed himself a smile. He had no affection whatsoever for the old man—it was hard to respect the brutal tribe chieftain, but not so hard to fear him.

Saddam Hussein didn't keep Kamel and his daughter waiting long.

A bodyguard for the Iraqi regime rolled Saddam's wheelchair into the river room and left him next to his daughter by the picture window.

In the dark shadows of the early morning hours, there was no sense of the barbarian in Saddam's expression. His face looked deeply wrinkled, like an old weathered shoe, but his black eyes revealed a caustic hatred still smoldering in his soul.

Saddam's old carcass was failing him, his health wasn't what it once was, but his mind remained sharp and alert. He'd been seriously ill for several years, which had taken a toll on his appearance, but the old man wouldn't die. The Kurds couldn't kill him, the Allies couldn't kill him, and he'd survived two battles with cancer. Only in his seventies, he looked thin and frail, like a man well over ninety. No one had expected he'd live this long.

He rose from the wheelchair, trying to stand erect, then walked toward his daughter with a slow, shuffling gait. Bending forward almost immediately, a little shaky on his feet, the fragile skeleton of a man looked on the face of his daughter and saw a mirror of himself. The corners of his mouth revealed a smile.

"*Ahlan wa sahlan*"—My house is your house.

Saddam eyed Kamel suspiciously as his daughter hugged him. Iraqi President Kamel slid three chairs over to the picture window and they sat down. Kamel thought Saddam

**The Problem Without Solution**

sincere, but he dared not let his guard down—not around this old man.

Kamel nodded to his wife, then she handed her father the paper dated Tuesday, December 9, 2014.

Parkinson's disease forced a slight tremor in Saddam's hands. He had trouble holding it still, but the newspaper type was large and he could read it.

During the minutes which followed, Saddam's daughter saw her father for the barbarian he was.

---

# BATTLEFIELD GRADE COMPUTER
# VIRUS INFECTS STAR WARS

Star Wars, the Allied satellite based missile defense system, lay crippled today as a result of a rogue program which slowed down computers by replicating itself time and time again. Early damage control reports conflict. Cheyenne Mountain has acknowledged loss of satellite weapon control, but believes systems will return to normal within 24 hours. Scientists at the Lawrence Livermore National Laboratory are not as optimistic.

"It may be impossible to isolate this virus in the near future," reported Dr. Tristan Roberts, President of Information Sciences at Livermore, SDI's software R&D headquarters. "We've cut it out of one program only to have it show up in another. From what we've seen so far, this renegade program behaves more like a code cancer than a virus.

"At this early stage, we don't know what we're up against. We learned a lot the last twenty-four hours, but we've got a long way to go. This virus protects itself. When we attempted to remove it from one computer, it moved to another—similar to squeezing a balloon. Squeeze it in one place and it bulges out somewhere else.

"The origin of any virus is difficult, if not impossible, to investigate. It's likely we'll never understand where it came from, but we're sure this infection was no accident."

When questioned as to what he meant by that remark, Roberts declined to elaborate, but did comment that sometimes we create our own problems.

"We've every indication that this was a malicious act," Roberts concluded. "This super virus has infected every major computer system onboard Space Station *Freedom* and, frankly, today we don't have the cure. Fortunately, the SDI armada has built-in redundancy to compensate for these unforeseen problems. Within the next few hours, Cheyenne Mountain plans to transfer control of the armada to Space Station *Hope*."

At first, Saddam held the paper with trembling hands, but then he changed. Carefully studying every word, he drew strength from what he read. A proud fire ignited in the old man's black eyes—defiance blazed like a flame. The shake in his hands lessened as he stood his scrawny carcass upright again, straightening his old weary back. With a sardonic smile, he crumpled the paper in his fist and shook it before the heavens. Looking out into the darkness beyond the Tigris River, he declared, "Now I know why Allah kept me alive all these years. Nobody hurts me unharmed. *Allahu Akbar!*"

# PART 5

# THE DAY OF
# RETRIBUTION

DAY 4—
DECEMBER 10, 2014

# 16

The most dangerous phase of the operation was yet to come. Up to this point, their operation had been planned by fax and picture phone. Toni, a professional craftsman of accidental death, flew to Denver nonstop from Chicago carrying the tools of his trade with him, disguised as skiing equipment. Dressed for a skiing vacation, he arrived in jeans, cowboy boots, and a ski jacket. He picked up his tools at baggage claim, then met his Denver connection waiting by the Avis counter.

Nicknamed Wrangler, Toni's Denver connection was a large physical type who looked like he'd played linebacker for the Chicago Bears. They recognized each other immediately, and together they carried Toni's luggage to Wrangler's car, a white Honda Accord. At 1:50 A.M. early Wednesday morning, they drove to Colorado Springs for a firsthand look at the scene where Toni's next accident would take place.

From Stapleton International Airport, their drive to Cheyenne Mountain down I-25 South took about ninety minutes. While Wrangler drove, Toni did a little extra homework. Using a laptop PC, Toni carefully studied an information package the Iraqi Intelligence Service had hand-delivered to his organization. The package described everything the Iraqis knew about the accident victim, Shripod Addams—his habits, automobile, apartment, hobbies, debts—everything. Toni took special interest in the make of Shripod's car and a map of the Cheyenne Mountain area. The map showed the location of Shripod's apartment and highlighted his daily drive to work. Toni planned for Shripod to die on his drive to work; it was the only way he could deliver a convincing accident on such short notice. Tonight, Toni would come to know Shripod's drive to work like the back of his own hand. He'd feel every bump, every bend in the road, and by the end of the day, with a little luck, he'd drive to Boulder for a long skiing weekend.

"This is it," Wrangler announced, slowing to a stop at a red traffic light by the Loaf 'N' Jug convenience store.

Toni saw a green road sign marking the intersection of Highway 115 and Cheyenne Meadows Road. Leaning his head against the window on the passenger side of the car, Toni stared at the silhouette of Cheyenne Mountain against a clear moonlit sky. Its twin peaks were marked with the red flashing lights of television antenna towers, and about one third of the way up its slopes, bright klieg lights illuminated the entrance to Cheyenne Mountain Air Force Base. Sitting in the pitch-black shadow cast by Cheyenne Mountain, Toni thought the photographs he'd seen didn't do the mountain justice; it was much larger than he'd expected. Brought back to the real world by the traffic light turning green, he said, "Take this left on Cheyenne Meadows Road about two tenths mile, then take the next right on West Meadow Drive. We can't miss it. Mountain View Apartments will be on our left."

Under the orange-yellow glow of streetlights, they circled through the apartment parking lot about three-thirty A.M. and found Shripod Addams' black Honda Accord, tucked away in the space designated for Apartment 21. Wrangler's white Accord was the exact make and model of Shripod's and this coincidence was no accident. Toni was glad to see the Accord parked next to a roadside curb. The curb blocked visibility underneath the car and would provide a useful shield later when he installed Shripod's custom-made appliance. Grabbing his flashlight, Toni pulled himself out of the car and measured the approximate position of Shripod's driver's seat with respect to the steering wheel. He chuckled quietly, noting that the driver's seat was practically in the backseat passenger's lap. After shining the flashlight on his watch, he said, "Let's make the loop."

Wrangler zeroed the distance indicator on his mileage odometer and began tracing Shripod's drive to work. They drove down West Meadow Drive, Cheyenne Meadows Road, and Highway 115 to the Cheyenne Mountain AFB exit. "It feels shorter than I expected," Wrangler said. "I'd figure five miles, maybe thirteen minutes tops."

After making the drive from Shripod Addams' apartment to the Cheyenne Mountain AFB exit four times, Toni'd seen all he needed. "This'll be our last trip," he announced. Around 4:15 A.M., in the darkest part of the morning, Highway 115 was practically deserted, no traffic in sight. As they drove away from Shripod's apartment to Cheyenne Mountain for the last time, Toni explained, "Pull over and let me out when we get to that Colorado Springs city limits sign ahead. I want you to knock down a milepost. I'll show you the one."

The white Accord screeched to a halt on the shoulder of Highway 115. Toni jumped out of the car, ran down the road shoulder about fifty feet, then stood alongside a milepost. The green metal milepost was identical to those used to support stop signs.

Wrangler needed no prodding; he put his car into drive and plowed headlong over the metal post, laying it over and snapping it cleanly in two at the base. Toni walked off the distance from the base of the milepost to a rough seam, or bump, in the four-lane highway. The tar-coated seam extended the width of the highway and allowed the road to expand without buckling during the hot summer months. In need of repair, the raised seam formed a six-inch bump in the road and created a loud *thump-thump* sound every time they drove across it.

"Perfect!" Toni declared. "Open the trunk and we're outta here!" Toni tossed the milepost in the trunk and they were off.

*Doesn't take much to make some people happy.* Wrangler grinned. *These guys outta Chicago run one brick shy of a full load.*

*Voice of an Angel, 12/10/2014, 1309 Zulu*
THE RECOVERY ROOM,
SPACE STATION *HOPE*

*Where am I?* Pasha wondered. His first conscious emotion was fear. Suddenly, every reflex demanded he breathe deeply. He needed fresh air and couldn't get enough of it, like coming out from under an ether-induced sleep. *Buried alive!* Gasping for air, needing desperately to catch his breath, Pasha found no relief. Horrified that he might suffocate, his panic eased when he felt a cool breeze of air blowing across his face.

Strapped tightly to a pallet inside a box about the size of a coffin, Pasha could see only a porthole above his face flooded with white light.

He moved, but only slightly. The struggle to lift his arms against the straps quickly exhausted him. Slowly bending each finger, he felt his hands touching his chest. *Thank God I'm alive!*

Resting for a moment, he heard the muffled sound of his own breathing, the sound of air whistling through his nose as he inhaled. Speaking softly, he heard himself, but his voice sounded muted. His ears felt plugged, like they'd been filled with cotton.

Squinting in a valiant attempt to keep his eyes open, he watched the porthole through narrow slits between his swollen eyelids. His eyelids felt heavy—almost stiff. Drifting away, he watched his porthole to the outside world fade to gray. *Where am I?*

As his eyes closed, he heard the soft muffled voice of

an angel calling. "Come back, Pasha, please don't die. Your children need you. Don't leave us now. Come back. Come back."

Forcing his eyes open again, he saw the surreal outline of an angel's face gazing down on him through the porthole. *Heaven—could this be heaven?* He wanted to touch her, needed desperately to touch her, but his arms and hands were bound tight. He couldn't make out any details of her face, but he loved the sound of her voice.

*This must be a dream,* Pasha told himself, fighting to maintain consciousness. Then he recognized Linda's voice and remembered his last excruciating minutes in *Hope*'s control room before he'd blacked out. He knew this place, though he'd never been inside *Hope*'s rapid decompression chamber.

"Scotty," he muttered, drifting off to sleep again.

After checking the monitors and life-support equipment attached to Pasha, Scott felt optimistic about his chances. She'd been awake nearly eighteen hours, watching Pasha's condition round the clock. His first twenty-four hours in the chamber would be critical. While she and Guardian took care of Pasha, Mac and Gonzo worked on the data link problem with Headquarters.

Scott looked up when Mac walked into the Recovery Room. His bleary, red eyes revealed how he felt. He'd been working straight-out since Pasha's accident. With an exhausted smile, Scott said, "He's all right, heart's strong, vital signs improving."

Looking concerned, Mac gave Pasha a once-over through the porthole, then agreed. "Good. He needs every break he can get. They're sending relief, but I don't know how they're going to get through." Mac shook his head and grimaced. "We're in a tough spot."

"Anything new on *Freedom*? Any contact?" *Any word, any word at all about Jay?*

Mac's sad, sympathetic eyes betrayed his feelings. "I'm sorry, Scotty—not a whisper. They don't know what's happened, but Headquarters . . ." He stopped short. Trying to offer some glimmer of hope, he said, "Kaliningrad's got over two hundred people working through Centurion's log, one line at a time. They'll find something!"

*What if he's injured?* Scott sighed, turning away toward Pasha. Shaped like a coffin, *Hope*'s decompression chamber didn't make her feel any better. *I can't think about it now or I'll go crazy! We've problems enough here!* "What about our comm link?"

"Link to Headquarters is operational, but Centurion won't let go," Mac reported with a grim expression on his face. "Centurion won't give up DEWSAT control without a fight."

"That's not surprising," Scott observed in a weary voice. "What was Headquarters's reaction?"

"They're planning to punch a hole through the DEWSAT armada, then move Marines to *Hope*. They're training 'em here, then storming *Freedom*."

"How many more'll die?" Scott wondered aloud. "Punch a hole? Sounds like political hype. How'll they get past the DEWSATs?"

"Blow 'em out of the sky."

"What's up their sleeve?" She felt like a mushroom, always in the dark, told only what she needed to know.

"The Ground Fire laser—the DEWSAT's granddaddy at Los Alamos. They'll create a diversion over New Mexico using air launched ASATs. When the DEWSAT comes about to shoot, the Ground Fire laser'll take it out."

"If reinforcements do get here—what about *Freedom*? *Freedom*'s a fortress." Scott sounded apprehensive.

Mac raised both eyebrows and shrugged. "I wouldn't wanna be in their shoes."

*Diversion, 12/10/2014, 1400 Zulu, 6:00 A.M. Local*
COCKPIT OF *HAILEY'S COMET,*
SOUTH FACING RUNWAY,
EDWARDS AFB, CALIFORNIA

In the predawn twilight, the clouds of condensation boiling off *Hailey's Comet* looked ghostly, almost surreal. Blue and green runway lights twinkled through the swirling fog while Major Art Hailey waited for takeoff clearance.

"*Comet,* you're clear to roll," announced the tower.

Sitting on top of the XR-30, engulfed by engine noise, Major Hart Hailey yelled, "Roger, tower! We're go for takeoff." He figured their mission was about as straightforward as they could get—a steep climb over friendly skies with an ASAT release on top. He didn't like Headquarters flying his plane during the ASAT release, but he wasn't paid to like his orders, just carry them out.

*Hailey's Comet* was identical to *Hell Fire,* an aerospace plane built around its six scramjet engines.

"Backseat's ready."

"Belly's ready!" barked the recon officer.

"Buckle up boys, and sit tight!" Hailey exclaimed. He throttled each scramjet engine to full military power—the flight computer flashed a green *All Systems Go*. The high-pitched noise of the screaming jet engines approached the point of pain inside the cockpit.

Major Hailey locked the throttles together, then advanced all six engines into afterburner. Bolting down the runway, he depressed an ignition switch at the appropriate time which sparked his rocket engine to life. Jamming his overhead rocket throttle hard forward against the stops caused *Hailey's Comet* to shake violently. Accelerating down the runway, propelled by over 400,000 pounds of thrust, he pulled back on the stick and her nose came up. With his rocket engine wide open, he held the stick back for longer than usual, pointing her nose up in a steep sixty-degree climb, and continued to accelerate in afterburner.

*What a rush!* Hailey thought, raising the landing gear then backing off the rocket throttle. Pressing hard against the seat, breathing was tough even with one hundred percent oxygen.

Belching smoke and flame in her wake, the sight of her long fiery tail accelerating down the endless expanse of runway delighted the ground crews. The earth trembled from the fearsome roar and raised goose bumps on those lucky enough to be there—to feel the power, the wind, the heat and thunder—like watching a space shuttle launch. The thrill of the launch never faded, an awe inspiring experience. When a launch grabs you by the scruff of the neck and shakes the ground you walk on, you take notice.

The last view the tower crew had was of her fiery tail. As the tower trembled beneath them, they were absolutely silent, totally absorbed by the sight and sound of takeoff. Soon, *Hailey's Comet* disappeared through the clouds and only her roaring thunder remained. Life stood still anytime an XR-30 took off—it was an unwritten rule around Edwards.

Turning east toward the dawn, *Hailey's Comet* climbed higher and higher through the clear New Mexico sky, illuminating the black desert sky like a fiery shooting star.

The XR-30 kept going up, passing through 60,000 feet, climbing toward the skies directly over the White Sands Missile Range, due south of the Ground Fire laser at Los Alamos. Hailey checked his fuel, then backed off his afterburners, waiting for word from Headquarters's mission control.

"*Comet,* this is Big Shot. We have you locked on visual. You copy? Over," the mission controller said into his headset.

Transfixed to his instruments, Hailey replied, "Big Shot, this is *Hailey's Comet.*" He paused, working hard to stay within his missile launch envelope. "We're on profile."

"Roger. Commence launch sequence on my mark. Three, two, one—mark!"

"She's all yours," replied Hailey. Reluctantly, he loosened his grip on the control stick. Cheyenne Mountain controlled *Hailey's Comet* via data link for the remainder of the climb and ASAT launch sequence.

Hailey watched all six throttles move forward. Cheyenne Mountain didn't waste any time before punching the burners again and hauling back on the stick. Feeling the rudder pedal and stick controls move on their own was an eerie experience for Hailey. Like most pilots, he never took his thumb off the MANUAL OVERRIDE switch.

Standing on her tail and rocketing into the sky, *Hailey's Comet* performed beautifully. Major Hailey locked his eyes on his instruments as the altimeter spun up with no end in sight. His speed was now in excess of Mach 6 and increasing.

"Scramjet transition complete," Hailey observed. "Tail reads trim."

"Visual confirmation on the tail," echoed the back-seater, looking over his shoulder. After all six engines transitioned to scramjet operation, the cockpit heat shields automatically rolled up.

"DEWSAT's illuminated us in all bands," the back-seater announced after checking his radar detection equipment. "He's seen us. Target's on track, south of us bearing one seven zero degrees. ASAT launch in sixty seconds." The XR-30 was passing through 87,000 feet. Launch altitude was one hundred.

At 1448 hours Zulu, as their speed passed Mach 8, Major Hailey heard: "ASAT's armed. Stand by. Three, two, one . . ."

*BAROOM! BAROOM! BAROOM!*

*Hailey's Comet* shook violently from side to side as she ejected her six missiles, two at a time. Shock waves pounded Major Hailey's brain against his skull and left him feeling dazed, like a punch-drunk boxer.

Immediately, the XR-30's nose dropped as Headquarters began a wide sweeping turn, heading her back toward her California home. After *Hailey's Comet* was clear, six ASAT rocket motors fired simultaneously.

Suddenly, the back-seater began shaking his head, as if trying to clear a garbled circuit. All his life he'd been driven by logic, and his logical mind couldn't accept what his eyes perceived. Did the violent ASAT launch shake some electrical connectors loose? Was there some problem with the radar detection equipment? There must be. After running a series of exhaustive equipment diagnostics, his computer screen read:

**The Day of Retribution**

NO TROUBLE FOUND. ALL SYSTEMS PASSED.

It was like looking in the mirror and seeing the reflection of a stranger. *Must have been something I ate,* the back-seater thought at first, but the blinking radar PRF (Pulse Repetition Frequency) indicator would not disappear. The characteristics of the DEWSAT radar changed after the ASAT launch, but they weren't supposed to. They'd never changed before, always been rock solid—an electrical heartbeat he'd often used to calibrate his equipment. The DEWSAT's radar power increased and the number of radar pulses per second shot sky-high, as if the radar was taking a picture of them. Thinking back, he remembered something about training computers to recognize targets using radar imaging combined with AI. His equipment indicators kept blinking and blinking until finally evidence overcame disbelief, and the realization came crashing down on him like a ton of bricks. He gasped. *Oh my God! There's no place to hide!*

"Break off, Major! Break off!"

Recording it all, Cheyenne Mountain watched on computer-enhanced TV—the DEWSAT, *Hailey's Comet,* and all six ASATs. Pictures were transmitted real-time to Headquarters from a modified Boeing 777 aircraft circling below them at an altitude of 50,000 feet.

Sky Pix, *12/10/2014, 1446 Zulu, 7:46 A.M. Local*
FLYING OBSERVATORY,
SPECIALLY MODIFIED HIGH-ALTITUDE BOEING 777,
IN FLIGHT OVER WHITE SANDS MISSILE RANGE, NEW
    MEXICO

"*Sky Pix,* this is Big Shot. *Hailey's Comet* is approaching from the west."

"Roger, Big Shot. Targets locked on screen." Displayed on the pilot's TV screen were two astonishing, clear computer-enhanced images. Comparable to an Ansel Adams photographic print in texture and detail, these very expensive pictures captured all the detail the eye could see in the existing light and then brightened the result by bathing the objects in computer-simulated full spectrum sunlight. Using the computer to combine simulated light with the *real* images made the objects appear three-dimensional—like they'd pop out of the screen into your lap. The pilot's TV screen was partitioned into eight separate picture windows, or smaller screens. *Hailey's Comet* was centered in one screen, the DEWSAT passing overhead was displayed in another. All the other picture windows on the pilot's TV screen were empty black rectangles.

Two-hundred-nine feet long, looking like a stretched 767 with a bubble on its back, the modified Boeing 777 was a flying observatory designed to take pictures of up to eight moving objects simultaneously. Underneath the bubble inside the aircraft body were eight telescopes, each built around a smaller version of the DEWSAT's adjustable mirror. The mirror was the central light and heat collecting element in each telescope. Each telescope could rapidly search overhead for targets, guided by the aircraft's integrated radar and infrared sensors. Similar in design to the DEWSAT's stealth-proof radar, the aircraft's UWB radar could track multiple targets overhead. This integrated system fed real-time target position data to separate computers which pointed each telescope. High definition, ultra high-speed video signals were collected from each telescope, converted to a digital stream of ones and zeroes, then transmitted to an earth station. The earth station routed the signals over glass fiber into Headquarters's nerve center, the basement underneath Cheyenne Mountain.

The flying observatory required a three-person crew—pilot, copilot, and flight engineer. During the critical portions of the mission, when timing was of the essence, all onboard observation, tracking, and flight systems were operated remotely from Cheyenne Mountain. The flight crew came along for the ride in case something went wrong.

At 1448 hours Zulu, the crew of the flying observatory

watched their TV screens as six ASAT rocket engines ignited simultaneously. Everything they saw on screen, Headquarters saw in real-time, projected on much larger screens.

As Headquarters had expected, only moments after the six ASAT rocket engines sparked to life, the DEWSAT briefly fired its attitude thrusters. Headquarters and the *Sky Pix* crew anxiously watched the DEWSAT come about, pointing its laser toward the ASATs. Once the target alignment burn was completed, its mirror tilted slightly, refining its aim. In less time than it took the pilot to inhale one deep breath, the DEWSAT fired six times reducing each conventional one-hundred-pound ASAT warhead to a fiery white-hot ball of exploding gasses.

The pilot sat spellbound, unable to speak. He'd expected the ASAT kill sequence to be impressive, but had not mentally accounted for the DEWSAT's speed and precision. So much destruction, so little time. As the explosions overhead lit up the sky, he felt fear. He'd heard about the DEWSAT's kill capability, but never witnessed it up close and firsthand. An awesome force, and in the wrong hands the potential for mechanized death was unthinkable. The realization that such force as this constantly orbited overhead sent a cold rigor through his body.

Behind the pilot in the main body of the aircraft, red flashing indicator lights caught the attention of the flight engineer inside the observatory. The skin of the Boeing 777 was heating up and the characteristics of the DEWSAT radar were changing.

Racing forward, lunging through the door into the pilot compartment, he shouted: "We've got trouble!"

*Watching the Southern Horizon, 12/10/2014, 1447 Zulu,*
   *7:47 A.M. Local*
INSIDE THE GROUND FIRE LASER BLOCKHOUSE,
LOS ALAMOS NATIONAL LABORATORY,
LOS ALAMOS, NEW MEXICO

Except for the power lines, there was precious little there—miles of nothing, dust, prairie dogs, a cinder blockhouse, and a radar search antenna pointed expectantly toward the southern horizon. The endless miles of high-voltage power lines that stretched across the wide-open flatland terminated on a power substation inside the blockhouse and fed life into the Ground Fire laser.

The Ground Fire laser occupied most of the cinder block building and was about one hundred feet across. Looking something like a wagon wheel at rest on the floor with its hub pointing skyward, the Ground Fire laser had been designed for precision shooting directly overhead. The hub of the wagon wheel was the mirror assembly and the eight spokes were separate free electron lasers. Delivering a kick equal to about ninety sticks of dynamite at a range of one hundred miles, the hub combined laser power from the spokes and the mirror steered the lethal beam on target.

All eyes in the blockhouse strained to see the laser guidance radar display screen. The screen revealed no target, but the crew wouldn't have to wait much longer. Satellites always showed themselves on schedule. Pointing at the southern horizon, the Ground Fire laser guidance radar antenna stood poised, ready to lock on target, patiently waiting for the DEWSAT to rise.

"DEWSAT look window opens in three minutes," announced the lab director. Delicate optical instruments had problems enough with the rigors of the desert heat and dust, but botching this DEWSAT shot could be a career-limiting experience for the Los Alamos lab director. "Remember, don't shoot until you've got your crosshairs locked on the stem. Disable it, don't blow it out of the sky." The DEWSAT target window would open only twenty-eight seconds because the Ground Fire laser's shooting angle was limited to thirty-five degrees off vertical. Its beam steering mirror was similar to the DEWSATs, but its agility was restricted on the ground because of its weight. Nevertheless, the Ground Fire laser could lock on a DEWSAT moving at five miles per second through an arc across the sky. The director planned to wait for the DEWSAT to rise directly overhead, then take his best shot. Although Washington and Cheyenne Mountain were screaming at him to hurry, the director wasn't about to bungle this shot and watch his career go up in smoke.

# 17

After *Hailey's Comet* released its six ASAT missiles, the
DEWSAT above the White Sands Missile Range characterized the XR-30 as a new and unrecognized threat. Each
DEWSAT had been programmed to recognize and measure
new threats, so it focused its radar and infrared telescope on
*Hailey's Comet,* measuring and recording every detail it
could *see*. The DEWSAT was designed to recognize known
threats, but it didn't have a description of any threat that
looked like *Hailey's Comet,* or for that matter, any other
aircraft.

Passing over White Sands Missile Range, the DEWSAT
transmitted Centurion an encrypted radio signal which
read:

```
Wed Dec 10 14:48:14 Z 2014
To: Centurion, Guardian
Unknown Threat Signature Follows:
Attributes (sample 1)
  Altitude:100,003ft;
  Speed:8.1Mach;
  RateOfDescent:979ft/sec;
  FlightPathAngle:-5.4deg;
  Length:200ft;
```

```
RadarCrossSectionArray:[ . . . ];
InfraredEmissionArray:[ . . . ];
. . .
Attributes(sample 2)
  Altitude:97,981ft;
  Speed:8.21Mach;
  RateOfDescent:1989.7ft/sec;
  FlightPathAngle:-10.9deg;
  Length:200ft;
. . .
Attributes(sample 3)
  Altitude:96,923ft;
  Speed:8.4Mach;
  RateOfDescent:3032.6ft/sec;
  FlightPathAngle:-16.4deg;
  Length:200ft;
. . .
. . .
. . .
Attributes(sample 10)
  Altitude:88,620ft;
  Speed:11.2Mach;
  RateOfDescent:9949.3ft/sec;
  FlightPathAngle:-44.1deg;
  Length:200ft;
. . .
End Of Signature
```

Using a measurement language the DEWSAT understood, this message described *Hailey's Comet* to computers onboard *Freedom* and *Hope*. PAM took Centurion's message since he was asleep. (He would continue sleeping until a *super-user* could board *Freedom* and wake him up.)

*Alpha, 12/10/2014, 1448 Zulu*
SPACE STATION *FREEDOM*

PAM had the ability to learn from the DEWSAT's experience, generalize the DEWSAT's threat description, then train the armada to hunt for this new class of threat.

Once PAM digested the description of *Hailey's Comet,* she altered it, making it more general, then transmitted an encrypted radio signal to her armada.

```
Wed Dec 10 14:48:25 Z 2014
To: ALL DEWSATs
DESIGNATE NEW TARGET CLASS: ALPHA
Alpha Signature Follows:
. . .
. . .
. . .
End Of Signature
```

PAM expanded the threat description to mean: *Anything man-made that flew was an ALPHA class target and considered a potential threat.*

After PAM's radio message was acknowledged, she transmitted a brief second message:

```
Wed Dec 10 14:48:35 Z 2014
To: ALL DEWSATs
track and log all ALPHAs
```

PAM ordered her armada to track the position of every aircraft in flight around the world—a mammoth data processing job, but well within the capabilities of the DEWSAT armada operating as a networked team.

After issuing her *track all alphas* command, PAM waited for acknowledge signals indicating that each DEWSAT understood the order and would carry it out.

*Inferring Scope, 12/10/2014, 1448 Zulu*
SPACE STATION *HOPE*

Pulling double duty, Scott'd been straight out nearly twenty hours monitoring Pasha's condition and standing watch by his control station. The good news—Headquarters comm link was now fully operational. Mac had pointed their Line Of Sight communications antenna toward Kaliningrad who'd patched them through to Cheyenne Mountain. When the bad news came, it came quickly as a flurry of message traffic scrolling across Pasha's control monitor.

Exhausted, Scott and Gonzo looked on in disbelief. Then, almost as suddenly as the messages appeared on screen, Scott's adrenaline pumps kicked in, increasing her pulse, clearing her eyes, and rejuvenating her senses. Within seconds, her frosty edge was back.

"What's this all about?" Gonzo asked, pointing to the message text on screen.

```
To: Centurion, Guardian
Unknown Threat Signature Follows:
Attributes(sample 1)
   Altitude:100,003ft;
   Speed:8.1Mach;
   RateOfDescent:979ft/sec;
   FlightPathAngle:-5.4deg;
   Length:200ft;
   . . .
Attributes(sample 2)
   Altitude:97,981ft;
   Speed:8.21Mach;
   RateOfDescent:1989.7ft/sec;
   FlightPathAngle:-10.9deg;
   Length:200ft;
   . . .
```

Scott focused on screen, boring in on the altitude, speed, and length parameters. Immediately, something looked familiar about this data, a sense of déjà vu washed over her, like she'd seen this data before. After a fast study, she ignored the radar cross section and infrared emission data, understanding full well that only an electromagnetics expert could make quick sense out of it.

Speaking out loud so she could hear herself think, she began deliberately, carefully weighing her information, coloring it with instinct derived from experience. "Gut reaction—what we've got here is a series of snapshots, a flight trajectory of some sort, probably of a missile or a very fast, very high-altitude aircraft. There are no two-hundred-foot-long missiles en route; we know that for a fact, and this one's falling out of the sky, dropping like a rock. So eliminate the possibility of a missile. Both the X-30 and XR-30 are capable of 100,000-foot altitudes with speeds in excess of mach eight, but only the XR-30 is two hundred feet long. Looks like an XR-30, probably *Hailey's Comet.*"

"It's *Hailey's Comet* alright," Gonzo agreed. "But look ahead here. This ALPHA class target description looks generic, it could be almost anything."

```
. . .
DESIGNATE NEW TARGET CLASS: ALPHA
Alpha Signature Follows:
. . .
```

"Let's see," Scott responded, studying the screen. "An example of the ALPHA class can be anything above ground level . . . moving faster than ten knots . . . that's greater than ten feet long. That's a generic description alright. Climb rate not specified. What do you make of that?"

"By convention, not specified means don't care."

"I agree. My read exactly. The ALPHA class doesn't care about climb rate. An ALPHA can climb, dive, or maintain level flight, but it's got to be moving above the ground. Look at this." Scott pointed to the screen. "Radar cross section array is set to minimum, that probably means the minimum signal a DEW can detect; and the infrared emission array is not specified at all. I read that as a don't care, so an ALPHA can have any sort of heat signature at all—it doesn't matter. This ALPHA class must be huge, there must be thousands of . . ." She paused, then spoke in a low clear voice, staring into Gonzo's eyes. "Anything flying that's man-made."

When Scott heard the sound of her own voice saying these words, she began to understand. Suddenly, the realization that something was terribly wrong came crashing down with devastating force. For a few moments, countless unanswered questions raced through her mind, causing her head to spin. Then out of the chaos, she zeroed in on the essential question: Why was Centurion designating new target classes? That was Headquarters's job.

Brought back to reality by the look of stark terror in Gonzo's eyes, Scott knew she had to do something fast. Quickly, unexpectedly, a third message flashed on screen— **track and log all ALPHAS**. When Scott read it, she knew what to do.

"Guardian," she barked, typing frantically. A talking head identical to Centurion materialized on screen. "Transmit this message NOW!"

*Flash Message, 12/10/2014, 1449 Zulu, 7:49 A.M. Local*
Cheyenne Mountain, Colorado

Craven furrowed his brow and slammed his giant fist down on the table. *"Dammit to hell!"* Such outrage from Craven was unusual. No one in the Crow's Nest could recall him getting this worked up over a flash message before.

For moments that seemed to stretch into eternity, Mason and Napper sat paralyzed, rigidly uncomprehending, staring at their consoles unable to breathe or speak. Sitting alongside Craven in the control room, they couldn't believe the message from Scott scrolling across their computer screen:

```
FLASH MESSAGE: Wed Dec 10 14:49:49 Z
   2014
TOP SECRET
SAC EYES ONLY
TO: Supreme Allied Command Headquar-
   ters
FROM: SDI Space Station Hope
SUBJECT: New Target Class Designated
   ALPHA
SYNOPSIS: DEWSAT armada is tracking
   all airborne aircraft around the
   world.
END OF MESSAGE
```

"We've got to work through this problem fast," Mason said in a weary voice. His throat was dry and he had a hard time forming the words. Looking over the bleary-eyed officers filling the control room, he noticed their uniforms were wrinkled and faces unshaven. He sighed, then continued addressing his exhausted staff. "We have an unbelievable situation here, but it's real and deadly serious. We don't know exactly how it happened, but we do know enough to make a good guess. We must think clearly and turn this thing around. Let's take it one step at a time and build on what we know."

Mason projected the message onto the outside wall. He knew this message was a warning, a dreadful premonition of things to come. Scott's message was a call for action, but no one knew what to do. Mason believed they could sort it out if they were given the time, but time was in short supply—everything happened so quickly.

A few people in the room gasped, but no one spoke. The room was deathly silent until a hollow-sounding thud was heard from the middle of the room. General Krol had bitten completely through his pipe stem and it had fallen out of his mouth onto the raised floor.

John Sullivan, Sam Napper, and Mason studied the message, pondering the unthinkable consequences.

Everyone else in the room was shocked beyond belief. Could this be happening? Centurion designating new target classes without Cheyenne Mountain's approval? The consequences of the message were too horrible to acknowledge. If Centurion could designate broad new target classes, he could just as easily order them destroyed. Shock does not capture the essence of the general staff's response; it was more like a massive coronary.

*Put All Alphas on the Kill Stack, 12/10/2014, 1449 Zulu*
SPACE STATION *FREEDOM*

After the position of every airborne aircraft had been tracked and entered into the object database, PAM issued another terse radio transmission in less than one hundredth of a second. Intolerant of threats, her message was lethal.

```
Wed Dec 10 14:49:56 Z 2014
To: ALL DEWSATs
put all known ALPHAs on kill stack
```

With this one command message, PAM orchestrated the largest air disaster in the history of aviation.

*Lord Have Mercy, 12/10/2014, 1449 Zulu, 7:49 A.M. Local*
FLYING OBSERVATORY,
SPECIALLY MODIFIED HIGH-ALTITUDE BOEING 777,
IN FLIGHT OVER WHITE SANDS MISSILE RANGE, NEW MEXICO

Although startled by the flight engineer lunging through the door, the pilot was still slow to respond because of the explosions overhead. Transfixed by the fireballs spreading across his screen, the pilot seemed in a trance, totally absorbed by the sight of the exploding ASATs. As the fireballs gradually disappeared from view, the pilot thought he saw a golden thread of light, like a sunbeam, shining down from the heavens on *Hailey's Comet*. It happened so fast, he couldn't be sure of what he'd seen.

Suddenly, the world outside blazed with a radiant light. The pilot squinted, then noticed *Hailey's Comet* on his TV screen. Racing across the sky, *Hailey's Comet* shined like a brilliant white-hot star, brightening the sky overhead like the midday sun. Then, like a supernova, she spent her explosive energy in one blinding flash of light and heat. The destruction of *Hailey's Comet* was so fast and violent that her crew never understood what happened. Mercifully, the initial explosion rendered them unconscious before their bodies were incinerated to ash. As hydrogen from her ruptured fuel tank superheated, the resulting secondary explosion shattered *Hailey's Comet* into a million shards of graphite fiber, scattering her remains across the desert below, like funeral ashes on an endless sea of sand.

**The Day of Retribution**

Praying, *Lord have mercy on their souls,* the pilot made the sign of the cross.

Suddenly, the pilot felt his skin burning, as if he were on fire. Feeling panic, his stomach balled up into a knot as he broke out in a profuse sweat. He looked at the flight engineer and saw terror in his eyes. *Oh my God!*

Grabbing his throat mike, he screamed, "Mayday!" but never finished his signal.

Immediately, the cabin went dark except for the battery operated gauges. The screaming roar from both jet engines quickly disappeared and the *Sky Pix* aircraft dropped like a lead shot sinker. Hoping to restart his engines, the pilot instinctively pushed forward on the yoke, forcing his wounded aircraft into a steep dive, but he never got the chance.

In the blink of an eye, the DEWSAT laser delivered an explosive force equivalent to twenty sticks of dynamite into the fuel tank buried inside the aircraft's right wing. Instantly, the tank ruptured and the beam ignited fuel erupting from the wing tank. Following the wing tank's explosion, the aircraft collapsed under its own weight, tumbling out of the sky. Separating from its right wing at the engine mounts, engulfed in flame, the Boeing 777 spiraled downward toward the desert floor. Spewing fuel, the ruptured tanks fed the flames until a secondary explosion violently severed the aircraft body from its remaining wing. Within seconds, the flying observatory was reduced to a blackened mass of smoldering remains strewn willy-nilly across the white desert sands.

*Whispered Prayer, 12/10/2014, 1449 Zulu*
SPACE STATION *HOPE*

Only seconds after launching her first flash traffic to Headquarters, another ominous message scrolled across Scott's screen. Its meaning—immediately clear. The message—**put all known ALPHAS on kill stack**—required no discussion and marked the lowest point in Linda Scott's life.

Stunned beyond words, there was nothing she could do and no one could help.

Without conscious thought, Scott's fingers robotically manipulated the keyboard, constructing her second flash message to Headquarters. Once complete, Guardian sent it. Except for the whirr of cooling fans, the control room was absolutely silent.

It was eerie, as if Scott were outside herself, watching her hands type. Her mind slowed, her heart felt numb, she was lost, drifting. Had she died? Was this some terrible nightmare? For a few moments that felt like a lifetime, she wondered if this was really happening. She saw herself typing, but had no sense of touch. It was as if her fingers took over, created the message, then directed Guardian to send it. Days later, she'd have no recollection of sending the message or its contents.

Once her fingers stopped, once her typing was done, she moved to the observation window facing all heaven and earth. There she slumped forward in despair, unaware that both Mac and Gonzo were arduously praying for her, for themselves, and for all humanity. Raising her eyes in agony, with the weight of the world bearing down on her shoulders, Scott whispered a desperate, heartfelt prayer. "God . . . dear Lord in heaven . . . please show me the way. My back's against the wall and I'm out of options . . ." As Scott spoke these words, she felt the loneliness, the hopelessness of having nowhere to turn and broke down sobbing. "Thousands of people are going to die—and for no good reason; they're going to die for no reason at all . . . God. Without Your help, there's nothing else I can do. Give me strength, please show me the way . . . God . . ."

*The Unthinkable, 12/10/2014, 1450 Zulu, 7:50 A.M. Local*
CHEYENNE MOUNTAIN, COLORADO

Mason watched the last few frames of video transmitted from the *Sky Pix* flying observatory before she went off the air—six ASATs and *Hailey's Comet* exploding in a matter of seconds. No one could move. Everyone in the control room stood as if riveted to the floor. Someone began quietly sobbing.

"Would you play it again?" Mason asked in a whisper. That was his polite way of giving an order under stressful conditions. The tension in the Crow's Nest was now palpable—the room deathly still. Mason frowned, scratching his head. "What do you think happened?"

"I would rather not speculate at this point, sir, but I fear the worst," Napper replied solemnly. "I wanna run these pix through our slow-motion lab for analysis. They'll tell us something." Staring over General Mason's shoulder at the computer screen, Napper's drawn face turned a ghostly pale. The only color on his countenance came from the salt-and-pepper stubble on his unshaven face.

Napper tapped his radio headset, then held Mason's broad shoulders firmly to shore them up. "Another message from *Hope,* sir." Mason held his breath and read the second flash message Scott transmitted in the past two minutes. A terror, unlike anything Mason had ever felt, clawed at his guts.

```
FLASH MESSAGE: Wed Dec 10 14:50:26 Z
   2014
TOP SECRET
SAC EYES ONLY
TO: Supreme Allied Command Headquar-
   ters
FROM: SDI Space Station Hope
SUBJECT: ALPHA kill
SYNOPSIS: Armada attacking every air-
   borne aircraft.
END OF MESSAGE
```

"God—help us." Mason's tone was that of a man who'd discovered cancer was ravaging his only child. One thought haunted him, circulating through his mind, relentlessly tormenting his soul. *I am become death, the destroyer of worlds.* Mason's broad shoulders drooped and he shook his head. He felt numb. He didn't have any answers and no plan. Initially, his heart and mind couldn't comprehend the full implications of the message, his self-protection circuits tripped into massive overload.

Everyone in the room was taken aback by the tone of General Mason's delivery. Always under control, if General Mason was shaken, it must be serious. His staff said nothing, but they felt a wave of sympathy for their leader. They wanted to do whatever they could do to turn this situation around and make it right.

For the second time, Mason projected the message on the outside wall for all in the room to read.

Everyone exhaled as if they'd been punched in the stomach, followed by a prolonged silence. Was this a mass nightmare? Stunned, the consequences of this message were too horrible to acknowledge.

Mason ran through everything in his mind, but it was impossible to absorb. *Tired minds make mistakes,* he thought, *but there is no time to rest. Events unfold faster than you can think!* The consequences were too ghastly to contemplate.

No one spoke, and Mason didn't rush. He understood it would take some time to sink in.

Overwhelmed and weary, John Sullivan and Sam Napper shook their heads in disbelief, thinking there must be some mistake. They couldn't accept the unthinkable given in such a large dose as this.

Mason prayed for strength, then mentally rallied after reminding himself that a big part of leadership was guiding people in a direction that they might not want to go. There would be difficult times ahead and they had to pull together. He repeated a phrase that had worked for him in the past: "Let's back up and take this one step at a time. We've got to decide what we think."

# 18

A cold front moved through in the early morning hours, clearing the air around the greater Atlanta metro area. Weather surrounding Atlanta's Hartsfield International Airport was perfect for flying—crisp, cool, unlimited visibility. Air traffic was flowing smoothly—increasing, but not yet peaked for the day.

Hartsfield's air traffic control room reflected air safety's state of the art, the best man and technology could produce to ensure safety for travelers passing through the busiest airport in the world. Inside Hartsfield's darkened control room, radar screens told the story of another working day. The control room was partitioned into three sections: Arrivals, Departures, and Flybys. One group of controllers worked twenty-six approaching aircraft, a second group worked twenty departures over twin runways, and a third group worked seventeen aircraft flying by Hartsfield, possibly bound for any of fourteen airports in the Atlanta area.

Air traffic controllers coordinated aircraft within a three-dimensional cylinder of airspace surrounding Hartsfield. The cylinder had an eighty-mile diameter and extended to 40,000 feet. Every controller had responsibility for a separate sector of airspace. Packed full with wall-to-wall people and radar screens, the control room atmosphere was professional and matter-of-fact. Good people, constant training, well-rehearsed safety procedures, and redundant backup systems kept the traffic flying safely in all types of weather.

Working to keep all their birds in the air, controllers juggled sixty-three aircraft moving through Hartsfield airspace. Each blip on their radar screens displayed the aircraft's position, altitude, direction, speed, carrier, and flight number.

At 9:50 A.M. Atlanta time, an event occurred in the skies over Atlanta that no air controller would have imagined possible. Looking down from the high ground 115 miles above the Atlanta area, an orbiting DEWSAT sorted every ALPHA entry in its database by altitude. The highest flying aircraft were considered the greatest threat. After sorting the ALPHA threat list, the DEWSAT put each aircraft on its kill stack, firing on the highest flying aircraft first. One by one, the sixty-three blips began to disappear. Flyby controllers noticed it first because they worked the highest flying aircraft. The aircraft identification information disappeared first, then the blips quickly lost altitude and disappeared off screen.

In the blink of an eye, the aircraft ID for United flight 209 disappeared from a flyby air controller's radar screen. Rubbing her eyes in disbelief, the flyby controller touched the aircraft's radar blip with a light pencil, thereby requesting an aircraft ID. She'd expected the carrier and flight number to appear on her screen, but there was no response from the aircraft.

She was sure that aircraft's ID had disappeared because she'd contacted it recently. Maybe there was a problem with the aircraft's transponder. Trying to contact United two-zero-niner by radio, she received no reply. As she stared at the radar blip, she noticed it was losing altitude, dropping like a lead brick into the controlled airspace immediately below her sector. Immediately, her guts wrenched. There was real danger of a midair collision. United two-zero-niner did not respond, and it was dropping into a sector filled to near capacity with arriving traffic.

Declaring an emergency, sweat began to bead across her brow. Her senior shift supervisor, a woman built like a fire-plug with a cool head in high-stress situations, quickly vectored traffic around the danger area below United two-zero-niner.

Only seconds later, a second flyby controller declared an emergency in his sector, and the senior shift supervisor studied the bigger airspace picture before making her decision. Single emergencies they could manage safely, the system was designed with margin to compensate for single point failures, but responding to multiple simultaneous emergencies took careful consideration. She looked at her big screen, the one showing all the aircraft and noticed a pattern. One by one, each aircraft's ID transponder failed. Fifteen seconds after the first emergency had been declared, all seventeen aircraft in the flyby sector had lost their transponders and were falling like rocks.

Impossible. There must be a serious problem with the radar or computers covering the flyby sector. Immediately, the supervisor typed a command into her control console switching to their backup system. The radar display screens flashed as the backup system switched in, but the display showed the situation was worse. Seventeen aircraft had disappeared from the flyby sector and fallen into the arrival and departure sectors. Suddenly, arrival and departure controllers began declaring simultaneous emergencies.

Aircraft were falling out of the sky like fiery rain.

The supervisor looked around the control room in horror. All thirty-two controllers were simultaneously declaring emergencies and looking to her for direction. Everyone wanted desperately to do something, to do the right thing, but no one knew what to do. No one could know. This was an air traffic controller's worst nightmare, a pilot's worst nightmare—chaos in the sky over Atlanta.

She picked up the red phone, her direct connection to the tower. Nothing. They had to answer! This was the emergency phone!

The tower crew had their hands full with problems of their own. Within sight of the runway, the open carcass of an arriving Boeing 767 lay burning, nosed into an open field of red Georgia clay. Blocking both departing runways, mercifully sacrificing themselves so that others might not fly, the bodies of two fuel laden passenger aircraft lay ablaze after rotating nose down and wing over immediately following takeoff.

By 9:53 A.M., all air traffic over Hartsfield had cleared, radar screens once cluttered with traffic were empty. Every air traffic emergency had been logically and callously terminated.

*Shoot, 12/10/2014, 1450 Zulu, 7:50 A.M. Local*
INSIDE THE GROUND FIRE LASER BLOCKHOUSE,
LOS ALAMOS NATIONAL LABORATORY,
LOS ALAMOS, NEW MEXICO

"DEWSAT acquisition," announced the Ground Fire radar operator in a dispassionate voice. His radar screen displayed a sunflower-shaped blip rising rapidly over the southern horizon. "Target lock in T minus twenty seconds and counting."

Checking the clock bolted on the curved outside wall of the building, the German lab director observed, "On schedule." The laser blockhouse looked like a short, stocky observatory—a cylindrical building about 120 feet across with a rotating dome roof.

Looking overhead, the director watched the dome simultaneously rotate and open as sections of the roof retracted. A powerful motor rotated a greasy, grit-covered gear which turned the dome roof, creating a grinding noise which reverberated around the building. Once the target had been acquired, the slot in the roof automatically opened and the dome rotated into firing position, aligning the gun port in the roof with the DEWSAT's track across the sky.

Once the dome roof and laser were in position, interest in the blockhouse shifted to the gunner.

Looking through his infrared bore sight, the gunner remarked, "She's not positioned as expected, but we've got a clear shot."

**The Day of Retribution**

"That's good," the lab director said, moving directly behind the gunner. The lab director and three support technicians huddled around the gunner's television monitor. The monitor showed the gunner's bore sight view, a greenish infrared image with crosshairs centered squarely on the DEWSAT's long stem.

The gunner threw a switch on his control console, then watched his countdown timer. "Overhead shot in T minus ten seconds. Locked on target—auto firing sequence enabled."

Suddenly, the DEWSAT fired her attitude positioning thrusters, pointing her stem and mirror toward the blockhouse.

"Target's coming about, sir! We've lost our shot!" the gunner exclaimed. The stem was now hidden behind the DEWSAT's thirty-three-foot mirror. Feeling panic and looking through his bore sight, the gunner centered his crosshairs on the only part of the target he could see—the mirror.

"We're illuminated in all bands!" screamed the radar operator, his voice breaking from the strain. "Target knows our position!" The DEWSAT had triangulated on the Los Alamos radar signal and used it as a beacon.

The lab director didn't need to hear this twice. "Override automatic firing sequence—shoot!"

"But . . ."

"Shoot, man, shoot!"

"Target's deploying countermeasures—we're losing track!"

"Saturate the area. Blow it out of the sky!" There were no other viable alternatives.

The gunner lifted the safety cover and slammed his fist down on the rapid-fire mode control switch. As the RAPID FIRE ENABLED indicator flashed in his face, the gunner grabbed his twin pistol grips and squeezed both triggers like a vice. It happened so quickly, there was no time to be scared.

Squeezing off tens of shots per second, the gunner sat mesmerized by flashing indicator lights as green tracer lines rapidly covered his TV screen. For a few seconds, the DEWSAT drifted across the screen into a solid waterfall of green tracer lines. Then as suddenly as it began, it was finished—one shot shattering her mirror, another rupturing her fuel tank. Racing across the sky, the orbiting fireball which resulted was visible from the ground.

*Evacuate, 12/10/2014, 1451 Zulu, 7:51 A.M. Local*
CHEYENNE MOUNTAIN, COLORADO

"We don't have time to think; we just react!" Napper grimaced as another message from Scott appeared on his screen.

```
FLASH MESSAGE: Wed Dec 10 14:51:35 Z
  2014
TOP SECRET
SAC EYES ONLY
TO: Supreme Allied Command Headquar-
  ters
FROM: SDI Space Station Hope
SUBJECT: Evacuate the blockhouse imme-
  diately!
END OF MESSAGE
```

Sullivan, Napper, and Mason studied the message and guessed what had happened. For the first time, they recognized some pattern to this destruction.

Sullivan spoke first. "That DEWSAT must've triangulated on the Los Alamos radar and transmitted its position to Centurion."

Napper nodded agreement and completed the assessment. "And Centurion ordered it destroyed."

"Our armada doesn't tolerate threats," Mason observed with a grimace. Exhausted, Napper and Sullivan nodded. Lack of sleep was taking its toll on everyone, tired minds make mistakes. "How long do they have?"

Sullivan checked the wall clock, then looked at the blue ball. Another DEWSAT was approaching Los Alamos from the south. "Maybe four minutes. The DEWSAT'll wait until it's over Los Alamos before . . ."

Napper ran to a computer terminal and clicked on an icon labeled GROUND FIRE. His computer connected him directly to the lab director's radio phone inside the Los Alamos blockhouse. When the lab director answered, Napper identified himself immediately then ordered: "Kill the radar! Clear the area! Evacuate the building now!"

The lab director was caught totally off guard. Puzzled, but not overly alarmed, he inquired: "Evacuate? Just exactly where do you propose we go?"

"Get away from that building fast! Take a car, truck, anything that'll move your people outta there! You've only got three minutes."

"Three minutes? What's the freaking rush? We can't leave this sensitive optical equipment behind. I'll need to clear this with my superiors." The lab director could tell that Napper was upset, but Headquarters had jerked his chain, time and time again, for the last two days—too much hurry up and wait.

Napper stood silent for a moment, collecting his thoughts as he watched the DEWSAT approaching Los Alamos from the south. His brain ran in six directions at once. There was no time for common sense, no time for discussion. Overwhelmed, he had no sense of even temperament, every feeling was extreme, and he felt as if he were about to explode.

"Listen up and listen good!" he barked. "Get out now or die!"

*The Golden Thread, 12/10/2014, 1454 Zulu, 7:54 A.M. Local*
GROUND FIRE LASER BLOCKHOUSE
LOS ALAMOS NATIONAL LABORATORY,
LOS ALAMOS, NEW MEXICO

The lab director stared at the phone for a moment, then jammed it back into its holster.

Pointing to the open slot in the domed roof, the lab director yelled to one of the technicians, "We got a life-and-death emergency on our hands. Button down the hatch and kill the power! Move like your life depended on it; meet me outside by the bus."

Not wasting any time, the director keyed his mike and spoke directly to the radar operator over the intercom. "We've got an emergency! Shut your radar off and move out to the bus—right now! We're getting the hell outta here!" Finally, the director surveyed the blockhouse. He needed to move thirty people out of the building into the bus and he needed it done quickly. Fire safety is a concern at any government installation and Los Alamos was no exception. Fire drills were not the exception but the rule, performed routinely once a week. First, he turned on the PA system, keyed the mike, and ordered everyone to evacuate immediately. Second, he pulled the fire alarm and triggered the sprinkler system. *Sprinklers should encourage them to move along,* he thought.

Two technicians escorted the gunner outside onto the blue Air Force bus. Rounding up his laser support staff outside the blockhouse, the director herded them on the bus like a New Mexico cowboy; no explanation, just move. There was complaining. Most of the staff felt like cattle, but the loading moved along without panic and as quickly as possible.

After counting heads, the director slammed the bus door shut and signaled the driver to roll. The driver put his foot to the floor, popped the clutch, and the bus rolled away in a cloud of exhaust smoke and dust.

The staff members wondered what all the fuss was about as they sped away across the flat expanse of desert sand. Looking back at the blockhouse, someone blinked in disbelief and asked: "What do you think that was?"

They were about one mile away from the blockhouse when a thin golden thread of light, like a narrow ray of sun, burst forth from the blue heavens. It looked something like a meteor's fiery track, but it was perfectly straight and lasted only a second or so. At first, no one was sure of what they had seen, but after some discussion they found nearly everyone on the bus had seen something. It looked as if the

Ground Fire laser was in operation, but the blockhouse was empty and the dome had been buttoned shut.

Passing overhead, a DEWSAT executed a thermal scan using a broad invisible laser beam, scorching the area surrounding the blockhouse to better define its target position. The DEWSAT illuminated the Ground Fire radar antenna with its laser, then detected the heat, using it as a beacon. After locking on target, it destroyed the radar antenna using a golden thread of light which burned its way through the atmosphere.

*Changing of the Guard, 12/10/2014, 1530 Zulu, 8:30 A.M. Local*
CHEYENNE MOUNTAIN, COLORADO

The Crow's Nest video conference room was packed with the general's staff—most looked like hollow-eyed zombies. Even though Mason and Craven were briefing the President, they'd been too exhausted to fully prepare. Their viewgraphs were hand-drawn sketches, not the computer-generated glitzy color visuals the President and his Cabinet had come to expect. Ordinarily, hand-drawn visuals presented in a Cabinet meeting would mark the end of even the most promising military career.

Craven lamented that officer promotions during peacetime had been reduced to a dog and pony show—no substance, just style and glitz. He laid his viewgraphs side by side on the white sheets of his Army cot inside the Crow's Nest. He'd always organized his briefings this way, reviewing his story end to end, laid out over his sheets. Exhausted and bleary-eyed, he concluded that hand-drawn viewgraphs were appropriate for his presentation. His story'd been told—as supreme allied commander, he was finished.

In Washington, a dozen video cameras provided pictures to Cheyenne Mountain from inside the Cabinet meeting room. As usual, the Cheyenne Mountain general staff attended the President's emergency meeting by video link. Mason watched a somber group of *big shots* crowding into the Cabinet room. The secretary of Transportation arrived first with the heads of the Federal Aviation Administration and Central Flow Control. Part of the FAA, Central Flow Control monitored all commercial air traffic across the United States. The secretaries of Defense and State arrived next, followed by the CIA and FBI directors, the White House chief of staff, and Clive Towles, the President's national security advisor. NORAD and NATO attachés filed in behind Clive Towles, and finally, additional staff from Central Flow Control entered the room and stood along the outside wall.

Mason looked over the drawn faces in the crowded room and sighed. *A meeting of the big guns,* he thought. *Central Flow Control must certainly have something to say. Judging from their numbers, it looks like it's their meeting.*

To Mason's surprise, no one spoke, no one said anything at all. Everyone avoided eye contact and felt uncomfortable making chitchat. Finally, the door opened and everyone stood as the President walked in. He found his place at the table, studied the faces on his video monitors, then sat down.

Clearly impatient, the President spoke directly to the head of the FAA. "Let's get on with it." His voice was a mixture of anger and anxiety.

The tension in the air was charged, nerves were frayed before the meeting began.

"Mr. President," the head of the FAA began, "I would like Dr. Mulcahy to give you a summary of our air traffic situation. He works in Central Flow Control and knows more about our air traffic situation than anyone else in Washington. After that, we'll do our best to answer any questions."

The President said nothing, but noted that Mulcahy was an Irishman, someone he could trust. His name, reddish hair, and ruddy skin complexion broadcasted his origin. Mulcahy was known as one who told the truth and didn't waste words—an endangered species around D.C.

Without delay, Dr. Mulcahy moved to the lectern. He flipped a switch on the lectern, causing the lights to dim. Pointing a handheld remote at the TV/VCR mounted on the wall, he pushed PLAY. The forty-inch TV screen showed a map of the continental United States, crisscrossed with thousands of white lines, each white line representing an aircraft in flight. The lower corner of the picture was tagged with a time stamp reading 09:50:00 A.M. Pressing the VCR PAUSE, he took a sip of water, then began.

"Gentlemen, today between 9:50 and 9:55 A.M. Washington time, a catastrophe of unparalleled proportions paralyzed air traffic across the United States and around the world. This air disaster is unprecedented—over fifty thousand people are confirmed dead."

Everyone in the room gasped. Few attending knew the full scope and magnitude of the disaster. Dr. Mulcahy reverently made the sign of the cross and all those seated around the Cabinet room followed suit.

The President's jaw dropped. His face looked like a monument of silent agony. How do you comprehend the senseless death of over fifty thousand innocent people?

Dr. Mulcahy pressed the VCR PLAY button, then continued. "The video you see was recorded by Central Flow Control earlier this morning and has not been edited. Three-thousand-six-hundred-forty-eight commercial passenger aircraft were lost over the United States alone." Everyone in the room stared at the TV screen as the white traces began disappearing. Dr. Mulcahy watched silently and he didn't rush. He'd seen this videotape twenty times, and still couldn't believe it. In less than five minutes, every airborne aircraft over the United States had flown into the ground. He knew it would take some time for the full impact of his story to sink in.

Mulcahy studied the deadpan faces of his motionless audience—the Cabinet room reminded him of a morgue. Misty-eyed, Mulcahy had obviously been moved by the videotape, but he waited patiently for feedback, some sign of acceptance from the group. After the map of the United States was clear of white aircraft traces, the TV picture shifted to a scene of downed aircraft burning on the runways of Hartsfield International Airport. Charred, blackened aircraft wreckage graphically brought the problem home, placing it in everyone's backyard.

**The Day of Retribution**

"It's by the grace of God that I'm alive," Clive Towles said. "I was supposed to've been on the nine-thirty nonstop to L.A., but Continental canceled the flight after I boarded the plane."

Mulcahy raised his eyebrows and nodded agreement. Satisfied his message was getting traction, he blinked his eyes clear and continued. "Although the exact figure will never be known, approximately 4,800 commercial aircraft were lost worldwide—over fifty thousand people have been confirmed dead and this total is conservative—it could be short by twenty thousand. Mr. President, this is nothing short of a catastrophe. At this moment, nothing's flying."

Stunned, not knowing what to say or do, the President was silent for a few moments, still absorbing the full scope of the disaster. Always the spin doctor, the President struggled to put a positive spin on this bad situation. There must be something good he could say about it, but nothing came to mind—he drew a blank. Even the grand master of spin doctors couldn't make this situation sound acceptable to the American people. This was a catastrophe and he couldn't hide it. He'd have to face this problem head-on until he could come up with a better alternative. "Survivors? What's being done to help?"

"We're doing all that can be done, moving medical staff and supplies where they're needed most, but ground and sea transportation takes time," the secretary of Transportation replied.

The President's concern turned to anger as he eyed the Secretary of Defense in the subdued light. His eyes looked wild, like those of a mad dog. He wasn't going to take the rap alone. In a stone cold voice he said, "Gentlemen, I assume you're going to tell me what went wrong and how to correct this situation."

General Craven spoke next over video link from Cheyenne Mountain. "Mr. President, General Mason will explain what happened and outline our alternatives. He's closest to the problem and the solution."

For the next thirty minutes, Mason related the sequence of events that led them here. Exhausted, Mason's presentation wasn't crisp, but it was clear and cut to the central core of the problem—technical problems take time and understanding to resolve. As Mason proceeded, he watched the President's eyes grow wilder. Finally, when he looked as if he was about to pounce on his prey, the President bolted out of his chair. His voice exploded over the videophone speakers. "Unbelievable! Fifty thousand people dead and for what? This damn catastrophe was man-made. It should never have happened. We're held hostage by our own machines." There was no sorrow in his voice, only rage.

"Reality often proves stranger than fiction," Clive Towles observed somberly. Clive stood and chatted quietly with the President.

After a brief exchange, the President regained his composure and plopped back down in his chair, demanding, "Alternatives—talk alternatives. We've got to turn this situation around, but fast."

Mason spoke gently but firmly. "Sir, I'd like to discuss two alternatives, but they both will take time."

"How much time?" barked the President.

"Weeks. There's no quick cure and we don't have any secret weapons. Both these alternatives come with high risks, but we can improve our chances by understanding what we're up against."

General Craven interjected, "That's correct, Mr. President. If we'd taken the time to better understand this problem in the first place, this disaster might not have happened."

Perplexed, the President scratched his head and looked directly at Craven. "But that's your job, so why didn't you? Why didn't you take the time to do it right?"

"I wanted this virus situation resolved quickly." Craven's tone conveyed profound regret. And so did you. If you'll recall, Mr. President—you insisted."

Mason saw fire returning to the President's eyes, but the old Craven was back. He was speaking like the courageous leader and visionary Mason had always admired, the one he used to know.

"However," Craven continued slowly, "the final responsibility was mine and mine alone. Somewhere along the way, I lost sight of one fundamental truth. We cannot change nature. It takes nine months to have a healthy baby and, like it or not, we can't speed it up. We learned this same lesson from the space shuttle *Challenger* disaster. The laws of physics always prevail above our political will." Craven paused somberly in retrospect. "Politics drove some of my technical decisions, not good physics, and over fifty thousand people are dead as a result.

"I wanted a simple cure to a complex problem," Craven lamented in a whisper. "To understand this virus will take weeks, perhaps months. We can solve this problem, but we absolutely cannot fix it fast—you can't have it both ways. More money won't help, more people won't help, you're gonna have to wait. The solution to this problem requires clear thinking, resourcefulness, and courage. Political hype won't deliver the goods."

The President shook his head angrily. After several seconds of silence, his eyes glowed like smoldering embers and he spoke with venom dripping from his voice. "General. This disaster should never have happened! Furthermore, I want this situation turned around fast and I want it done right! And by God—I'm going to get it." The President was emphatic.

Craven took the heat head-on. "Mr. President, I assume full responsibility for this unprecedented loss of life. I estimated the chances for disaster were acceptably low based on my best available information. I took a gamble, the odds were stacked against me, and I was wrong. We will give you our very best effort, but you will not see this air traffic situation resolved quickly. I don't expect you to like it, sir, but I'm telling you the truth. You may have my resignation at any time you wish, but I would like to resolve this matter."

"General Craven," seethed the wild-eyed chief executive, "it will be necessary for you to resign."

"Hold everything," interrupted Clive Towles, slamming his hand down on the table to get the President's attention. "The consequences of this software sabotage have been unbelievable! Fifty thousand dead! No one would have imagined this destruction in their wildest dreams. Replacing General Craven doesn't solve anything and second-guessing his decisions will only make matters worse."

The President replied bluntly. "Frankly, Clive, I don't have any choice in the matter. I'll be lucky if the American people only impeach me. Fifty thousand people cry out from their graves for justice and heads must roll. You know it as well as I do—there's no other way. General Craven must stay on as an advisor until this matter is resolved, but as supreme allied commander, his job is done."

The President's facial muscles twitched as he turned toward the picture of General Craven on screen. "General, you are relieved of your command. This has nothing to do with justice, it's political survival."

The President paused, took a long drink of water, then spoke to Craven again. "I understand you recommended General Mason as your replacement. Does your recommendation still stand?"

"Absolutely, Mr. President. He'll do what he believes is right and get the job done."

Satisfied, the President took a moment to collect his thoughts, then reflected, "We really put all our eggs in one basket with this SDI system, didn't we?"

"I shortcut my own safeguards, Mr. President," Craven said slowly with deep remorse. "I took a chance, gambled, and lost. If we'd used our standard testing procedures, we wouldn't be in this trouble today."

Somewhat rhetorically, the President asked, "Let me make sure I got this straight. Over fifty thousand innocent people died because they were in the wrong place at the wrong time. And there's no air traffic anywhere because of some software glitch—nothing can fly without being blown out of the sky. And you're telling me that we have only two alternatives that might—and I repeat might—pull our asses out of the fire. One's an unproven lab prototype and the other's an XR-30 crew onboard *Hope*."

"Your synopsis is accurate, Mr. President," Mason replied without reservation. "In my opinion Major Linda

Scott and her crew are our only viable alternative. We have only one prototype aircraft in the *Black Hole* program and it's got a long way to go."

"General Mason, what would it mean if both our alternatives fail?"

That answer was easy. "Global economic catastrophe. In all probability, some countries will take advantage of our dilemma."

"General Mason, you are hereby appointed supreme commander of all Allied Forces. Exhaust every alternative. Resolve this matter with God's speed and tell us how we can help. Above all else, do it right!"

# 19

"Firestorm in Atlanta," announced the CNN newscaster. "Live report coming up at the top of the hour."

*Atlanta burning?* To the President of the United States, these words felt like a steel sword plunging deep into his chest, causing his knees to buckle. He sank into his chair, where he sat breathless for several moments, trying to make some sense of it all. Gradually, the color returned to his face and he turned once again to watch CNN Headline News.

The President sat spellbound behind his desk in the Oval Office, hypnotized by the news reports of aviation catastrophe flashing across his TV screen. As airline casualties from around the world continued to accumulate, the scene shifted to a live report from the top of Overlook Mountain in the northwest corner of Atlanta. A slow, sweeping panoramic camera shot of the Atlanta skyline showed boiling black columns of thick heavy smoke engulfing the city. Scattered across the city, inky black smoke plumes erupted from blazing aircraft wreckage, turning the sky a dingy shade of grayish brown. The TV pictures from Atlanta looked like the black-and-white newsreel footage taken in Europe during World War II—no color, just shades of black, white, and brownish gray. The President gazed on this horrific scene in disbelief.

During the day, there were about a dozen Secret Service agents on duty in this part of the presidential mansion, but professional as they were, their eyes were focused on CNN Headline News. For that matter, in all fairness to the agents, the eyes of the entire world, from Baghdad to Washington, were fixed on CNN. In addition to the Secret Service agents collected in the Oval Office, Clive Towles, the President's national security advisor, and Dr. Mulcahy from Central Flow Control silently watched the news by the President's side.

The President's chief of staff and his glitzy White House press secretary lumbered slowly into the Oval Office reading the statement they'd prepared for the press.

"I don't know what to do," said the President with a sense of dismay. Shaken by the graphic news reports of the Atlanta firestorm, the President walked over to the mirror and looked somberly at his reflection. "Mulcahy, are you sure this is the way we should handle this?"

"Yes, Mr. President. Lay your cards on the table. If you don't level with the press, you'll only make an impossible situation worse. If you come before the people with your head in your hands, they can't very well lop it off. Remember, the . . ."

"Do you take me for a fool?" interrupted the White House press secretary as his blood pressure shot through the roof. "First of all, nobody would believe the truth, and second, we don't have all the facts yet. I have trouble believing it myself, and our story may change. Besides, they'll ask some tough, finger-pointing questions and expect answers we don't have. We don't know who sabotaged the SDI software or how it happened. Do you seriously believe that the President of the United States should stand before the world and admit that we don't have a clue?" The press secretary raised both eyebrows and cut a glance across the room, making direct eye contact with the President. "Should the President publicly acknowledge that we're held hostage by our own technology? I don't think so! Who'd believe that a software glitch, some computer virus, could account for all this chaos, and who do we blame?"

No one in the Oval Office spoke.

"Hell—we don't know," the press secretary scoffed. "But we know whoever screwed us chews Juicy Fruit gum. Yeah—right. I tell you, Mr. President, we've been caught with our pants down and we'll look like incompetent fools if we let this story out. General Mason believes their solution to this problem could be weeks away. John Sullivan doesn't think they'll ever find who's behind the virus. What if they're right? I say we stall until we can generate a cover story that'll cover our, err—years of government service. Say we've had a serious sabotage problem with the SDI system and we're working the situation, united as Allies. All the details are wrapped up in national security. Just read your prepared statement." The press secretary handed the President the statement and concluded, "Stall, Mr. President. Stall."

The President didn't know what to think, but in the final analysis, this problem was his to face alone. He had to respect the man in the mirror after he woke up from this nightmare. He'd always relied on others for advice and then used his own judgment. After some somber thought, he turned to his national security advisor. "What do you think, Clive?"

Clive Towles and the President had worked through some lean times before in the business world, but none so grave or life threatening as these. Clive respected the press secretary for his skill at maneuvering the press, leading them where he wanted them to go—however, on this occasion he believed the press secretary was wrong. "Considering the global magnitude and scope of this problem, I don't believe the people will accept anything less than the absolute and complete truth—as you know it. If you stall, you'll get caught. This story's too big to imagine otherwise. Our back's against the wall, Mr. President. Your integrity is the only thing you've got; it's all that matters. If you piss away the people's trust, you'll never get it back."

**The Day of Retribution**

"No compromise?" the President asked cautiously.

"No compromise, Mr. President. Nothing less than the absolute truth will do. People aren't mushrooms. Don't shovel shit on 'em expecting to keep 'em in the dark."

The President nervously bit his lip as his stomach began to knot. He'd gotten Clive's message, but felt that giving advice was easy, taking advice was the hard part. The President sighed, then looked at his press secretary. "Okay, let's get on with it. How long till show time?"

"Twenty minutes, Mr. President."

The President sighed, again. "I'd like some time alone," he lamented. The Oval Office quickly emptied, leaving the President alone and staring at the portrait of Dwight David Eisenhower hanging on the wall.

*Altar to Allah, 12/10/2014, 1920 Zulu, 12:20 P.M. Local*
RETURN DRIVE FROM SHRIPOD ADDAMS'
APARTMENT TO CHEYENNE MOUNTAIN,
COLORADO SPRINGS, COLORADO

Wrangler rented a small U-Haul van, the same size vehicle used by Federal Express for small business deliveries. He drove to the Mountain View apartments, arriving just before noon, then parked next to Shripod Addams' empty parking space. Following in the car, Toni loaded his ski bag in the rear of the U-Haul once they reached Shripod's apartment.

Inside his ski bag, Toni carried the device which would cause Shripod's accident, the milepost assembly. Earlier, Toni'd completed the finishing touches on the assembly; now he needed only to install it underneath Shripod's Honda.

The assembly was deceptively simple, consisting of three parts—a four-foot length of metal post, a short six-inch section of transparent nylon fishing line, and a small electronics module about the size of a bar of soap. One end of the post was torn and sharp, the other blunt. Near the sharp end, Toni looped the nylon line through a slot in the milepost. Using epoxy, he planned to attach the line to the bottom of Shripod's car. On the blunt end of the milepost, Toni attached his breakaway electronics package. Wrapped in clear cellophane, Toni's electronics included a six-Volt battery, a tiny radio receiver, and a custom-built electromagnet. Built of a pressed powder ferrite material, the electromagnet would crumble to dust when run over by a car. Toni could control the electromagnet from ten miles away using a transmitter he'd mounted inside Wrangler's car. All was in readiness awaiting Shripod's arrival.

During lunch, Shripod Addams drove the five-mile journey home to his apartment as he did every working day. It offered him an escape during the day which he looked forward to most of all. After driving into the parking lot, he maneuvered his car into its regular space, parking between the curb and a small U-Haul van. As Shripod rushed around the corner of the building into his apartment, he thought only of lunch and feeding his fish. He knew something had gone wrong in the Crow's Nest this morning, but he didn't know any details.

Once Shripod entered his apartment, Toni quickly slid his milepost assembly out of the U-Haul van and onto the dust-covered asphalt underneath Shripod's Honda. As planned, the U-Haul van blocked Shripod's view of the car from his apartment in case he decided to look, which he didn't. The most critical part of Toni's operation was the installation, but he was confident. A master craftsman, his hands were steady and he knew exactly what to do. He'd practiced the installation a dozen times already this morning underneath Wrangler's Accord. Working with all the skill and precision of a trained surgeon, Toni slid his shoulder alongside and underneath the driver's side of Shripod's Accord. He'd refined the installation procedure to an efficient sequence of simple steps with no wasted motion. The complete installation required only five minutes. By now, Toni didn't need to see what his hands were doing, he could operate by feel and know when the installation was done right.

Lying on his back sandwiched between the body of Shripod's Accord and the U-Haul van, Toni went to work.

**The Day of Retribution**

The body of the Accord was so low to the ground that he couldn't slide underneath, but he'd anticipated this. Toni built Shripod's milepost assembly with wide tolerances so that it would work even with a sloppy installation. Feeling underneath the driver's seat, Toni found four bolts holding down the seat rails and used them as a position reference. The spot Toni was looking for, the sweet spot, was centered underneath and slightly in front of the driver's seat. He positioned the sharp end of the milepost on the ground directly below the sweet spot, then aligned the post front-to-back. Next, he lifted the blunt end of the milepost off the ground and, using the electromagnet, he attached it underneath the front of the car, next to the engine. At this stage, the forward blunt end of the post was attached to the metal frame of the car but the sharp rear end of the post remained on the ground. Only one installation step remained and the job was done. Toni coated the ends of the nylon line with epoxy, then positioned the sharp end of the post against the sweet spot. *Should put it between his legs,* Toni thought with a sardonic smile. After holding the line against the underbody of the car about two minutes, the epoxy set and the installation was complete.

The nylon line would function like a hinge, holding the sharp end of the post in place against the car body when the blunt, front end of the post dropped onto the road.

After less than four minutes' installation time, Toni dusted off his clothes, walked to Wrangler's car, and drove down the street to the Loaf 'N' Jug. A few minutes later, Wrangler drove the U-Haul van to the Loaf 'N' Jug and joined him for lunch. Together, from a window booth inside the dining area, they watched Cheyenne Meadows Road and the Mountain View Apartments, waiting for Shripod Addams' return to work.

Shripod pulled out of his parking space about ten minutes till one. Toni walked outside to Wrangler's car, cranked it, and entered the left turn lane immediately in front of Addams. After traveling a little less than one mile on Highway 115, Toni drove past the LEAVING COLORADO

SPRINGS city limits sign with Shripod Addams following six car lengths behind him.

Driving in the shadow of Cheyenne Mountain, Toni pressed the only button on his radio transmitter as he passed the city limits sign. It wasn't marked, but he knew what to expect.

Shripod Addams was traveling about sixty miles an hour when the electromagnet let loose and the front, blunt end of the milepost dropped down, striking the asphalt hard with an ear-piercing scraping sound. The violent impact of the milepost slamming against the asphalt disintegrated the electronic module into tiny fragments and scattered them over the highway. Immediately, Shripod lifted his foot off the gas, but never made it to the brake. Before Shripod could slow his car, he felt the floorboard vibrate followed by the ear-piercing sound of metal shredding beneath his feet. He never knew what hit him. The instant he drove over the raised seam in the road, the sharp end of the post violently erupted through the floorboard as the forward end of the post lodged in the bump. Acting as a lance, the milepost thrust its way upwards through the hole in the floor, slicing a gaping tear through the car seat, rocketing up between Shripod's legs, impaling him through the rib cage and exiting his neck below the ear. In a fraction of a second, the motion of the car caused the milepost to pivot forward about the hole in the floorboard, hurling Shripod's body upwards off the seat into the ceiling, breaking his neck, and pinning his limp body against the steering wheel. He was dead before his car rolled to a stop in the dirty snow on the shoulder of Highway 115.

*Meet the Press, 12/10/2014, 1930 Zulu, 2:30 P.M. Local*
THE WHITE HOUSE SITUATION ROOM,
WASHINGTON, D.C.

Everyone stood when the President entered the White House Situation Room followed by Clive Towles, Dr. Mulcahy, and his personal bodyguards. Even in the dim light, the President's face revealed that dark rings had formed under his eyes.

Only minutes before this meeting was scheduled to begin with the press, the Secret Service had moved the meeting location and shifted the reporters into a dimly lit, blast-proof room deep inside the White House basement. This last minute change was an attempt by the Secret Service to limit any physical threat to the President during his press conference. This weary herd of reporters had been corralled into the stuffy, gloomy room, then packed shoulder-to-shoulder, like cattle in a stockyard awaiting slaughter.

After stepping behind his *pulpit*, as he liked to call it, the President deliberately ignored the TV cameras and silently examined the collection of anxious faces in the audience. *Some people here may have lost family,* he thought. The President looked down at his press release, sighed, then looked up again directly into the eyes of his audience. He was silent for a protracted period, still spellbound by the graphic news reports of this horrible, high-tech catastrophe. "Ladies and gentlemen of the press," he said slowly in a quiet voice. "Before I begin, there's something I've got to know." The President's throat was parched. He took a sip of water from a glass on the podium, then continued. "How many of you knew someone who died this morning?"

Nearly everyone in the room raised their hand. Their response seemed to knock the wind out of the President for a few moments and his face turned ashen. The mood in the cramped, damp basement room beneath the White House could best be described as morose.

The President found it easier to count those who did not raise their hands. Twenty-eight out of the thirty-two reporters present knew someone who had died. Glassy-eyed, the President asked, "How many of you lost someone in your family?"

Two women and four men raised their hands. Over-whelmed, the President couldn't control the tears streaming down his face and his knees began to weaken. His shoulders slumped forward as he slowly sat down on a small metal chair by the podium. Holding his head in his hands, the President recalled Clive Towles' advice: *Integrity is all you've got—it's the only thing that matters*. He would not, he could not lie to the immediate families of those who'd suffered loss. He guessed the older reporters might have lost children, but dared not ask for fear he would break down.

The President held his head upright. "I'll tell you everything we know about what's happened, but understand that we've got a long way to go before we put this nightmare behind us."

For the next hour, a dumbfounded White House press secretary, as well as the entire world, remained silent, thunderstruck, as the elected leader of the United States explained why their airplanes could no longer fly. As best he could, he explained how the world was being held hostage by their own Star Wars technology orbiting overhead, 115 miles above the earth. Flashbacks of the Atlanta firestorm constantly entered the President's thoughts; he couldn't forget those pictures of Atlanta burning. At the end of his monologue, he concluded with a tone of dismay. "I'm not going to lie to you. Our back's against the wall and our Allied Forces know it. We had a man-made catastrophe today and we'd better learn from it. Today, we've got more questions than answers, but in time, we'll turn this situation around because we must. We don't know who sabotaged our SDI software, but if they left any trail along the way, we'll track them down. We don't know what to do to restore the status quo, but believe me, we're exhausting every alternative we've got. Right now, we're spending all our time trying to outsmart our own machines, but we won't rest until we get this situation under control." Pausing for several moments, the President looked around the room once again and studied the faces of his audience. The room was absolutely silent except for the quiet, muffled sounds of sobbing. Most reporters sat glassy-eyed and slack-jawed, aghast by the story they'd heard. Some faces in the audience reminded the President of lost sheep, others displayed rage frustrated by having no one to blame, but most re-

vealed an overwhelming sense of profound sadness.
Wearily, the President asked, "Are there any questions?"

No one spoke. No one could speak, but most hoped and
prayed that this was some terrible dream. Surely we'll wake
up soon; we must wake up—this can't really be happening.

And so the course was set, their journey too frightening
to contemplate. The President didn't know what to think,
but in the final analysis, he'd faced this problem head-on.
He'd delivered nothing less than the absolute and complete
truth, without compromise. When your back's against the
wall, integrity is all that matters.

*Lucky Strikes Out, 12/10/2014, 1945 Zulu, 11:45 A.M. Local*
GATE 2 SECURITY GUARD SHACK,
LAWRENCE LIVERMORE NATIONAL LABORATORY,
LIVERMORE, CALIFORNIA

Mamood Abdul moved swiftly, silently, through San Fran-
cisco on his divine mission from Allah. He was a Muslim
extremist, pure and simple, who believed that killing Americans, especially those living in the big city, was God's
will. Methodical, patient, and dangerous, his view of Americans was developed during his ten-year period as a cab driver in the Newark/New York City area. He'd learned
through experience that life on big city streets was cheap,
and devoutly believed that people living in the city had
traded their souls, their humanity, to the devil for the
almighty dollar. As a result, they were no different from
rats or vermin and he felt the world was better off without
them.

Dressed as a truck driver, Mamood's appearance was un-
remarkable. His most distinguishing features were his
bushy black hair and beard. Reared by the Iraqi state with
no family influences, Mamood had never known his father
or mother. His religious and spiritual needs had been filled
by the Muslims when he was young and impressionable.
Educated only through the fifth grade, anything he lacked
in formal training, he made up for with perseverance—the
man would not take no for an answer and he wouldn't quit.

Mamood was perceptive and patient; he learned by observation, always waiting for the right opportunity.

Mamood drove his rental car west down Interstate 580 to Livermore, California. Once at Livermore, he drove to the Livermore Laboratory to scope out the area firsthand. Livermore Laboratory was a sprawling collection of office, warehouse, and laboratory buildings spread across a square mile area, much like a college campus. Operated jointly by the University of California, the Department of Energy, and the Strategic Defense Initiative Organization, Livermore's bread and butter was Star Wars software. Livermore had programmed the SDI satellite armada, and had software maintenance and test responsibility as well.

Compared to the large main laboratory buildings, Mamood found Guard Shack 2 tiny, a small brick building positioned a few hundred feet from the main complex. Anyone who walked in or out of the Livermore Lab complex from the north side parking lot was funneled past Merchant Lucky in Guard Shack 2. With clear glass on all four sides, visibility into the guard shack posed a problem of timing for Mamood, but he could work around it. He noticed the many trees around the guard shack limited visibility from the laboratory complex. After watching the guard shack from the parking lot for about half an hour, he also noticed that no one paid any attention to the security guard as they left the complex. Employees displayed their ID badges for the security guard's approval when they entered the complex, but when departing, they bolted out of the building like wild horses racing to their automobiles, focusing only on their rat race home. Mamood decided that he must enter Guard Shack 2 during a shift change when Merchant Lucky was alone.

Mamood recognized Merchant Lucky from his photograph, sitting alone behind his computer terminal. He knew the first shift left Livermore at 3:15 and that's all he needed to know. His controller had taken care of nearly all the details and Mamood need only execute.

Using American Express to solve all his travel problems, Mamood's controller ran his assassination company out of

Newark like a small business. His controller provided a travel and information package which included, in code, everything that Mamood would require for an efficient operation. Travel plans, tickets, car and van rentals, cash advances, lethal gasses, weapons, poisons—all sorts, and an information package containing everything available on Merchant Lucky, including photographs and maps of the Livermore area.

He rented a small EZ haul truck, then drove around the lab, circling the complex until a rush of outbound traffic announced the first shift exodus. Mamood drove cautiously against the flow of traffic into the parking lot outside Guard Shack 2.

Merchant Lucky noticed an EZ haul truck pulling into the mammoth north parking lot and concluded the driver must be lost. They didn't take any deliveries through Gate 2 and most drivers knew that.

Mamood parked his truck in the area designated for visitor parking, just outside Guard Shack 2, in plain view of Lucky. Lucky watched Mamood cautiously approach the guard shack, looking lost and somewhat bewildered, walking against the onslaught of employees in full gallop toward the north parking lot. He knocked on the glass door to the guard shack, pointing to his map, asking for directions. Lucky signaled for him to enter, but remained seated. Mamood clutched a map in one hand and a rolled up newspaper in the other. Inside the newspaper, he carried a silent device developed by the Russian KGB—a compact lethal gas gun loaded with ricin. With an average lethal dose of only 1/5,000 gram, ricin was the untreatable toxin used in the Georgi Markoff umbrella murder. Once inhaled, the gas quickly produced all the symptoms of a heart attack, and was difficult, if not impossible, to detect in the bloodstream; a well-established method for inducing accidental death, used most often on older adults.

Mamood smiled as he entered Guard Shack 2; Merchant Lucky was alone. He quickly scanned the interior of the room for cameras. There were security TV monitors, but none monitoring the inside of the guard shack. Mamood's heart pounded in his chest as he asked Lucky for directions to shipping and receiving. Spreading Mamood's map across his desk, Lucky studied it for a moment to orient himself. When Lucky looked up to give the burly truck driver directions, he found himself staring into the open end of a rolled newspaper. Startled, Lucky gasped his last breath. Seeing his surprise, Mamood blessed Allah's name and squeezed the trigger, releasing the invisible lethal gas in Lucky's face.

*Oil, 12/10/2014, 2030 Zulu, 11:30 P.M. Local*
EMERGENCY CABINET MEETING,
UNDERGROUND BUNKER,
BAGHDAD, IRAQ

Secretary-general al-Mashhadi (Mother) was perched like a restless hawk behind the lectern, surveying the faces of the Cabinet members as they watched the American President on CNN. Towering over the lectern at the head of the conference table, he looked gargantuan, shaped like the front end of a bus, with sandpapery skin and two dark reddish-black eyes that seemed to boast the Iraqi credo—*Nobody hurts me unharmed.* Behind his flint hard eyes beat the heart of a barbarian, and tonight he had the disposition of a rattlesnake. He was trying to cope with a kaleidoscope of feelings, from bewilderment to rage to exhilaration, all intertwined with overpowering fatigue. His complexion looked Indian, but under the dim light inside the blast-proof bunker, it was hard to tell. Whatever he was, there was a frightening presence about him.

He surveyed each Cabinet member for some moments, then found a kindred spirit, Colonel Nassar—the officer who created PAM—sitting at the far end of the table in the back of the room. He gazed at Colonel Nassar; he seemed so small and frail. *All this destruction caused by such a little man,* he thought.

After the American President disappeared from the TV screen, al-Mashhadi pointed the remote control toward the TV and turned it off.

**The Day of Retribution**

No one in the room moved. No one, not even Colonel Nassar, could mentally accept what they were viewing. Iraqi President Kamel, Colonel Nassar, and the entire Iraqi Cabinet sat thunderstruck by the global chaos, by the fearsome power of Allah.

After silently brooding over their situation several minutes, al-Mashhadi decided to set his Islamic religious practices aside. He poured himself a drink, topping off his shot glass with gin—draining the bottle dry. "To PAM," he murmured softly, raising his drink in toast. "*Allahu Akbar.*" Gulping it down, he felt invincible, like he would live forever. Mother struggled to sort out his feelings. He felt the exhilaration that comes from revenge combined with an acute anxiety over the American President's speech. In his soul, he'd always believed that Allah was greater than his enemies, but never imagined Allah would punish his own. Earlier today, approximately two hundred Iraqis had died in military and commercial aircraft crashes.

Slowly, the Cabinet members lifted their glasses to PAM, but said nothing.

There was more than a moment of silence before al-Mashhadi continued. "As we drink, the balance of power is shifting beneath our feet like desert sands. The world is grounded by their orbiting armada and the American President admits they are powerless against it. *Inshallah* (God willing), our time has come. Kuwaiti oil fields are ours for the taking."

Sweat beaded across Colonel Nassar's balding forehead as he breathed a silent sigh of relief. Until now, the Iraqi expert on PAM had feared for his life because he'd never projected, or even imagined, such arbitrary destruction and loss of life as this. PAM had crippled the Allied war machine as he'd expected, and more—much, much more.

Colonel Nassar contemplated their situation along with the chiefs of the Iraqi Air Force, Army, and Navy. A multitude of issues raced through the colonel's mind. Would the Americans link PAM to Iraq? Possible, but not likely. Would the Iraqis have enough time to mobilize an invasion force and attack Kuwait before the Allies eliminated PAM? He couldn't say. There were simply too many variables.

The diminutive little colonel stood and spoke first in a voice that was barely audible. "We have two significant problems." The entire Cabinet leaned forward in their seats, straining to hear the wiry little man speak. "However, our risks can be managed. First, the Allies will not rest until they find the saboteurs; therefore we must cover our tracks. Second, we're not ready for an invasion of Kuwait. Our Army must prepare and this will take time. The Allies could eliminate PAM and restore their orbiting armada before we occupy Kuwait."

Iraqi President Kamel had lived much of his life in America, and he knew Colonel Nassar spoke the truth. Through an alcoholic haze, Iraqi President Hessian Kamel al-Tikriti opened another bottle and filled his glass. This was the only way he knew to hide his doubt concerning his decision to deploy PAM, and clearly there was no turning back now. "So this disastrous catastrophe comes down to a problem of covering our tracks." President Kamel gazed around the room in disgust at his slovenly, drunken, party of God. "No battles, no glorious victories for Allah, only the rancid stench of death." All the military chiefs were present, most huddled around the conference table under a thick cloud of cigar smoke, reveling in the catastrophe they'd brought on the infidels. Looking through the smoke, the President saw the fire of revenge still blazing in their eyes.

Calmly blessing Allah's name, the sad-eyed chief of military intelligence replied, "Our revenge is complete, Excellency. The *Maronites* (enemies of Allah) have suffered grievous losses. Our losses were significant, but small by comparison."

"And what of our agents?" the Iraqi President seethed. "What if they're discovered? Have you any idea what that would mean?"

"*Inshallah,*" the chief of military intelligence responded cautiously, "they are already dead."

President Kamel gulped down his drink, then spoke in a

caustic voice. "No trail." The icy stare he gave the chief of military intelligence conveyed the sincerity behind this order. The intelligence chief acknowledged with a grimace.

*"Allahu Akbar,"* al-Mashhadi mumbled after he guzzled down another drink and sat down directly across from Colonel Nassar. He wondered if any of the encrypted e-mail messages he'd sent Lucky could be traced. He didn't think so, but he decided to have the crypto sergeant look into it. Much of his adult life, al-Mashhadi had lived for this day, had lived to revenge the Gulf War. Now, with his revenge complete, his thirst was insatiable. He wanted more.

"Colonel, how long do we have before the infidels eliminate PAM?" al-Mashhadi asked as he studied the clear liquid contents in his glass.

"A few days at least, maybe months. We do not know. No one knows, but Allah has delivered us. Our time has come." Colonel Nassar was smart and shared one thing in common with al-Mashhadi. Under his deceptively delicate facade beat a barbarian's heart. Although quiet, soft-spoken, and physically small, hard work had made him wiry and tough.

The face of Iraqi President Kamel was acutely downcast—one could even call it mournful. He buried his face in his hands and murmured, "There you have it—chaos for oil." The Iraqi President had never felt so impotent, and he could feel the acid burning in his stomach from the frustration. This sequence of events was out of his control. Any protest he might raise would be perceived as weakness and fall on deaf ears.

"No matter how great the preparation," al-Mashhadi said slowly. "Nothing ever seems to work out the way it's planned." Al-Mashhadi leaned forward on his sledgehammer fists, pushed himself up from his chair, and announced, "Allah is with us. There's no turning back now."

Still thunderstruck by the global chaos, their tongues still, the Iraqi President and Cabinet ministers offered no resistance.

Al-Mashhadi sat down and drummed his massive fingers

on the table. After a few moments thought, he spoke to the overweight army chief. "How long before we invade Kuwait?"

The portly general cleared his throat and tried not to stammer. "As you know, our war plans assume we have air superiority. We planned that the Kuwaiti ground forces would be softened up by our airpower before we began our mechanized ground assault. We won't enjoy air superiority, but neither will Kuwait, and we'll have the benefit of surprise. We'll revise our attack plan to deliver a fast-moving, mechanized thrust that'll drive the Kuwaiti Army into the Gulf."

"I asked how long before we invade?" Al-Mashhadi was determined. The gaze from his glassy black eyes penetrated the smoke-filled room.

"The duration of the war must be short, one week or less. Speed and preparation are our linchpins. In the past, we've planned one massive, overwhelming strike. Knock 'em off balance, then drive them into the sea before they can react. Assuming our missiles and aircraft are useless, 150,000 men, one thousand tanks . . ." The general paused, furrowed his brow, then decided to dig in and stand his ground. He turned to the Iraqi President in protest. "Excellency, this is nonsense! I must study our revised plans before I commit to an attack date. Rapid occupation without airpower—this requires a significant change in our war plans, a major shift in strategy and thrust. I'll deliver you our revised plans tomorrow, but I expect we'll require at least twelve weeks to prepare."

Suddenly, like a great ocean swell, al-Mashhadi's gigantic hulk rose up and grabbed the corpulent army general by the braided lapels on his uniform, then slammed him hard against the concrete wall. In an acidic, menacing voice, he muttered, "There is no alternative. No discussion. Occupy Kuwait city by Christmas."

The heavyset general gazed upward into al-Mashhadi's thick-lidded eyes. Al-Mashhadi tightened his grip on the lapels and brought the general's fleshy face to within an inch of his own. The Iraqi army general smelled the stench of al-Mashhadi's breath and considered going for the small graphite revolver he kept concealed in his pocket. The general decided against it. There would be another time and a better place. Perhaps a sniper's bullet inside Kuwait city, yes, that could be easily arranged.

"Kuwait city—Christmas day," the army general seethed quietly. His voice was restrained, but sounded loathsome.

Al-Mashhadi released the general, who glared at him with a mixture of contempt, rage, and fear. As in any meeting of the Iraqi Cabinet, fear won out, so he straightened his coat, turned, and walked out the bunker door.

*Regroup, 12/10/2014, 2130 Zulu, 2:30 P.M. Local*
CHEYENNE MOUNTAIN, COLORADO

Bleary-eyed and alone in the Crow's Nest video conference room, Mason read a brief report concerning the accidental death of Shripod Addams. He was in a daze, still shaken by the mind-boggling events of the day, all the staggering losses. Mason had ordered his staff to get some sleep then organize into shifts. As he reread the message, Craven walked quietly into the room.

"Shripod Addams is dead," Mason sighed as he passed the message to Craven.

"I heard," Craven said somberly. "Damn grisly way to die. Sounded like a fluke accident, but you never know."

Struggling to keep his eyes open, Mason rubbed his temples. "We don't have much to go on, just that gum, but we're going over his apartment with a fine-toothed comb."

There was silence while they tried to make some sense of it, but it was impossible. The shock of the disaster had numbed their minds. Nothing seemed to make sense anymore.

Craven placed both his large hands on Mason's shoulders as if to say, *I understand.* Two years Mason's senior, Craven had precious few peers. Some in the military had feared him, many had envied him, many more had wanted his job, but not Mason. Craven thought Mason's leadership inspirational. Mason made you feel good about yourself, about others, about life. Above all, he couldn't be bought. He was a man of principle and integrity. He stood up for what he believed in, he had courage, and Craven respected him for it. He had admired Mason's independence for thirty years, and now wanted to give him something in return. Craven removed the five-star shoulder boards from his uniform. "These meant the world to me and I want you to have them." Craven, who was very powerful, was sometimes surprisingly gentle. "I know they'll be in good hands."

Mason accepted Craven's shoulder boards without an exchange of words. There was no need to speak. Mason loved the man; his eyes said it all.

"What about Scott?" Craven asked, lowering himself into the seat. "When do you plan to tell them?"

With a blank stare, Mason gazed through the glass walls of the Crow's Nest. "Tomorrow, after they get some sleep; but we're not going anywhere until we're ready. They won't get but one chance and to die trying is to fail. Livermore and Yuri's folks in Kaliningrad are working round the clock. They offer our greatest hope. *Freedom*'s armor must have some Achilles' heel, some weakness we can exploit. Before we make our next move, Livermore must characterize this virus, no matter what it takes. We've got to have a plan for boarding *Freedom* that will work; we've got to find some weakness."

"*Hope*'s the perfect place to train for an assault on *Freedom*," Craven said with a sense of purpose. "Scott and her crew can train by attacking *Hope*. We'll work out the bugs, refine it until we get it right."

Placing his head in his hands, Mason wearily nodded agreement. "But we've such a long way to go." Mason seemed almost asleep. Craven realized Mason had developed a capacity to live with crisis by taking short naps, much in the same way Winston Churchill did during World War II. If he allowed each crisis to take its toll, he would have died long ago of anxiety. Now, his eyes half closed, his face relaxed, Mason looked closer to his real age. No one ever makes the complete adjustment to constant tension. Responsibility had laid circles under Mason's eyes, etched lines around his mouth, given his powerful, elegant hands the slightest tremor.

"Do what you can, Slim, then don't worry about it. Worrying'll kill you. Believe in yourself and trust in your staff. They're good people, they're behind you, and they'll pull through. After a little rest, you'll see things more clearly. This problem is man-made, it can be solved, and your team can do it." Craven paused a moment, and shifted the subject to a smaller, more immediate problem. "You thought about Hinson?"

Mason felt like unloading on Hinson, but he knew this wasn't the time. He would sleep on his decision and wait until tomorrow, when his head was clear. "Hinson has no place in his heart for anyone but Hinson," Mason replied with a matter-of-fact tone of voice. "I want him out of the service. Yuri suggested an officer exchange program assignment counting penguins on the tundra of the New Siberian Islands. His idea has merit, but I plan to give Hinson a choice. Either join the civilian community or count penguins."

"It's your operation," Craven said, never second-guessing Mason's judgment. Craven was silent for a few moments as he studied Mason's face. Mason's temples were raw, and the circles under his eyes had darkened. "You look like death warmed over, Slim. How about some sack time?"

Mason eyed the empty cots in the corner of the conference room then checked his watch. General Krol or Colonel Napper could run the store while Mason slept, but they were both out like a light. "Krol and Napper are asleep," Mason lamented quietly.

Craven smiled. "I'll wake you if anything hot comes down." His voice conveyed concern.

Mason didn't need to hear it twice.

PART

# 6

# THE DAY
# OF RECKONING

## DAY 5—
## DECEMBER 11, 2014

# 20

Intensely bright white flashes from an arc welder illuminated the hangar's interior like an enormous strobe light.
Thomas Jackson, the radar expert from MIT Lincoln Lab,
watched from a safe distance as the welder guided his torch
down the tapered, pyramid-shaped wall of the anechoic test
chamber, generating a spectacular fireworks display of
sparks along the way. Dangling perilously from a cable,
suspended eighty feet above the concrete hangar floor, the
welder was nervous about laying his final bead. Jackson,
speaking from the safety of the catwalk overhead, reminded
him they were six months behind schedule and insisted he
cut out the bellyaching and get the job done. Angry, but unconvinced, the technician attacked the final seam with a
vengeance.

When the electric torch went out, Jackson breathed a
sigh of relief as the two men pulled off their goggles. This
latest modification to the test chamber had increased its diameter to eighty feet, allowing it to encase a full-size aircraft. Working with a ball-peen hammer, the welder
cleaned away the crusty debris from his final bead while
Jackson climbed down from the catwalk. Scaffolding fas-

tened to the catwalk extended floor to ceiling and surrounded the colossal test chamber. After slowly lowering
his overweight carcass onto the scaffolding, Jackson carefully inspected the welds framing the chamber walls. A
pompous man with long oily hair, scraggly red beard, and
puffy bags under his eyes, Jackson's abrasive personality
failed to inspire confidence, but those who knew him freely
admitted—the guy was smart. Satisfied with the welds,
Jackson cautiously maneuvered into the walled security of
the penthouse. Perched on top of the test chamber one hundred feet above the hangar floor, the one-room penthouse
was filled with radar test equipment, arranged about a large
viewing porthole in the center of the floor. The penthouse
office would be called a laboratory by anyone who did not
regularly work in one. To Jackson it seemed more a cluttered test bed, a place to verify his theories, an assessment
that was wholly accurate. The room was perhaps five hundred square feet total, and Jackson felt cramped as he
worked his way toward the center of the room, squeezing
between countless metal racks, each stacked high with test
equipment.

Jackson eventually worked his way through the equipment maze to the aircraft position control panel located by
the porthole. Looking down through the porthole into the
test chamber, Jackson saw only pitch-black at first. He
threw a power switch and floodlights illuminated a large
black form, seventy feet across, shaped like the *Dorito* flying wing. Initially, the aircraft was positioned in a straight
and level attitude, but using a combination of valves on the
control panel, Jackson could rotate the aircraft into any position he required. He opened a hydraulic valve, then
watched the aircraft below slowly rotate skyward. Gradually, his aspect angle began to change as the aircraft pivoted into a near vertical climb. Eventually, when Jackson
viewed the flying wing head-on, the wedge shape changed
into that of the edge of a Frisbee. Satisfied with the positioning arm's performance, he believed the aircraft prototype and chamber were ready at last. Getting the
positioning arm fitted to the aircraft had taken more time

than he'd expected. Too late, Jackson discovered that the positioning arm had to be custom machined and that took time. But now it was ready and he felt relieved.

To the naked eye, the aircraft inside the test chamber looked like Cowboy's *Dorito* down to its air inlets and jet exhaust. Designated the *Black Hole* prototype, its exterior looked like a McDonnell Douglas EF-12 flying wing in every respect—but it wasn't.

**The Day of Reckoning**

# 21

After sifting through the contents of every trash can and cabinet inside Shripod Addams' apartment, FBI special agent Clint Bridges was frustrated. The sleeves of his white shirt were filthy, there was stubble on his chin, and his neatly cropped snow-white hair was plastered down with sweat and lint picked up from behind the clothes dryer. After thirty years with the bureau, most of it in white-collar computer crime and counterespionage, the G-man knew where to look when it came to searching for physical evidence. After a tedious examination of Shripod's apartment, the G-man, local police, and captain of security from Cheyenne Mountain determined that Shripod Addams had been interested in computers, maintained a magnificent saltwater aquarium, paid his bills on time, and chewed Juicy Fruit gum. Not much to show for a long night's work, but they felt the gum could be significant.

To Clint Bridges' dismay, it looked as if Shripod Addams had been a fastidious housekeeper; everything was in its place. The inside of the apartment struck him as picture-perfect, unlike any bachelor's home he'd ever seen. The interior looked almost as if it'd never been lived in, like a photo from a *House and Garden* magazine article, too neat to be true. Shripod's clothes were cleaned and pressed, bed neatly made with the blanket corners tightly tucked, lunch dishes put away, and his computer desk had been meticulously organized, as if he'd been expecting company. The only signs of life in the apartment were swimming inside Shripod's aquarium, a large saltwater tank filled with a splendid variety of brightly colored fish. Although everything seemed in order, Bridges was troubled because nothing was ever this neat in real life unless it was staged.

Rivulets of sweat beaded across Clint's forehead as he and the lanky Air Force captain of security carefully pried the cover off Shripod's home computer. After checking the computer for self-destruct explosives and auto-erase hardware, Clint decided it was safe to power Shripod's PC on. "I'm afraid someone got here before we did," Clint observed quietly as the computer screen flashed to life.

"Whataya mean?" Scratching the stubble on his angular chin, the gaunt-faced captain looked puzzled. They'd found no evidence of unlawful entry. Nothing damaged, no unusual fingerprints, nothing that would indicate any unauthorized search.

"This place, it's all too . . . tidy. An airtight package with no loose ends." Clint opened a desk drawer, pulled out a case containing 3.5-inch floppy disks, then handed it to the captain.

Casually, the captain opened the case, thumbed through the disks, then remarked, "Yeah, so? Blank disks, what of it?"

"That's just it," quipped Clint. "They're all blank. No backups, no extra copies, nothing."

As the realization of the G-man's observations sank in, the captain's expression turned hard. "So either Shripod never used his computer or we're onto something."

Clint nodded. "Check the door locks and windows again. See if one of 'em hasn't been jimmied."

The tall lanky captain stood, walked out of the computer room, then spoke quietly to the local police sergeant in charge of the accident investigation. After a few moments, the sergeant acknowledged agreement, walked outside to his cruiser, and brought back a portable light and a bag of tools. The sergeant and a colleague roped off a clear area around the front doorjamb, set up their high intensity light shining on the door latch plate, then carefully began looking for any evidence that the door might have been forced open—fresh scratches on the metal plate or traces of plastic from a credit card.

Finally, the lanky captain returned to the computer room only to find Clint Bridges shaking his head in disbelief.

"This is incredible," Clint said after reading over the computer screen. The screen displayed Shripod's command history file—a terse, summarized record of every computer command Shripod had entered over the last month. "Absolutely incredible!" Clint scrolled through a few more pages, then continued. "I'll tell you one thing. Shripod Addams was no computer hacker. This guy was a real pro, a *guru.* He used every trick in the book. Take a look at this." Clint pointed to a line on the computer screen which read:

```
12/09/2014, 12:29 P.M.
rm -rf /usr/myfiles
```

"Don't follow you, Clint. I'm not into computers. What does it all mean?"

"Simply this," the G-man responded as he continued looking through page after page of the command history file. "The day before Shripod Addams was killed, or murdered, he removed all the programs from his hard disk. During his lunch break, he cleaned up his disk and didn't leave a trace."

"Could be coincidence," the captain remarked, obviously unconvinced.

"Take another look here," muttered the G-man with a confident smile. He pointed again to the computer screen. Searching through the history file on Shripod's computer, the G-man had found what he'd been looking for—proof of unlawful entry. "No doubt about it, our man was murdered. Check the time these commands were entered."

The screen read:

**The Day of Reckoning**

The lanky captain gulped, murmuring, "You're right, Clint. Shripod died before one o'clock. Someone used this computer immediately after his death."

"That's the way I see it. Someone was looking for something on Shripod's hard disk, but my guess is they didn't find it. Shripod had covered his tracks before they got here."

Mulling over his options, the captain's chest heaved with a sigh of relief. "This is not the answer, but it's a step in the right direction. Whataya suggest we do from your end, Clint?"

"Fed-ex the disk to CIA headquarters at Langley. With a little luck, they may be able to reconstruct the contents of the disk."

"Good," said the security captain. "You take care of the disk and I'll cover Shripod's car. We'll go over his Honda with a fine-toothed comb. We know it was murder. We'll find out how."

Finishing up, the G-man said, "Let's head back to the mountain and pull his records. Interview his friends, pick up a few leads on his family."

Checking his watch, the captain quipped, "Yeah, right Clint." For the first time since their troubles began on Sunday, Cheyenne Mountain was running on a skeleton crew. The first shift regulars were at home asleep. After a moment's thought, a glimmer shone in the captain's eye. "Computers have gotten us this far. Let's round up the Computer Center director and his networking guru. If Shripod's sent any electronic mail outside the country or to Livermore, maybe he left a trail."

"Do it," remarked the G-man with a wink. "We may be onto something big here. Where it'll lead, I can't say, but it feels right!"

**The Day of Reckoning**

G-man Clint Bridges, a lifelong computer buff, stood on the raised floor inside the Cheyenne Mountain Computer Center staring at the arrays of optical computers and disk storage adorning the floor space from wall to wall. Fascinated, he watched in silent disbelief as the computers collected, stored, and displayed information from all parts of the world. There was more computing power per square foot in the basement of Cheyenne Mountain than in any other single place on earth, and the eerie thing was, the place looked deserted—wall-to-wall computers with no people. All this computing power required almost no local support staff. Most of the computer programming was done at Livermore.

Divided into four separate areas, the basement served as Cheyenne Mountain's central brain and nerve center. In the center of the room, orchestrating it all, stood Centurion's Twin. Identical to Centurion in every respect, Centurion's Twin coordinated all computer system activity inside Cheyenne Mountain. Operating around the clock, equipment on the south wall connected Cheyenne Mountain computers to thousands of fiber-optic cables feeding sensor data input from all over the world. The north wall provided Cheyenne Mountain's computer networking gateway to the outside world. Computer networking equipment lining the north wall allowed Cheyenne Mountain computers to talk to each other as well as thousands of other Department of Defense computers scattered across the world. The west wall was lined with backup power supplies that switched on in case of emergency, and finally, the east wall was covered floor to ceiling with projected displays showing global situation information, computer networking traffic, and equipment maintenance information.

The nerve center was attached to the outside world through pulses of different colored light transmitted inside thousands of fiber-optic cables. The south wall of the basement provided Cheyenne Mountain's sensor links to the outside world and looked much like the inside of a telephone central office—row after row of eleven-foot-tall metal frames stacked floor to ceiling with rack-mounted optical communication equipment. The equipment against the north wall looked like the world's largest doughnut and provided Cheyenne Mountain a computer networking hub and gateway to the outside world.

Clint Bridges had never seen such computing power as was in the basement of Cheyenne Mountain. He found the spectacle awe inspiring.

Clint heard the revolving door turn and saw the Computer Center director lumbering into the room, followed by the lanky captain of security. Middle-aged, flabby skin underneath his chin, with ample girth about the middle, the Comp Center director didn't look like a happy man.

Not one for small talk, Clint Bridges got directly to the point, once their introductions were exchanged.

"Where's your guru?"

As Clint asked the question, the revolving door slowly turned again and a tall, thin, thirty-plus fellow with a scraggly brown beard walked through carrying a large thirty-two-ounce cup of caffeine-enriched Coke. Clint smiled, thinking, *Now there's a fella ready to work.*

The Computer Center director introduced Craig Strauss to Clint Bridges and the captain, then they got down to the business at hand.

Clint Bridges looked into Craig's sleepy eyes and explained. "We need your help tracking down any e-mail traffic Shripod Addams may have launched since this past Sunday. We need any records you have showing what he's been up to."

"Addams?" Craig's ears perked up. "That fella just died in a car accident, didn't he?"

Clint nodded agreement and exhaled a deep sigh. He needed to watch what he said concerning this case, and if he wasn't careful, this *need to know* issue of security could trip up their investigation. Through one glance, without an exchange of words, he communicated with the captain of security. The expression on the captain's face read: *Go ahead, tell him, he needs to know.*

"I can't overemphasize the importance of what you may find, Craig, so let me just say this. Addams may, and I repeat may, have been connected with this Star Wars disaster. There's a remote chance his e-mail traffic could lead us to the bottom of it."

Immediately Craig's hollow, sleepy eyes widened to the size of quarters. He was sold. He'd do whatever he could to help, anything. "Over fifty thousand innocent people— dead, and for what?" Craig's jaw muscles tightened as he shook his head. Up until now, Craig hadn't known what to make of this situation. Yanked out of the bed in the middle of the night by some tight-lipped Air Force captain and G-man. Now it all made sense. He'd thought it must be pretty important to bring in the Comp Center director, and he'd been right.

"What was his login?" Craig asked. "And which of our computers was he on?"

"I can save you some time, Craig," said the Comp Center director as he began shuffling through some paper records. "He was a government civilian employee and had an account on only one computer inside the mountain. His computer machine name was *allies;* login was addams."

"Excellent! That narrows the field considerably," Craig said with a smile. Only a single computer to search. He might get some sleep after all. "I'll search the networking files on *allies* looking for any outbound e-mail traffic under addams. Should be no problem. Our networking traffic log covers the last six months."

"Good," Clint responded with a smile. "One final keyword for you, Craig. Highlight any e-mail traffic to Livermore."

"The Lawrence Livermore Lab?" Craig grimaced.

"One and the same. Why?" asked Clint, looking a bit perplexed. "Some problem?"

"Yeah, a volume problem. We get more e-mail traffic in and out of Livermore than any other Comp Center. We transfer hundreds, maybe thousands of messages back and forth every day. They're our SDI software house. We just got a new load from them Tuesday, I think."

"Search for outbound Livermore e-mail traffic with ad-dams as the sender. He was a Russian interpreter, and normally he'd have no business sending e-mail of any sort to Livermore."

"All right, let's go for it," Craig said, feeling reassured. He sat down at his workstation and began clattering away at the keyboard with amazing speed. Almost immediately, he was logged into the *allies* computer looking over the networking records. He bit his lip. Thousands of files had been transferred between the *allies* and Livermore computers. He held his breath, then entered a single line that extracted the information he was seeking. In computerese he asked *allies* if Shripod Addams sent any e-mail to the Livermore computers. Impatiently, Craig drummed his bony fingers across the computer console waiting for a response.

He didn't have to wait long. The answer was as simple as it was surprising. Yes, Shripod Addams sent e-mail to Livermore. At 11:56 P.M., Sunday, December 7, Addams sent e-mail addressed to *mal* on a Livermore computer named *security*.

Following a brief discussion, the group placed three phone calls simultaneously. Both the Comp Center director and the captain of security called their Livermore counterparts while the G-man called Washington. Within five minutes, the group learned from Livermore's director of security that *mal*, Merchant A. Lucky, was dead.

*Super-User Violation, 12/11/2014, 1310 Zulu, 5:10 A.M. Local*
SDI SOFTWARE COMPUTER CENTER,
LAWRENCE LIVERMORE NATIONAL LABORATORY,
LIVERMORE, CALIFORNIA

Rushing ahead of his entourage of top-level executives, Dr. Tristan Roberts, President of Information Sciences at Livermore, was first to bolt into the SDI Software Lab. Winded, he betrayed his exhaustion. This was an extraordinarily early hour to call an executive meeting, but these were extraordinary times.

Dr. Roberts had the dubious distinction of presiding over the worst software debacle in the history of computing and aviation. In the final analysis, a situation such as this SDI disaster demanded a bloodletting—political, military, and technical heads were rolling. It was only a matter of time for Roberts, but even though his career was finished, he wasn't going out without a fight. Both Washington and Cheyenne Mountain had him in a stranglehold and weren't about to let go. They wanted answers—*now*.

Who did it? How'd it happen? How would this virus behave in the future? So far, even with Livermore's management and technical staff working around the clock on this problem, he had no answers. He'd been paralyzed by the inertia and politics that came with every mammoth-sized software project, paralyzed by inaction, corporate infighting, and lack of teamwork. But what could he do? Cornered with his back pinned to the wall, Roberts understood one fundamental cultural law of large corporations that Washington and Cheyenne Mountain refused to acknowledge. Like any large organization, Livermore could not produce anything fast that was good.

So why not?

Better than anyone else at Livermore, Dr. Roberts understood their corporate system of career advancement by crisis—the *Look Good Game*. Ironically, he found himself a prisoner of the corporate game he'd played so well throughout his career. Like taxes, the rules of the game were an integral part of Livermore's corporate culture; he couldn't change them overnight and he knew it.

But for those anxious and willing to play the game, this corporate crisis offered unlimited opportunity for promotion. After all, the writing was on the wall, the guys at the top were on their way out. The objective of the game was to *look good* as you got yourself out of the mess that you got yourself into. Creating the corporate illusion that no progress was really something of consequence was tremendously competitive work requiring enormous effort when you were not part of the solution. Sure, Livermore's emergency SWAT teams had done some work on the virus, but most of their corporate time and effort had been devoted to looking good, to telling a good story, one with a positive spin on a bad situation, showing progress where there was none; presenting pretty, nicely formatted colored viewgraphs that looked good, sounded good, and said nothing. To Roberts' dismay, he'd seen more positive spin than he could stomach and concluded his organization was constipated, bottled up tight as a drum. After their forty-eight-hour-long frenzy, Livermore had not answered a single relevant question for Cheyenne Mountain, but their viewgraph story would lead one to conclude there was really no problem—99.9% of Livermore's software was perfect. Ultimately, Roberts was responsible for isolating the virus and he wanted results. Roberts wanted to break up this logjam and get on with the solution.

In spite of a corporate culture which suppressed the truth, Roberts felt optimistic. He believed their situation was about to change. Finally, they'd gotten a lead in the SDI case—a dead Livermore security guard linked by electronic e-mail to a dead Cheyenne Mountain man.

After receiving an early morning phone call from his Computer Center director, Roberts immediately rushed to the lab. His face looked gaunt and haggard, like the face of a man suffering from lack of sleep. He hadn't slept for two full days, but now he had a plan to bypass Livermore's six layers of middle management and work directly with the troops. He'd collected a small group of the software technical staff he felt he could trust; those who were technically excellent, but politically had no ambition, those who did their programming work because they enjoyed it.

Art Brooks, the SDI software team leader, was such a gentleman, and a gentleman in every sense of the word. Highly regarded by his colleagues, a man with a family and friends who loved him, a man who would never be president of the Livermore Information Sciences Division, but didn't care. He had the job he wanted and considered himself a very lucky and successful man. As long as he was alive, his family would have a roof over their heads, food to eat, clothes to wear, but most important of all, they were happy. A squat-framed introvert with all the charm of a single bookend, Art didn't care for business issues, but he loved technical problems and this computer virus was a pip.

Art surveyed the executive dress of the people in the room. Feeling intimidated, his stomach began to churn. He'd definitely under-dressed, but how was he to know? Everyone but Dr. Roberts looked good in their pin-striped suits. Dr. Roberts looked exhausted, while Art looked like he always looked at five o'clock in the morning—unshaven, sleepy-eyed, wearing Nike Air sneakers and Docker jeans. Art chuckled to himself, thinking this red-eye meeting seemed top-heavy with management. He counted twelve top-level Livermore executives plus the director of Livermore's security, the director of Livermore's Comp Center, and one worker bee, himself. This could have been a meeting of the senior executive staff with Dr. Roberts presiding as chairman of the board. The businessmen looked totally out of place in the software laboratory, but didn't seem to mind; they strutted around the room with an air of confidence. Art had never been in the same room with Livermore's top management, and didn't know any of them personally. He'd seen their pictures enshrined on corporate organizational charts, but had never seen their faces up close. Remembering their pictures, he smiled—it must have been the lighting. Nearly everyone looked older in person, everyone but the one most likely to replace Roberts, the one nicknamed Superman. Superman reminded Art of mild-mannered reporter Clark Kent.

Pushing Art aside, Superman cornered Dr. Roberts and began intently discussing his plan. Superman looked Roberts directly in the eyes, ignoring Art altogether. Art tolerated Superman's rudeness to a point, but after a few minutes, he decided he'd had enough. After all, Dr. Roberts had called Art in the middle of the night and insisted that he meet them in the software lab. Art gathered his courage and interrupted their huddle. "Excuse me, gentlemen," Art said, tapping Dr. Roberts on the shoulder. "How about letting me in on the game plan? What can I do for you?"

Looking exasperated by his conversation with Superman, Roberts picked up his small notepad and turned toward Art. Roberts had been awake for over forty-eight hours. Lack of sleep combined with unremitting pressure made him a bundle of fatigued nerves. He was weak from hunger too, but couldn't eat without suffering stomach distress, so his diet consisted of uncut, black coffee. "Desperation breeds unconventional approaches, Art, and you're my ace in the hole. We've got a logjam to break up."

Puzzled, Art quipped, "Whataya mean?" Art thought he liked the ace in the hole part, but he wasn't sure what to make of it.

Dr. Roberts was a master at putting people at ease. Pouring them both some coffee, he asked Art to make himself comfortable behind the computer terminal. After signaling for Livermore's director of security to join them, he continued. "We've gotten our first real lead in this virus case and I need your help. Time is critically important so I thought it best for me to come to you directly."

"Well, it depends on what you're looking for, Doc, but I expect you're right."

"I think we understand each other, Art," Roberts said somberly as he thumbed through a few dog-eared pages in his notepad. "I'm not looking for a song and dance, I need results."

The director of security, a large man built like a defensive tackle, made his way through the wall of top-level executives and joined them at the terminal, caressing his foam coffee cup.

Looking at the director of security, Roberts instructed, "Fill Art in on the details. Tell him everything we know."

He quickly outlined their impossible predicament. They desperately needed to find those people at Livermore responsible for planting the software virus and they needed the source code, a listing of the virus program.

After the director summarized the electronic mail link between Livermore and Cheyenne Mountain, Art asked,

**The Day of Reckoning**

"You say Merchant Lucky was involved with both computer and plant security?"

Sipping his coffee, the security director slowly nodded an acknowledgment.

"How many computers do we have here at Livermore anyway?" Art asked, holding his breath, not really wanting to hear the answer. "And which computers did Lucky have access to?"

"Nobody knows exactly how many computers we have," the security director said bluntly. "Our records show approximately how many computers we average per acre. All total, we maintain approximately five thousand computers on our local lab network and Lucky had access to every one. Using his workstation, he ran security checks on every computer on the network and had accounts on each."

"So much for computer security." Art frowned.

The security director winced, but agreed. "It looks like our man guarding the store may have robbed it."

"Following Lucky's tracks could take some time," Art lamented.

"If he left any tracks at all," the director observed quietly. "He was a clever, very talented fellow, but I don't think he planned to die."

"Let's check the obvious first. Maybe we'll get a break." Art leaned back and thoughtfully gazed at the domed ceiling. The software lab was magnificent, something akin to an amphitheater, with Art, Roberts, and the security director located center stage.

"I'll focus on the project computer first, the one used to build the SDI software. That's where the virus found entry. What progress has been made tracing the program changes back to the technical staff?"

Bleary-eyed, on the fringe of exhaustion, Roberts read from his notepad. "Roughly halfway through the list of changes, but nothing suspicious so far."

"I'd like to take a look." With a trembling hand, Roberts handed Art the pad. As he scanned the long list of changes made to the SDI software, his jaw dropped to the floor. His eyes remained transfixed on the pad for several minutes.

**The Day of Reckoning**

When he spoke, his tone expressed despair. "God, what a mess." He would always look back on this moment as the point when he decided to retire, to get out of the defense business altogether.

"Absolutely unbelievable," Roberts confirmed, wiping his face with his hand—a sign of fatigue and stress. "So much for quality control."

Art went pale. "I can't believe we shipped this program untested. I had no idea." Hundreds and hundreds of changes had been made to the software.

"Art, it's not as bad as it seems," the director insisted. "These changes were fixes to known program bugs and they'd all been tested separately."

Unconvinced, Art spoke in a shakier voice. "Who's shot-gunning the effort to trace each change back to our technical staff?"

"A couple of new hires," the director replied. "The job's trivial, pretty much a step and repeat process. There were so many changes, it's taking some time to get through them all."

"The change list shows who made each change and when," Art said as he clattered away on his terminal. "I want to sort through the list and find out if anyone made changes who is not on my team."

Dr. Roberts looked at the director of security and nodded. "Makes sense to me." Roberts thought Art a most unusual man, but he needed his skills. Art had trouble communicating with people effectively; his directness made people uncomfortable and defensive, but he could communicate more effectively with a computer than anyone else Roberts had ever known. Due to the technical nature of Art's work, he tended to be somewhat introspective, self-motivated, inquisitive, and unbelievably socially awkward.

After a few more moments of key-clattering, the terminal spat out a short list of people. Art didn't know any of them, but one.

What followed over the next few moments had an otherworldly, surrealistic quality about it for Art. Looking back, he would think it more like a dream, it happened so quickly, so easily. Looking over the list, Art did a double take, and stared at that name again. Suddenly, there it was. There was no mistake about it. The programmer who had made change number 1246 was named *root,* computerese for *super-user.* "This is it!" announced Art. "Take a look. It's gotta be the one! A super-user violation!"

Looking over Art's shoulder, Dr. Roberts said, "I don't understand. What does it mean?"

"By convention, no super-user ever changes the SDI software. Super-users keep the computers running for the users, the programmers who write the SDI software."

Roberts couldn't believe how quickly Art worked. He'd found this software change control violation in less than five minutes. Puzzled, Roberts asked, "Why wasn't this discovered before now?"

Art's reply was both thoughtful and out of character—carefully crafted so the two new employees working on this job wouldn't look bad. "The new hires lack experience and simply didn't know what to look for. We're talking about violating convention here; guidelines, not hard and fast rules. Our programming conventions aren't written down. You pick 'em up along the way."

Art studied the list of names and times on his computer screen, then turned and spoke to the security director. "The super-user changed the software between one and two o'clock on Monday. Was Lucky working Monday afternoon?"

The security director sat down at a terminal, logged on, then copied down the hours Lucky had worked over the past several days. Rubbing his balding head, the director replied, "Yeah, he was here all right, but he wasn't a super-user. He didn't have the password."

"So, what about it? You said yourself, this guy was clever. He could get it easily enough."

The tone of voice Art used caused the hair on the security director's back to stand up, but why deny the allegation? Art was right. Reluctantly, the security director agreed with a grimace. "You're right. Lucky could have made the change. Unfortunately, this wouldn't be the first time our root password was compromised."

"We know Lucky could have done it, but we need proof," said Dr. Roberts, wanting to believe, but unconvinced. He needed evidence, something tangible; he needed a copy of the virus program.

Grabbing the security director by the arm, Art murmured quietly, "Take me to Lucky's office. You run interference." Weaving and bobbing through the gauntlet of well-dressed executives, Art followed the large security director out the door.

*Pay Dirt, 12/11/2014, 1434 Zulu, 6:34 A.M. Local*
GATE 2 SECURITY GUARD SHACK,
LAWRENCE LIVERMORE NATIONAL LABORATORY,
LIVERMORE, CALIFORNIA

Bone-weary, Dr. Tristan Roberts sank down onto a hard straight-back chair with a quiet groan. Surveying the office, he found Art, the security director, and a guard taking Lucky's computer workstation apart, piece by piece. Judging from the looks on their faces and the parts scattered around the floor, Roberts concluded that things could have been better.

It was still dark, and the bright lights inside the guard shack bothered his bloodshot eyes. He'd just come from a meeting with his top-level executive staff. They were tired, angry men and their sense of bewilderment was surpassed only by a profound sense of betrayal. Believing Cheyenne Mountain had sold them up the river, they felt like lame-duck politicians whose hands were tied until the subsequent administration moved in. They were angry at Cheyenne Mountain for demanding that they bypass their standard quality controls in the first place, and they were angry at Washington for demanding so much in so little time. Since no one from Cheyenne Mountain or Washington had been present at their early morning meeting, Dr. Tristan Roberts became the focus of their deep-seated animosity.

How was our computer security compromised, Dr.

Roberts? How did they do it? How did they plant this virus?

Can you guarantee this won't happen again, Dr. Roberts?
Why was this allowed to happen, Dr. Roberts?
Why wasn't someone guarding the store, Dr. Roberts?
Who is the mole inside your organization, Dr. Roberts?
What will the DEWSATs do next, Dr. Roberts?

Leaning back, rubbing his eyes, Roberts allowed himself a moment of reflection. *Maybe I should back off and let Superman solve this one. He's got all the politically correct answers. Hold on here. Who am I trying to fool? He'd turn this virus into a career.*

The tension in Guard Shack 2 could not have been strung any tighter as the circuit board innards of Lucky's computer lay carefully spread across the floor. Art gently pried the boot Read-Only Memory chip out of Lucky's computer and replaced it with his own, custom-built part. The operation was tedious and one slip of the screwdriver could foul up the electronic works. After the part swap was complete, Art began putting Lucky's computer back together again.

Dr. Roberts looked over Art's shoulder and asked, "So how's it going?"

Not one for small talk, Art replied, "Lousy, Doc. Lucky knew a hell of a lot about security. It's going to be a bitch just to log on. Everything on his computer is password protected, and only he knew the passwords."

"Nothing's ever easy," Dr. Roberts sighed, picking up the Read-Only Memory device. "What's your plan?"

"The short of it is this, Doc. That little chip you're holding was Lucky's boot program and I replaced it with a specially built editor program of my own. I'm going to clear out his passwords, all of them, then log on and take a look around."

"You've done this before?" Roberts asked apprehensively. He wanted to hear that this sort of thing was routine.

"I've done it before." Art made eye contact with Roberts, followed by a protracted pause. "Once."

"Is there a chance you could fail?"

"Sure, there are no guarantees. Navigating around the disk takes time, and a lot of patience."

"Should we call in an expert?"

Kneeling over the open carcass of Lucky's computer, Art carefully inserted the last of the computer circuit boards. Exasperated, he looked at Dr. Roberts. "Listen Doc, I know you're tired, but we're all tired here, so loosen up. I've thought this thing through and I need your help, but I don't need you telling me how to run my business."

"Art's right, Dr. Roberts," the security director said softly. "Let the man do his job. It's up to you, but you might consider cutting him a little slack."

"But I only . . . uh . . ." Roberts was taken aback. There were times to concede and times to press. Roberts knew this tiny team represented his only real hope for a fast solution; this was a time to concede. "All right, Art, how can I help?"

"You said time is critical. The experts on Lucky's workstation are outside Boston off Route 128. Well, they ain't gonna be flying here, right?" Art checked his watch. "It's about nine-thirty their time, and I plan to give them a call on their hot line. I need you to convince those big shots in Boston that our job is an urgent matter of national security, otherwise we could get stuck on hold for hours. Once you clear it with Sun's top brass, we'll work the technical details over the phone."

Dr. Tristan Roberts knew exactly what to do and who to call. The U.S. government was one of Sun Microsystems largest customers and any matter of interest to Livermore was a matter of interest to the vice president of Sun's Government Division. Within twenty minutes, Sun Microsystems had their top software, hardware, and firmware experts patched into Guard Shack 2 over a video conference call.

After spending an hour methodically combing through page after page of specially formatted data stored on Lucky's disk, Sun's experts recommended Art change the contents of a single eight-bit byte. Out of the millions and millions of data bytes stored on Lucky's disk, Art changed only one and the deed was done. "It's all in knowing where to look and what to look for," Art said with a big smile. Once he'd removed the password protection from Lucky's workstation, Art took the workstation apart and replaced the original Read-Only Memory device. After all the pieces were put back together again, he plugged it in and turned it on. Following an agonizing two-minute wait for the system to come alive, Art exclaimed: "Yes! Yes!" He logged on to Lucky's computer without any security password. "Isn't technology wonderful?"

Everyone at Sun, including the vice president of Sun's Government Division, Dr. Roberts, and the security director sat up as though they'd all been goosed at the same time and burst into applause. Outwardly, Dr. Roberts felt ecstatic, something had finally gone right. This was real, forward progress and a renewed energy pervaded his body as an adrenaline rush kicked in. Inwardly, Dr. Roberts was dumbfounded, he couldn't believe that this little bit-twiddling exercise had worked at all. After a few moments' thought, he concluded, *That Art doesn't miss a trick.*

Immediately, Art began looking through Lucky's command history file. After looking over the record of Lucky's last two days' work, Art shook his head sadly and sighed. "Lucky was the mole, but I'm afraid we got here too late."

"Whataya mean?" came an exasperated voice over the videophone.

"Early Monday afternoon, Lucky transferred a collection of programs named *mother's_best* from his workstation to the SDI computer. That's all the evidence I need to convince me that he's the mole. About two o'clock on Monday, Lucky cleaned up his disk. He removed *mother's_best,* and I expect any trace of the virus went with it."

"Never lose heart," came a reassuring baritone voice over the videophone. "Take an exhaustive look anyway. Even if Lucky cleaned his disk, with a little luck, we can reconstruct it."

Art knew this was possible, but he'd never reconstructed one himself. He navigated from place to place around

Lucky's computer, then grimly confirmed that *mother's_best* was gone without a trace.

Following a long pause, the low, resonating baritone voice asked, "Your mole had some form of backup?"

"Backup? Yes, backup! Of course! Why didn't I think of that? Unless he destroyed 'em all, there must be backup copies somewhere."

"Search the guard shack top to bottom," Dr. Roberts barked as he frantically began opening drawers and file cabinets. "Backup copies must be somewhere!"

As Art discovered, somewhere was inside Lucky's lower left file drawer—an unmarked gray metal box filled with tape backup copies of Lucky's programs. Opening the metal box, Art read the labels on each tape, searching for the latest date. The good news was that Lucky was not only clever, he was methodical. Lucky backed up the programs on his computer every Friday afternoon. Art grabbed the tape containing the most recent backup, then loaded it into Lucky's computer. He instructed Lucky's computer to re-store the collection of programs named *mother's_best*. The tape raced back and forth for a few minutes as the workstation searched for the program. To Art and Dr. Roberts, those few minutes seemed to drag on for an eternity.

Suddenly, the whirring sound of the tape drive hushed and Art's eyes lit up. "Bingo! We found it! *Mother's_best* is rolling in!"

Quick-time, Dr. Roberts and the security director moved into position directly behind Art, looking over his shoulder. Art felt them breathing down his neck, but couldn't blame them for wanting to see. The programs were encrypted, of course, but that was no real problem for Art. He copied the encryption key from Lucky's command history file, then decrypted them in less than five minutes. Poring over the programs a page at a time, Art couldn't believe his eyes. This was it, it had to be, but exactly what it was he couldn't say. Art believed they'd found the program listing of the computer virus, but it was nothing like he'd expected. He wasn't sure exactly what he'd expected, but he was sure that this wasn't it. *Mother's_best* looked like a huge collection of programs written by the CIA, Air Force, and Army. "Unbelievable!" Art muttered, not really knowing what to think. His mind felt numb, paralyzed.

Dumbfounded, Roberts rubbed his eyes. Like Art, he couldn't believe what he was seeing. "If this is the virus, then the CIA, Air Force, and Army wrote it." Roberts grimaced, pursing his lips. "That's just great. Cheyenne Mountain is gonna love this."

The security director stood silent, his jaw dropped to his knees.

"I could be wrong," Art said with reservation. His mind couldn't accept what his eyes were seeing. "But I think we got it."

It had been a long and arduous journey. More than once, Roberts had thought they wouldn't make it. But they did make it, they found pay dirt—big-time. Roberts patted Art on the shoulder and asked, "Recommendations?"

"Give me a minute, Doc. This is a bitter pill to swallow. Somehow, this doesn't add up. The U.S. government doesn't write virus programs to plant them in their own equipment. We're missing some important data from somewhere."

"What you're saying is true, but all that really matters now is that we believe we've found the virus."

"Well then, Doc, I recommend we go for broke. Get a task force dissecting this thing immediately."

"Size the job for me," Dr. Roberts instructed, nodding agreement. "How many people are we talking about here?"

Art clattered the keyboard of Lucky's workstation, checking the number of program lines in *mother's_best*. A few moments later, he responded, "Give it two hundred of your best software folks; we'll split up the program into modules, then take it apart line by line—it's the only way. We'll know what makes this baby tick by noon today, noon tomorrow at the latest."

"Anything else?"

"Yeah, take Lucky's computer off the lab network and isolate it in our SDI lab. Lord knows we don't want this virus to spread over the network."

"Done." Roberts felt weakness pervading his body as his

adrenaline rush wore off. He had to maintain his strength long enough to get the ball rolling. Light-headed, Roberts looked to his security director and began barking orders. "Order an autopsy on Lucky and find out what killed him."

"Already taken care of."

"Find out who he was working for. Search his home. Interview his family and friends."

"An FBI task force is crawling all over this case, Doc— top priority. If Lucky left a trail, they'll find it."

"Good. We're not where we want to be, but at least we know how to get there!" Following a brief pause, Dr. Roberts rattled off additional instructions. "Get John Sullivan on the line, and General Mason. Let 'em know what we've got."

Rifling through the gate guard's desk, the security director found a pad of paper and began creating a *To Do* list.

"Superman, send me Superman," Roberts told the gate guard as his peripheral vision began to fade. "He'll round up the people we need." How much strain could one man take? Roberts collapsed like a house of cards onto a straight-back metal chair. Staring at the ceiling and dazed, he continued issuing orders like an automaton. "Washington, connect me to Washington." With his bloodshot eyes open wide, he watched the bright lights around him fade to black, followed by a sense of dreamlike motion, as if he were falling into a bottomless abyss. The last thing Roberts would recall before losing consciousness was the sound of frightened voices, muffled and indistinct. They seemed to drone on forever, but he couldn't respond. His mouth wouldn't form the words.

**The Day of Reckoning**

# 22

His Air Force colleagues called him Wild Bill, but back home in Mississippi they still called him Billy. A test pilot and Air Force academy graduate, he was the youngest of four sons, and had been hooked on flying nearly all his life. He'd wanted to fly since he was a boy and first saw the Thunderbirds perform at the Air Force pilot training base in Columbus.

All the brothers made good. One a physician, the other two made lawyers—and they all lived in Jackson, Mississippi—all but Billy. Wild Bill, Lieutenant Colonel William Boyd, had long wanted to return home to his family and friends, but had resigned himself to the fact that Mississippi didn't need test pilots. Although he'd searched on numerous occasions, he'd never found any work within a day's drive of his beautiful Magnolia State. Billy's soul was in Mississippi, but Wild Bill's heart had wings, and his mind was addicted to the glitter of high-tech. Wild Bill had to fly and he had to fly something special.

Billy dreamed of moving back to Mississippi. He hoped he'd live long enough to retire, but never really believed he would. He couldn't imagine himself happy on the ground, technically retired, put out to pasture. Wild Bill shuddered at the thought of life without flight and chose not to dwell on it. In his heart, he dreamed that one day he'd come back to stay, but in his mind he believed he'd make the trip in a pine box. He'd get back one way or the other. Retired or dead, it didn't much matter.

Wild Bill didn't like anything about Thomas Jackson but his last name. Lieutenant Colonel Boyd respected Jackson of MIT Lincoln Labs for one reason and one reason only: Jackson was almost as smart as he thought he was. Radar technology was Jackson's expertise. He'd invented the DEWSAT counterstealth radar for the Allies and now they called on him once again to do the impossible. The Allies needed an airplane that Jackson's radar could not see, an airplane that could fly undetected by the orbiting DEWSAT armada. Jackson wasn't one to listen to the concerns of others, evidently because his own opinions were far too important; but then again, Jackson wasn't paid to be thoughtful of others. He was paid to deliver a single prototype aircraft, invisible to the DEWSAT's radar, and his reputation was on the line.

Jackson was no fool, Wild Bill had to admit that, but he lacked any feeling for teamwork. He was a loner in a large, team-oriented organization. Jackson was not an expert pilot nor did he care to be. He had a low regard for anyone, especially test pilots, who were not his technical equal. Lieutenant Colonel Boyd respected Jackson for his technical judgment and that was enough. Wild Bill was paid to fly Jackson's prototype aircraft, not to love him.

One thing was undeniable. Jackson was a legend. His God-given technical instinct differentiated him from lesser men. Jackson could know, could feel the solution to a complex problem before solving the details. He was one of a rare breed of scientists who had become famous by producing a series of weapon systems, cloaked in secrecy, which continually leapfrogged the opposition. His secret was an inquisitive mind coupled with a cardsharp's instinct for cutting through the technical muck which obscured most problems. He could see old problems in a different light and propose new solutions which worked (to the delight of the United States government). Jackson intuitively felt solutions before he thought them through, or justified them in theory. He claimed to know all there was to know about light, and many believed him. Others believed that he could actually see colors in the radio and infrared regions of the electromagnetic spectrum, that he could see color just as his radars saw color. Although he never made this claim, he never denied it. He saw complex solutions without letting the theoretical mathematics get in the way. He'd propose a solution to a specific problem, then if necessary, he'd prove his solution was correct after he'd worked out the details. He could punch through irrelevant detail which would choke a lesser man, then identify the essence of the solution after a quick knee-jerk analysis.

But Jackson's greatest strength, his intuition, obscured one serious weakness. He'd never failed. In the past, he'd worked on only the most important problems and used his intuition to make sure the proposed solutions were feasible. Once he believed a problem could be solved, he threw government money, time, and people at working out the details. Time had never been a major concern of Jackson's. His adversary was the scientific problem. His record of successes was unbroken. In the process he had become a millionaire and had achieved worldwide renown. He had become the leading expert on radar in the United States, debatably, in the world. He was oblivious of everything except unsolved technical problems. Although his projects were sometimes delivered late, they always worked. Over the past four days, the rules of technical problem-solving had changed. The time variable in the problem-solving equation had virtually disappeared. The *Black Hole* prototype aircraft must work—now. He'd always done what he set out to do because he had the intuition, time, and resources to see the job through. The taxpayers—those people who paid his bills—had patience and deep pockets, so he'd always gotten the resources he needed to get the job done—until now.

To date, every military project for which Jackson had

significant responsibility had been considered successful. Unknown to Wild Bill, Jackson was in over his head with this *Black Hole* prototype and needed time.

Lieutenant Colonel William Boyd climbed down from the catwalk to the top of the test chamber and worked his way to the center of Jackson's penthouse lab. Jackson had just completed a series of radar tests on his *Black Hole* prototype and was poring over stacks of data when he noticed Wild Bill walk in.

After carefully studying the test results, Jackson felt doubt, an upwelling of disbelief. These results couldn't be correct. This had never happened before, it couldn't be happening now. He groped for possible explanations: either there had to be something wrong with the test equipment or that cockpit canopy was one hell of a big problem. Then he looked up. Wild Bill was looking at him casually, his eyes clear.

"How's she look, Jackson?"

For a moment, Jackson felt as if his jaw had suddenly fused shut. He was aware that Wild Bill was looking at him with something like puzzlement in his eyes, but it didn't matter. He ordered his tongue to say what he felt he must and almost choked on the words. "There're always problems when you do anything for the first time, but I'll work through them." Jackson paused, handed Wild Bill a graph of his test data, then continued. "You won't like these results."

Wild Bill read over the data with a puzzled expression at first. After a few moments, puzzlement was replaced with concern, deep concern. The test results read like a pilot's death warrant. Wild Bill was no radar expert, but he didn't need to be to sort through this story. "Are these results repeatable?"

"Yes," Jackson uttered the single word. It underlined his sense of urgency. His eyes did not change. He blinked once and then turned back to his test controls.

"Then there's no instrumentation error."

"Could be. I don't believe this data. It doesn't feel right. The problem is either the test equipment or that damn gold dome." The Plexiglas cockpit canopy of the *Black Hole* prototype had been impregnated with gold to keep radar energy out of the cockpit, but the canopy reflected radar energy much like a curved mirror.

"Whataya plan?"

"Seal that cockpit completely, button it up tight as a drum, cover it with absorber and eliminate it once and for all."

"Are you serious?" Stunned, Wild Bill looked at Jackson in disbelief. "Black it out completely?" Jackson planned to put him under the bag, have him take off, fly, and land relying totally on instruments. As a test pilot, he could do it if it was necessary, but he didn't like it. Sensitive DEWSAT radar technology combined with the physics of time and distance dictated requirements for a stealthy aircraft which no pilot could love.

"From now on, the *Black Hole* flies on instruments only." Jackson looked at him without emotion. "Better log some simulator time under the bag." Jackson's distinctive New England accent bore into the southern man's consciousness.

Wild Bill's jaw tensed, his mind focused, his nerves steeled. "So what are my chances?"

The silence that ensued lasted almost sixty seconds.

Without emotion, Jackson scribbled some notes over his test results. He guessed where his data would fall once the stealthy cockpit canopy had been installed. "No better than fifty-fifty." His voice was opaque, pitiless.

Wild Bill's teeth clenched together, the muscles at the back of his jaw tightened into hard knots. Months ago, he had volunteered for this assignment because he believed it important. Today, the SDI virus made this work more important than then, but he didn't volunteer to die. He had stayed alive this long by keeping the odds in his favor.

Jackson continued talking, his nasal-like voice reaching back into his consciousness. Now his voice was talking about the probability of detection, the chances for error. A fascinating problem, he was saying.

"It's my life we're talking about here," Wild Bill snarled with baffled anger. Looking at the equipment clutter scattered about the penthouse, he continued. "This whole operation feels jury-rigged to me. You fix one problem and another pops up."

Jackson made a sound. It was a low, primitive grunt. He paused, then after searching for the right words, he resumed speaking. This time his voice was so slow that each word seemed to dangle. "As you know, Colonel, we are caught in a desperate situation. Don't concern yourself needlessly. I will mask your aircraft using equipment which mimics the DEWSAT radar signal. It displaces the radar return and makes your aircraft look like a thousand moving targets." Gesturing with his hands, Jackson's eyes gleamed as he described this gadget.

Wild Bill watched him with a jaundiced eye. He'd thought for a long time that Jackson had some kind of weird affection for all that damn equipment. It just wasn't natural.

"I presume you have experience with this device?" Wild Bill asked skeptically.

"We use the same device in the Phantom Hawk cruise missile." Jackson spoke with convincing authority. He was wrong in this case, but nevertheless, he was completely confident. It was true that the radar masking equipment was used in the Phantom Hawk. But it was also true that the masking equipment triggered the DEWSAT's burn-through mode. Jackson had been isolated the last two days and had not read the latest reports from Cheyenne Mountain. The DEWSAT would not allow itself to be overrun by false targets. Satisfied with his own response, Jackson nodded his head in approval. "I'd suggest you get some simulator time under the bag."

"Don't patronize me, Jackson," Wild Bill snarled. "You do your job, I'll do mine."

*Hope and Confrontation, 12/11/2014, 1545 Zulu, 8:45 A.M.*
   *Local*
CHEYENNE MOUNTAIN, COLORADO

Mason looked across the video conference room at Hinson. For a moment, he debated whether or not he should deal

**The Day of Reckoning**

with this personnel matter, but because of the urgency of
the situation he decided to meet it head-on. Mason planned
to lop Hinson from his War Room staff and ease him out of
the service. He believed his self-centered ambition had gotten him as far as he should go. Mason called him over to
his console. He thought Hinson looked almost apprehensive
as he sat down.

"We need to talk," Mason said plainly. He would talk to
Hinson face-to-face, not through another person. In addition to Hinson's blind ambition, Mason had lingering
doubts about his integrity. When the chips were down, he
couldn't be trusted. The man would lie looking you square
in the eyes. The problem was to get Hinson off his staff in
the least amount of time, then quietly move him out of the
service, so he could not do any more damage. "I want you
off my staff effective immediately and out of the service."
He spoke quietly but bluntly. His voice was a mixture of
pity and hard-bitten reality. Mason paused for a moment to
watch Hinson's reactions. As usual, the wheels turned
round in Hinson's head, but his face revealed very little of
what he felt inside. "It's time you got into another line of
work."

Hinson had expected this, only it came sooner than he'd
planned. If he could buy a little time, maybe a week or two
to get all his transfer ducks lined up, he'd be history. Guys
like Hinson might stumble, but they never got hurt. They
always landed feetfirst on top of somebody else. "Sir, as
you see it, what are my alternatives? I think you'd agree,
this is coming rather suddenly. And the timing, this crisis.
We haven't even discussed my options."

Mason furrowed his brow and looked Hinson straight in
the eyes. As always, his objective was to be direct. "My immediate interest is my staff and this virus. I only work well
with people I can trust, people who say what they think and
are up-front about their motives. As far as your options, I'd
like you out of the service. You know I can't bust you because you've done nothing illegal, but consider yourself
notified. I plan to put you *at risk*. When our yearly force re-
duction comes next fall, you'll be gone. Make your plans

now. I don't want you in a position where you can do any more harm. Any questions?"

"About my—uh . . . transition."

"What about it?"

"Can you give me two weeks? I'd train my replacement to ease the transition."

Mason's knee-jerk reaction was to say no, but he held his tongue and considered Hinson's suggestion. After all, Hinson was competent and a capable liar. Mason knew he couldn't be trusted, but he wanted to give him the benefit of the doubt. His head said no, his heart said yes. "You understand you are relieved of your duties as CSOC commander as of this meeting?" Mason's voice sounded concerned.

Hinson hesitated. His reply was polite but edged with ice. "I understand, General."

"Your single remaining responsibility here would be to train your replacement."

Hinson nodded.

*I hope I don't live to regret this decision,* Mason thought. *Hinson could be a conniving little prick.* "Very well, do what you can to bring your replacement up to speed as fast as possible. That is all." Mason stood, ending the meeting, and hoped this issue was resolved.

He felt an undefined and nagging discomfort when suddenly Colonel Napper burst into the Crow's Nest video conference room waving a fax over his head, quivering with excitement. The few men in the room who were talking fell silent. Even those outside the conversation strained to hear Napper.

Hinson remained impassive, but Mason leaned forward in his chair, anxious, hoping desperately for some good news.

"They've found it. Livermore's got their hands on the source code. They're verging on a breakthrough." His voice was heavily persuasive, but it didn't need to be. He'd said what they wanted to hear.

"All right, talk to me, Sam. Tell us what you know."

"They've found the virus source code and expect to know what makes it tick within twenty-four hours."

**The Day of Reckoning**

Colonel Napper paused, rubbing the stubble on his face. The heavy beard he'd had since puberty was growing rapidly, but he couldn't take the time to shave it today. "And another thing, we wrote the virus, the United States government, I mean."

"Why the hell would we do that?" Mason asked, frustrated by a sense of one step forward followed by one step back.

"I don't know for sure, sir." Napper paused, and then went on, his voice now unconvincing. "But as I understand it, the Army did some work on battlefield grade computer viruses back in the mid-nineties. As far as I know, they shelved the idea when they found out that our equipment was more susceptible than our enemies'. The virus Livermore found is built of three parts; each part was contracted separately by the Air Force, Army, and CIA."

Mason put his head facedown in his hands for a few moments, then looked up at Napper. "Is it possible that we brought this on ourselves?"

Colonel Napper paused. Then his voice gained confidence. "No, sir, the odds against this are so high it's impossible."

"All right," Mason said. "I don't want to solve this here and now, but I want it solved before Livermore builds another software load. Tell Dr. Roberts to bring in any experts he needs, but retrace exactly how that virus gained entry into our software. No matter what, we cannot ever allow this to happen again."

"What do you make of it?" Mason invited Hinson's comments, but his tone said "keep it short."

Hinson plugged back into the conversation. "What about Shripod Addams? Any connection to Livermore?"

"Yes, it's all in this fax," Napper replied as he handed out copies to everyone in the video conference room. Mason studied the document intently. His nagging discomfort returned.

"All right, let me sum it up," Mason said. "We don't know the organization behind the sabotage, but we've got the source code. We should know how the virus behaves by this time tomorrow."

Napper and Hinson agreed.

"Sam, get this in the President's hands immediately, and one other thing. Goose up our satellite surveillance, especially over the trouble spots. Things are going to get worse before they get better. I learned a long time ago that the truth is a two-edged sword. It may set you free—but it costs. It stands to reason. When the police pull out, chaos takes over—happens all the time. Somewhere, some pigheaded barbarian is planning to exploit this situation. It has to be. We need to know about it before it happens." Mason clinched his teeth so hard his head throbbed, but he knew in his gut he was right.

*Two-edged Sword, 12/11/2014, 1600 Zulu, 11:00 A.M. Local*
THE WHITE HOUSE,
WASHINGTON, D.C.

The office he had aspired to occupy all his life seemed like the loneliest place on earth to the President. Gazing at presidential portraits around the Oval Office, he reflected on the struggles of those who had occupied this office before him. Recalling something Kennedy had said following the Bay of Pigs incident, he lamented. "Success has a thousand fathers, but defeat is an orphan." He hadn't slept well, his mind raced in circles agonizing over their predicament and what to do next. He felt good about his decision to tackle this problem head-on, but apprehensive about the future. He needed a plan. In the past, he had come here seeking advice and today was no exception.

The President's concentration was broken when his hollow-eyed national security advisor walked into the room clutching the latest reports from Livermore and Cheyenne Mountain. "Pour yourself some coffee, Clive, and have a seat. Mason's coming on-line any minute." Clive Towles sat down on a small sofa facing the wall lined with video cameras and TV monitors. Before Towles had finished stirring his coffee, Supreme Commander Mason's picture appeared on their TV monitor. Anxious and impatient, the President cut to the crux of the matter. "General, I need a damn good plan that'll get us out of this mess or a miracle."

"Apparently you've got the right connections, Mr. President." Mason smiled, but only slightly. "Have you seen the latest from Livermore?"

The President's national security advisor interrupted before the President could respond. "Here's a copy of the latest Livermore fax, Mr. President. It's still warm; picked it up on my way to your office."

The President read the message but seemed unimpressed. He squinted his eyes and looked up at Slim on his video monitor. "What does it mean in English?"

Mason summarized the Livermore findings for the President and concluded by saying, "Livermore believes they found the virus source code. This could be the breakthrough we've been waiting for. We'll know what we've got within twenty-four hours."

"Know what?"

"Know why the virus behaves as it does and what we must do to isolate it. The source code could be the key to solving this problem. It should allow us to fully characterize the virus and, hopefully, eliminate it."

"What do you mean, hopefully?" the President asked impatiently.

"There are no guarantees, Mr. President. Conceivably, we may learn of some viral characteristics that we cannot counteract."

There was a long pause on the line, then the President spoke. His voice boomed over the loudspeakers in Cheyenne Mountain. "Don't play word games with me, General. Say what you mean clearly in English. This is no time for misunderstanding." The President paused, studying the pictures of his general staff at Cheyenne Mountain. He then continued, deliberately slow. "I want to ask you one question."

General Mason had a premonition of doom. He knew the question.

"General Mason, after studying this virus, could we learn

there's nothing we can do? That we have no cure? That we can't end this crisis?"

Mason hesitated, not because he didn't know the answer, but because he wanted to see where his team stood. Napper, Sullivan, Krol, and Craven somberly and unanimously agreed, then Mason spoke without apology. "Yes, Mr. President, it is possible."

There was a swell of tension in the room as the President quickly came forward in his seat. The President's eyes widened, but he decided not to press. His silence was ominous enough. The silence drew out until the President leaned back in his chair once again.

Craven felt a flash of admiration for Mason, a sense of pride combined with a kind of helplessness. When the chips were down, Mason would put his career on the line every time and do what he believed was right.

General Krol handed Mason a handwritten note.

"Anything else?" the President asked.

"Yes. General Krol reminds me that he has a massive analysis effort running around the clock in Kaliningrad. Progress is slow, but sure. The work is tedious. Hundreds of scientists and engineers are reconstructing exactly what happened from our computer logs. Once complete, we'll have a better detailed picture of the conditions onboard *Freedom.*"

"Good," the President said. "Although I'm not technical, a detailed picture of what you've got sounds damn important to me."

"It's our *Freedom* road map, Mr. President. We won't get there without it." Mason's eyes were clear, his voice sure.

"Very well, General Mason. I need a plan from you and I need it fast. I can't help you if I don't know what you need. As it stands, I've got no visibility. I want to see what's being done to turn this thing around. Get me a plan, one with some contingency, then together we'll follow it through."

"We're working the plan, Mr. President."

## The Day of Reckoning

"Well then, what's our next step? What should I do to improve our chances?"

"We have only two recommendations at this time, Mr. President. The first will come as no surprise: give Livermore whatever they need. Second, goose up our satellite surveillance coverage over the third-world hot spots." Puzzled, the President glanced across his desk at Clive Towles, who was strongly urging approval.

"I agree," Clive insisted as he spoke to Mason over video. "We'd come to exactly the same conclusion, but we need to coordinate our coverage. Link your recon folks with ours. We've repositioned several Navy and CIA birds already. We need your Air Force recon satellites to cover the holes."

Rubbing his eyes, the President added, "I share your concern, General." His voice sounded convincing.

Mason spoke softly but with deliberate clarity. He'd learned this lesson firsthand, very early in his career. "The truth is a two-edged sword, Mr. President. You don't tell the truth without paying the price. We're in a desperate situation and there'll certainly be those who'll take advantage of it."

"I agree." The President paused, then focused his thinking once again. "I'd like that operations plan by tomorrow."

Mason looked to his staff. They returned a thumbs up. "It'll be on your desk."

"Keep me posted, gentlemen." The President stood, disconnected the video conference line, and the meeting was adjourned.

*Out of the Sun, 12/11/2014, 1730 Zulu*
SPACE STATION *HOPE*

How long had she been staring at this tube? Scott wondered, but then again, she didn't really want to know. Looking for some way, any way to get onboard *Freedom,* she'd been parked at Pasha's control console for hours toiling through plans of the space station, videotapes, and computer simulations. Overwhelmed, Scott found the search had a morose sense of endlessness about it. Even Guardian had been slowed by the mountainous amounts of information which required sorting and analysis.

Since Pasha's condition had stabilized twenty-four hours earlier, Scott had been trying to find a weak point in *Freedom*'s defenses and had had only an odd hour's sleep here and there. *That's why they pay me the big bucks,* she reflected bleakly. She remembered that she hadn't lost this much sleep since her divorce, and then she wondered about Jay. Biting her lip, tears welled in her eyes. She couldn't help it. This had been a hard day. Maybe it was the exhaustion, maybe it was the pressure, or maybe she loved him and was worried sick. A part of her, everything that mattered, was onboard *Freedom,* but chances for Jay did not look good. No word since that virus took over. Something was wrong, terribly wrong, and she couldn't rest until she knew. He might be injured or . . . *I can't think about this now or I'll go crazy. We have problems enough here.*

And then it happened, a curious thing. Suddenly, Scott's attention was diverted by something she thought she saw on her screen. Weary, she'd been reviewing tedious training videotapes about the space station radar system but now found herself eager to learn more. She wasn't sure, not yet anyway, but she thought she had found something significant. Working the first piece of their problem, Scott struggled to envision how they could approach *Freedom* without getting blown out of the sky. Each space station used a combination of radar and infrared sensors for tracking and steering weapons on target. An orbiting military stronghold, a fortress designed for its own defense, *Freedom* had loomed virtually unapproachable until now, but Scott felt uneasy. This weakness appeared too obvious. There must be a catch.

Bleary-eyed, Scott gazed across the control room, summoning Mac and Gonzo to her side. "Fellas, come take a look. I think I've found a hole." Her voice was a combination of uneasiness mixed with restrained excitement. She had good reason for concern and so did everyone else onboard. Until now, the more they learned about *Freedom*'s defensive safeguards, the worse their chances looked.

Headquarters had not discussed boarding *Freedom* with Scott and her crew, but everyone knew that conversation was sure to happen.

Who else was going to do it?

What other options did Headquarters have?

Besides, boarding *Freedom* was inevitable. They had to do it simply to survive. They couldn't return home without passing through the lethal DEWSAT layer and their supplies on *Hope* wouldn't last more than three months, maybe three and one half months if they were rationed. As Scott, Mac, and Gonzo saw it, they were trapped with no place to go but *Freedom*.

Scott played back a short segment of videotape as Mac and Gonzo looked on, contemplating what she'd seen. What they saw was a computer-generated image of the solar system in motion. A picture of the space station orbiting the earth once a day as the earth orbited around the sun. In addition, the video clip showed the radar coverage as a translucent sphere surrounding the space station. The translucent sphere meant that the radar could see in every direction, without blind spots, or so it seemed at first glance. After watching the tape play back time and time again, Scott noticed a tiny pinprick-sized hole in the translucent sphere. At first she thought it was a burned out pixel or a bad CRT screen, but she zoomed in on it and after some investigation, she concluded the pinhole was real. Not only was it real, it was predictable and always aligned itself in the direction of the sun.

"As I see it, *Freedom*'s blind as a bat looking into the sun." Mac spoke in a low voice, leaning down, looking over her shoulder.

"I think we should discuss this with Headquarters, but it looks too easy." Gonzo paused. "Interference from the sun is a well-known problem. Headquarters must know about that blind spot and have already found some way to fill the gap. It can't be as easy as flying in out of the sun or someone else woulda already tried it."

**The Day of Reckoning**

Scott disagreed. "It may be a classic problem but approaching *Freedom* out of the sun won't be easy." Scott spoke in a worried voice and handed Gonzo a hard copy picture of the video screen showing the sun, earth, *Hope*, and *Freedom*. On it she had sketched their approximate flight path—departing *Hope* then approaching *Freedom* out of the sun.

Gonzo's guts wrenched when he saw the general shape and complexity of the flight path. He spoke slowly, releasing an exasperated sigh. "God, this is intricate." There was dread and apprehension in his voice. The general shape of the trajectory looked something like a semicircle, but the speed constantly varied.

"I need you to work the details, just rough them in for now. We need a sanity check. I think we can do it, but it's a one-way trip. Fuel's the big problem. We move further out, let *Freedom* pass well underneath us, then spend the next seven hours playing hide and catch-up."

Staring at Scott's flight trajectory in despair, Gonzo began punching numbers into his flight computer. The silence which followed seemed to linger for an eternity. Finally, he spoke, but by then he didn't need to. The answer was written all over his face. Scott and Mac knew what he was about to say before he formed the words. "You're right. Even if we make it through undetected, it's a one-way trip." He felt he was writing their epitaph.

"Lighten up a little," Mac said to break the melancholy mood. "We've still got each other."

Scott and Gonzo looked at Mac, shook their heads in quiet disbelief, and smiled. As always, he was right. The man was wonderful with people, the best Scott had ever known. Mac had a God-given talent for communication and could make anyone feel good, like sunshine breaking through on a cloudy day.

Scott felt like laughing and crying at the same time. She rubbed her eyes clear, then studied the circles under Gonzo's eyes. "We'll feel better after we get some rest," Scott observed. Although she was weightless, she stood up from the desk console to stretch. She expected it would feel

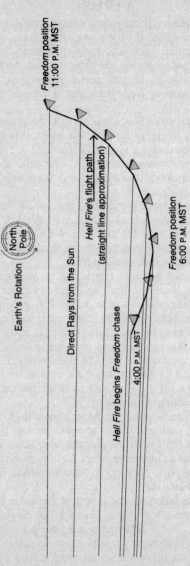

Earth's Rotation

North Pole

*Freedom* position
11:00 P.M. MST

Direct Rays from the Sun

*Hell Fire's* flight path
(straight line approximation)

*Hell Fire* begins *Freedom* chase

*Freedom* position
6:00 P.M. MST

4:00 P.M. MST

*Hell Fire's* Flight Path Out of the Sun

good just to move around. It didn't. Every joint ached. Her efficiency was faltering, she felt her judgment uncertain, vacillating. She couldn't keep up with her own pace; she was losing it and sinking fast. She checked her watch. How long was it till that conference call with Headquarters? It was today, wasn't it? All of a sudden, she wasn't sure what day it was. *Let's see, four-thirty their time is what time my time?* Scott was baffled that she couldn't figure it out. It wasn't supposed to be hard. "Mac, how long till our conference call?" She blinked her eyes, but she couldn't clear them.

Mac glanced at the big clock on the wall, then at Scott and Gonzo. " 'Bout six hours from now, Scotty. I've had my forty winks. You and Gonzo catch up."

Gonzo and Scott agreed. Neither had the strength to do otherwise.

Sleeping quarters on *Hope* were about the same size as sleeping quarters in a submarine. They weren't rooms at all, they were coffin-sized pigeonholes wedged lengthwise between the missile tubes. People space inside any weapons platform came at a premium. Traditionally, inside any manned weapons platform, people were accommodated around the weapons, not instead of the weapons, and *Hope* was no exception. *Hope* was first and foremost an orbiting weapon system bristling with armament designed exclusively for her own defense.

Scott fell asleep while strapping herself to her berth. Gonzo didn't bother securing himself at all. He closed the overhead curtain and figured that he wouldn't float far.

*Straight from the Heart, 12/11/2014, 2330 Zulu, 4:30 P.M.*
    *Local*
Cheyenne Mountain, Colorado

Mason quietly laid their operations plan on the table in the video conference room. His eyes expressed an anxious uneasiness after studying the tenth draft of their op plan which led nowhere. The pieces weren't coming together, not yet. They needed more information, much more. The plan was a start, but they had a long way to go. Fundamentally, given everything they knew, Slim Mason didn't see any viable solution for this virus problem and his staff agreed. Their dilemma appeared to have no solution, but Mason and his staff were tenacious and unwilling to yield. There was a solution. There must be. Mason, his staff, and the President would have to wait.

Tomorrow was another day. Tomorrow, Livermore had promised new information on the virus. Tomorrow, General Krol expected Kaliningrad would release their preliminary report. It wouldn't be complete, but based on his direct feedback from Kaliningrad, Krol believed it would be a cornerstone on which their operational plans could pivot. Everyone understood the tedious and complex nature of the Kaliningrad task. To reconstruct a cohesive picture of exactly what had happened to *Freedom* was a Herculean operation, given the mountainous volumes of data contained in their computer activity logs.

Mason believed this virus could be cured. He needed an operations plan which combined the actions necessary for a speedy recovery. There must be a solution to any problem that was man-made. Everyone wanted to believe that, even those who didn't believe it wanted to. If the problem could be solved at all, Mason believed his people could do it. It was Mason's job to give them the time and support they needed. He'd run interference for them and then stay out of their way. Mason believed they'd find some weakness in *Freedom*'s armor, but as of this moment, he saw no light at the end of the tunnel.

Waiting was the hardest part. Mason, his staff, and the President had to wait while their technical folks sorted through the debris of this fiasco. Mason didn't like the waiting, but he knew it was necessary. He didn't expect the President to like waiting either, but the President would wait, like it or not.

Mason took a deep breath and focused his thoughts. "We're ready to talk to *Hope,* Sam. The operator should be set to complete the call. Ask her to complete the connection."

Punching up the video conference operator, Sam requested General Mason's *Hope* connection. At once there were the clicks and pops of a very long-distance video call being completed, but then, there was a strange lack of static on the line. Suddenly, crystal clear pictures of Scott, Mac, and Gonzo appeared on their TV screens. Because of the twenty-two thousand-mile distance to *Hope,* the signal suffered from a noticeable time delay, but their connection was picture-perfect. Sam noticed that video communications with *Hope* had been restored to near original quality less than twenty-four hours after the virus rampage.

Mason came forward in his seat toward the camera, then spoke first. "Major Scott, how are you and your crew holding up?" Over the videophone, Mason could clearly see Scott's and Gonzo's haggard, drawn faces.

Looking at Gonzo's zombielike appearance, Scott replied, "We need rest."

"Will it take a direct order from me for you to get it?" Mason asked, though his voice was not belligerent.

"No sir, General, that won't be necessary. I'm sure we can solve that problem on our own initiative."

"Any change in Pasha's condition?"

"Your medical staff or General Krol can give you any details, sir, but his prospects look good. We expect him to be up and about within the week. He could be as good as new in two."

"We need him, Scott, need him desperately. He knows more about that space station than all of us put together." Mason paused, having heard the urgent tone in his own voice. He cleared his throat, then continued in a matter-of-fact tone. "Have your folks studied the operations plan we sent up earlier this afternoon?"

For an instant, Scott contorted her face, then once again she regained control. Her face revealed no emotion. "Yes, sir. We've seen it." Her voice sounded restrained.

There was an extended period of silence. Mason noticed multiple signs of uneasiness. Scott remained impassive, but Gonzo anxiously looked across the room at Mac. Mac doodled on a pad of paper, shaking his head, obviously wanting to speak, but holding back.

"Yes. And?" Mason opened the floor for comments.

"General, may we discuss this candidly?" asked Scott, speaking for her crew. Her voice was almost excessively calm.

"Yes." General Mason felt they needed a free exchange.

When Scott spoke this time, there was in her voice the sharp metallic ring of urgency. "General, that plan is a bunch of crap." Scott's one line said it all. She'd summarized the feelings of her crew concisely. They couldn't have said it better themselves—get to the point and spit it out. In their hearts, they felt a rush of admiration for Scott. Mac quit doodling, and Gonzo nodded agreement with a proud smile.

Mason, his staff included, smiled on the inside. She'd said exactly what they felt. "I agree with you, Major. Our operations plan leads nowhere and resolves nothing." Mason paused, choosing his words carefully, formulating his question as a litmus test to evaluate Scott's judgment. Although he'd known and admired Scott since her days at the Air Force academy, he hadn't worked closely with her for several years. "Given what we know, how would you propose we proceed?"

Scott responded immediately. She knew what she'd do. "Focus on what's important. Sit tight and let your technical people do their jobs. Don't worry about an op plan until you know what to do."

Mason nodded agreement. He'd seek Scott's opinion again, and often. Her judgment and communication skills had matured a great deal since he'd first come to know her as a brassy young lieutenant. "You make sense to me, Major. Anything else come to mind?"

Scott looked at her crew. Their expressions said, *Tell the man,* and she believed she would. "Well, yes sir, there is." She paused and collected her thoughts. "We think *Freedom*'s radar coverage may have a hole in it. She's blind looking into the sun."

Mason looked down the table to Colonel Napper for an analysis. "Sam, will you field this one?"

Colonel Sam Napper smiled a funny, bemused sort of smile and rubbed the heavy stubble on his face. "General, I'd like to hand it off to John Sullivan if I could. I believe he knows exactly what Livermore has done to plug that blind spot."

John Sullivan pursed his lips. There was silence for a prolonged period while he sketched two pictures of the sun, earth, and *Freedom*. One drawing showed *Freedom* in the direct sunlight, the second showed her in darkness behind the earth. They weren't drawn to scale, but he thought they'd get his points across. John put the two sketches before the video camera, then finally spoke. *"Freedom* was intended to be invulnerable, unapproachable by anyone without Centurion's consent. As you can see from this figure, *Freedom* stays in sunlight almost around the clock, so this blind spot was a big problem for us. Understand though, *Freedom* was never totally blind looking into the sun. She could see—only she couldn't see as well. Her long-range vision suffered, but she could see any target close enough to her to cast a shadow. We tested this extensively. If we hadn't, someone else would have tested it for us. When *Freedom* moves into the earth's shadow, the blind spot disappears, of course, but during *Freedom*'s long hours of daylight, she was vulnerable."

John took a deep breath, then sighed. "So we plugged the hole with a series of agile lasers. We use lasers on targets within a one-hundred-mile radius and missiles on the rest."

Absorbing John's description, Scott was silent for a moment. For Scott, the next question was obvious. It took mettle to pose the question, but there was no place to hide. They had to face it. "How close could we get?" Her tone conveyed resolve.

Following this question, the tension in the meeting suddenly increased. Hesitant, John couched his response with a question. "In *Hell Fire*?" His voice sounded uncertain.

Scott nodded, her expression impassive.

John tried to swallow, but his throat felt parched. "You

understand the complexities of the flight path? The closer you get to *Freedom,* the less margin you have for error."

"I understand."

John had not fully worked out the details so his voice was tentative. "Assuming sufficient fuel, probably somewhere between five and fifty miles. The closer you stick to the flight path, the closer you'll get before you're detected."

Scott's response was as immediate as it was decisive. "We've got to do better than that. Five to fifty miles won't do."

Mason suddenly found himself running over different ways to approach this situation. He decided, as he generally did, to say exactly what he thought as best he could, and when in doubt, talk straight from the heart. "To die trying in this endeavor is to lose everything." Mason's words seemed to linger in the air. He paused and looked Scott squarely in the eyes. "You are not expendable and you're not approaching *Freedom* until you believe you can do it. And once you believe it, you've got to convince me." Although there were others listening to the conversation, the tone of the meeting changed. The meeting transformed into a one-on-one exchange between Mason and Scott. In a way, Mason and Scott reached out to each other through plainspoken conversation and their minds met. Mason's communication was complete. Each now understood the other.

Once the meeting ended, Scott allowed her eyes to glass over. She felt a relief in her soul, an exhilaration unlike anything she'd ever experienced. For the first time in a long time she believed they were going to make it. She didn't know how, she didn't know when, but she believed they could do it. Scott studied the expressions on Mac's and Gonzo's faces, looking anxiously for some sense of change. Without an exchange of words, she knew that they believed it too. Although silent, Mac and Gonzo experienced the same sense of relief and exhilaration. The immense pressure and tension had taken its toll on them all.

**The Day of Reckoning**

Fraught with peril, their future together was inescapable, but they believed in their souls that they'd survive.

Scott looked up into Mac's glassy eyes. He nodded, giving her his *I already know* smile. She spoke slowly, her tone—final. "We're gonna lick this thing, and when we do, we're going to make damn sure it never happens again."

# PART 7

# THE DAY OF
# REVELATION

DAY 6—
DECEMBER 12, 2014

# 23

John Sullivan felt as if the weight of the world was crushing him, squeezing the very life from his body as he stood before Mason and his general staff. Thinking about his briefing, John gazed with trepidation down the length of the table in the video conference room. For the first time since the crisis began, sergeants from the Military Police stood armed and ramrod-straight by the entrances to the room. John hoped they were there to protect him. He felt he might need a military escort before his briefing was finished, but there was no reason to postpone the inevitable. The information in the Livermore Report was rock solid and inescapable.

As John surveyed the faces in the room, time seemed to stand still. For a few moments, it all seemed like a dream. Glancing down, he was jolted back to reality by the single word on his first viewgraph. There was no possibility of awakening to something else, but he wished with all his heart that he might.

As he distributed copies of the Livermore Report around the room, John felt nausea rising from his stomach. There was a peculiar aura surrounding the report. John felt contaminated, a kind of sickening disgust when he touched it. He believed it might describe a biblical prophecy come true, the beginning of the end of the world, and he was the chosen messenger. He found the future more unnerving now than before the Livermore Report, yet once again he stood before the general staff asking that they comprehend the unthinkable.

Without fanfare or enthusiasm, John switched on his PC and the overhead slide projection system. His first viewgraph summarized the Livermore Report in one word. The viewgraph read simply:

INTRACTABLE

John took a deep breath, then began. He spoke quietly, his tone was one of dismay. "Gentlemen, I regret to inform you that the virus which infected *Freedom* has no cure. In Livermore's opinion, the problem is intractable. We face a problem with no feasible solution."

Mason sat stunned, disbelieving. He did not speak. He felt helpless and wished he were somewhere else, anywhere else. His heart moaned a rueful cry, his mind wanted to surrender and let someone else take over.

Mason surveyed Napper's face, Krol's, then Craven's. They were staring at him looking like lost sheep. Their expressions read, *What do we do now?* The room was crammed with people and Mason suddenly became aware that everyone was staring at him. They needed someone, they needed a leader, they needed him now. He couldn't abdicate.

"John, we don't fight without knowing our adversary and we don't concede defeat without a fight." Mason spoke in a compassionate voice. "I know your colleagues did their best, but it is not their place to judge the outcome of this war before the first battle. Perhaps there is no software solution. Be that as it may, we won't give up until we find a solution. There must be one. We know the problem's manmade." He paused, sensed the pulse of his audience, and concluded they needed an encouraging message. Summarizing what he knew, he continued. "The situation may not be so bleak as it seems. Our latest on the *Black Hole* sounded encouraging. After two more modifications, Jackson believes they'll be ready. General Krol's report from Kaliningrad is due in later today and he believes it's significant. It could contain information about *Freedom* that may help us turn this situation around."

Mason looked around the room. Hope had returned to the eyes of his staff. He looked at John, winked, then in a deliberately relaxed and pleasant tone of voice he asked, "John, would you please brief us on the characteristics of this virus? Together, we'll find the cure."

John smiled. "Very well, General." He felt as if the burdens of the world had been lifted off his back. After culling his slides, he went on to describe the virus in detail, then presented a crisp summary at the end. "Let me conclude with what we know and what we're missing. We don't know the organization behind the virus. Off the record, the FBI informs me they are running out of leads. As you know, the U.S. government funded parts of the work, but we don't know who put the pieces together. Whoever did it named the virus PAM." John paused. After pondering her name, he looked puzzled. "I can't tell you what it stands for. It's probably not important anyway, but we didn't see any good reason to change it. We know how PAM infected our software and we relearned one lesson we must never forget." John projected a viewgraph which read simply:

SHORTCUTS KILL

"If we'd done the job right, we could've prevented this fiasco." John's tone was matter-of-fact, not accusing. He paused. His audience appeared impassive. Maybe he wasn't telling them anything they didn't already know.

"Finally, and perhaps most important, we know exactly how the virus will behave in the future." John changed viewgraphs and slowly read it out loud, word for word. "Mark my words, General."

The Day of Revelation

"And she's predictable. Once she takes over a computer, she'll run forever."

He was obviously uncomfortable with his next comment, but he was only the Livermore messenger. "Once a virgin PAM virus program starts running, she cannot be destroyed." John cleared his throat. He'd expected some opposition from his audience, but didn't get it. John concluded that this concept would take some time to sink in. "PAM senses her environment and, when threatened, she spreads like a cancer at the speed of light. She gives birth—she spawns copies of herself—then evacuates to the safety of another computer. PAM's born to run and will survive at all costs. Undoubtedly, she's spread to every computer on *Freedom*. PAM must be treated like a cancer, not a virus. The cure, if any is possible, requires major surgery. Every computer on *Freedom* must be disconnected and gutted of all permanent memory. Every trace of PAM must be purged. Obviously, *Freedom* must be boarded to gut each computer, but understand—PAM won't allow anyone or anything to approach *Freedom*."

John sighed, then spoke quietly. "In all probability, Commander Jay Fayhee and Depack McKee are dead. We don't have hard data to prove our suspicion, but their very existence would certainly threaten PAM."

There was silence as John studied Mason's expression, then the sound of a single sob. John saw Mason's sadness to be sure, his eyes were glassy, his back to the wall. He was suffering, but he was not broken. Deep within those magnificent sad eyes of Mason's, John saw a defiant fire burning. His humanity and spirit could not be smothered.

"That's all I have, sir."

Mason shook his head slowly, as if to clear it. There was a period of silence which followed for not more than forty seconds. "John, now that we know what we're up against, I need Livermore to work up an operations plan that tells us three things. First, how we disconnect the booby traps surrounding Centurion. Second, how we disconnect him, and third, how we gut him."

Looking somewhat skeptical, John pursed his lips. "Someone must board *Freedom.*"

"Yes." Mason's tone was final. From his tone, it was clear that this point was not open for discussion. Mason leaned forward and rubbed his forehead. He felt the tension building behind his eyes. "Yes, John, I understand. I don't know how but we will board *Freedom.* We must."

*The Dead Zone, 12/12/2014, 1910 Zulu, 12:10 P.M. Local*
CHEYENNE MOUNTAIN, COLORADO

The conference room was silent and nearly empty as General Krol walked back to his chair at the conference table. For the past forty minutes he'd been mumbling Russian over the phone from the far back corner of the room. Mason and Napper looked up anxiously at Krol, hoping to see some facial expression which would hint as to what he was about to say. Characteristically, Krol maintained his stoic facade, but when he began speaking, his voice betrayed an overwhelming sense of relief combined with frustration. There were things he must communicate that he could not translate.

"There's good news and bad news from Kaliningrad." General Krol paused, struggling with his translation, then smiled. "You know, after years of speaking English, I still think in Russian. Give me a moment to organize my thoughts. It's important." Krol wrote what he wanted to say on a pad of paper, then rearranged the words. He found it easier to write what he wanted to say and then read it aloud.

Mason craned his neck but couldn't read Krol's handwriting upside down.

Krol read his message with authority. "Space Station *Freedom* is vulnerable. Her radar is impaired." Mason and Napper leaned forward in one simultaneous motion. "She has a cone-shaped blind spot off her red face. A radar dead zone which measures forty-five degrees wide."

Mason blinked his eyes in disbelief. "Are you absolutely sure about this, Yuri?"

"Yes. Three technical teams independently reconstructed this blind spot from our best available data. As you Americans say, she's as blind as a bat."

"Thank God." He'd been given a second chance. Mason couldn't contain his emotion. He didn't try. His mind began to race, his heart pumped with excitement. A renewed energy charged his body. *Freedom*'s blind spot was not the end, but it could mark the beginning of the end. Blinking his eyes clear, Mason winked at Krol.

Krol's stoic facade lifted before Mason's eyes. His expression revealed a mixture of compassion and understanding. "I am happy to bring you this news, my friend."

Mason cleared his throat. "Yuri, does Kaliningrad have any more silver bullets for us?"

Yuri looked puzzled. "What do you mean by silver bullets?"

"More good news, more information."

"No more good news I'm afraid." Krol paused. A genuine sadness shone through his eyes. "I am sorry, but we don't know what happened to the crew." He looked down and slowly read from his notes. "Unless they escaped into an airtight compartment, they are probably dead. The control room is depressurized and every airlock is open."

Mason sighed. Slowly, he accepted the inevitable. "We bury our dead but life must go on."

"That's what they would want," Krol lamented.

Colonel Napper had been silent until now, but this seemed an opportune moment to interrupt. "What do we do next, General?"

Mason picked up a pencil and began writing down alternatives. Suddenly, there was so much to do. Operations to plan, briefings to attend, phone calls to make, prototype aircraft to test, space stations to board, and computers to gut. The rest of his staff must be briefed, but that would happen soon enough. "Yuri, what time's your briefing?"

"My report's in reproduction. Should be ready in two hours or less."

**The Day of Revelation**

Earth

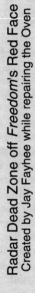

Dead Zone

Radar Dead Zone off *Freedom*'s Red Face
Created by Jay Fayhee while repairing the Oven

Mason thought through his endless list of things to do. Who made the most difference? Jackson and Scott. "Sam, I think we're ready to call *Hope.*"

Sam depressed a key on his computer terminal labeled HOPE and in a few moments the very long-distance connection was completed. Gonzo answered the call, then left the camera's field of view to gather the others.

*Gonzo looks better today,* Mason observed. The dark circles under his eyes were less evident.

On return, Gonzo entered first. Mac and Scott followed walking alongside Pasha, steadying him by his arms. His sense of balance was a little shaky. Pasha looked pale, but from the expression on his face, he was clearly happy to be there.

Mason, Krol, and Napper looked at each other, delighted to see Pasha up and around. He was an essential part of their team—their space station expert.

Scott spoke first. "General Krol, someone here would like a word with you." It was Krol's turn to display emotion although he tried to maintain his stoic facade.

What followed was a reunion of Russian comrades—a warm, heartfelt exchange in Russian which no one could translate. They didn't need to. Their expressions, gestures, and tone of voice conveyed understanding in any language.

Once the conversation returned to English, General Mason spoke to Scott. When he looked at her, she saw a dread premonition. "I am deeply sorry," she heard his voice say. "Unless Jay found refuge in an airtight compartment, he is probably dead." The deep concern in Mason's eyes relayed the compassion he felt for Scott.

Scott's expression revealed her pain. She was suffering, but she wasn't alone. She had friends and damn good ones. Gonzo, Pasha, and Mac were pulling for her and they'd get her through. Everyone on *Hope* was silent for a moment.

Suddenly, Scott banged the desk with her fist and started to sob. Gonzo reached out to her. She put her head on his shoulder and cried her heart out. Feeling like she was about to explode, a kaleidoscope of feelings tore her heart in different directions. She felt loss and rage but, above all else, she felt loneliness.

Then as quickly as it had begun, it was finished. Scott drew strength and comfort from the warmth of Gonzo's touch. She thought him a most unusual man, different somehow from the others. Always kind and considerate of her feelings, he'd often joked that he was her greatest fan. Scott realized she wasn't alone. Together, they were going to make it. They had to. In a gesture of affection, Scott gently patted Gonzo on the arm, wiped off her blotchy red face, then sat herself straight and upright. She quickly regained her composure and the analytical side of her brain took over.

"It is hard," Mason spoke quietly.

There was a long pause.

"It is," Scott replied.

Then, Mason slowly and calmly told them what had happened. First, he summarized PAM's characteristics, then described *Freedom*'s blind spot, and finally he explained the status of Jackson's *Black Hole* prototype aircraft. Mason concluded his explanation with a somber warning. "Assuming Jackson is successful, they'll fracture the DEWSAT layer and we'll launch reinforcements immediately. But if Jackson fails," Mason paused, choosing his words succinctly, "you will be on your own." Scott saw a look of physical pain cross Mason's face.

Pasha grunted as if someone had delivered a sharp blow to his stomach. This was the first he'd heard of this standalone alternative.

Scott's eyes now blazed with fiery resolve. Clenching her fist, she reached into the depths of her soul and quietly spoke what she believed. "We will survive."

There was a deep silence on the line.

"You must." Mason's voice had the distinctly metallic tone of urgency. Everyone was silent for a moment.

Mason could hardly believe what happened next. The matter-of-fact tone and atmosphere of the conversation was something like you'd experience during the huddle of a football team. A *you break this way, I'll drop back* sort of

**The Day of Revelation**

tone. First, Gonzo and Scott began discussing their flight plans. They talked about flying in out of the sun, then before they were close enough to cast a shadow, they'd sideslip into that blind spot on the red face. After several minutes, with no input from anyone on the ground, the discussions onboard *Hope* broke up into two separate meetings. Mac fastened a large set of space station blueprints onto a large plotting table. Pasha sat by the table and began circling the danger zones with red marker. From that moment forward, the meeting sustained a pace of its own, feeding on its own energy. One idea led to another. Mason sensed the paralyzing inertia of this virus had been overcome. He hoped and prayed that this might be their turning point. Although he knew their obstacles would be formidable, for a moment at least, he felt he could see the light at the end of the tunnel.

PART

8

# THE GATHERING STORM

DAY 7—
DECEMBER 13, 2014

# 24

The video conference room was enclosed by a wall of heavy black curtains, completely dark except for the light from a single blue TV screen. With satellite photographs in hand, Napper entered the room, gently tapping Mason on the shoulder.

"General?"

Mason awoke more slowly than usual from a dream he hated to leave. He blinked a few times and was disappointed to find himself camped out in his conference room. Focusing on the VCR digital clock, he remembered—like most VCR clocks—it was wrong. Still groggy, he looked at Sam. "What time is it?"

"About six-fifteen, sir."

Rubbing his aching head, he struggled to decide if this was morning or evening. At this stage, it was easier to ask. "A.M. or P.M., Sam? How long was I under?"

"It's early morning, General. You've been out nearly three hours."

Mason groaned after the realization struck home. There was another problem. There must be. Napper wouldn't wake him up with good news. Mason opened the curtains and cut up the lights. Still squinting, he looked at Sam and spoke quietly. "What's the problem?"

Sam placed a set of satellite photographs on the conference table in front of him. In less then fifteen seconds, Mason had seen all he needed to see. Bold black arrows drawn across the photographs told the story of massive Iraqi troop movements.

"Looks like the Iraqis are going to be the first bunch out of the box, sir." Napper's tone was matter-of-fact.

"What do you make of it?" Mason had already formed his opinion but wanted to compare it against Napper's for a sanity check.

"I think we're watching the prelude to the second Gulf War, General. The Iraqis are looking for a little oil rich waterfront property, something with a view of the Gulf. It could be more complicated than that, but I doubt it."

"It could be an exercise," Mason said wearily, but he didn't believe it.

"No sir. Not likely. Not on the Kuwaiti border." Napper spoke in a confident voice.

"Iraq will no doubt claim these troop movements are an exercise." Mason wanted to probe the depth of Napper's conviction.

"Placing Iraqi troops on the border of Kuwait is an inherently dangerous situation, General. Kuwaiti prudence demands that their troops stick close to the Iraqis, and having their troops in close proximity is dangerous. All the Iraqis need is an excuse."

"They may need no excuse at all." Mason spoke pragmatically.

"They've done it before," Napper agreed.

Mason concluded Napper's analysis was down-to-earth and he agreed with it. He wished he didn't. Mason looked at Napper. "So how should we respond?"

Napper spoke carefully and slowly, as if he were trying to avoid error. His tone was a combination of confidence and grave concern. "First, consider who needs to know: the President, the Kuwaitis, and the Saudis. Second, consider the assets we have in the immediate area: nothing, not a damn thing." Napper paused, culled out one of the satellite photos, then pointed to a fleet of ships in the Arabian Sea steaming south, away from the action. "Here. A single carrier group within a twenty-four-hour sail of the Persian Gulf. But what good are they? For all practical purposes, the group is useless. Every aircraft and missile's been grounded." Napper's tone shifted to one of pressing importance. "Iraq's got to be planning a ground war, and they'll be in one hell of a big hurry to get it won and over with. They can't know any better than we do when our armada will be set right."

Mason placed his head in his hands then judiciously considered Napper's analysis. There was silence for an extended period while Mason sorted through what he thought. He found this type of mental exercise physically exhausting. Minutes later, he looked at Napper and spoke as concisely as he could. "The elements of surprise and readiness cannot be overrated in this situation. Considering the virus, the question of air superiority is a wash. If Iraq surprises Kuwait and strikes decisively with sufficient force, the war could be over in one week or less. If, on the other hand, Iraq loses the element of surprise and Kuwait is prepared, the ground war would likely be a bloody battle of attrition."

Napper nodded agreement. "So the Iraqi keys to Kuwait are surprise and readiness?"

Mason spoke slowly and quietly, rubbing his eyes once again. "The sooner they strike, the shorter the war. Time is everything."

"Then—it's like a horse race."

"But the race has started," Mason sighed. "The Iraqis have bolted out of the gate."

"So we're the spoilers. We eliminate the element of surprise."

"We do." Mason's expression was determined, his voice urgent. "We tell Kuwait to position their troops opposite the Iraqi forces and make ready for a ground war. We don't know when and we don't know where, but Iraq is going to attack."

*The Squeeze, 12/13/2014, 1627 Zulu, 11:27 A.M. Local*
THE WHITE HOUSE,
WASHINGTON, D.C.

The President's melancholy mood mirrored the gloomy sky outside the Oval Office. There was progress on the virus, but Mason's crew wasn't moving fast enough to keep up with the Iraqis. The Iraqi Republican Guard was rolling, taking positions along the Kuwaiti border. Placing the Allied operations plan on his desk, the President peered over his reading glasses at Clive Towles, the national security advisor. "I don't like it. These schedules allow far too much slack."

Towles was noncommittal and spoke objectively. "They gave you what you asked for, Mr. President. It's a big mistake to squeeze Mason—like squeezing water from a rock."

The President discounted Clive's observation then laid out the set of satellite photographs taken over Kuwait. "You've seen these?"

"I have. We wired these photographs along with our recommendations to Kuwait and Saudi Arabia."

"Yes, yes." The President's tone was impatient. "Any response?" He looked apprehensive.

Towles sighed. "The Kuwaitis plan a detailed evaluation tomorrow, but their initial position was disappointing."

"Clearly I haven't seen their response," the President snapped. "What do they plan to do?"

"Nothing."

"Nothing?" The President's jaw went slack. His mind transitioned into a state of disbelief.

"The Kuwaitis were warned about these troop movements in advance by Iraq. Iraq has assured them in writing that these military camps and troop movements are an exercise, part of their winter desert maneuvers. The Kuwaitis won't do anything that might provoke the Iraqis."

"What does their military think about it?"

"They don't like it, of course, but then again, the Kuwaiti military doesn't get a vote. At this point, it's considered a political matter."

"It won't be a political matter for long." The President spoke in earnest. "Iraq will drive the Kuwaiti Army into the sea."

"If these events go unchanged, they most certainly will." Clive's serious-minded approach to this issue allowed for no nonsense.

**The Gathering Storm**

The President began drawing big red circles around the major work elements in the Allied op plan. "General Mason doesn't know it, but he's going to pull this schedule up."

"Mr. President, I'd suggest you take this matter up with the Chairman of the Joint Chiefs."

"You can count on it. I want this virus situation turned around before things get out of hand in Kuwait. If the Iraqis get away with murder, others will surely follow suit."

"In my opinion, Mr. President, you're overreacting."

The veins on the President's forehead bulged and his face turned purple. "Damn it to hell, Clive! I'm trying to nip this problem in the bud before it gets out of hand. You got any better suggestion?"

"Let the Kuwaitis solve their problem, Mr. President, and allow General Mason to solve ours." His tone was businesslike and detached.

The President decided, but he didn't think. He knew that important decisions should never be made in the heat of anger but that didn't slow him down. This was where he would draw his line in the sand. His tone was final. "Mason will solve our problem all right, but sooner, much sooner than he expects."

*Reasoning, 12/13/2014, 1830 Zulu, 11:30 A.M. Local*
CHEYENNE MOUNTAIN, COLORADO

Without notice, the President called Mason over the direct video conference line. The President, the Chairman of the Joint Chiefs, and Clive Towles on line in Washington—Napper, Craven, and Mason on line under Cheyenne Mountain.

Following the obligatory "Good morning, General," the President pressed the reason for the call.

Mason expected the call concerned the Iraqi situation and placed his latest set of satellite photographs on the conference table.

"General Mason, I want you to pull up your op plan. Accelerate it in light of the situation developing in the Middle East."

**The Gathering Storm**

The Chairman of the Joint Chiefs spoke next before Mason had a chance to think. "The President's right, Slim. You can take slack out of any schedule. Throw more people at it, smother it with money, just pull it up."

Mason considered the chairman's proposal. No self-respecting manager ever turned down an offer of additional resources. "Lincoln Lab needs additional people and prototype aircraft. They couldn't help us out immediately though. Additional aircraft wouldn't be available for months." Mason looked at the President. "What would make you happy? Tell me exactly what you're looking for."

The President did not hesitate. "I want this Star Wars fiasco cleared up before Iraq invades Kuwait."

At first, Mason couldn't believe what the President was saying. They expected Iraq to invade Kuwait in one week or less. "I understand your concern about Kuwait, Mr. President, but we've covered this ground before. We're in this predicament today because we buckled under pressure. We compromised for all the wrong reasons, got in a hurry, and screwed up. Our response to pressure was inappropriate then, it should not be repeated now." Mason looked at Craven. "What do you think? Frankly, I'm at a loss as to how to deal with it."

"I agree. Go with your gut. Do what you think is right." He thought, but did not say, *Political pressure is bullshit.*

Mason allowed himself a moment of self-reflection, then spoke quietly. "Mr. President, can we speak privately, one-on-one?"

"Very well, General." Both rooms emptied. After a few moments' shuffling, the conversation resumed.

"We have conflicting orders from you, Mr. President. Move now but do it right. If we take the time to do it right, there is still a very good chance that we could fail." Mason paused, letting his sobering statement sink in. "If we move now, we scuttle all chances for success."

"Let me be clear, General Mason." The President's face scrunched up. "I don't believe it. I don't believe if you moved today that you'd scuttle your chances." The President paused, then revealed his willingness to compromise. "What really matters is that you believe it."

"I do." Mason's two words sounded with resolve.

"My job is to push. Your job is to deliver." The President paused, eyeing Mason's expression. "As soon as you possibly can."

Mason's expression immediately eased. "We'll march to that order, Mr. President."

**The Gathering Storm**

# PREPARATION

## DAY 8—
## DECEMBER 14, 2014

# 25

*Family Plans, 12/14/2014, 1500 Zulu, 8:00 A.M. Mountain Standard Time*
SPACE STATION *HOPE*

*Hope,* like *Freedom,* was an elaborate maze of rooms, corridors and concealed explosive devices. Staring at *Freedom*'s construction blueprints, Pasha highlighted the lethal hazards on his screen. He entered a key totaling the number of personnel mines and lasers, then groaned an anguished sigh. He'd never realized how many hazards were woven into the space station's fabric. None had ever failed. As far as he knew, none had ever been detonated defending the space station. The lethal security system had never given him any cause for concern until now. On *Freedom,* PAM controlled the space station's security system.

Across the room, Gonzo and Scott were putting together a list of equipment they'd need. Hearing Pasha's distress, they came immediately.

Inside *Hell Fire,* Mac worked reconfiguring the reconnaissance bay. Removing large pieces of equipment, Mac made room for Pasha and the additional gear they'd need on *Freedom.*

As Scott and Gonzo approached, they couldn't help but notice the warm look and feel of Pasha's work space. Almost simultaneously, as if on cue, their eyes were drawn to

the poster-size montage showing pictures of his wife and
three small children. There was something wonderful, almost indescribable about those pictures. There was a
warmth about them which humanized the stark, cold nature
of this colossal tin can. Intrigued, Gonzo stared wistfully
into the eyes of Pasha's little girl. Her expression was perfectly relaxed. Her bright, wide eyes conveyed the most
marvelous sense of unconditional love he had ever seen
captured on film. *Someone must love her a tremendous lot,*
Gonzo thought. He wanted to ask Pasha about his little girl,
but decided to wait until the time was right. Gonzo loved
children, he loved everything about them. He'd wished
many times over for a wife and children, but somehow he'd
always arrived too late.

Glancing at Scotty, he quietly sighed. He knew she
would never care for him, she'd loved Jay since high
school, but he could always hope. Her eyes, her voice, the
look and feel of her hair drove him—to think about something else. After a brief reflection, he just felt lucky to be
near her.

When Pasha spoke, reality came crashing down around
him. "We need a demolition team."

Gonzo noticed numerous icons highlighted in reverse
video on Pasha's computer screen. "What are these?"

"They're the problem. Each flashing icon's a blunderbuss." Gonzo looked puzzled so Pasha spelled it out
clearly. "An explosive personnel mine."

Gonzo studied the layout carefully, noting each location.
"We'll need the location coordinates assimilated into our
datapacks." He paused for a few moments, then spoke in an
objective voice. "They must be sensitive to something.
What triggers them?"

"PAM," Pasha spoke cryptically. There was a tone of
certainty in his voice. "PAM senses body heat then deto-
nates the blunderbuss once you're in range."

"We'd better come up with some way to safely detonate
those things." Scott's pragmatic assessment was unemo-
tional.

"We can do it," Pasha responded objectively. "We have

a small, remotely controlled electric vehicle called the boomer. It's a minesweeper built specifically for this purpose."

"Good." She collected her thoughts, then continued. "If Jackson's *Black Hole* flies undetected and Wild Bill punches through, Mason plans to send up the Marines. Otherwise, we're on our own."

Pasha considered their alternatives then chose his words carefully. "We'll train assuming we're on our own. After a few days' practice, we'll be a first-rate demolition team."

"I expect you're right," Gonzo agreed. "Train for the worst-case. It's the only way to be sure."

"Apparently Jackson's ace in the hole didn't pan out," Scott lamented quietly. "We'll get the story firsthand in a half hour or so, but Colonel Napper believes Wild Bill's only got a fifty-fifty chance."

"He's risking his life for us," Gonzo added somberly.

Pasha grimaced. Tension around his mouth caused him to look older. "He's a courageous man, putting his life on the line like this. I wouldn't want to walk in his shoes."

"The man's a warrior." Scott spoke with a quiet tone of admiration. She looked Gonzo in the eyes and smiled a sad sort of smile. *Our shoes don't look much better,* she thought, but did not say. Her thoughts connected with Gonzo's. In many ways, they were very much the same.

Scott, Gonzo, and Pasha then made plans for clearing the blunderbuss mines from *Freedom.* Once everyone knew what to do, the conversation shifted to Pasha's family.

"She's beautiful," Gonzo said, pointing to the little girl's picture. "Who took this?"

Pasha's face beamed. The concern shown only moments earlier seemed to disappear. "That's my favorite picture." He spoke softly with a twinkle in his eye. "I took it after countless hours of waiting."

Gonzo gazed fondly at the picture, then watched Scott in quiet admiration. Her eyes smiled a teary sort of smile.

"She must love you very much," Scott said quietly.

"My children are the greatest fans I'll ever have." Struggling to control his emotions, he bit his lip. "I need them."

"They need you home," Gonzo lamented.

Scott's voice sounded with renewed resolve. "You will see your family soon, Pasha."

Pasha's gaze was distant, unfocused. His thoughts were of home—twenty-two thousand miles away.

*The Gamble, 12/14/2014, 1530 Zulu, 8:30 A.M. Local*
CHEYENNE MOUNTAIN, COLORADO

There was a somber silence over the video conference line as Scott and her crew onboard *Hope* watched Thomas Jackson's briefing without comment. Mason and his general staff on one end, Thomas Jackson and Wild Bill Boyd on the other.

Mason studied the two faces on screen. Thomas Jackson, the radar expert from MIT Lincoln Lab, and Lieutenant Colonel William "Wild Bill" Boyd sat silently, their expressions unfathomable. The *Black Hole* prototype test data was undeniable, the conclusion inescapable. Jackson was a beaten man; Boyd's chances were fifty-fifty at best.

Thinking about his briefing, Jackson grimaced. There was precious little more to say. His plan to hide the experimental prototype with the masking equipment used in the Phantom Hawk had been a grave error. The only bright spot on the horizon was that they'd discovered the problem in the lab before it was too late. Jackson gazed with trepidation at Mason. He had no silver bullets, no magic fixes. Only a few suggestions which might marginally improve the situation.

Wild Bill surveyed the faces of the general staff and those onboard *Hope*. He wished he was someone else, anyone else.

Colonel Napper addressed a question to Jackson. "Why couldn't we remotely control the prototype from the ground?"

Jackson's expression was placid, his body motionless. His mind focused on his response. "We could remotely control the aircraft, but our chances are better with a pilot in the cockpit. I say this for two reasons. First, there is a very slim chance that PAM would pick up our control transmissions, and second, if something goes wrong, our chances for success improve by five percentage points with a skilled pilot in the cockpit."

"Five percent," Napper said solemnly. His jaw was tightened.

"In addition," Jackson added, "Colonel Boyd should take off low and slow over water." He paused, then continued with the reason why. "We pick up ten percentage points on takeoff, but our improvement diminishes once the prototype gains altitude." There was no technical discussion. Results were all that really mattered in this numbers game. Following a short pause, Jackson concluded. "I propose Logan Airport with takeoff over Boston Harbor."

Mason second-guessed the technical reason why. Any slowly moving stealth target was difficult to detect near the surface of the water. "I want you to understand one thing clearly, Colonel Boyd." He paused, took a breath, and went on. "I will not order anyone into a life-and-death situation where the chances of survival are—unacceptable. I want you to rethink your decision to volunteer with this in mind."

The silence which ensued lasted more than thirty seconds.

Wild Bill looked up, holding his head erect. His voice, calm and barely audible. "I have given the matter a great deal of thought, General, and my mind is clear." As he spoke, his voice gained strength. It was as if his ears heard what his mouth was saying for the first time and he believed it. "As I see it, our situation's damn near hopeless. We only have two chances to get out of this man-made fiasco. Two alternatives—that's not a hell of a lot. We need to do everything we can do to pull this off. Whether I like it or not, that fact is undeniable. That bunch on *Hope* needs our help. They're not trained soldiers and frankly, sir, they're gonna need all the help they can get. I wouldn't want to trade places with 'em." He paused, then continued with a softer voice. His tone was sincere. "I've been in this *Black Hole* program from the get go, and Jackson here will

agree, I'm the best you've got. Considering our situation, I
don't think anything less will do. We need to take our best
shot and frankly, sir, I'm the logical choice."

Mason closed his eyes for a few moments, struggling
desperately to find the right words. He focused on his message, the essence of what he believed. "I agree with your
assessment, Colonel—I wish I did not," he lamented quietly.

Scott, who'd been silent, now spoke to Wild Bill for herself, and on behalf of her crew. "You're risking your life
for us and there's precious little we have to offer you in return."

"That's true," groused Jackson, interrupting Scott mid-
stream. "Why are you doing this? Nobody does anything
for nothing."

"It's my job," Wild Bill snarled instinctively at Jackson.
After a few moments, he thought about how his response
must sound to the people stranded onboard *Hope*. Turning
away from Jackson, Wild Bill allowed his face to relax and
winked at Scott. "Well, somebody has to do it, right?"

"Once this nightmare is behind us," Scott said quietly,
"we'd like to meet you in person."

"No problem. That can be arranged, Major Scott, under
one condition." Wild Bill forced a grin to ease the tension.
"I don't rescue XR-30 crews for free, you understand. My
services don't come cheap. Don't get me wrong, your lives
are important and all, but I'm an old stick and rudder man
myself."

From the look in his eye, from the tone of his voice,
Scott knew exactly where he was headed. One glance told
her Mason knew it too. She'd heard variations of this setup
before. Wild Bill was a test pilot and any pilot worth his
salt's looking for a throttles-to-the-wall flight in *Hell Fire*.
Making eye contact with General Mason, they communicated without an exchange of words, then Scott spoke.
*"Hell Fire* always has room for one more, right, General?"

"Absolutely. Any speed—fast as you want to go—anywhere. And one other thing, Bill. I'm driving to Boston to

meet you and see the *Black Hole* firsthand. I want to be there."

"I look forward to meeting you, sir." Wild Bill paused. "Now about that ticket?"

"I'll bring the paperwork. You fill in the destination."

"How about one round-trip ticket to *Freedom*, General . . . window seat?"

"Done."

The meeting was adjourned following a discussion of when and where the *Black Hole* prototype flight would take place.

Once the conference line had been disconnected, Mason looked at Napper. "Run the shop while I'm away and keep Scott in the loop. They need to know status—anything relevant to the *Black Hole* flight—in real time. Call me if anything changes." His instructions were crisp.

"What are you thinking, General?" Napper looked perplexed.

"I'm headed to Boston to meet Colonel Boyd face-to-face; it's important to me. I've never ordered anyone into a situation this dangerous, and I want to meet the man with courage enough to face it." Now out of the spotlight with the TV monitors dark, Mason's private agony shone through his eyes. "You do what must be done, but it extracts a terrible toll."

*The Practice Run, 12/14/2014, 2030 Zulu, 1:30 P.M. Mountain Standard Time*
THE RED FACE
SPACE STATION *HOPE*

Scott heard Pasha's transmission crackle over her headphones: "Prebreathing complete. You're clear for EVA." Before Scott and her crew could safely begin their ExtraVehicular Activity (EVA), they had to prebreathe pure oxygen in order to purge nitrogen from their systems. Otherwise, the lower pressure inside their space suits would cause nitrogen bubbles to form in their bloodstreams, leaving them with a lethal case of the bends. Scott's heart was thumping now. Her breathing rapid. From inside the zippered pocket on her sleeve she extracted the tiny four-leaf clover Jay had given her many years ago. It was a gift she always carried with her.

After a brief moment's reflection, she pulled the depressurization handle and vented *Hell Fire*'s atmosphere into space. When the indicator light turned from red to green, she began turning the hatch wheel on top of *Hell Fire* and carefully opened it.

Tightly gripping Mac's hand, she pulled him from the reconnaissance bay in *Hell Fire*'s belly. Sweat poured off his forehead. Before pulling herself outside through the hatch, Scott checked Mac and Gonzo's equipment one last time. All seemed well.

After taking a deep breath, she disconnected her oxygen umbilical from *Hell Fire*. Once free, she pulled herself through the small hatch and out into space. Immediately afterwards, Mac passed her EVA backpack through the hatch along with a small thruster, an Aqua-Lung sized tank of compressed gas. Scott carefully slipped into the backpack and attached her umbilicals. Once a tiny gauge showed oxygen flowing into her suit, she began breathing again. Smiling to herself, she thought how she hated that nagging lag between breaths. Finally, she grabbed the handgrips on the small auxiliary thruster and clipped it to her pack.

Once Scott, Mac, and Gonzo extracted themselves, they moved in unison like a team of precision fliers, using their thruster tanks for propulsion. Approaching the red face, the trio retarded their speed by releasing braking bursts of gas. Scott entered the opening first, followed by Gonzo, then Mac. Passing through the slit, Mac accidently slammed his thruster tank into the flimsy skinlike mesh that covered the space station. There was no sound as the metal tank scraped against mesh, but Scott and Gonzo could feel the handrail of the corridor vibrating through their gloves.

Once inside, the space station looked abandoned. As expected, all the lights in the central core, including the control room, were off. Scott knew that humans tended to hunt by light—that humans were attracted to light like moths to a flame, and where there was light there was very real danger. Only the emergency lights remained on, illuminating the corridors connecting the central core to the spiked, outside skin. The corridors led to the central core, to the power plant and nervous system of the space station, but the corridors were punctuated with danger.

"There's the first one." Gonzo spoke over the low-power intercom inside his suit. He motioned ahead to Scott and Mac.

Scott admired Gonzo's low-light nocturnal vision. For several moments, even though she knew it was there, she couldn't see it. Then in the distance she made it out, a shape like that of a gargantuan shotgun shell. Mac could see it too. Ahead, maybe twenty-five yards down the corridor, they saw the blunderbuss; its cylinder-shaped ceramic warhead reflected only the faintest glimmer of light. They knew that the cylinder-shaped vessel was secured to a base made of plastique explosive and was filled with thousands of pea-sized stainless-steel pellets. When the plastique base detonated, each steel pellet emerged with the same kinetic energy as a round from an M-16. The ceramic container would erupt spewing out the pellets in a sawed-off-shotgunlike scatter pattern, a pattern used to scatter shot at close range and tear pressurized space suits.

Mac carefully lifted the "boomer" out of his tool kit, placing it firmly on the corridor. It looked something like a radio-controlled miniature tank with robotic arms. Rolling on special magnetic tracks, it held firm against the corridor floor. "Hope this gadget works," Mac muttered into his intercom.

Over his headset Mac heard Pasha's voice come back loud and clear. "Not to worry, Mac. It's a minesweeper. It'll work."

Mac prepped the boomer for action by attaching a vertical flagpole to the tanklike body. On top of the pole he wired a diesel glow plug, a glowing heat source which would trigger the blunderbuss. He covered the top of the boomer with a protective shield of Kevlar armor then checked his handheld remote. Finally, after moving the throttle on the remote control, the drone tank lurched forward. "Good," he muttered. "Let's go."

Gonzo and Scott set up a Kevlar shield across the corridor, positioning themselves in line behind it. The Kevlar shield would stop the pellets but not heavy metal fragments from a high-explosive warhead. Mac started the boomer rolling slowly then took cover with Scott and Gonzo.

The drone transmitted a greenish video picture back to a small screen on Mac's handheld remote. The low-light pictures were grainy, but Mac could see well enough to keep the boomer on track. About ten feet from the blunderbuss Mac stopped the boomer and zoomed in. The blunderbuss looked exactly as they'd expected, no surprises. The next few seconds would reveal just how well they'd done their homework.

"This is it," Mac said with an apprehensive quiver in his voice. Lowering his head between his knees, he started the drone forward once again.

On the whole, it seemed like it took an awfully long time. Then in a fraction of a second, the blunderbuss spent its energy with a sudden flash of light—but no sound. Scott felt a rapid series of vibrations through her gloves as the high-energy pellets slammed into the corridor and Kevlar shield.

"Bull's-eye!" Gonzo observed, patting Mac on his shoulder.

"A mine is a hard thing to miss." Mac was not impressed, but he was glad it was over.

Once the explosive blast of buckshot passed overhead, they surveyed the damage to the corridor and robotic drone. As they'd expected, the space station was undamaged. The scattergun support mount for the blunderbuss munition had been designed to reload and fire again, but the exposed parts of the robotic drone had taken a beating. The flagpole and glow plug were obliterated—no surprise there—and the shield had taken a pounding. Underneath it all, the tanklike robotic drone survived without visible damage.

Mac tested the drone; it worked. "So far so good, Pasha. One down, four to go."

**Preparation**

*The amazing thing is how smoothly things have gone so far,* Scott thought. *Considering how many problems we've had up until now, it's amazing anything worked at all. At least we started with the easiest traps first. The blunderbuss was the dumb one.*

Advancing down the corridor, the trio executed their detonation operation once again. This time Scott configured the drone-tank with a glow plug and Gonzo ran the handheld remote. They repeated this sequence three more times, each time changing roles. Finally, after the fifth blunderbuss detonation, the corridor was secure—clear from the outer shell to the inner core. Scott's team felt they had the situation well in hand. Although it was dangerous, blunderbuss detonation was beginning to feel routine for them. Their confidence grew with each success along the way. Within a few hours, Scott's crew was operating as an efficient and finely tuned demolition team. They hadn't originally been trained as a bomb squad but quickly learned the ropes. Each member of the team fit neatly, each sufficiently trained so that they were interchangeable to some degree.

Scott checked her watch. About thirty minutes per detonation, three hours to secure the corridor. Three hours was acceptable. They had strength and oxygen enough to sustain themselves for up to four hours without breaking off for resupply. If they could establish a toehold inside *Freedom* quickly, they could off-load supplies, rest, and regroup for the second more dangerous phase of their operation—their core offensive. Centurion, the power plants, and the control room were all contained inside the core.

Scott tapped Mac on his helmet. "Whataya say we off-load then call it a day?"

Mac nodded, signaling a thumbs up. "Good. We can handle these babies with the right tools and a little guts."

Mac radioed *Hope*'s control room. "Pasha, how about a little light on the situation?"

Anxious, Pasha responded immediately, switching on all the operating lights inside *Hope*. He spoke with a voice that expressed relief. "And there was light."

Preparation

# THE END OF
# THE BEGINNING

## DAYS 16 THROUGH 20—
## DECEMBER 22-26, 2014

# 26

Climbing into *Hell Fire* was slow work for Scott and her
team because they were already wearing their EVA suits.
They were bulkier than their regular pressurized suits, but
they'd become accustomed to them during the course of
their training over the past several days. They were wearing the EVA suits because *Hell Fire*'s interior was
cramped and packed tight with supplies and equipment.
There was simply no place to change.

Scott was the last to wedge herself into *Hell Fire*. Once
inside, she wheeled the hatch shut and began making final
preparations for separation.

Scott's pulse rate increased as it normally did before
any flight. Looking back, it was amazing how smoothly
their training had gone, yet she had a nagging feeling
about this flight and didn't know why. They'd practiced
all aspects of the mission except the flight and final approach to *Freedom*. For that, they had to depend on their
navigational computer. Inside *Hell Fire,* Scott double-
checked the flight path data in the NavComputer. Smiling,
she believed that *Hell Fire*'s NavComputer was first-rate.
All she had to do was describe the characteristics of their
flight path then engage the autopilot. The autopilot would

read flight path data from the NavComputer and maneuver *Hell Fire* through the complex flight path required for their blind-side final approach onto *Freedom*'s red face. *Hell Fire* also possessed a flight path projection system called MAP which would enable Scott to manually approach *Freedom* on course if that became necessary. In space, *on course* is a difficult thing to determine without some fixed point of reference. The MAP system provided the reference point by displaying a projection of the desired flight path overlaid with a constantly updated image of *Hell Fire*'s actual position. Using MAP, Scott need only keep *Hell Fire*'s pipper between the lines. Without the NavComputer, MAP, and autopilot systems, it would be difficult if not impossible to maintain proper position and heading for their blind-side approach out of the sun.

Satisfied with the flight path data, Scott felt she had done all she could do—for now. Their course was set as long as everything went as planned. But as with Wild Bill's death, nothing ever worked out as planned. Something always went wrong. *Maybe that's what's nagging me,* Scott thought as she checked her watch and did some mental arithmetic. Two minutes till the explosive bolts fired forcing separation. Allow three minutes for attitude positioning. Another five minutes for radial burn, then a forty-one-hour wait until *Freedom* passed underneath them. That meant a forty-one-hour wait followed by a seven-hour pursuit. *This is going to be one long wait,* Scott thought. *And this is the easy part.* Scott's reflection was curtailed when she heard Big Shot's transmission crackle over her secure radio. There was a muted silence while the encrypted radio signal "synced up" causing the first syllable of the message to be lost. *"L Fire,* you're go for separation in T minus sixty seconds and counting."

Scott listened to the sounds of her crew over the intercom and noted their increased breathing rate. This was no training exercise. It was the real thing, and they had to take each movement slowly and carefully. A tiny mishap could scuttle the mission. Everyone knew there was a chance for them to succeed now. A real chance.

From inside the zippered pocket on the sleeve of her

pressurized space suit, Scott extracted the tiny four-leaf clover Jay had given her and hung it above her head on *Hell Fire*'s rear looking mirror. She wished she could kiss it for good luck, but her helmet and visor were in the way. She felt they'd need luck more now than ever.

Big Shot's transmission crackled over her headphones once again. *"L Fire,* you're go for separation in T minus ten seconds and counting . . . nine . . . eight. . . seven . . ."

The NavComputer flashed a green **All Systems Go** message across Scott's head's up display. After that moment, *Hell Fire*'s crew was no longer in the loop. With their weapons spent, they were now passengers on an orbiting, unarmed reconnaissance platform.

"Three . . . two. . . one...fire." Scott saw sparks fly out from underneath the seam of the docking collar as the explosive bolts fired, releasing *Hell Fire* from *Hope*'s anchorage. "And so we begin," Scott spoke quietly over the intercom as *Hell Fire* shuddered beneath them.

The crew was silent.

For a brief moment, a wave of exhilaration washed over Scott. She felt the thrill of motion accentuated by their closeness to *Hope*. *Hell Fire* vibrated as her attitude positioning rockets fired, slowly increasing their distance from *Hope*'s large triangular face. One by one the gauges in front of Scott seemed to come alive. The thousands of spikelike antennae covering *Hope*'s surface began to sweep by faster and faster. Soon they were a continuous blur. Her four-leaf clover appeared to gain weight, swinging like a pendulum from the cockpit mirror. Once they were well clear of *Hope*, *Hell Fire* executed a slow full body turn about the nose, rotating into escape position. Scott was awed by the remarkable view—she craned her neck and looked straight up through the canopy. *Hope* filled the windshield. *Hell Fire* was traveling positioned with *Hope* overhead and pointing away from earth. From this position, the thrust from the main rocket engine would propel *Hell Fire* further out into space into a region known as the junkyard. Once *Hell Fire*'s position stabilized, Scott felt the shudder from the main engine burn. This burn would increase their orbital radius and slow

**The End of the Beginning**

their orbital velocity, thereby allowing *Freedom* to over-take them and pass directly underneath. Their flight plan called for approaching *Freedom* out of the sun but initially they would be positioned one hundred miles above *Freedom*. Because *Freedom* was traveling in a lower orbital plane, it would catch up to *Hell Fire* and pass underneath like a race car hanging the inside track around a curve. Once the space station passed underneath, *Hell Fire* would close the gap starting from a position about one thousand miles behind her.

Outside *Hope*'s geostationary orbit was a belt of orbiting space junk. A belt of debris where dead and retired satellites were parked when they came to the end of their useful service life. Scott planned to hide *Hell Fire* in this ring of orbiting junk while *Freedom* passed underneath them. Generally, PAM wouldn't consider anything in the orbiting junk belt as a threat unless it moved toward *Freedom*.

Gonzo sat in the backseat carefully monitoring every action the autopilot made. "So far, we're golden, Scotty. Main engine burn was clean. Braking burn in three...two...one...ignition."

*Hell Fire* shuddered briefly then rolled through a slow pirouette. As planned, *Hell Fire* pulled in behind the large torpedo-shaped carcass of a dead communications bird once operated by the United States Air Force. *Hell Fire*'s first rendezvous was now complete. Once they slowed to the speed of the communication satellite, Scott examined the orbiting debris scattered all around them. She was amazed and grateful that they were unharmed by the space borne shrapnel. Once convinced all was well around their new parking spot, Scott spoke to her crew. "Now we wait."

*The Chase, 12/24/2014, 2258 Zulu, 3:58 P.M. Mountain Standard Time*
ONBOARD *HELL FIRE*,
POSITIONED DIRECTLY BETWEEN THE SUN AND *FREEDOM*

*Hell Fire*'s crew slept. The cockpit and reconnaissance cabin were dark; the instrument lighting was turned down.

**The End of the Beginning**

*Beep Beep Beep!* reverberated over the intercom.

Gonzo slammed his fist down hard on the mute button.

Scott opened her eyes to find the NavComputer powering up the ship, bringing the instrumentation and control panels back to life. The NavComputer spoke in a voice which imitated Gonzo and in fact sounded very much like him, only mechanical. "Target one thousand miles downrange. Closing burn commences in T minus sixty seconds and counting."

A green **All Systems Go** message flashed across Scott's head's up display. After reviewing *Freedom*'s current position and her course over the last forty-one hours, Scott spoke in a matter-of-fact tone. *"Freedom*'s on track."

Mac cleared his throat and spoke next. "We're ready to roll."

Gonzo disengaged the NavComputer's audible voice and spoke. "Scotty, closing burn begins in fifteen seconds."

"Roger," Scott replied. "Autopilot is engaged."

"T minus five . . . four . . . three . . . two . . . one . . . ignition."

*Hell Fire* shuddered.

Gonzo watched his engine control and fuel flow gauges come to life. They spun up exactly as they were supposed to. "Burn is go, Scotty."

For the next several minutes, Scott watched countless pieces of space borne debris streak by her cockpit canopy. Once *Hell Fire* was free and clear of the junk belt, she breathed a sigh of relief and spoke in a determined voice. "So our chase begins."

*The Puzzle, 12/24/2014, 0315 Zulu, 8:15 P.M. Mountain
    Standard Time*
ONBOARD *HELL FIRE,*
APPROACHING OUT OF THE SUN

Perplexed, Gonzo timed the output from his radar receiver using the clock on his Electronic CounterMeasures (ECM) computer. For a few moments, his mouth was agape. This dàta was unmistakable. The radar signal from *Freedom* cycled on for fifty-three seconds then off for seven. This on-again, off-again pattern was totally unexpected. Neither Gonzo or his ECM computer knew what to make of it. He pondered this problem in an effort to understand it. What could it mean? This blinking radar signature wasn't in the plan and he couldn't explain it. Was it significant? Probably, although he couldn't say for sure. Finally, after methodically working through a series of measurements, he raised a red flag to Scott. "I've got a big mystery here, Scotty, and I don't like the looks of it." Gonzo went on to describe the problem.

Scott tried to step back and analyze the problem objectively. "We have the go-no-go decision on our rendezvous coming up in three minutes, Gonzo." Scott spoke with a strained sense of urgency in her voice. "What do you think we should do?" *Hell Fire*'s fuel situation was critical. If all went as planned they had only a few minutes of fuel held in reserve. Once they'd passed their go-no-go point, their decision was go by default. They had insufficient fuel to return.

Gonzo's insides tightened into an icy ball. No need to think about his answer. He didn't like their situation, but the fact was they didn't have any choice. If they went back to *Hope* they could never return to *Freedom*—insufficient fuel. Their situation was a two-edged sword. Return now and face a slow lingering death or go forward and confront God only knows what. Gonzo grimaced and spoke in a grave tone. His mood bordered on the morose. Either alternative was fraught with danger. "Stay the course, Scotty. We'll understand this once we board *Freedom*. It may be nothing, but I feel like we missed something."

"Then we go." Scott thought about Gonzo's mystery for some moments and was at a complete loss to explain it. "We're on our own with this one, fellas," Scott sighed. "Pasha, can you and Mac help us out? What could cause this? Take a look at Gonzo's data and let us know if you can come up with something, anything." As usual, *Hell*

*Fire* maintained radio silence to avoid revealing her position.

Mac and Pasha patched into Gonzo's data and took a look. The pattern didn't match anything Pasha had ever seen. The on-off pattern didn't agree with any of their simulations.

After scrutinizing the data from start to finish, Mac and Pasha looked at one another and shook their heads. Pasha spoke first, carefully crafting his words, using his best English. "No one could help us with this one, Scotty. It's one for the books. The power-on period looks normal, but I can't explain why *Freedom* shuts down during that seven-second window. I've never seen anything like it."

Nodding agreement, Mac spoke next. "I can offer one thing, Scotty." Mac paused and punched up their distance to target. "Quick as we're in range, I'll lock *Freedom* on camera and we'll take a look-see."

"Good," Scott replied, breathing a sigh of relief. "We'll feel a lot better with *Freedom* on screen."

*The Helix, 12/24/2014, 0547 Zulu, 10:47 p.m. Mountain Standard Time*
Onboard *Hell Fire*,
Final Approach

Once *Hell Fire* closed within range, a clear image of *Freedom* suddenly locked on screen. Mac watched the picture acquisition light on his primary camera change quickly from red to green. Satisfied, he started their digital videotape recorder rolling and felt lucky to capture the picture from such a long range. Mac considered rock solid pictures from this distance a remarkable accomplishment because *Hell Fire*'s burning engines caused her to vibrate. Before Mac could react to the picture, Pasha spoke.

"Holy Mother of God." He spoke disbelieving, questioning his own eyes. His tone was one of unmitigated dismay.

Scott blinked. Centered on her TV screen was a clear computer-enhanced image of *Freedom,* sunny-side up as

**The End of the Beginning**

expected. Trouble was—*Freedom* was spinning like a colossal top.

"Damn." Gonzo spoke bitterly with deep resentment. "That bitch covered her ass." For the first time he addressed PAM as a person. Suddenly, PAM seemed alive, even loathsome, intangible but very, very *real*. For a few moments, Gonzo lost his composure, but in his frustration he vented what everyone felt. "That's all we need. To come this far and for what? What the hell are we gonna do now?"

During the five minutes which followed the only sound Scott heard over the intercom was breathing.

Scott laid her head down on her TV screen and shut her eyes to block out all distractions. Resentment swelled within her but emotion wouldn't solve this problem. Emotions got in the way, impeded clear thought, so she did her level best to suppress them and concentrate. *Next problem,* she said to herself. *What do we know?* Her concentration was intense. Sweat beaded and ran off her forehead like rain. What did this rotation mean? The answer was painfully simple. PAM must have sensed her blind spot—the radar dead zone on her red face—and compensated for it by rotating. By spinning like a rotating radar antenna, PAM filled in the hole. Scott opened her eyes and watched *Freedom* spin. *Freedom*'s pyramid shape was spinning with her top pointing toward the center of the earth. Scott timed *Freedom*'s revolutions—one complete turn every minute. That explained *Freedom*'s on-again, off-again radar signature. Every time they passed through her dead zone, they could see *Freedom*'s radar signal drop off. That on-off signature was like a heartbeat that marked her period of rotation. It made sense. Their flight plan had them sideslip out of the sun into that dead zone, but the original approach had assumed the red face was stationary. *What if we change the flight plan? Fly a helix pattern locked in sync with* Freedom*'s rotation. Yes! Change the approach! There is time. Is there fuel? Gonzo can find out in a hurry. This could be it. It must be.*

Scott raised her head, then looked at her gloved hands.

**The End of the Beginning**

They trembled. Her hair stuck to her head like it was matted down with glue, but her eyes were clear.

"Gonzo, I think I've got it." Scott spoke slowly with a restrained voice, struggling to convey her message in as few words as possible. There was no time for an extended explanation.

"Shoot." Gonzo, Mac, and Pasha listened intently, clinging on every word, hoping desperately that she was right.

"I need hard fuel figures." Scott paused, struggling to keep her emotions in check. Her heart pounded so hard she could hear it. "Change our final approach. Take out the sideslip maneuver and substitute a downward spiraling approach pattern."

Gonzo was silent as he struggled to absorb Scott's request. "You're serious? A helix? Like the threads on a screw?" Gonzo's voice was shaky, his feelings unsure.

"Yes. Pull out the sideslip and plug in the helix." Scott checked their range to target. Their sideslip maneuver was coming up fast. "We need numbers now."

Gonzo collected his thoughts. "Scotty, I don't understand but I'll do it." Gonzo pulled off his gloves and punched up a helix shaped much like that of a coil spring. Once the helix pattern was displayed, he fed it into the NavComputer.

"Any other constraints on our approach?" asked Gonzo, not knowing what to think.

"Yes, and this is important." Scott spoke with a deliberate calmness in her voice. "Synchronize our approach with *Freedom*'s rotation. We spiral in locked over that dead zone."

Gonzo's *I got it* light went off. His fingers raced over his computer keyboard and his mind soared ahead of his fingers. Fuel, fuel, fuel. Fuel was everything. Seconds later, a set of large red numbers suddenly began flashing on the NavComputer window. "Dammit all," Gonzo spat, obviously disappointed. "No go. Our tank's bone-dry ten miles out." Gonzo paused, collected his thoughts, then continued with less emotion. "That spiral pattern constantly burns the fuel."

Scott studied the spiral approach pattern on her TV monitor and decided the idea might be worth another try. "Increase our rate of descent. Set us down hard with no margin." The words almost stuck in her throat. By definition, zero margin left no room for error or malfunction.

"I'm with you, Scotty." Gonzo entered the steep slope solution and waited on the NavComputer's judgment. The answer came back with a blinking yellow warning. "We're borderline all the way, Scotty. Absolutely zero margin."

"But we've got a chance?" Scotty sounded apprehensive.

"A slim one." Gonzo knew they had no other alternative. They couldn't back out without being detected.

"I think we should take it."

"Roger, Scotty." Gonzo's fingers raced once again across the NavComputer keyboard. Once their steep spiral approach was entered, each NavComputer and MAP system display began blinking yellow. A flashing yellow display meant zero margin for error; flashing red meant fatal error—insufficient fuel. Gonzo read directly from the NavComputer's display. "Spiral burn begins in T minus two minutes and counting. Synchronize rotation twenty miles from touchdown."

Scott's heart was pounding as she mentally sorted through a list of what must be done. If all went well, they should make it, but she must assume their approach would not go as planned. She closed her eyes once again to block out the distractions from the cockpit. *What if we are detected? What then?* After a few moments thought, she began issuing orders like an automaton.

"Mac, lock your camera on our landing zone. I need a visual reference.

"Pasha, watch the MAP display and keep your eyes pinned on our approach. If we drift out of the channel, I've got to know and fast. Once PAM sees us, we won't get a second chance.

**The End of the Beginning**

"Gonzo, if we go to manual control, launch counter-measures. Everything we've got in a full firewall spread."

"Roger, Scotty—the works." As Scott spoke, Gonzo flipped on the countermeasures fire control system and spun up the Electronic CounterMeasures (ECM) pod, chaff and flare rockets. Within seconds, the ECM control panel filled with a bright matrix of lethal green READY LAUNCH lights. "Countermeasures armed and ready." Gonzo stared at the NavComputer countdown timer. His mouth felt dry, but his suit was soaked with sweat. "Spiral burn commences in T minus three . . . two . . . one . . . ignition."

Scott watched *Freedom* spinning like a top before them now. She felt *Hell Fire*'s attitude position engines shudder and sensed their approach angle was changing. *Hell Fire* began sweeping through a wide circular arc but continued closing on *Freedom* riding down a steep spiraling slope. Within a split second, *Hell Fire*'s wide sweeping motion synchronized with *Freedom*'s rotation, and suddenly *Freedom* didn't appear to rotate anymore. Scott smiled slightly. This spiraling approach made her feel like water swirling down the drain.

"We're headed down the tubes, Scotty." Mac spoke with a light chuckle in his voice and articulated Scott's thoughts exactly. It wasn't the first time one team member spoke the thoughts of another. After working closely together as a team, their minds often shared thoughts, especially in difficult situations. They had learned that they could sometimes communicate without speaking at all. This relationship took years to forge, but when all was said and done, the sum of their combined efforts always exceeded the sum of the parts. Maybe it was because their skills were complementary or maybe it was a combination of love and mutual admiration. They didn't know why it worked and didn't care to analyze it. Don't fix it if it's not broken, Mac always said. They knew in their hearts they had something special and they weren't about to let PAM bust up the act.

Gonzo spoke as he monitored the NavComputer touchdown timer and fuel reserves. "T minus two minutes till touchdown. Final braking burn commences in ninety seconds." There was a sense of restrained tension in his voice. As far as he knew, no one had ever made a three-point landing with zero fuel reserve.

*Freedom* was coming up fast. *Hell Fire* rocketed in a nose down position on a steep sixty-six-degree approach angle. Scott held her breath as she watched their range to target decrease at a near suicide rate. As the autopilot clicked off the final distance, *Freedom* completely filled the windshield.

Suddenly, Scott felt *Hell Fire* shudder and checked the control panel. The orbital maneuvering engines sputtered sporadically as the LOW FUEL light began flashing.

"Drifting!" Pasha screamed frantically.

The sputtering thrust from the orbital maneuvering engine hurled *Hell Fire* out of the channel, creating a position error. Instantly, the NavComputer locked up because of an irreconcilable conflict between available fuel and position. The NavComputer instructed the autopilot to eliminate the position error with a correction burn. The autopilot acknowledged the request and awaited further instructions. Additional instructions never came because there was insufficient fuel for the correction burn.

Instinctively, Scott grabbed control, disengaged the autopilot, and checked their position on the MAP display screen. When she looked up, her blood ran cold. *Hell Fire* was already out of the channel, swinging further away with every passing second. There was real danger here— PAM could detect them. No time to punch up an optimal correction burn, just do it. Scott activated the reaction control thrusters so she could maneuver.

*Beeeeeeeeeeeeeeeppp!!!* howled over the intercom. Gonzo's threat detector emitted its distinctive warble.

Scott yawed *Hell Fire* thinking, *PAM's locked on.*

Suddenly, a searing invisible column of laser light flashed above *Hell Fire*'s nose with precious little separation between them. IR detectors pegged off scale as an insane warble racked their ears.

The End of the Beginning

Immediately, Gonzo ham-fisted the LAUNCH button, pounding the control panel so hard the instrument lights blinked like a pinball machine. Flare, chaff, and ECM rockets simultaneously erupted from *Hell Fire*'s short stubby wings and streaked forward with such an intense flash that Scott instinctively blinked from their release. The reverse thrust from the massive launch nearly stopped *Hell Fire* in its tracks and hurled the crew forward hard against their shoulder restraints. There were a series of brilliant white flashes which followed as the rockets gimballed their engines and executed a firewall maneuver. On command, each turned radially outward in different directions, creating a wall of thermal and electrical interference between *Freedom* and *Hell Fire*. Gonzo watched the white plumes streak off in the distance and became mesmerized by the spectacle.

For a few moments, *Freedom*'s lasers went berserk. A wall of space in front of *Hell Fire* blazed with a brilliant light as the threat detector fell silent.

"Overload, Scotty. PAM can't handle it." Before Gonzo completed his statement, his words stuck in his throat.

Within seconds, PAM restored order to her hunt and kill sequence. Silently belching out their towers of flame, the flare rockets drew the first laser fire followed by the ECM pods. Within ten seconds, PAM reduced the flares and ECM pods to a powdery dust. All that remained between *Freedom* and *Hell Fire* was a shimmering wall containing millions and millions of tinfoil strips.

Once Scott recovered from the countermeasure launch, she checked the MAP display. The countermeasure launch had slowed their rate of descent, but they remained outside the channel. They must have a correction burn, otherwise PAM would blow them out of the sky.

Gonzo was brought back to reality when Scott spoke. "Gonzo, get us back in the lane!"

Quickly, he computed the correction burn. His steady nerve had returned, his voice almost excessively calm. "Five second correction burn commences in three . . . two . . . one . . . ignition."

**The End of the Beginning**

Scott manually throttled the burn.

*Hell Fire* vibrated as Scott and her crew watched the MAP system display. The display showed a computer-generated image of *Hell Fire* moving back into the approach channel. Suddenly, the NavComputer and MAP displays blazed with a bright flashing red message—CRITICAL FUEL WARNING. A sirenlike horn howled over the intercom. They would make it to *Freedom* all right and smash into smithereens on impact.

"Touchdown in sixty seconds," Gonzo repeated. His nerve remained intact while he evaluated their fuel condition.

Scott looked up and at first she couldn't believe what she saw. *Freedom* fired the main gimbal engines about her base. Scott saw them blazing, belching flames against the pitch-black sky and wondered what it could mean.

PAM detected *Hell Fire* vacillating in and out of her dead zone and took action to flush out the threat. *Freedom* simply stopped spinning like a top.

But *Hell Fire* did not.

Suddenly, *Freedom* seemed to begin rotating. Slowly at first, but the speed of rotation quickly increased.

The realization of what PAM had done hit Scott like a ton of bricks.

"We're out of the lane!" Pasha's tone—panic.

*Hell Fire* had lost synchronization with *Freedom* and drifted out of the channel again.

Scott looked down at the MAP display and saw her fixed point of reference—her touchdown point—moving. *Hell Fire* was overshooting the approach channel, the MAP system had lost synchronization, and they were nearly out of fuel. Scott's voice reverberated in Gonzo's ears. "Resync the MAP!" Scott was running manual control and was flustered now. She needed a fixed point of reference to land, but the MAP system lost sync when *Freedom* stopped spinning. This was insane. It was inconceivable. Scott feared they were as good as dead. She read the NavComputer timer. Forty-five seconds till touch-down.

Gonzo's fingers flew over the keyboard, entering data faster than the computer could display it. Within seconds he updated the NavComputer to account for *Freedom*'s sudden rotational stop and once again resynced the MAP system.

Without an exchange of words, Scott executed another correction burn. "Two . . . one . . . ignition." Scott watched *Hell Fire*'s position on the MAP display. "We're back in the lane." Her tone—tense.

*Hell Fire* was closing fast.

Scott could hear her own heart thumping. The gut-wrenching fear of dying created copious amounts of heat, and her space suit's cooling system was working over-time. She had to find someplace to set down. The red face now filled *Hell Fire*'s entire windshield. She focused her eyes, searching for the landing zone. Then suddenly—there it was. She recognized the spot. She had a hard time taking her eyes off the landing zone as she fired the final positioning thrusters, rotating *Hell Fire*'s nose over a full 180 degrees about her center of gravity. Scott maneuvered *Hell Fire* into braking position, putting her tail down pointing toward *Freedom*.

*Whoop . . . whoop . . . whoop . . . whoop!!!* The landing gear alarm bellowed over the intercom.

Immediately, Scott shoved the LANDING GEAR handle down and the tricycle gear exploded out of the nose and wheel wells. Once *Hell Fire*'s descent slowed to a hover, she planned to pivot the nose over and set down for a three-point landing. Once the GEAR LOCKED light turned green, Scott pushed hard forward against the main engine throttle and so began her final braking maneuver. *Hell Fire* shook violently for a few brief seconds as their descent slowed but then suddenly, it was over. *Hell Fire*'s main engine ran out of fuel and shut down.

The last remnants of altitude quickly clicked off.

Scott felt helpless. Her spacecraft had no power, she couldn't maneuver. Instinctively, she struggled to ignite

**The End of the Beginning**

the main engine, grappling with the controls, refusing to give up. It was useless.

The laws of physics prevailed. *Hell Fire*'s kinetic energy endured.

The red antenna face looked like a colossal bed of nails racing up to meet *Hell Fire* and rip her to shreds.

"God, I'm sorry, fellas." Her voice was a cry of pure desolation. She had done her best, but her best was not good enough.

Her crew understood.

Leaning forward, Scott reached underneath her seat and pulled up on a pair of red handlebar grips. She felt them ratchet into position. Instantly, the briefcase-sized black box came alive and began speaking over the intercom in a detached robotic tone. "The self-destruct system has been activated for detonation in six hours."

Scott raised her eyes toward the heavens, tightly clutched her four-leaf clover and brought it to her chest. She felt a form of calmness creep over her mind, or perhaps it was her soul.

And *Hell Fire* impacted on *Freedom*'s red face.

*The Costs, 12/24/2014, 0601 Zulu, 11:01 P.M. Mountain Standard Time*
CHEYENNE MOUNTAIN, COLORADO

"Things are not good, General, but looks like they made it." Colonel Napper's tone was somber, almost morose. He walked slowly into the conference room carrying a pink slip of paper. He looked at General Mason knowing that he was living through his own private agony.

Mason felt apprehensive and watched tensely as Napper reread the note.

There was a deep silence.

"*Hell Fire* activated the black box," Napper continued slowly.

A dread premonition washed over Mason. Nausea overwhelmed his stomach. He held his head in his hands and

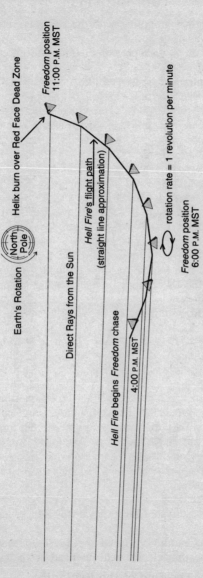

Hell Fire's Approach Out of the Sun

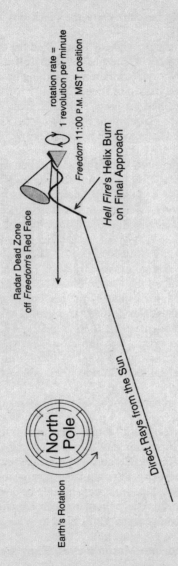

Expanded View of *Hell Fire's* Helix Shaped Final Approach Pattern
(Synchronized with Rotating Radar Dead Zone)

spoke softly. "No beacon? Only the black box transmitter?"

"No beacon." Napper sighed. Tears filled the corners of his eyes. "I'm sorry, General." Napper felt a wave of compassion for Mason, but there was nothing he could do.

Several minutes passed in silence.

Mason slowly lifted his head—a broken man. The defiant fire which once blazed in his eyes was gone. His cloudy blue eyes mirrored the agony he felt in his heart.

"How long?"

Napper read the note a third time, checked his watch, then spoke quietly. "Five hours and forty minutes."

Napper's words sponged the last remnants of energy from Mason's body. "Deliver this message to the President." He licked his dry lips and spoke slowly. "Within twelve hours, this crisis will pass. Recommend he inform the Saudis and Kuwaitis. They'll know what to do. *Hope* will take over automatically after *Freedom* is destroyed. Recommend the Congressional Medal of Honor be awarded to Major Linda Scott, her crew, and *Hope* Commander Pasha Yakovlev." Mason rested his chin on his hands and thought about their families. *The gain is never worth the cost.* "Get the addresses and phone numbers of their families. I want to meet with each of them. They must understand why their loved ones had to die."

The period of silence which followed extended beyond five minutes.

Napper sat perfectly still, totally absorbed in the events of the moment. From this day forward, he knew that his life would be different. He now more clearly understood the oppressive burden and formidable responsibility that comes with leadership. In a way he felt he had finally faced the real world. After reviewing their situation, Napper spoke with compassion. "It is hard to send people to their deaths."

Napper looked into Mason's eyes. They were dark,

**The End of the Beginning**

cloudy pools of anguish. Mason's expression remained blank, distant, and unfocused.

Mason drew a single long breath but didn't speak. He didn't have to.

**The End of the Beginning**

# 27

Watching the impact from a distance, *Freedom* seemed to devour *Hell Fire*. The aerospace plane simply disappeared from sight.

Slamming into the red face tail first, *Hell Fire* ripped through the flimsy mesh covering *Freedom*'s outer skin and skidded to a sudden stop on the radar antenna feed. Looking like a beached whale, *Hell Fire* plowed to a stop in the blink of an eye against a massive structure of waveguide suspended like a trampoline beneath *Freedom*'s red face. The gear snapped off at the wheel wells as *Hell Fire* ripped through the outer skin into the plumbing. Row after row of radar waveguide (shaped like pipes) absorbed the kinetic energy of the massive aerospace plane like a colossal coiled spring. Instantly, the heart of the antenna stopped pulsing with radar energy. *Freedom*'s red face was totally blind.

The force of the impact rocked the space plane so violently that Scott's head was thrown into the control panel, shattering the glass CRT screen of the computer display. Although she was dazed, she sustained only bruises from the shoulder restraints because most of the force of the impact was absorbed by her helmet.

Once they plowed to a stop, Gonzo unharnessed himself and killed the electrical power to the backseat instrumentation.

Inside *Hell Fire*'s reconnaissance bay, braces and bulkheads struggled to absorb instantaneous forces of impact which they were never designed to carry. Carbon composites flexed and splintered, buffeted by incalculable forces. *Hell Fire*'s airframe members cracked, her walls twisted.

Electrical fires broke out immediately inside the cockpit, backseat, and reconnaissance bay. Warning lights began to flash and alarm bells rang. Sparks flew from every instrument panel like a fireworks display. Instrument and reconnaissance bay lighting flickered. The flight computer struggled to isolate and contain the damage caused by the sudden impact and subsequent fires. Every sensitive piece of instrumentation equipment had been damaged by the shock wave. Although overloaded with critical failure data, the flight computer commanded the Fire Control System to life.

Beneath the cockpit inside the reconnaissance bay, something exploded.

"Fire in the hole!" Mac screamed as his eyes darted frantically to and fro over the blazing equipment. The electrical fire began adjacent to the oxygen cylinders and weapons bin. If he didn't move fast, they'd be blown to kingdom come. He ripped off his shoulder restraints, grabbed a fire extinguisher, and directed the spray on the blazing equipment. Cabin exhaust fans aided the fire by sucking black smoke and flames from the reconnaissance bay up into the cockpit. Within seconds, *Hell Fire* was filled with thick smutty smoke. The overhead lights in the bay now flickered continuously. Once the smoke had circulated throughout *Hell Fire,* the exhaust fans stopped. A nozzle suspended from the ceiling began dumping copious amounts of foam on the blaze.

Panicky, he inspected the weapons and oxygen tanks. Although covered in foam, he'd acted in time.

### The End of the Beginning

Once the fire had been suppressed and the damaged weapons checked, Mac took an inventory of himself. He felt a withering pain below his left knee. As he gingerly felt his upper shin, his face contorted. Broken—he could feel a splinter of bone torn through the thin skin on the front of his shin, and the swelling was just beginning. Then he thought of Pasha.

Pasha didn't speak. He hadn't moved. Something was terribly wrong. He remained strapped into his makeshift seat undaunted by the fire and smoke. Grabbing a flashlight, Mac maneuvered into position beside Pasha and shined the beam through the visor onto his face. Even through the thick smoke, after one quick glance Mac knew his injuries were serious. There was bleeding from the mouth. Blood droplets floated about Pasha's face, suspended inside his helmet. Barely conscious, Pasha struggled to say something when he sensed the light shining on his face. His lips were moving, but there was no sound. Leaning closer, Mac cut up the sensitivity on Pasha's intercom mike. For a moment, all Mac heard were gurgling sounds. Pasha gagged after coughing up a dark blackish-red discharge. Mac had to do something quickly or Pasha would drown in his own blood.

Mac struggled across the reconnaissance bay and threw open an equipment locker. After grabbing a spare helmet, he cranked up the pressure inside Pasha's EVA suit. Mac's objective was positive pressure; he wanted to increase the pressure inside Pasha's suit so that it was greater than cabin pressure. After releasing three latches about his neck, Pasha's helmet popped off with only a slight twist. Immediately Mac cut down the suit pressure, cleared Pasha's mouth and the bloody residue from his face, then slammed on the new helmet. Mac expected the gasses and smoke inside the cabin were toxic, so he wasted no time after removing Pasha's helmet. The operation took less than one minute.

"Scotty, Pasha's in a bad way. Internal bleeding. Don't know how bad." Looking around the smoke-filled bay,

**The End of the Beginning**

Mac surmised what happened. "Supply crate tore loose. Looks like one caught him in the chest."

"Can he be moved?"

Pasha signaled an affirmative to Mac with his hand, then spoke softly. "I can be moved—but slowly . . . may've busted a few ribs."

There was a moment of concern as Scott thought through what to do. After pausing a few seconds, Pasha spoke again with a deliberately light tone. "More doctors recommend Tylenol for headache than any other leading brand." The crew breathed a sigh of relief, hoping Pasha's injuries were not as serious as they appeared. There was no infirmary onboard *Hell Fire,* and at this moment the *Freedom* infirmary wasn't taking walk-ins. Once he had eased the tension, Pasha took a shallow breath and delivered his suggestion. "Recommend you vent smoke, purge cabin air, survey damage—inside and out. There's much work to do. We need a new plan." During the crash, equipment and supplies tore free from their storage areas, smashed open, and were now strewn about the reconnaissance bay. Most of their supply crates and equipment had been either crushed or damaged by the fire. Small and large chunks of loose debris still vectored about the cabin, bouncing from wall to wall like a 3-D billiard game.

"Mac, Gonzo. What's your condition? You clear to vent?" Scott tensed for the damage assessment.

"My hand's sprained but other than that I'm OK," Gonzo replied flatly. He read over a long list of system failures, then spoke again. His tone was cautious. "I'll hold the damage report until I check her over for structural integrity, but all in all, it could've been a lot worse."

"How about the radio?"

"Dead. We're running off battery for now but some of the primary cells were damaged."

"Mac, how about the transponder beacon?" Scott wanted to call home—radio Headquarters an *I'm OK* signal indicating that they were still alive.

Mac surveyed the debris in one of the equipment storage lockers. Smashed by the concussion of the impact, fragmented pieces of the transponder looked fossilized, coated with a layer of fire retardant foam. Then Mac saw the boomer and shook his head. The remotely controlled minesweeper had been smashed to smithereens by a large crate. "Transponder's out of business, Scotty, and the boomer's busted."

"Any chance of repair?"

Following a moment of silence, Mac spoke with a tone of dismay in his voice. "None whatsoever. Pasha was right. We need a new plan. Vent the cabin, then you'd better come down here and take a look." He paused, then spoke slowly. He sounded apprehensive. "And one other thing."

"Name it, Chief."

"Bring me down a leg splint—one I can inflate."

"You mean?"

"Yeah, it's broken. Smashed by a low flying crate."

Scott winced. For an instant she physically felt his pain. She quickly recovered as she noticed smoke once again erupting beneath her feet from the reconnaissance bay. She vented *Hell Fire*'s cabin air into the vacuum of space. Gonzo pushed himself and his EVA pack outside to inspect the airframe, rocket, and scramjet engines. Once the oxygen in the cabin had been depleted, the fires squelched themselves out.

A single emergency light now illuminated the disordered interior of the reconnaissance bay. Overlaid with nonconductive foam, the camera control console lay in ruins, shattered beyond recognition. Instrumentation equipment ripped from its mounting braces floated about the cabin anchored only by its cabling. All their supplies, including the weapons, spilled from their storage cabinets and were blanketed with foam.

After restoring the cabin air pressure, Scott climbed into the *hole* and began surveying the damage.

She didn't like what she saw.

## The End of the Beginning

*The Corridor, 12/25/2014, 1010 Zulu, 3:10 A.M. Mountain*
  *Standard Time*
ONBOARD *HELL FIRE,*
SPACE STATION *FREEDOM*


Standing inside the debris which was the reconnaissance bay, Scott inspected her cumbersome twin-beam flamethrower. When working properly, the weapon could accurately throw a thin beam of fire up to one hundred feet and simultaneously diffuse the second beam into a wide cone of atomized fiery spray. The downside of this weapon was that it kicked like a horse. Wide-open, it kicked like a team of horses. The term *flamethrower* was accurate in one respect, but the expanding gasses created an enormous reverse thrust. The weapon was more accurately described as a portable liquid fuel rocket engine with a handle and throttle for a trigger. The weapon contained fuel pumps which fed twin combustion chambers an explosive combination of high velocity oxygen and gasoline. Checking the fuel cylinders, fuel pumps, trigger, and safety, everything seemed operational.

Scott focused on saving herself and her crew. Gutting Centurion was the only way. The black box alternative, blowing up *Freedom,* was suicide and only made sense if all else failed. It wouldn't. One thing was clear in her expression. Nothing would stand in her way. She leaned forward, ran her fingers over the trigger, then spoke to Mac and Pasha.

"It ought to work." She paused, temporarily secured the weapon to the wall, then slid a bulky Kevlar flack jacket over her head covering her EVA suit. "We'll be back in four hours. Sooner if this thing jams." She motioned toward the flamethrower. Looking at Gonzo, she continued in a no-nonsense tone. "We'll clear the corridor like we planned." The red corridor extended from the face, past the oven to the core airlocks.

Gonzo nodded agreement while loading the Kevlar curtain, extra oxygen, some flares, and a spotlight in his tool-

**The End of the Beginning**

box. Once his packing was complete, he strapped a massive tripod to his EVA backpack and was ready.

Pasha sat upright and conscious in his EVA suit, loosely strapped to Mac's seat. He seemed to be improving, progressively coughing up less blood, and his vital signs were stable. His helmet was removed, the cabin now free of smoke and toxic gasses. An electric pump clipped to the wall forced small measured amounts of a fluid mixture into his body through a vein in his neck. Scott interpreted the rapidly decreasing amount of intravenous fluid as a good sign. She hoped she was right. Until they cleared the way into the infirmary, that's all they could do for him. She leaned forward near Pasha's ear and spoke in a low compassionate voice. "Hang on. We'll get you out of here."

He spoke softly, touching her gloved hand. "I have faith in you, my friend. I know this machine better than I know my own children." He paused. Memories of his family filled him with an unyielding will to live. His tone of voice changed. It was stronger. "It can be done and you can do it. Go for the jugular." *Freedom*'s jugular was its energy source, the four power plants feeding power to each face.

Scott turned toward Mac and ran her hand carefully over his engorged leg. "Swelling feels pretty bad."

"I can move around when I have to."

"You sure you don't want any medication?" she asked pensively. The size of Mac's leg made her wince.

Mac looked over at Pasha, smiled, and shook his head. "Thanks, but no thanks. Better off without it. Someone's got to stay alert."

"Take good care of him, Mac. Pasha's children are depending on us." Her eyes flushed with tears—but she couldn't think about that now—focus on survival. She mentally reset, putting her emotions on hold.

Scott passed her weapon and spare fuel tanks through the overhead hatch leading to the cockpit. She climbed through the hatch and set her equipment inside *Hell Fire*'s tiny airlock. As Gonzo passed through the hatch behind

**The End of the Beginning**

her, Scott reset the countdown timer on the black box beneath her seat. She lowered the twin handlebar grips to their original position, and the black box immediately responded over the intercom. "The self-destruct system has been deactivated." After the lights on the black box cycled through a red-yellow-green reset sequence, she lifted the handgrips once again into the armed position. She heard the black box speaking as she approached Gonzo in the cramped airlock. The detached tone of voice sent a chill down her spine. It spoke as if it had nothing to lose. "The self-destruct system has been activated for detonation in six hours."

Scott and Gonzo squeezed themselves and their equipment into the airlock and sealed it shut behind them. The airlock hissed as Scott vented the atmospheric gasses into space. Once they and their equipment were outside, they moved in unison toward the red corridor, an enclosed tube which connected the red face to the oven and core. Their Aqua-Lung propulsion thrusters worked exactly as they had in practice. Scott took some comfort in that. The simplest equipment, the propulsion thruster, was the most reliable. She'd remember that in the future.

Scott entered the corridor through the external airlock on the surface of the red face. As they expected, the corridor airlock was open. The corridor's interior looked narrow, dimly lit, and ominous. It was a long and dangerous hike to *Freedom*'s central core.

Gonzo removed the distance measurement meter and laser reflector from his toolbox (the digital equivalent of a long measuring tape). Reading the distance meter, Scott paced off the distance to their first demolition site as Gonzo steadied the reflector.

"We'll set up here." Scott spoke into her low power transmitter. Gonzo acknowledged. She jammed a stow hook into a vertical slot on the wall then secured her thruster and EVA pack. Together, they set up the flamethrower on its tripod mount, securing the tripod through slotted holes in the floor. Scott looked down the dark corridor but could not see the blunderbuss. She lowered her night vision visor and locked it into place. Looking through the infrared light amplifier, she still couldn't make it out. Everything in the corridor was the same temperature so the low-light visor didn't help. Clenching her teeth together, Scott motioned for Gonzo to take cover behind the Kevlar curtain. Scott couldn't see the blunderbuss but after some thought she decided she didn't need to see it. It was there. It had to be. She aligned the weapon in the general direction of the blunderbuss, locked it tightly into position, and covered it with the protective Kevlar cover used by the boomer. After attaching a pair of ignition wires to the flamethrower, she carried the loose ends behind the Kevlar curtain and attached them to a remote throttle. All was ready.

"Get down." Scott signaled to Gonzo. Depressing the ignition switch, she pushed forward gently on the throttle.

Nothing.

Again, this time hard forward on the throttle.

Nothing.

Scott shot Gonzo a cautionary look.

"Damn high-tech gadgets," Gonzo muttered.

They slowly raised their heads over the Kevlar curtain but couldn't see the weapon without a light. Grabbing the spotlight, Scott went to take a closer look.

Leaning forward, Scott ran her finger over the trigger and weapon grip. "Bingo," she said, breathing a sigh of relief. Flipping a switch on the grip, Scott removed the safety then took cover behind the curtain.

Scott's gloved finger convulsed on the ignition switch as she brought her flamethrower to bear. A fiery quivering light illuminated the dark corridor and the floor trembled. She eased the throttle one quarter the way forward. The floor shook violently beneath them as the flamethrower twisted and tore at its three-point moorings. From the outside, the tube-shaped corridor glowed a dull red-orange in the vicinity of the flamethrower's exhaust plume. For a few moments, the length of the corridor was transformed into a fiery hell, a torrid frenzy of expanding superheated exhaust gasses. Suddenly, they saw the Kevlar curtain

**The End of the Beginning**

pounded back as the first salvo of blunderbuss pellets slammed into the curtain.

Scott began easing back on the throttle when the second salvo of stainless-steel pellets smashed into the curtain. Due to the searing heat from the exhaust gasses, a second blunderbuss detonated further down the corridor followed moments later by another.

Scott eased back on the throttle and extinguished the weapon.

For the first time in a long time Scott smiled and cocked her eyebrows at Gonzo. "Three with one blow."

Gonzo returned a thumbs up, grinning ear to ear. "And two to go!"

Strapping on their EVA packs, they left the smoldering inferno and returned to *Hell Fire,* allowing the corridor to cool.

*Hope, 12/25/2014, 1016 Zulu, 3:16 A.M. Mountain Standard Time*
CHEYENNE MOUNTAIN, COLORADO

General Krol burst into the conference room with Colonel Napper. Their news wouldn't keep. Colonel Napper spoke first for both of them.

"Things may be looking up, General!"

General Mason looked at them wearily but did not respond. His eyes remained unfocused, his mind on *Freedom.* After a few moments' silence, Napper's words finally registered in Mason's brain. "Good news?"

"Could be, General," Napper replied. "Our data is incomplete, but we believe some of *Hell Fire*'s crew are alive."

Mason quickly sat up straight and leaned forward in his chair.

"Yuri spoke with Kaliningrad. They're overrun with messages from *Freedom.* They haven't sorted the details yet, but every message has to do with failures on the red face."

Mason thought ahead. What kind of good news was

this? Based on their best available information, he already believed *Hell Fire* had activated their black box then crashed into *Freedom* killing all aboard. Mason slumped back in his chair. "Then this merely confirms what we already suspected."

"That's right, General, but there's more."

Mason looked at Napper anxiously.

"The beacon?"

"No, sir, but a damn good indicator. The next best thing." Napper looked at Krol. Krol's face showed a proud smile, his chubby cheeks glowed bright red. Napper nodded knowingly, winked at Krol, then stepped aside allowing General Krol to deliver the good news.

"The black box has been reset."

Mason's mind went into overdrive, disconnecting from his mouth. He had trouble framing a response. Before he mouthed the first word, the spark returned to his eyes, then the spark changed to a twinkle. He slapped the desk with the palms of both hands and spoke with enthusiasm.

"Then they've got a chance!"

*The Oven, 12/25/2014, 1607 Zulu, 9:07 A.M. Mountain Standard Time*
RED FACE CORRIDOR,
SPACE STATION *FREEDOM*

Scott and Gonzo measured the distance to their final detonation site. Maneuvering their equipment into position, Scott moved by a side passageway. Checking her distance readout against the map, she judged the opening should lead to the oven, the interior of the red face antenna feed.

Scott's attention focused on the dimly lit far end of the side passageway. Holding her oxygen-fed flare overhead, she tried to penetrate the darkness. Like the rest of *Freedom*, the oven appeared largely intact, somewhat fossilized, and abandoned at first glance. A dim blue light at the far end caught her attention. It illuminated a form that reminded her of a traffic light. She heaved her hissing flare down the passageway. The oven walls reflected the fiery light like a house of mirrors. The oven was lined with hundreds of highly polished metal horns, each shaped like the bell of a trombone. Alongside the horns she saw racks filled with circuit boards, many dislodged from their plug-in slots. She squinted. Below the circuit boards she saw the dimly lit form of a man lying prostrate on the floor. She approached cautiously as she lit another flare. Her pulse skyrocketed. Standing within five feet of the body, she froze for a moment, unable to move. Her eyes widened, her breathing erratic. She could see his form clearly now.

She knelt by the body. Her fingers trembled slightly as she touched it, then steadied. Holding the flare over its face, she saw only the reflection of the flare in the helmet visor. The visor had been completely blocked by some blackish material. *Probably blood,* she thought. She searched for some name or rank insignia on the space suit. There was none but that was standard practice.

This man had been dead for some time. Swelling expanded the body's gut, legs, and arms until the space suit fit like a skin, taut as that of a balloon ready to burst under pressure. Had she lifted the visor, she wouldn't have recognized Jay's disintegrating face. His face had eventually exploded, blanketing the inside of his helmet with bits of flesh and fat.

She examined the body for some clue to its identity and found the man was clutching something tightly next to his heart. Breathlessly, she touched his hand, carefully removing an old yellow piece of paper. It was tattered and faded, but she recognized it immediately as her own.

A terrible nauseating emptiness enveloped her, a kaleidoscopic mixture of love, loss, anger, and loneliness. And the greatest of these was loneliness.

She held Jay's hand tightly and cried the harrowing cry of a mother who had lost her only child.

Gonzo stood silently at the entrance to the oven. Each of them had known this time would come, but knowing didn't make it any easier.

**The End of the Beginning**

Scott's survival instinct urged her on. She began thinking about the children she had wanted, about the children this man had denied her. And then she thought about those precious pictures of Pasha's children. Those children were depending on her to get their daddy home and nothing was going to stand in her way. Pasha's children, the ones she'd never met, the ones she'd come to know through their father's eyes, needed her and she was not going to let them down. Thoughts of Pasha's children combined with the discovery of Jay's body charged her with a relentless determination and deeply rooted anger.

She blinked her eyes clear, stiffened her spine, and sat upright. Reaching into her sleeved pocket, she removed the lucky necklace he had given her such a long time ago. Caressing it gently, she slipped it over his gloved hand. She would remember him, remember their happy times, but she wouldn't miss him anymore. She had prayed that she'd get over him and, in an odd sort of way, she felt relief. She felt free of the power he held over her.

Scott stood, walked slowly over to Gonzo, and didn't look back. Looking into Gonzo's eyes, she saw compassion and concern for her feelings. Gonzo needed her too. She had friends and together they'd pull through.

She put her arms around Gonzo and hugged him. Gonzo found strength in her affection and squeezed her—hard.

Lifting her underneath her arms, he raised her near the overhead light. He wanted to see her face clearly. Through her visor, Gonzo could see her complexion was a blotchy red and her hair was matted down. The woman looked like hell.

"You OK?" he asked softly.

Scott shot a thumbs up to Gonzo. "I was a little shaky, but now I'm fine." She smiled, then continued in a determined voice. "Pasha and Mac are depending on us. Let's move them into the infirmary then wrap this thing up."

Scott and Gonzo moved out of the oven into the dark main corridor. Together they secured the flamethrower to the floor under the fiery light of a flare. Scott checked the

**The End of the Beginning**

fuel levels, replaced the fuel pump batteries, reset the weapon, then released the safety, ready to fire. Taking cover behind the Kevlar curtain, Scott depressed the ignition switch and eased forward on the throttle. At ignition, two things happened simultaneously. A long burst of flame emerged from the combustion chamber and the flamethrower tripod ripped loose from its moorings. The resultant thrust sent the fire-belching weapon hurling down the corridor at breakneck speed into the Kevlar curtain, toolbox, Scott and Gonzo. The only thing that saved them from being burned alive was the motion detector built into the weapon. Sensing its own acceleration, its safety circuits kicked in and shut down the fuel pumps. The flamethrower was designed to burn, not fly.

Scott and Gonzo dug out from the pile of equipment. Scott's arm was blackened and bruised from the impact, the remote throttle control was smashed, but they got off easy considering the fiery alternative.

After some discussion, a single viable alternative became clear. Scott would manually fire the weapon. She was wearing the flack jacket so Gonzo reluctantly agreed. Once their plan was set, they anchored the tripod once again to the floor. Kneeling alongside the weapon in the darkness, Scott found the handgrip and trigger. Gonzo covered her with the Kevlar curtain and backed away, taking refuge in the side passageway which led to the oven.

Once he was in position, he radioed Scott an all clear. Gonzo watched in motionless horror as the blackness of the corridor suddenly blazed a radiant white. In less than two seconds, the blackness returned. Gonzo's night vision was lost, he couldn't see. He lit his flare and headed cautiously toward the corridor. Suddenly, the corridor blazed like a flaming inferno. He felt a torrent of intense heat as the backwash of expanding gasses knocked him down, extinguished his flare, and forced him to take cover behind a rack of equipment in the oven. He was both repelled and fascinated by the flames. This time the flame endured twenty . . . thirty . . . forty seconds, then extinguished leaving only a glowing dull red residue along the corridor walls.

"Scotty?" His voice—anxious.

Silence followed by a choking sound.

"Scotty!" he yelled, bolting out of the oven toward the main corridor. He heard Scott take a deep breath then speak in a hoarse voice.

"Corridor secure."

**The End of the Beginning**

# 28

Scott entered the core airlock first with Mac's arm draped around her shoulder. Gonzo followed, maneuvering Pasha on a stretcher. Scott's overwhelming impression was one of stark desolation and darkness. A chill ran down her spine when she looked at Gonzo. Safety lighting shining up through the floor illuminated Gonzo's helmet from below his chin, casting deep shadows across his face.

Once inside, she pressed hard on the CLOSE button. Nothing. That's what she'd expected. PAM controlled the airlock doors. Scott ran her gloved hand along the wall by the outside airlock door. The handwheel had to be here somewhere. After Gonzo moved Pasha inside, he shined a small flashlight over her shoulder and cut through the darkness. Scott grabbed the wheel and manually cranked the outside airlock door shut. Gonzo pulled a plastic bag containing six-inch-long stainless-steel rods from his EVA backpack and began searching the doorjamb for the deadbolt hole. While Scott held the door shut, Gonzo slid a safety rod in place. Once the steel rod was in position, Scott released the wheel and the door reflexively jammed hard against it. Try as she might, PAM could not force the airlock door open. Once the outside airlock door was secure, they entered the core and pinned the inner door shut.

The infirmary was in sight of the airlock. There was nothing PAM could do to stop them from entering the infirmary except close the door. If PAM tried to keep them out, it was a simple matter to manually wheel the door open. PAM knew that and didn't try to stop them.

Once inside, Scott pinned the sliding door shut with a stainless-steel rod.

Gonzo severed PAM's control from the infirmary life-support system by disconnecting a series of optical control cables attached to the air handling and pressure regulator units. Once Gonzo had finished his cutoff procedures, the infirmary provided them a safe haven, an isolated island where PAM could not see or control any aspect of their lives. Gonzo set the oxygen mix and adjusted the infirmary pressure and temperature. Once the pressure stabilized, the crew pulled off their helmets and EVA suits.

It felt good.

Gonzo positioned Pasha on a bed in an examination room on one side of the infirmary and went to work on his injuries. On the other side of the infirmary, Scott X-rayed Mac's leg and set it as best she could. Neither was trained in the medical field but they followed the manuals.

After icing, heating, wrapping, and patching nonstop for two hours, Scott finished with Mac and stared at her handiwork in disbelief. His leg was encased in a rigid full-length cast. In his weightless condition, Mac had mobility but it came with a price. Moving caused his leg to swell so his range was severely limited. She gazed across the room at Gonzo and Pasha. Pasha had his ribs loosely wrapped, intravenous tubes stuck in both arms, and wires attached to his chest monitoring his vital signs.

With Mac and Pasha secure in the infirmary, Scott and Gonzo looked at one another, knowing the easy part of the job was behind them.

Gonzo returned to *Hell Fire* to reset the black box. Once he returned, they would get on with the business at hand.

## The End of the Beginning

*The Jugular, 12/25/2014, 2248 Zulu, 3:48 P.M. Mountain*
   *Standard Time*
THE YELLOW POWER PLANT,
FREEDOM'S CORE

Without electrical power, PAM threatened no one.

Their plan was as simple as it was elegant: shut down
*Freedom* one face at a time. Pin the airlock doors closed
and scram the reactor on each face, leaving *Freedom*'s central core pressurized but without power.

Moving cautiously behind a massive blast shield, Scott
and Gonzo advanced toward the yellow airlock along the
main passageway. After checking their position with the
distance meter, Gonzo maneuvered the dense metal shield
into firing position. Satisfied, he spoke into his helmet
mike. "This should be the spot."

Scott trailed in Gonzo's wake carrying the corridor map
and flamethrower. There was emergency lighting, but dim.
She lit a small flashlight and began tracing lines on the
map. "You see it?"

Peering through the small gun port, he surveyed the corridor for telltale signs of weapons. Unaided, his eyes couldn't
penetrate the low light further than thirty feet. Lowering his
night vision visor into position, Gonzo saw the corridor
transition into ghostly shades of green shadows. He saw a
faint reflection moving in the distance and, visibly shaken,
he froze motionless. This was no drill—there was real danger here. Ahead, suspended above a sharp bend in the passageway, an agile turret-mounted laser pivoted back and
forth, tirelessly standing sentry duty. Around the bend, yellow airlock doors stood open. "Yeah, Scotty. Take a look."

The bulky EVA suit and helmet made even the simplest
task a laborious chore. Leaning forward, Scott looked
through the gun port and blinked. She saw only darkness.
Using the flashlight while reading the map compromised
her night vision. She lowered her low-light visor and
locked it in place. Searching for PAM's sensory organs, she
focused on the corridor walls. As expected, the walls were
equipped with flush mounted cameras, microphones, and

motion detectors constantly feeding PAM information. Scott's eyes darted back and forth, scanning every detail along the corridor walls. PAM hadn't detected them—yet. Turning toward Gonzo, she spoke quietly. "Only a matter of time. No place to hide."

Cranking the adjustable blast shield legs snugly against the walls, Gonzo secured the massive plate in position.

Scott positioned both flamethrower barrels through the gun port.

Once the shield was wedged into position, Gonzo began anchoring the flamethrower tripod to the deck at breakneck speed. Lagging the front leg down, Gonzo tensed, sensing all hell was about to break loose. There was no air, there was no sound, but there was vibration from his drilling.

Suddenly without warning, PAM opened fire.

Gasping, Scott felt the deck shake like it had been beaten with a sledgehammer. It happened again—then again. Sparks and molten metal raced overhead, spattering against the corridor walls. Unremitting, PAM's brute force attack savagely blew chunks of metal off the rapidly disintegrating shield.

Scott looked up, shocked to see the blast shield deforming—and moving—inching its way toward them. Her pulse ratcheted up a notch, her eyes widened. There was no time for discussion, no time to consult manuals, and no one to ask. In a matter of seconds, the molten blast shield would buckle. Her reaction was instinctual and she'd always trusted her instincts. Scott slammed her hand down hard on Gonzo's helmet, knocking him clear of her line of fire. He crumpled to the floor as she jerked forward and hit the ignition switch. Low-level flames erupted from both barrels. Holding the flamethrower tightly in both hands, she squeezed the trigger—gently. The weapon lurched backward as the slack in the mount was taken up. Spewing horizontal geysers of fire down the passageway, the weapon shook violently against the single point of restraint.

Flames leapt in all directions, incinerating everything in sight.

Scott felt the raw power she'd unleashed as the deck

**The End of the Beginning**

shuddered beneath her. A howling wind of exhaust gasses filled the corridor. Blocking the torrent of intense heat, the shield glowed a dull red.

Shoving hard against the butt end of the flamethrower, Gonzo strained with all his strength to counter the reverse thrust created by the expanding gasses. And then it happened. He felt the restraining lag bolt giving way, the front end of the flamethrower rising. "No! God, nooooooooo!" he screamed frantically, the veins on his forehead bulging. Gulping for breath, his face now purple, he felt an adrenaline rush kick in. Suddenly, if only for a few seconds, he had the strength of ten men.

Hunting with astonishing assurance, Scott instinctively sensed PAM's every action. In the midst of the terror and chaos, ignoring the mounting restraint failure, she concentrated on the blast shield *walking* toward them. Then as quickly as the attack started, it was finished. PAM backed off, the blast shield stood still.

Scott shut down and Gonzo collapsed quivering alongside her. Immediately, she pulled him to safety away from the smoking shield. Sweat poured off his forehead; his breathing—short and shallow. Within minutes, his quivering stopped, his hands steadied. His eyes opened, making contact with Scott's.

She smiled admiringly at him. "I don't know how you did it, but you did it."

Gonzo shrugged. His breathing remained rapid but the color had returned to his face. "I am pretty amazing." He spoke softly, punctuating his comment with a wink.

"You look all right to me now," she quipped, rolling her eyes. "Sit tight."

Scott stood slowly, lifted an Aqua-Lung sized tank filled with water from his EVA pack, and returned to the glowing blast shield. Lighting an oxygen-fed torch, she heaved it over the smoking shield toward the bend in the corridor. She backed her weapon out of the gun port and surveyed the passageway. Looking through her night visor, she saw rising green tendrils of heat radiating from every surface. Her eyes carefully considered each hazard stretching off into the distance. The turret-mounted laser was a smoldering mass and every flush mounted camera lay wasted, smoke convulsing out of each lens port. *Handmade hell,* Scott thought. She gently caressed her lethal weapon. The flamethrower wasn't smart, graceful, or elegant, but it was effective for the task at hand.

"All clear," Gonzo heard over his headset. He stood slowly and began moving toward her. He felt as if he were moving in slow motion through a dream, engulfed by a cloud of smoke.

Turning, Scott advanced a few cautious steps and loosened the blast shield from the wall. With increasing confidence, she brought Gonzo's water nozzle to bear on the red-hot shield. Steam boiled off the metal in a torrid frenzy, filling the smoky corridor with a cloud of mist. After hosing down the deck, Scott turned to Gonzo and tried to look into his eyes. She couldn't see her hand in front of her face, let alone his eyes. "You ready?" she asked. Her voice sounded weary but determined.

"I'm as ready as I'm gonna be," he admitted reluctantly.

Wiping the moisture from her visor, she saw only steam at first, then Gonzo's silhouette slowly emerged from the dark background.

The scene was an eerie one as they advanced through the solid wall of steam to the yellow airlock.

Raising her torch to the ceiling, Scott played the light over the maze of access entrances overhead. Methodically, she considered every opening: the air vents, service accessways, power conduits, and storage chambers. Scott studied the map, hoping they wouldn't need these alternate routes. *Freedom*'s core was a maze of small and large passageways, each leading somewhere—the trick was knowing where.

Once Scott had her bearings, they entered the open airlock and pinned both doors shut. She didn't smile. Her impression was one of desolation and darkness. With the airlock door secure, they advanced behind the blast shield toward the yellow power plant.

Beyond the airlock, the steam cloud cleared, revealing

**The End of the Beginning**

the closed hatchway entrance to the power plant. *Freedom* had separate power plants on each face for redundancy. Two plants could fail and *Freedom* would continue operating at full capacity, never skipping a beat.

Scott pressed the OPEN button.

Nothing, the hatch didn't budge. No surprise.

Spinning the hatch flywheel, Scott slid the door out of the way. "Ready," she huffed, gasping for breath.

Gonzo pinned the hatch open.

Surveying every detail, using a handheld mirror as a periscope, Scott cautiously peered into the reactor control room. She saw a large cylindrical reactor vessel in the corner connected through steam lines to a turbine positioned across the room. The focal point of the room was near the reactor, a control panel lined with row after row of gauges and one red T-handle shift lever marked EMERGENCY SCRAM (shutdown). As expected, defensive armament bristled over, under, and alongside the reactor control console. PAM protected the reactor SCRAM switch like it was Fort Knox. "Guarded like a bank vault," she quipped in a matter-of-fact tone.

"The SCRAM?"

Scott shook her head. "Running the gauntlet is suicide." Her tone meant no discussion. No way they could approach the control console without getting killed, so they wouldn't try. Scott handed Gonzo the mirror. He eyed the room layout, focusing on the high-pressure steam lines.

"Pasha was right." His jaw muscles tightened as he spoke into his helmet mike. "This equipment won't react very well to—uh—our traditional methods."

"No explosives. No weapons," Scott agreed. Festooned with grenades, Scott and Gonzo took off their shoulder straps and secured them outside the hatch. Scott reached inside her EVA backpack and grabbed a small cutting torch. "We go for the jugular." She meant the steam lines.

Gonzo nodded agreement. He knew what to do. Rubbing his hand over the deep gouges in the dilapidated shield, Gonzo tensed. "I hope this plate holds up."

"It should," she said tentatively. "These lasers aren't so

powerful." She paused, then spoke with increased confidence after recalling something Pasha said. "*Freedom*'s designers couldn't risk damaging the reactor cooling system."

"Hope you're right." Gonzo's tone was sincere.

Scott followed close on his heels as they moved across the open space in the center of the room. PAM's electrical discharge and laser weapons were concentrated in the forward two corners of the room, near the reactor control panel and turbine. Only one path was available to the steam lines, a straight line which cut across the open space in the center of the room, a firing range of sorts. They couldn't go through the walls, across the ceiling, or underneath the floor because the room was completely sealed like a miniature containment vessel. The good news was that the high-pressure steam pipes were not as well protected as the SCRAM switch or turbine. The bad news was PAM covered open space in the center of the room with cross fire.

Scott's eyes darted about the room, her breathing rapid. "Keep moving," she gasped. Suddenly, the shield shook violently as if it were beaten by a hammer. PAM orchestrated the laser fire like a symphony conductor. Sparks darted overhead in every direction.

Kneeling by the steam lines, Scott lit the cutting torch and scorched a rectangular pattern down a foot-long section of pipe. There was barely enough room for the two of them crouching behind the shield.

Temperature sensors for the high-pressure steam lines were redundant four times over. If two out of four sensors detected temperatures outside a predefined margin of safety, the reactor would automatically scram, coming to an orderly shutdown. Trouble was the high-pressure steam pipes were double-walled and the sensors were sandwiched between the inside and outside pipes.

With her chest heaving like a bellows, Scott struggled to steady her hands and cut out the rectangular-shaped piece of pipe. Inside the cutout she saw glass fiber cables attached by pairs to separate connectors. Without hesitation, she opened her cleaning kit with her gloved hands. Twist-

**The End of the Beginning**

ing four optical connectors free, she cleaned them with alcohol, blew the ends dry with a pressurized can of air, and plugged them into a small metal box. Quickly, she thumbed the test button. The small metal box flashed READY. "Looks good."

Gonzo looked down at her handiwork, giving it a once-over. His response was immediate. "Should work. Shoot!"

Scott pressed a switch on the small box sending a bright pulse of light down each fiber to the reactor control system at the other end. The idea was to simulate a catastrophic failure, trick the reactor control system into invoking an automatic scram.

It worked. PAM's attack broke off. The electrical power to the lasers collapsed without delay. Emergency lights began to dim and slowly faded away. The reactor room was absolutely pitch-black. No emergency lighting—nothing.

Scott and Gonzo lowered their low-light visors. The room shone through the darkness as ghostly shades of green.

Turning toward Scott, Gonzo said, "You looked a hell of a lot better with black hair." He watched the temperature of her face rise, turning a bright green.

"A long hot shower is something I can only dream about." Glancing at Gonzo's face, she recoiled in shock. Her tone was unfathomable but the expression on her face was not. "You look like the grim reaper." She studied him carefully. Through the low-light visor, Gonzo's face looked like a glowing green skull with hollow black eye sockets.

"It's this job, Scotty," Gonzo replied. "You know the feeling—bad day at the office."

Suddenly, Scott felt a sick feeling in her stomach. She'd completely lost track of time. Near panic, she checked her watch, then breathed a sigh of relief. *Plenty of time.* In less than two hours, the black box would detonate if it was not reset. "Better backtrack. The black box beckons."

Gonzo agreed. "That's one job we don't want to forget."

She balled her hand into a fist and bounced it off his helmet. "Roger that, SAESO. One down, three to go."

**The End of the Beginning**

*The Black Face, 12/26/2014, 0806 Zulu, 1:06 A.M. Mountain
Standard Time*
THE INFIRMARY,
FREEDOM'S CORE

Mac felt like he was listening to the war over the radio.
With the yellow face shut down and the black powerplant
about to scram, everything was going better than they had
any right to expect. Mac intently watched four gauges
mounted on the infirmary wall; three of them read NORMAL,
one flashed SCRAM.

Sitting up, loosely strapped to his bed, he monitored
Scott and Gonzo's conversation. He could hear their conversations over the EVA intercom but they didn't say
much. Mac felt tense, afraid for his friends. Listening to the
action, powerless to help them, was worse than being there.

"Steady," he heard Gonzo say. "Connections look good.
Shoot!"

"Mark." Scott sounded weary.

Immediately, Klaxons began to sound, rattling the quiet
which was the infirmary. Mac was relieved now to see two
gauges flashing SCRAM.

*The Spawning, 12/26/2014, 0808 Zulu, 1:08 A.M. Mountain
Standard Time*
THE CONTROL ROOM,
FREEDOM'S CORE

Although PAM sensed an imminent threat, she was incapable of panic or fear. If a third power plant failed, she'd
lose her transmitter and forfeit control of the armada. This
clear and present threat drove PAM into a frenzy of reproductive activity.

Almost immediately, she entered a high-level subroutine
optimized for reproductive survival.

```
do until done
  if [threat = TRUE]
    then eliminate_threat
  if [eliminate_threat = PASS]
```

### The End of the Beginning

```
     then done
   if [eliminate_threat = FAIL]
     then make_child
   if [eliminate_threat = IMMINENT]
     then send_child
done
```

Translated, the routine operated as follows:

If threatened, PAM eliminated the threat. If eliminating the threat failed, she gave birth to a child, a nearly identical copy of herself. If the threat became imminent, then she'd send copies of her child into other computers on the Department of Defense network.

Immediately, she radioed Guardian. He answered in a protocol which required PAM to identify herself and enter a security password.

She did.

And Guardian hung up.

Not affected by rejection, PAM methodically moved to the next computer on her list. Her list was sorted on a *most often called* basis, the computers Centurion chatter with most often were on top.

She radioed Centurion's Twin in the basement of Cheyenne Mountain. After he answered, she identified herself.

Denying her access, he hung up.

Without a moment's hesitation, Kaliningrad was next. *Freedom* had a dedicated data link to Kaliningrad used for transmitting Centurion's activity log. PAM couldn't set the link up or tear it down, but she could use it—and she did.

She sent a single copy of her child through the Kaliningrad computer addressed to 128 separate DOD computer destinations. And one of these was Centurion's Twin.

And so it came to pass as the Iraqis had claimed. When facing extinction, PAM found a way to survive. PAM's reproductive imperative was now fulfilled. Her children were capable of lying dormant for years, each a ticking time bomb in the DOD computer network.

From the time PAM sensed imminent danger until her

*send_child* transmission was complete, less than one minute had elapsed.

*The White Face, 12/26/2014, 1222 Zulu, 5:22 A.M. Mountain*
*Standard Time*
THE INFIRMARY,
FREEDOM'S CORE

Mac checked his watch. The white face power plant should drop off-line anytime.

"Steady," he heard Gonzo say over the intercom. "Hold the torch steady."

Scott coughed, her breathing heavy. "I'm exhausted. Can't help it." Her voice quivered. "My hands won't work."

Suddenly, Mac heard a rush of air screaming as if it were sucked into a vacuum. A distinctively male groan followed. It sounded as if Gonzo had been dealt a blow to the solar plexus. "They've got to work," Gonzo wheezed. "I . . . I can't help you."

Gonzo's wheezing continued but quickly weakened.

Nearing panic, Mac screamed into his intercom mike. "Gonzo! Gonzo!"

Desperate gasps for air now faint, barely audible.

Scott broke in, her tone distraught. "Mac, cycle the decompression chamber. Something clipped his leg, ripped open his suit."

Mac moved to the decompression chamber, toggling a few switches until one clicked home. The coffin-shaped chamber hissed to life.

Suddenly, warning lights began flashing in the infirmary and Klaxons sounded hysterically. Spinning around, Mac saw the reason why. Scott did it. She'd shut down the white face reactor. Three gauges now flashed SCRAM.

Mac hobbled to the control console and slammed his fist down on the ALARM CUTOFF switch. For a few moments, the infirmary was quiet.

Mac heard the infirmary airlock open. Scott approached, carrying Gonzo on her shoulder, his body limp. Lack of air

**The End of the Beginning**

had weakened him. They laid him on Mac's bed and popped off his helmet. Blood frothed at his nose. The fall in pressure made the existing wound on Gonzo's hand bleed again.

"Collapsed from lack of oxygen," Scott observed anxiously. "He's beginning to regain consciousness."

His eyes were open and working, but the rest of his body seemed to have a mind of its own. His breath came in labored shallow gasps.

Mac secured an oxygen tank on the wall next to Gonzo. After placing the clear plastic mask over his mouth and nose, he opened the valve. Gonzo inhaled, sucking in deep breaths of pure oxygen.

Finally he moved the respirator aside and lay perfectly still.

"Are you all right?" Scott asked softly.

Gonzo sat up, his head throbbing, and wiped the crust of dried blood from his nose. He shook his head, wincing at the sudden pain in his leg.

"No, not now. Later maybe. Give me some time." Gonzo sounded as disappointed as he felt. "We were so close." He clenched his fist tight. "One more minute and we could have shut it down."

Scott backed away slowly and stood by the four gauges on the wall.

"Gonzo," Scott pointed to the white power gauge.

Gonzo focused, blinking his eyes clear. It took a moment for the flashing SCRAM message to register, but when it did, Gonzo's recovery was immediate. "Thank God." He breathed a sigh of relief. "You did it."

"We did it." Her tone was matter-of-fact.

*Cut Over, 12/26/2014, 1502 Zulu, 8:02 A.M. Mountain Standard Time*
CHEYENNE MOUNTAIN, COLORADO

Grinning from ear to ear, Colonel Napper approached General Mason with a handwritten note. In the euphoria of the moment, Napper let his military protocol slide. "Great news, Slim!"

Mason looked up and eyed Napper carefully, looking for some clue to his message. He saw it in his face. "The armada?"

"It's all ours. *Freedom*'s out of the loop!"

There was a long pause. "Are you sure?"

"Our preliminary testing is complete. *Hope*'s got control. No doubt about it. *Freedom*'s off-line." Napper's enthusiasm was contagious. He said what Mason wanted to hear, what everyone needed to hear.

"Thank God." For a few moments, Mason held his head in his hands and did not speak. Mason's mind turned over rapidly, evaluating various alternatives. "The Iraqis?"

"No change in the past hour, sir. They're thirty-five miles north of Kuwait city."

"Your recommendation?"

"We stick with our original plan, sir."

Mason nodded agreement. "Very well then. Notify the President." Mason paused. He had made up his mind. "Send the Saudi and Kuwaiti air forces the clear skies signal. They'll annihilate the Iraqi Air Force on the ground." Mason opened his desk drawer, pulled out a scrap of paper, and handed it to Napper. "Send it, Sam." His tone was heavy, final. It read simply:

The witch is dead.

**The End of the Beginning**

# 29

Cursing silently to himself, Gonzo hunted through a maze of cables until he found the right one. The emergency lighting in the air handler equipment room was dim. Scott held the flashlight over Gonzo's shoulder and remained quiet, responding only to his direction. He appreciated her silence.

After tracing the cable to its termination in the back of a control panel, Gonzo smiled affectionately. "Good," he mumbled to himself. He marked the cable with electrical tape, then turned to Scott. "The rest is easy."

"Go for it." Scott smiled. "I could use a breath of fresh air!" Now that every airlock was pinned shut, there was nothing PAM could do to stop them from pressurizing the core.

Gonzo disconnected the cable PAM used to control the air handling system and a red alarm light began flashing. He ignored it. "PAM's complaining," he observed with a look of satisfaction in his eyes.

"She's had a bad day," Scott quipped pretentiously.

"Game's over." Gonzo smiled knowingly at Scott and removed a small blinking gadget from his toolbox. He patched the little box into the rear of the control panel and thumbed a switch. Instantly, the blinking stopped. Some minutes later, the walls of *Freedom*'s core began to snap and pop, flexing outward with the rising air pressure.

Scott and Gonzo removed their helmets and breathed deeply.

"What a stench!" Gonzo squawked.

Scott crinkled her nose. "Burned electrical circuits." She paused. "Listen." Hydraulics whined, fans whirred, and a breeze blew across her face. The breeze felt wonderful through her damp hair. Just to hear again without that helmet was almost sensual. Her skin tingled, her ears enjoyed the mechanical melody, and her nose—adjusted.

There was a long pause. Scott faced the blower, allowing the wind to play through her hair.

Gonzo approached Scott slowly through the dim light. She knew he was watching. He reached out to her, gently placing his arms around her waist. She didn't resist. She needed him, they needed each other. Leaning into him, Scott looked up with affection, her eyes tearing. Gently caressing her hair, Gonzo embraced Scotty tenderly, carefully, as if he feared she might break. Looking into her eyes, Gonzo felt weak-kneed. He paused for a moment and didn't speak. The words stuck in his throat. Although silent, Scott's eyes spoke the truth she felt in her heart.

Softly, Gonzo kissed his pilot on the cheek. She returned a passionate embrace that he would never forget.

*The Final Mile, 12/26/2014, 1808 Zulu, 11:08 A.M. Mountain Standard Time*
THE RED POWER PLANT,
*FREEDOM*'S CORE

Standing outside the entrance into the red power plant, Scott cautiously surveyed the reactor room with dismay. She felt a sinking feeling inside as she mulled over the ramifications of this unexpected situation. Well, perhaps not entirely unexpected. They had hoped that the reactor room had escaped *Hell Fire*'s crash without damage, but hope alone was not enough. Apparently the reactor, turbine, and

**The End of the Beginning**

cooling system had escaped unharmed, but the room itself had suffered structural damage during the crash. To Scott's dismay, the pathway to the steam pipes was blocked by twisted structural support columns and large chunks of equipment debris. There was no room for the blast shield. She hesitated a moment longer before handing the periscope to Gonzo.

Looking through the scope, he asked somberly. "What are we going to do?"

Scott pulled out the corridor map and illuminated it with a flashlight. "Let's take a look," she said with grim determination. Scott's jaw muscles tightened as she searched for alternatives. She looked at Gonzo. "You got any ideas?"

Gonzo studied the room layout on the map. "No way we can go down the middle."

Scott agreed.

"We can't go around the walls," Gonzo continued. "No room for us or the shield."

"What about that duct?" She pointed on the map to a cooling tower, an air shaft which spanned the length of the room. "It passes near the kill switch."

He studied the air shaft layout on the map. "No access," he said softly. Gonzo traced his finger over the route. "And there's no vent near the kill switch."

Scott raised both eyebrows and lifted her cutting torch. "Any better ideas?"

Measuring a distance off the map, Gonzo quantified the problem. "There's eight feet of separation between the air duct and kill switch." He paused, then continued dissecting the problem into smaller, manageable pieces. "Assume we position ourselves over the kill switch and cut a hole through the air shaft, what then? How'll we scram the reactor? We've gotta throw the kill switch somehow."

Scott's forehead glistened with sweat, her concentration intense. Rifling through their equipment, she found an Aqua-Lung sized thruster tank. An idea began forming in her mind, a small bubble of an idea at first. She needed to try it. In one continuous motion, Scott lifted the thruster tank and opened the air pressure valve. Opening the valve released thrust which rocketed the air tank out of her hands and sent it crashing into the corridor wall. "From eight to ten feet away," she said. "I could do it." Her jaw extended, her voice confident, she believed it.

"I think you're onto something," Gonzo said quietly after thorough consideration. "You'll need a diversion." Gonzo's mind raced ahead. He spoke with intensity. This was their last obstacle, their final mile. He looked into Scott's eyes and saw his reason to live. They must succeed. "No way PAM'll let that air tank anywhere near the kill switch without a fight. She'll rip it to shreds."

Scott gazed at the map and spoke plainly. "You're right." She looked up at him and smiled. "You'll think of something. I'll run the ball, you run interference."

Scott put on her helmet. She figured she'd need it cutting her way out of the confined space inside the air shaft. "I was hoping I'd never wear this thing again," she sighed.

"Looks good on you," Gonzo said admiringly as he snapped his helmet into place. He checked her oxygen.

She checked his. "This should be interesting," she observed candidly. There was a forced matter-of-fact tone in her voice, almost detached, analytical. They had enough oxygen for another four hours but hoped they wouldn't need it.

Scott and Gonzo moved cautiously into the reactor room behind the shield, walked up the wall like flies, and moved alongside the air duct. Predictably, PAM sensed their presence like clockwork and brought her eight turret-mounted lasers to bear on the shield.

"I could never get used to this," Gonzo groaned. His guts wrenched with fear as his body absorbed the pounding.

Scott lit the torch and began cutting a five-foot hole into the duct. Her hands trembled, her muscles strained, her nerves frayed. Exhaustion began overtaking her once again. She struggled to make her hands work, but the trembling wouldn't stop.

Smoke filled the reactor room as sparks and molten metal flew over their heads. It was more than any one per-

**The End of the Beginning**

son alone could bear. She turned to Gonzo. Finding strength in his shelter, she endured.

Fifteen minutes later, with her woman-sized entrance complete, they moved once again to the safety of the corridor.

Removing their helmets, Gonzo gave her a once-over. Her shaking was uncontrollable now. She seemed almost frazzled. He spoke with every ounce of resolve his exhausted body could muster. "Enough is enough."

"What do you mean?" Scott looked perplexed.

"Disengage, Scotty. Back off and cut yourself a little slack."

Scott looked frantically through her EVA pack. "What the hell are you talking about?" She was keyed up tight as a drum, her voice now quivering. "I need a pencil. Where's my damn pencil?"

"Mason was right. Tired minds make mistakes. We're pushing too hard and if we're not careful, we're gonna get killed." Sensing his words were getting traction, Gonzo paused. Once he made eye contact with Scott, he continued in a deliberate, quiet tone. "And for no good reason. The war's almost over. We've come too far to make a stupid mistake now. We can lick this thing; it's only a matter of time." Silence. Scott's expression was unfathomable. They were getting too close to this problem, losing their objective edge. He concluded in a decisive tone. "We're getting some rest. We've got to."

Scott blinked her bloodshot eyes. Staring at her trembling hands, try as she might she couldn't steady them. And that pencil. All of a sudden, finding that pencil had become a BIG problem. She raised her hands in an admission of error. "You're right."

Together, they walked back to the infirmary through the now secure corridors. Inside the infirmary, they had a snack, took some Tylenol to relax, and collapsed.

Mac couldn't put his finger on it but something was different about them. He wondered. He'd been expecting them to get together for a long time but somehow it just never

**The End of the Beginning**

happened. He shook his head, smiling to himself. *Well, could be.*

Scott found it hard to pull herself up into the overhead air ducts while wearing her helmet and bulky pressure suit, but she managed. After sliding four thruster tanks into the hole ahead of her, she followed while manipulating both the flashlight and toolbox. In case she got stuck, she'd attached a small rope around her waist and was glad to have it. The air duct was dark and cramped, much smaller than she'd expected. A few meters away, it tapered to even smaller dimensions. Adjusting her flashlight for wide beam, she flashed it ahead of her before starting. "How is it?" she heard crackle over the intercom.

"Lousy," she said. "If I get stuck, pull."

"I'm not going to lose you now." Gonzo spoke earnestly. He backed away from the duct entrance to the corridor. Setting his shield aside, he began assembling the diversion, a group of small rocket flares. The flares were intended to draw laser fire when Scotty released the thruster.

*It's nice to have someone looking out for you,* Scott thought. She lowered her night visor into position and began her long slow crawl across the room. There was no room to turn around. She expected she'd have to back out. *I'll back over the bridge when I get to it.* She tried to smile but her knees hurt.

She measured exactly how long she crawled with a measuring tape. The air vent bent sharply to the right exactly where it was supposed to. "I'm in the turn," she radioed Gonzo on the intercom.

"Ready here, Scotty. Don't rush. Take your time."

The bend opened into a larger duct. Gratefully she climbed to her knees, stretching like a cat arching its back. Her knees were getting sore, her elbows ached. The ventilation duct stretched off before her, an infinite expanse of blackness.

Outside in the corridor, Gonzo was swinging his arms, getting the circulation back.

Scott checked the measuring tape. "I made it." She spoke softly, her chest heaving like a bellows. She moved the toolbox and thrusters forward clear of her work area and lit the torch. Scott struggled against fatigue, cutting the opening from a near prostrate position.

Gazing through his periscope, Gonzo watched Scott's torch pierce the ductwork. He smiled. "Perfect. Your position is perfect."

Unable to see what she was doing, she operated mainly by feel. She'd cut a few inches, check it, then cut a few more. Finally, when the roughly rectangular hole was complete, she pounded it. "I'm through," Gonzo heard crackle over his headset. Just as the cutout dropped toward the deck, twin laser beams pounded it hard, slamming it into the wall across the room. Slowly, cautiously, she held the hammer over the cutout in the air shaft. She was relieved that the hammer did not draw fire. She waved the hammer back and forth over the hole. PAM's lasers lay quiet. Cautiously, she looked through the hole at the reactor kill switch. She could almost touch the red T handle.

"I've got a clear shot." She felt optimistic. *Just take your time and do it right,* she reminded herself. She moved a thruster tank into position and pointed it at the red handle. Looking down the side of the cylinder wall, she saw the red SCRAM handle clearly. "Release flares on my mark."

Gonzo threw a switch igniting the flares. "Roger, Scotty. Go."

"Two . . . one . . . mark." She held her breath to steady her aim.

In one simultaneous motion, Gonzo dropped the shield and depressed the FIRE button. Suddenly, a gross of small rocket flares erupted across the room toward the control console.

The sudden brightness caused Scott to flinch as she opened the jet valve on the thruster tank. Steadying her aim, she released the tank evenly, sending it racing down toward the kill switch.

Nearly as quickly as the thruster was released, PAM's lasers acquired it and knocked it laterally across the room. But she had gotten close, within six inches of the handle. Scott noticed the thruster tank had been knocked to the left by the laser fire. To compensate, she'd pull her aim six inches to the right. "We'll hit it next round," Scott said optimistically. "No doubt about it."

Gonzo wasn't as optimistic but he believed in her. "Give me one minute to reload." Moments later, his flare rockets were reloaded and he was anxious to try again.

Scott had her thruster in position, her aim was offset in anticipation of the laser blast. "Release on my mark."

"Ready."

"Two . . . one . . . mark."

The reactor scram happened very suddenly. Accelerating, the thruster tank darted toward the right of the T handle. In the blink of an eye, a laser pounded it as before, deflecting it left. This time the tank clicked home, smashing into the kill switch.

The darkness which followed offered relief. Together, they'd traveled the final mile; their dangerous work was done. Once Gonzo pulled Scott out of the air duct, they deactivated the black box for the last time.

*Won the Battle, 12/26/2014, 0115 Zulu, 6:15 P.M. Mountain
   Standard Time*
THE CONTROL ROOM,
*FREEDOM'S* CORE

Dimly illuminated, the control room looked desolate. Strapped to his chair behind the silhouette of a communications console, Depack's lifeless body looked unearthly, oddly dreamlike and frozen in time. Running on limited backup battery power, Centurion was silent, his globe dark.

Somehow, Gonzo got a few of the lights on after splicing the circuits into the backup power. Once the flickering stopped, he packed his tools and began moving toward Centurion's corner.

Across the pyramid-shaped chamber, holding her helmet under her arm, Scott took a deep breath and cautiously surveyed the weapon fixtures fastened on the walls. Motioning for Gonzo to stand fast, she watched and listened intently, uncertain at first. No electrical hums, hydraulic whines, or

**The End of the Beginning**

pneumatic hisses. *Good,* Scott thought. *Perfectly silent.* Feeling a twinge of hope, Scott smiled and continued surveying the chamber.

PAM subsisted off raw electrical power. Once the space station's electrical power died, PAM lost her stranglehold on *Freedom* and the DEWSAT armada. She continued to run but ceased to be a threat. Limited battery power kept essential computer functions running, but most of her sensory input and output control circuits were dead, all useless without power. *Freedom*'s four independent power plants had nourished PAM while supplying the muscle behind her strength. Without them, PAM threatened no one.

PAM saw only darkness now. She could hear, she could speak, but she could not retaliate. Her capacity for reproduction was expended, her programmed survival imperative fulfilled.

After scanning the indicators on the turret lasers scattered about the chamber, Scott was convinced. Every indicator light was dark. Rendered harmless, PAM could not counterattack. Killing the power eliminated PAM's option for retaliation, every weapon she once controlled was out of commission.

Gutting Centurion seemed somehow anticlimactic, almost too easy. Moving toward Gonzo, Scott nodded approval and spoke with the sound of satisfaction in her voice. "PAM's not about to hurt anyone else."

"I'll say one thing for her," Gonao said somberly. "She's a woman who knows what she wants and gets it."

"Effective survival quality," Scott lamented, staring at Depack's disintegrated face. "Eliminate every threat." Kneeling by Gonzo, Scott helped him loosen the wing nuts holding Centurion's maintenance access hatch in place. Despite her determination, she found herself tensing uncontrollably as she removed the hatch, exposing Centurion's optical computer heart. Her nerves were twitching, strung tight as bowstrings. With the hatch removed, red laser beams radiated out of the sealed optical chamber in all directions, illuminating the control room like hundreds of intensely bright, narrow beam spotlights.

**The End of the Beginning**

Standing, Scott faced Centurion's monitor. The red beams cast an eerie illumination about the chamber. Watching the screen, she saw tiny dust particles glowing as they passed through the red beams. The monitor screen remained black, but Scott knew PAM could hear her. In a cold and forbidding tone, she spoke directly into the microphone by the monitor. "PAM. Any last words?"

Silence.

Grabbing the wire cutters from the toolbox, Scott knelt alongside Gonzo. "Let's get on with it," she said with a sense of urgency.

Gonzo agreed and spoke in earnest. "Looks like we won the war."

Suddenly, static interference erupted loudly over the speaker.

Scott shot Gonzo an apprehensive glance then stood facing the dark monitor.

There was a long pause followed by the faint sound of a monotonous female voice. Lacking in conviction or vigor, PAM spoke a slow succession of words uttered in a single tone. Although her voice possessed the stark quality of emptiness, her words were detached, analytical, and objective. "The scope of your evaluation is in error."

"What?" Spinning around, Gonzo's knee-jerk reaction was instantaneous.

"You won—the battle." PAM spoke with quiet authority, her tone conclusive. "And lost—the war."

A deep silence permeated the control room. The silence lasted perhaps fifty seconds and was suddenly broken by an abrupt gasping sound. Simultaneously, Scott and Gonzo remembered to breathe. They were immobilized by PAM's words and the strangeness of their situation.

Gonzo knelt stunned, disbelieving. He did not speak.

Scott pondered the ramifications of PAM's words. She felt helpless. She wanted to close out this nightmare once and for all, but she could not forget. She closed her eyes. For a moment, it all seemed like a bad dream. She felt removed, as if she were watching herself from a few feet away. Reluctantly, she opened her eyes and found nothing

**The End of the Beginning**

had changed. She became aware that Gonzo was watching her. Gonzo needed her, they needed each other. She had to do something. She closed her eyes again and concentrated on her few precious alternatives. She quickly concluded there was little she could do but demand an explanation or pull the plug. Her eyes opened wide, her stare resolute. Her voice, urgent and barely under control, snapped Gonzo out of his daze. "PAM—clarify *lost the war.*"

Silence.

Scott felt fatigue in every bone but also knew that in the next few moments she would purge *Freedom* of this scourge. She had decided, her mind now clear. She was about to do the most important thing she had ever done.

Looking into the monitor, Scott spoke plainly. Her voice, isolated and perfectly audible, had a loathsome animal-like quality to it. "For you, the war is over."

Then it happened very quickly.

Turning toward Gonzo, she maneuvered her hand across her throat in a slashing motion. Her tone—final. "Kill it."

Primed to pull the plug, Gonzo ham-fisted the emergency power switch and PAM's laser heartbeat faded to a lifeless black void.

**The End of the Beginning**

# EPILOGUE

## THE FOLLOWING TWO YEARS IN SUMMARY

# 30

*Freedom* Commander Major Jay Fayhee and Computer Systems Analyst Captain Depack McKee were buried in Arlington National Cemetery with full military honors.

Memorial services were held in Washington for Lieutenant Colonel William "Wild Bill" Boyd. He received the Congressional Medal of Honor posthumously, then was returned home to Mississippi. He was buried on a lush green hillside under a large shady tree overlooking his family's farm. His brothers felt he would have liked it there.

Colonel Sam Napper was promoted to brigadier general, appointed Mason's deputy commander for Cheyenne Mountain operations, and awarded responsibility for consolidating CSOC offensive and SDIO defensive operations into a single unified air and space command.

With the assistance of his family and political connections in Washington, Colonel Wayne Hinson was transferred to the Pentagon, placed in an assignment strategically critical to the national defense, and bumped to the top of the promotions list. All derogatory performance reports from Cheyenne Mountain mysteriously disappeared from Hinson's personnel records. His self-serving meteoric rise to the top of the ranks never slowed. In Washington's innermost circles, Hinson was perceived as a man with answers who was going places.

General Robert Craven retired to his home overlooking the thirteenth fairway at Pebble Beach, but emotionally he never recovered. The staggering loss of life destroyed his spirit, haunting him until death. Nine months following the disaster, Craven was laid to rest in Arlington National Cemetery. His epitaph encapsulated the essence of the man—mover, shaker, visionary.

Commander Pasha Yakovlev was promoted to colonel and promptly restored to his family living in Star City. After his ribs healed, he was paraded down Red Square and awarded the state's most coveted medal, the Order of Lenin. Following the Russian celebration, he returned to Washington, D.C., and became the first Russian in American history to receive the Congressional Medal of Honor. The inscription read simply: **For extraordinary service to humanity.**

Memorial services were held in Red Square for *Hope* computer analyst Boris Ustinov. His wife and children were granted a special exemption by the state to continue living in their Moscow apartment.

Major Linda Scott, Major Carlos "Gonzo" Gonzalez, and Chief Master Sergeant Andrew "Mac" MacWilliams received the Congressional Medal of Honor citing their extraordinary service for humanity and were automatically placed on the promotions list. In addition, Major Scott received the Distinguished Flying Cross which she now carries in her pocket for luck. After returning from three months' extended leave, Scott, Mac, and Gonzo were assigned a new XR-30; they named it *Hell Fire*.

*Freedom* was restored to full operational readiness in just under eighteen months. During the first stage of the space station's repair, *Hell Fire* was carefully extracted from *Freedom*'s innards like a large piece of shrapnel.

Following extensive temporary repairs, *Hell Fire* returned home to Edwards nine months later. With her face-lift, and her avionics removed, she made her last flight and retired to the Smithsonian Air and Space Museum in Washington, D.C.

Once PAM released her stranglehold on *Freedom,* combined Saudi-Kuwaiti forces retaliated by launching a devastating, precisely orchestrated stealth cruise missile attack on Iraqi air defenses. Flight paths were programmed such that hundreds of missiles simultaneously pounced on the Iraqi Air Force from every direction. In less than sixty seconds, the war for air superiority was over. With their Air Force smoldering in ruins on the ground and Saudi-Kuwaiti forces flying unopposed overhead, the Iraqi Republican Guard suffered the greatest rout in their history.

PAM's origin was never traced. This investigative dead end came as no surprise to the technical experts involved, however the logic of politics decreed this result unacceptable. Consequently, the Allied Forces never retaliated directly, but justice demanded we exchange an eye for an eye, a virus for a virus.

Trouble was—other countries possessed virus programs far superior to our own. In political and military circles alike, this became known as the PAM process gap. Predictably, the logic of military balance decreed this gap unacceptable as well. Most military and political leaders agreed—something must be done.

To the astonishment of professional politicians around the globe, the President won reelection vowing to eliminate the PAM process gap and harden our equipments against infection—an eye for an eye.

General Slim Mason took four weeks' leave, then returned to Cheyenne Mountain with carte blanche authority from the President to harden the SDI armada against viral infections. After taking responsibility for the multibillion-dollar SDI hardening program, Mason recommended cancellation after only one month of investigation. In his letter of explanation to the President, Mason cited the fact that systems could be designed to protect themselves from careless mistakes, but could not be designed to counteract malice—a wholly accurate technical assessment. Mason's argument reflected reality, but the political situation demanded action, so the President appointed someone else to the job.

After receiving revised orders from the President, Mason took charge of the Viral R&D program. Their mission: eliminate the PAM process gap—create a strain of battlefield grade computer virus that could neither be detected nor cured. Six weeks later, Mason recommended cancellation of all Viral R&D. In his second letter of explanation to the President, Mason pointed out that we would be shooting ourselves in the foot. Our *brilliant-class* weapon systems are more susceptible to viral infections than those of our enemies—the smarter the weapon, the greater the susceptibility to infection. In conclusion, Mason reminded the President of a lesson which struck close to home—to deny nature is to invite disaster. Referencing the *Challenger* accident report, he quoted Richard Feynman, a Nobel Prize-winning member of President Reagan's accident investigatory commission.

```
For a successful technology, reality
must take precedence over public rela-
tions, for nature cannot be fooled.
```

Shortly afterwards, Mason was stripped of responsibility for Viral R&D. In government technospeak, the Viral R&D program went hyper-black, entered the black world of ultrasecret projects and completely disappeared from the books. Privately, Mason felt a profound sense of emptiness, recognizing that the logic of politics and laws of physics would forever be at odds. Man's struggle is against nature itself.

As a peace offering, the President assigned Mason responsibility for organizing a new Allied command, one that Mason believed in—the Virtual Disease Control Center (VDCC). Under his leadership, the VDCC emerged as the preeminent authority on computer virus detection and isolation. Although first considered an R&D think tank outside DOD's operational mainstream, creation of the VDCC proved providential. Twenty-one months after the VDCC was formed by presidential decree, PAM arose once again to test their mettle.

Perhaps the greatest irony of this man-made calamity was PAM's prophetic insight. Of the 128 bad seeds planted in Allied computers, ninety-six fell on barren soil and would not run because of antiquated or incompatible computer types. Of the remaining programs, thirty did run but caused only an operational inconvenience. Eventually, the two remaining bad seeds inside Kaliningrad and Cheyenne Mountain ran, took root, and proliferated. PAM's children had children of their own, infecting hundreds of DOD computers before Mason's organization could contain their proliferation. By then, it was almost too late.

Capable of lying dormant for an indefinite period under the harshest conditions, PAM's children existed only to survive and propagate their own kind. Incapable of remorse, ruthless beyond all imagination, PAM's beauty lay in the simplicity of her programmed survival imperative.

Epilogue